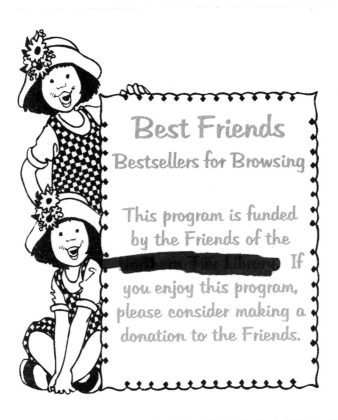

Best Friends
Bestsellers for Browsing

This program is funded
by the Friends of the
████████████████ If
you enjoy this program,
please consider making a
donation to the Friends.

Also by Tony Hendra

Father Joe

The Book of Bad Virtues

Brad '61 (with Roy Lichtenstein)

Going Too Far

THE MESSIAH OF MORRIS AVENUE

THE MESSIAH

OF

MORRIS

AVENUE

a novel

TONY
HENDRA

HENRY HOLT AND COMPANY   NEW YORK

Henry Holt and Company, LLC
Publishers since 1866
175 Fifth Avenue
New York, New York 10010
www.henryholt.com

Henry Holt® and ® are registered trademarks
of Henry Holt and Company, LLC.

Distributed in Canada by H. B. Fenn and Company Ltd.

Library of Congress Cataloging-in-Publication Data

Hendra, Tony.
    The messiah of Morris Avenue : a novel / Tony Hendra.—1st ed.
    p.cm.
    ISBN-13: 978-0-8050-7964-7
    ISBN-10: 0-8050-7964-5
    1. Journalists—Fiction. 2. Spiritual life—Fiction. 3. Preaching—
Fiction. I. Title.

PS3608.E528M47 2006
813'.54—dc22   2005044736

Henry Holt books are available for special promotions
and premiums. For details contact: Director, Special Markets.

First Edition 2006

Designed by Victoria Hartman

Printed in the United States of America

2   4   6   8   10   9   7   5   3   1

THE MESSIAH OF MORRIS AVENUE

PROLOGUE

FORT OSWALD, TEXAS. An early summer storm roils the sky. Lightning crackles between fat thunderheads. They lurch over the flat plain, roly-poly gun-metal-gray giants, thousands of feet tall, occasionally spitting thin streams of dazzling light at the ground.

Abutting the vast air base's southern boundary is a brand-new maximum security prison, one of thousands that dot the Lone Star landscape, as familiar a sight as forests of oil rigs once were, back in the bad old days before God returned to America.

The prison is a sprawling complex covering dozens of acres. It consists of identical rectangular compounds, each formed by three rows of titanium-reinforced twenty-foot chain-link fence, topped with dense rolls of razor wire. The gap between each row is packed with more razor wire. The wire bristles with countless thousands of tiny blades. When lightning flashes overhead, they flash too.

The prison's full name is the Risen Lamb Correctional Facility. Its directors call it a Christian prison, one that respects the retributive power of Church and State: the right of the judiciary to exact punishment, the right of the Lord to vengeance. The men and women incarcerated here aren't "inmates" or "prisoners" but "sinners." Those convicted of capital crimes are called "cardinal sinners." But the God of vengeance is also the God of forgiveness. This prison differs from all others in the fervent efforts that are made to help cardinal sinners repent before they're terminated; to be born again before they die.

At the center of the complex is its spiritual heart: a circular two-story rotunda containing ten lethal-injection chambers. No other facility in the world has such multiple capability. If necessary, ten cardinal sinners can be terminated simultaneously.

From the center of the rotunda rises a colossal 150-foot rotating crucifix: one full rotation every sixty seconds. Front and back, the arms of the cross bear a scrolling LED readout. On one side the legend reads CHRIST DIED FOR YOUR SINS! When the opposite side comes around, it reads NOW IT'S YOUR TURN!

It's been an auspicious morning for the new facility. At noon it executed its very first cardinal sinner, a young non-Caucasian male, and for an unusual crime: treason. Every effort was made to bring him to the Lord before he went to the execution chamber. Alas, he was unrepentant.

Owing to the inexperience of the staff, he underwent considerable trauma: The lethal drugs took some time to effectuate termination.

But all is well. At 12:45 P.M. he was declared dead and his remains were cremated. The ashes will be placed in a simple container and, before nightfall, delivered to his mother.

✦

The years haven't softened the image of him, lying dead on the gurney. The memory is as raw as the long bloody gashes the IVs had opened in his arms. Each time I see him there, the pain still roils me, as the storm did the sky.

I put him on that gurney. I was his Judas.

ONE

IN THE BEGINNING . . . I knew him only as the Mysterious Stranger.

I first came across him at a low point in my career—well, *the* low point, actually—lower, as they say in Texas, than a snake's belly. Clinging to the underside of said reptile was where you'd find me, Johnny Greco, in the middle of the second decade of America's Millennium, or Christ's Millennium—which by then were interchangeable terms.

I was entering if not the twilight, then certainly the happy hour, of a long career that had begun in youthful idealism at the Columbia School of Journalism and proceeded more realistically through the ranks of the newspaper of record, reaching its peak when I was forty-something and the descendants of Mr. Joseph Pulitzer bestowed one of their baubles on me for investigative reportage. This was when that still meant something: before they began awarding Pulitzers for In-Depth Gossip and Best Rumor.

From then on my path led downhill to its nadir: a senior post at something called the *New Jersey Inquiring Mind*.

According to its proprietors the *Inquiring Mind* was a newspaper, but it had no connection to news or to paper. At a time when most real newspapers had gone out of business, the term had the cachet of the obsolete. The *Inquiring Mind* was a newspaper in the same sense that, when I was a kid, a pimpmobile was called a brougham.

The home page was topped with tasteful line art depicting a crusader on whose shield was emblazoned the proud word TRUTH. Below this logo was a bottom-feeding web-zine, pumping out old-fashioned streaming video and chockablock with blinding ads for sex aids, bankruptcy lawyers, homeopathic cancer cures, intercontinental "dating" services, and astrology-based investment strategies.

There was an identical *Inquiring Mind* in every other state of the Union and in scores of nominally English-speaking countries. The whole world-wide web-net of rock-bottom sleaze cost almost nothing to run and made a fortune. It was owned by three guys in Bangalore. Alas, they didn't call themselves Three Guys from Bangalore. If only. They called themselves NewsWeb and were listed on the Nikkei Multi-Bourse. One of them is now prime minister of India.

The *Inquiring Mind* was premised on an obvious if depressing reality. Whatever global computer literacy was doing for understanding among nations, it had added hundreds of millions of people to the happy throng of those willing to do anything in front of a camera. Now everyone in the world had the chance to act like a fubar senior on spring break. Whether it was a Sherpa trying to Rollerblade down Stage 2 of Everest or an ordinary Joe from Canton, Ohio, with size 14 feet so webbed that from the butt down he looked like Donald Duck, the freaks of Planet Earth found a warm welcome at the *Inquiring Mind*.

Like all the others, the New Jersey "edition" was essentially a strip-mining mechanism that scoured our territory for freaks. The only remotely newspaperlike aspect was my half-dozen stringers around the Garden State, doing the scouring. If they found something promising, they forwarded their video to me; if I liked it I would "report" it: that is, insert myself in the video (thanks to some miracle of digital editing beyond my print-bred brain) and slug it into the appropriate department. It could run regionally or nationally, or—that pinnacle of journalistic prowess—globally.

The top-rated department was the Nut Log, which brought our reportorial scrutiny to bear upon rampant cases of mental derangement. (It wasn't exploitative or anything—perish the thought.)

Many Nut Log candidates were religious nuts, which wasn't surprising, given the improvements Christian fundamentalists had introduced into the American way of life. The Ten Commandments now appeared helpfully in schools, bars, planes, restrooms, gyms, and nightclubs; on cigarettes, alcohol, prescription drugs, lingerie advertising—anywhere temptation might slither up and bite your ankle. This theocratic concern for American souls was widely seen as a good thing. In a national *Inquiring Mind* Insta-Poll we'd run, 86 percent of the respondees believed *theocracy* was spelled "The Ocracy"; 89.9 percent of *them* said they didn't know what an Ocracy was, but they knew it was good.

The most powerful effect of the Ocracy on the deranged was its constant drumbeat that these were the Final Days. For someone with a limited supply of marbles, the urgency of the end-time message had a very specific result. Instead of developing some more normal abnormality like barking from trees or directing traffic in their boxers, they zeroed in on being God—or close to it.

My favorite Nut Log nut was a former professor of archaeology at Rutgers. An obliging angel of the Lord had informed him that he was the reincarnation of Simon Stylites, a saint who'd spent the best years of his life atop a fifty-foot pole, sustained by bread and water.

St. Simon the Sequel had constructed a similar perch in his yard in Asbury Park and had been living up it in a loincloth for a while when the Nut Log crew caught up with him. His wife would shin up a ladder every morning to bring the Saint his bread and water.

We shot this ritual from a neighboring tree; the very first time, St. Simon snarled, "Damn you, woman, I said *stale* bread! And this water is *clean*!"

That did it for me. But what sold him to the Nut Log was an hour later, when the time came for his self-mortification. The appearance of his helpmeet had given him a fine erection, which he proceeded to pound with a mallet against the floor of the platform for a good half hour.

Then there were the messiahs. In theory, messiahs were a gold mine. Problem was, they were largely indistinguishable. The Manson eyes, the unkempt hair, the beard with bits of food in it, the occasional robe—they'd all been watching the same movie. When you get right down to it, fanatics aren't that funny. Except for the King James garble coming at you nonstop, most Christs could just as easily be animal activists, Roswell geeks, classical bassoonists, or wine writers.

So when I first got a report from my stringer in south Jersey about some guy wandering around with a bunch of disciples, performing miracles, I didn't pay much attention. Messiahs were a dry hole. But other stringers in other parts of the state began to hear things on their grapevines: a man cured of TB in a supermarket parking lot in Phillipsburg, a kid with MS made to walk in a schoolyard in Mount Laurel; more than one report of young women cured of full-blown AIDS, no location given.

I began to wonder a little, but not whether miracles were happening; quite the opposite. These "miracles" had a familiar ring. They sounded like retooled versions of old tent-revival laying-on-of-hands scams: autosuggestion temporarily alleviating symptoms of serious disease. You had to know your way around not to be fooled by them, but desperately sick people often were. Then they'd find out there'd been no cure and fall apart.

Hardly what Nut Log fans wanted to see on their carputers in morning traffic.

Messiahs fell into two categories: nuts or hustlers. This guy sounded like the second, and I wasn't about to give him any publicity. He was probably doing enough harm as it was. On the other hand, he didn't seem to want publicity, which was puzzling. Nuts or hustlers, messiahs were always ravenous for attention; even the most severely unhinged sought us out day and night.

One of my stringers, a funny energetic Asian kid named Kuni, was intrigued enough to start keeping a record of the "miracle" messiah. There weren't that many sightings, perhaps five in as many months. All were after the fact. There was no way to predict where he was going to pop up. He seemed to be operating in the tristate area, but he was hard to track because he moved in the underground of the truly poor: the toughest neighborhoods of hard-hit cities like Elizabeth, Trenton, Bridgeport. Once or twice a stringer got wind that he'd materialized somewhere, but the neighborhoods where he appeared weren't easy or safe to navigate, and by the time someone got there he was on his way again, leaving behind talk of cures and second sight and people changed by his words. The inaccessibility of these places then made it hard for stringers to find and check for people who'd been "cured" or "changed by his words."

Kuni kept at it. One source said the miracle worker's people called him Jay and they all traveled together in a beat-up van. He sometimes preached in Spanish. He never took up collections, as other messiahs invariably did. One source said he had a real slow way of talking that "made you feel peaceful-like." Kuni said someone told him she thought he'd got his start in Camden. *That'd* be news, I said: getting your start in Camden.

I remember this conversation because it was the first time Kuni called him the Mysterious Stranger. I liked that. It was a very cool putdown. From then on, in the way that happens when someone anonymous acquires a handle, he became more real. I asked Kuni about him regularly, not because I planned to run a story but just so I could say, What's new with the Mysterious Stranger? It always made me smile.

It wasn't a nice smile. The term Mysterious Stranger had a derogatory, derisive overtone. It could even be code, indicating to those who moved in the antifundamentalist samizdat that you did too; you too resisted the dictatorship of the holytariat, worked for the overthrow of the Church-State.

✦

The term was in vogue that year, thanks to a man I'm proud to say I loathed, one of the few men in terminally compromised, culturally homeless, morally destitute America who was evil enough to make the stump of my lefty conscience tingle.

The Reverend James Zebediah Sabbath embodied in every respect Christian America's long journey from the heathen wilderness of the mid-twentieth century into the Promised Land of the early twenty-first: a faith-based, morality-valuing, Bible-believing America, where theocracy and democracy were synonymous; where the executive, legislature, and judiciary were Father, Son, and Holy Spirit, distinct, omnipotent—not to mention omniscient—persons of the ruling triune God.

The Reverend had been Spiritual Adviser to three presidents, enjoyed the rank of two-star general as chaplain-in-chief of the U.S. Armed Forces, and had twice been reappointed Spiritual Clerk of what he first dubbed the Supreme Court Under God. He was arguably one of the most powerful men in the nation—certainly the CEO of fundamentalist Christianity, which by the second decade of Christ's Millennium was the only kind left standing.

Our paths had crossed twice. Once face-to-face—for me, disastrously—and once electronically, earlier that year, when the Reverend had achieved a decisive victory in a war he'd fought for decades: the conversion of that last nest of paganism in God's Chosen Land, Hollywood.

Hollywood had fought back. Hollywood had thrown everything it had at him, but finally, to use his favorite phrase, Hollywood had cried uncle. After a furious internal debate and scores of angry resignations, the Academy of Motion Picture Arts and Sciences had invited the Reverend to host the first faith-based Academy Awards in history.

TWO

WELCOME, PLANET EARTH, to a NewsWeb exclusive: the Eighty-eighth Academy Awards. The big news this year is that for the very first time in motion picture history, this Oscar ceremony is dedicated to the Lord our God! I'm Johnny Greco reporting to you live from backstage at the fabulously refurbished Grauman's Christian Theater."

Actually, I was three thousand miles away in Fairlawn, New Jersey, sitting in a tiny suite off the local NewsWeb server with Kuni at my side to help with the technology. Thanks to some miracle of digital technology only Kuni understood, my scrawny kisser did appear to be backstage at Grauman's.

"High in the hills above this glittering scene, with beauty and talent inside the theater and ecstatic crowds outside, sits something else that's been refurbished, perhaps one of the best-loved signs on earth."

Kuni clicked on the clip and there it was, shining out over Laurel Canyon, Beverly Hills, Santa Monica, the Pacific, the world: the familiar sign with a new diamond-dust finish that dazzlingly reflected the hyper-halogens. Its letters glowed with an ethereal corona of light, except that now there were only eight, not nine:

HOLYWOOD.

Of all the depredations—or, depending on your point of view, improvements—the Reverend had inflicted on the movie capital over the last few years—control of budgets, final review of scripts, and veto of studio heads, to all of which it had eventually succumbed—the sanctification of the Hollywood sign was where it dug in its heels. Only by dint of massive bribery had the Reverend's patsies on the LA city council prevailed. With days to spare, the offending *L* had been hauled down and, it was rumored, sold for a fortune to a movie producer in Bombay.

"Hosting the Oscars tonight, by special invitation of the Academy of Motion Picture Arts and Sciences," I said still supposedly backstage, "is the spiritual adviser to the president, the Reverend James Sabbath!"

The backstage video feed panned to Sabbath, standing in the wings, impeccable in a perfectly fitted tux, the only color on his person a narrow blood-crimson bow tie and a discreet triangle of matching cummerbund peeping from his jacket.

"A few minutes ago, I asked the obvious question," I said, before turning to an attentive close-up of the Reverend (it had just been MP-9'd to countless other reporters around the world who were all, right now, asking the same thing). "This is your first Academy Awards, Reverend. You nervous?"

The familiar face, slightly fleshy, slightly tanned, with its slightly unruly head of black hair, cracked in a friendly smile. The uncanny thing about the Reverend was how ordinary he seemed, how unthreatening, how neighborly. You'd be happy to have him living right next door, yes, indeedy. Only his eyes belied the impression: They were a washed-out brown, without affect, pale as virtue.

"Nervous? Heck, no." He chuckled. "I'm . . . cotton-pickin' . . . *terrified*!"

Onstage, the show began. Band and chorus cracked into a spirited gospel version of "Hooray for Holywood." The show's voice-over announced its illustrious host and segued into a bio-montage of his life. The earliest black-and-white footage was of the Reverend in his teens, as Little Jimmy Sabbath, Archangel of Alabama, youngest and glibbest layer-on-of-hands the revival circuit had ever seen. Then— still in black-and-white—came the full-bearded young Jim the Baptist, prophet of doom, immersing terrified hippies in a toxic-looking stretch of the Mississippi. Next, in washed-out eighties color, was the clean-shaven, blow-dried televangelist James Z. Sabbath, a zealot so extreme even his friends called him the Talibangelist. Then, on to the nineties and the Oval Office, posing with Sparrow 1, his first presidential charge. Now he'd reinvented himself as Pastor Jim, publicly a serene Evangelico-Pentecostal, privately a ruthless power broker and vote getter-outer. In the early years of Christ's Millennium, reinvented yet again as the (self-ordained) Reverend Sabbath, he was arm in arm first with Sparrow 2 and then with Sparrow 3, the current incumbent, looking ever more sleek and corporate and incorruptible. Finally, he was seen reading scripts, peering through viewfinders, sitting in director's chairs. The biopic ended on another long shot of the refurbished sign with its heavenly halo and that lonely *L*.

Tension crackled in the air as the live Reverend walked out onstage. There were many holdouts in the industry who made no secret of their hatred for him. At their core was a group called the Hollywood Hundred and Ten who lived in lavish exile in Baja, Cuernavaca, and Acapulco, writing angry anti-Christian screenplays that would never be produced. At the other extreme were those who saw him as the movies' only hope. But the majority of the permanently beautiful people in the theater that night were on the fence; they welcomed the work he'd brought, even paid him lip service. That didn't mean they had to like him. The Reverend, whether he knew it or not, was being auditioned.

He stood at his podium for a long moment, head humbly bowed as the dutiful applause died. "OK," he said, looking contrite. "I'm sorry about the *L*."

Appreciative chuckles from the rich and lovely. At least the guy was willing to grasp the nettle.

"But I'm told it's found a good home. From now on Bollywood will be spelt with *three L*'s."

Raucous laughter, loud applause. Bollywood, which had stolen much of Hollywood's foreign market, especially in Asia, was widely hated in Los Angeles. Even liberal luminaries who'd spent their lives on the front lines fighting ethnic prejudice would voice rabidly racist comments about its product.

The Reverend went into a passable version of the Indian accent everyone used when dumping on the competition. "B-o-l-l-l-y-wood!" he added.

It was a brave attempt to be cool; it was professionally done, it was a gamble. In short, it was Hollywood. Grauman's Christian gave him another laugh and a big hand, and all the tension was gone. The old bastard had done it again.

✦

Why was the Reverend, of all people, standing at the podium that evening? Because he'd pretty much single-handedly raised Hollywood from the dead.

The early twenty-first century saw the Web metastasizing into private webs as macro-content providers started charging for what they'd previously offered free. Flush with cash, these webs proceeded to eat every medium in sight, from paper to pay-per-view. Meanwhile, Hollywood blockbusters were tanking, thanks to the monumental narcissism of their stars and their obsession with computer-generated death. The *box* in box office was fast becoming a coffin.

How did the Rev walk this Lazarus from its tomb? The good old carrot and stick.

The stick was the passage of new blasphemy and witchcraft laws. To the utter dismay of Hollywood, who'd given their neosocialist egalitarian all to prevent it, Sparrow 2 was reelected by a landslide to a third term, in the tsunami of patriotism that had swept the nation after the bombing of the UN building.

The new administration then passed the Christian Right's fondest dream: federal laws against blasphemy, sodomy, and witchcraft. The third of these wasn't quite as medieval as it sounds. Witchcraft did mean Wicca and *Bewitched* reruns and British boy wizards; but mostly it meant paganism, aka "worship" of flora and fauna, aka environmentalism and, by simple extension, evolution.

Striking right back, the private-jet Left announced a maxi-budget blockbuster called *The Origin of the Species* based on the life of Charles Darwin. Dozens of superstars climbed aboard the good ship *Beagle.* As one Wall Street Hollywood analyst said, the subject had "all the box-office appeal of a duck-billed platypus," but that wasn't the point. It was a flexing of cultural muscle and, as it turned out, old Hollywood's last gasp, despite a triple-platinum, superdanceable love theme, "Random Selection."

A week before *Origin*'s premiere, the Reverend went after it with a vengeance, condemning it as a pagan outrage to hundreds of millions of creationist Christians and suing its principals for blasphemy and witchcraft. To Hollywood's shock and horror (you'd think they would've learned by now), he won all the way to the Supreme Court. *Origin*'s British-born producer Neil Bending went to jail, numerous screen careers went south, and two major studios were ruined.

That was the stick. The carrot was to offer the dying industry a huge and loyal audience who went to movies because they were told to: the Reverend's vast flock and those of his like-minded brethren. The superstars and megadirectors moping around their Malibu beach homes, waiting for foreclosure notices, could have their lights, cameras, action, and even lifestyle back (cleaned up, of course), provided they were willing to make movies for Christians.

Why did the Reverend want Hollywood? Because beating his traditional enemy was the old way. The new way was to convert this bastion of secularism, socialism, and sin. He was a missionary in a heathen land; there were souls to be saved. And there was a dramatic parable in Hollywood's redemption. Dead, it was a mere corpse. Resurrected as Holywood, it was a triumphant example of what the Reverend could accomplish in God's name: a shining city on a hill—or, more accurately, hills.

The most important thing, however, for the serried rows of glitterati in Grauman's Christian that night was that the Reverend had breathed life back into stardom. Many had been reborn, demure and wholesome, to keep their names above the title. For stardom, the private-jet Left was happy to become private-jet Baptists or private-jet Evangelicals.

The Reverend waved to them from the stage. "Merle . . . Susan . . . Barry . . . Steve . . . hey, Neil, welcome back!"

Heads craned a little higher, people sat up straighter in their seats, hoping to be recognized—men and women who'd once raised countless millions to put this man out of business or made impassioned speeches to huge rallies, denouncing him as a heartless monster.

"Looking fine tonight! Especially you ladies! Lordy!" The Reverend shook his head roguishly. "There's a *lot* of temptation out there tonight! If I wasn't happily married to my sweet Jeanine. . . . Hoooboy!" The Reverend made a great show of waving an imaginary Satan behind his back. "Get thee behind me! Get thee behind me!"

In the front row, his wife, Jeanine, a vibrant redhead who'd been married to him for thirty years, laughed right along. So did Evan Whittaker, sitting next to her. The former star wide receiver for the Atlanta Patriots, now born again, was a key member of the Risen Lamb team. Evan's splendid baritone was the sound of the Reverend's weekly *Sabbath Hour*. With Jeanine, Evan cohosted the nation's number-one morning webcast, the *Risen Lamb Prayer Breakfast Club*.

The Reverend was just kidding about being tempted, of course. He waited for the fun to die down. "Before we get started, if you'll forgive an old preacher man the habits of a lifetime, I'd like to say a little prayer. . . ." He bowed his jet-black head and clasped his hands. Throughout the auditorium, coiffed and Botoxed skulls bowed also; lavishly beringed hands clasped in designer laps.

"O Lord, we know that the arts of pretense and imitation, the amazing ability to project oneself into another character, can be used to deceive and confuse, even to possess the innocent. But we know also, Lord, as You do, that in the right hands, like those before You in this hallowed place, these arts can open the gates of the human soul into a garden of profound truth and understanding—of Your world and Your people.

"That is the simple, honest work of Your servants gathered here tonight, Lord. Bless their work! Help them to use, for Your ends, the awesome talents and astonishing gifts, the matchless physical beauty and prowess You have bestowed upon them in such abundance!

Above all, bless the winners who sit amongst us! Smile, as we surely will, on those to be honored here tonight, the very best of the very best in all Your creation! Amen!"

At this fervent and gentlemanly tribute, the entire audience—even the doubters and fence-sitters—rose to its feet in thunderous applause. For the Reverend, for the Lord their God, and most of all for themselves.

◆

The Reverend was a great host. He made 'em laugh, he made 'em cry; he provided gravitas when it was called for; he punctured winners' ego balloons when they overinflated. Not only did he front the show, he ran every aspect of it behind the scenes. Once, when stars thanked God for their Oscars, you giggled about it at the *Vanity Fair* party. Now it was required of every nominee—or no Oscar.

He'd done a brilliant set piece, Bible in hand, about the "Second Renaissance" Holywood was embarking on, harking back to the first Renaissance and its most brilliant exponent, Michelangelo. Grauman's Christian was delighted to gaze on a giant hologram of Michelangelo's *David*, tickled to death that their work might be in the same category. Then the Reverend brought it home: David wasn't just some pal of Michelangelo's called Dave but the David who was about to slay Goliath, the David in *this book*! And he'd slapped the Bible with his free hand.

"I would never tell anyone what to write—God forbid," he'd continued, "but I do suggest to you, dear colleagues, that all human drama can be found in *this book*. Birth, death, love, yearning, loss, redemption. Patriotism and betrayal, heroism and cowardice, war and peace. There's poetry, there's narrative, there's dialogue. It's all here in the Screenplay of screenplays!"

Around the auditorium, several born-again Santa Monica screen-writers were heard crying, "Amen! Amen to that!"

Typical Reverend, flattering his audience while promoting him-self. One of the two favorites for Best Film that night was *A Man Comes to Cheyenne*. It was the fourth in a series of Westerns (all had *Man* in their titles) produced by the Reverend's Risen Lamb Films. All had broken box office records.

Their plots were identical. A frontier community is under siege, from outlaws or corrupt government or peddlers of sin. A stranger shows up. He has no name and wears no guns. He speaks in mono-syllables. He has mysterious medical skills with which he heals some desperately sick person, often a beautiful child. At least one painted hussy throws herself at him, to no avail. He works hard (as rancher, farmer, or grubstake miner) but can't prosper because of the bad guys. Finally, pushed too far, he unpacks the guns he vowed he'd hang up forever. In the ensuing bloodbath, the bad guys are sent to Hell and the stranger is mortally wounded. He dies in the dust of his final shootout, surrounded by grieving townspeople who, in-spired by his sacrifice on their behalf, go on to build America.

Christ, the Reverend was fond of saying, was a man slow to anger, a man of few words, but who, once roused, destroyed his en-emies without mercy. Christ was Gary Cooper.

In the underground, these hokey, creakily symbolic films were a running joke, as was their unnamed hero, known as—ethereal voice de rigueur here—the Mysterious Stranger. Much ribald speculation took place about his backstory and his sexual proclivities were a sta-ple of satiric theater, which was why Kuni's using the term about our mystery miracle man always made me smile.

That the Bible could breed hits was borne out by other contenders for Best Film. All took a holy half-turn on a classic Hollywood genre.

Final Warming was a big-budget disaster movie, except that global warming, and the global carnage it caused, was a sign that the Second Coming was at hand. For Christian audiences, this was a happy ending.

The same was true of *Sophie's Free Choice*, essentially a Christian payback movie. Sophie, a young mother pregnant with twins, is told by her (feminist) doctor she must abort one of them or die. Sophie does, despairs, finds Jesus, and becomes an instrument of divine retribution. The final bloodbath is knee-deep in feminist gore.

But the Reverend's principle didn't quite hold for the other favorite of the night. It was certainly Bible-based, but it was hard to place in a genre.

"And now," I announced, "the runaway favorite for Best Film: *Dan's Inferno*, written and directed by the Reverend Sabbath's archrival, Pastor Bob, First Shepherd of the White Light Evangelicals. For those of you eyeballing us from abroad, the White Lighters are the second largest fundamentalist denomination here in the U.S. The Reverend's Pure Holy Baptists are the largest, but only just."

An ex-surfer from Long Beach and a generation younger than the Reverend, Pastor Bob had been his nemesis for years. His Church of White Light in Colorado Springs had been growing like kudzu since he founded it twenty years earlier.

Frequent political allies, the Reverend and Pastor Bob mostly saw eye to eye. In some matters, like race, Pastor Bob was even farther to the right. (As a youth he'd been an avid member of the AKA, the Aryan Knights of America.) But in style they were chalk and cheese. Pastor Bob was loose and laid back. The Reverend believed God wore a suit. The Reverend liked the old hymns, preferably played by a large black woman on a harmonium. Pastor Bob wrote his own New Agey anthems and played them on a Stratocaster. The Reverend had a team of joke writers; Pastor Bob had briefly been a stand-up comic. If someone mentioned the Reverend in his presence, Pastor Bob would say he was the Irreverend.

And while the Reverend had done all the heavy lifting in taking over Hollywood, it was Pastor Bob who'd cleaned up. He was younger, cooler, and—for Hollywood—a local boy. If they had to work for far-right Christians, better an ex-surfer from the Southland than an ex-angel from the South. Pastor Bob's production company, White Light Camera Action, dwarfed the Reverend's Risen Lamb Films.

Dan's Inferno was as close to comedy as Christian entertainment got. Due to a mix-up in the celestial bureaucracy, blameless young evangelical accountant Dan Forte dies at exactly the moment Dan Forte, Mafia hitman, is supposed to. Evangelical Dan is condemned to Hell for his namesake's sins and, trying to escape, passes through all its nine circles, encountering many celebrities and politicians undergoing appropriate punishment for their earthly misdeeds. In the ninth circle, impaled on a spit, being nicely browned by demons, is a soul bearing a startling resemblance to the Reverend.

Just a casting mistake, Pastor Bob insisted.

The Reverend appeared for the final segment, holding high the envelope containing the winner for Best Film. "Dear colleagues, I hear that every Christian in America has seen *Dan's Inferno* so often their lips move along with the dialogue. So I say, let's skip the clips and get to the envelope. But first, a quick story. There's this young accountant dies before his time? Gets up to the Pearly Gates, and while St. Peter's checking the Book of Life, he looks inside Heaven. There, on a big old throne, is . . . Pastor Bob! He says to St. Peter, 'Gee, I didn't know Pastor Bob passed away.' St. Pete says, 'Oh, that ain't Pastor Bob. That's God. He just *thinks* he's Pastor Bob!' . . . Come on up here, brother!"

Pastor Bob, lanky, deeply tanned, with long gray-blond tresses, in an electric-blue silk evening jacket, plain white T-shirt, and a rough-hewn ironwood crucifix hanging around his neck, ambled up onstage. The rival messengers of the Lord embraced carefully.

"When you see these two great Christian leaders side by side," I said, "Pastor Bob looks like the future, doesn't he? As Satchel Paige might say to the Reverend tonight, 'Don't look back. Someone's always gaining on you.'"

"Jimmy," said Pastor Bob, in his surfer drawl, "the Good Lord has taken us some weird places. This is the weirdest yet!"

"It ain't the ninth circle of Hell, Bobby."

"Now why would God-fearing men like us be in the ninth circle of Hell?" drawled Pastor Bob, getting a sycophantic laugh from his jewel-encrusted workers. "Come on now. Open the darn envelope and take your Oscar home. It's late."

They tussled back and forth over the envelope, two old pros whipping up the tension. There wasn't much to whip up. Everyone knew the envelope would give the Oscar to the wacky Christian blockbuster that even the town's refuseniks found funny. Eventually, the former surfer ended up with the envelope and made a show of opening it as slowly as possible, mugging outrageously like the comic he once was. He drew out the Academy's decision.

"And the winner is," he said, not a muscle stirring in his leathery face, "*A Man Comes to Cheyenne*."

Over startled applause, orchestra and chorus cracked into a rousing reprise of "Hooray for Holywood."

"A big surprise," I said to the world, "but a fitting climax. For tonight is the Reverend's night. If there was any doubt that the Reverend has won his battle with the movie industry, it's gone now! The ever-beautiful people here tonight are sending a powerful message. However he's done it, the Reverend is one of them—a star!"

THREE

"**I DON'T GET** it," said Kuni. "If they know you hate the guy so much, why did they make you report the Oscars?"

"Because when you're fifty-plus-plus and not exactly employable, you do what the boss says—even if his name is Mohandas."

We were sitting in Fairlawn's legendary no-star eatery, the Dish of Food, having a beer to wash away the memory of the Reverend's triumph. I couldn't take my eyes off the four-foot-high Ten Commandments displayed behind the bar. Perhaps it was the Reverend's talk of temptation, but Number Seven was jumping out at me tonight. How long, O Lord, since I'd even had a shot at adultery?

"It seems totally sadistic," said my young friend, toying with the meatballs on the bar. I moved them out of his reach. You couldn't risk it, with mad pig everywhere. And now mad chicken.

"Corporations *are* sadistic," I said. "They're like any herd; they despise the weak and wounded. They know my history with this guy, so they torture me by forcing me to say nice things about him."

"I never understood this hard-on you have for the Reverend. I know he's the Enemy, et cetera, et cetera, but it seems . . . personal."

I stared into my beer, wondering if I should explain. Why not? He was the only under-thirty who'd ever shown any interest in my hopelessly outdated politics. He said he wanted to be a reporter. It'd be a cautionary tale.

◆

It was back when I was still at the newspaper of record, basking in the afterglow of the Pulitzer I'd won ten years earlier.

With the blasphemy-sodomy-witchcraft statutes in hand, the first thing the Christian Right did—even before they went after Hollywood—was to start suing major post-progressive newspapers. Any story in which Christianity or Christians were mentioned (proposals, strategies, activities, initiatives, anything) triggered a blasphemy suit. They were mostly nuisance suits and were thrown out over and over on First Amendment grounds. But they kept coming, costing newspapers—who were already sweating about declining circulations—millions they could ill afford. Right-wing papers, naturally, were immune.

The tricky thing about being accused of blasphemy is that the accuser has enormous freedom to define the extent of your guilt. It's like sexual harassment. Unless actually witnessed, it's judged on the emotions. He said/she said? The guy's probably guilty. He said/God said? Same thing.

The big papers started backing away from stories about Christianity. But far-right Christians were running the show everywhere: the judiciary, the military, the legislatures, the budget, foreign policy. News and Christians couldn't be separated. The papers' coverage became spottier and spottier, and readership declined even further. This Big Chill was exactly what was intended.

I should've seen my demise coming. I'd just lost my editor of twenty years, Ted Kaminski, a good friend despite his being as skewed to the right as I was to the left. He saw the writing on the wall and fled downtown to Wall Street, where the writing was safer. If he'd stuck around, he'd never have let me write myself into a hole the way I did.

Although our news was getting softer and softer, with back sections of the paper—fashion, dining, lifestyle, the arts—becoming front sections, we were still the newspaper of record. If the fundos (as we called them) went too far, we'd have an obligation to cover them, whatever the legal consequences. Came the day that obligation arose.

The Christian Right had long maintained that sex was for one thing only: making babies. Halfway through Sparrow 2's third term, the Reverend began pushing the more radical notion that any other kind of sex was a form of abortion (since a baby-making op had been deliberately averted). He christened the movement Pro-creationism. With *Roe v. Wade* a distant memory, this meant that anyone who made the beast with two backs for—God forbid—pleasure could go to jail. How could you catch the sex-crazed bastards? You couldn't. But you could remove from the culture all those pernicious stimulants that cause even nice Baptist couples to claw feverishly at each other's clothes as soon as they get home from church.

Of course the initiative wasn't aimed at Baptists but at every kind of sexual activity the Right hadn't yet got its mitts on, extramarital or birth controlled, sex education, the ever-popular porn industry, suggestive advertising, cinematic sex scenes. (Straight sex scenes, anyway; gay sex was already a felony.) Most of the areas we still covered would be affected, even wining and dining, if you consider a good dinner with a bottle of wine a form of foreplay.

The newsroom watched the debate with slack-jawed disbelief: Were they really going to make sex illegal? But the subject was a minefield. We clung to the hope that lunacy this extreme would, for once, shoot itself in the foot.

Driven by the Reverend, the debate morphed into concrete pro-posals. Pieces of Pro-creationist legislation began making their way down the streams and creeks that flowed into the great sea of salva-tion. Most were bans on something, all were fascinating insights into the right-wing Christian libido. There were to be no lipstick ads where lipstick was shown in contact with lips, no shampoo ads where hair swung in slow motion, no images of two or more people in a hot tub, no close-ups of the snap in pro football coverage. There were proposals to clothe the nether regions of male pets and farm animals and numerous bans on apparel: ankle bracelets, pointy shoes, pants with things written on the butt. Iowa wanted to outlaw grain silos with rounded tops. Anything that got right-wing Chris-tians hot was facing the Big No.

The tipping point had come. My editorial board decided that outlawing sex was so outrageous it couldn't be allowed to pass. A major piece on the ultra-extremism of Pro-creationist proposals was planned, mainly to arouse public indignation. I lobbied hard for the assignment.

It was a conscientious piece. I gave a dispassionate account of the ongoing debate and detailed the potential impact of Pro-creationist bans on lifestyles, advertising, and the arts. I interviewed countless religious lunatics, bending over backward to be balanced (which is a pretty interesting posture to be in, believe me).

Where Kaminski would've stopped me dead was my going a step farther—into the Bible. Ironically, I was trying to be fair to the Pro-creationists by quoting the biblical basis for their proposals. I found a basis for many of them: For example, St. Paul would definitely have had a cow about female hair swinging in slow motion. But I did write, after exhaustive research, *The Bible is silent on condom use.*

It seemed an innocent enough statement. Our blasphemy attorneys cleared it, the fact-checkers double-checked it. The editors ran the article deep inside the A section as a lifestyle piece. But it wouldn't have mattered how deep it was buried. Within days we were in the middle of the perfect shit storm.

The furious responses came from every quarter—though we soon discovered the Reverend was coordinating the whole thing. They all boiled down to the infallibility of the Bible. There was a chasm between the two sides. For us, if the Bible was silent on condom use, it meant there was no prohibition. For them it meant condoms didn't exist in God's plan for man.

The paper braced for the inevitable lawsuit. Or lawsuits: one against the paper and one against me. In questioning the Bible's infallibility, we'd caused chronic spiritual trauma to, and grossly infringed on, the freedom of worship of the plaintiff, a young and telegenic Pure Holy Baptist mom from Indiana, personally selected, I'm sure, by the Reverend.

In other words, the First Amendment was being used against the First Amendment. (For legal historians, this was several years before Sparrow 3 suspended the First Amendment with the First Emendment.)

Our blasphemy attorneys said we could win, but the fight would be protracted and expensive. After so many battles, the paper had no stomach for another. They'd counted on arousing public outrage, but the public didn't seem to care. There was an election coming up in a year. . . .

You never knew.

✦

The Reverend was in an expansive mood that windy March morning in the tenth-floor boardroom. He was riding into the very heart of the enemy camp to issue his terms to the Antichrist. The moment brought out the good ol' boy in him. He'd chosen to wear Tony Lama boots and sat with them up on the boardroom table, his teeth clenched in a triumphant leer as our attorneys went into their good-cop bad-cop routine. After a few moments, he shut them up with a wave of his hand, jumped to his feet, and leaned on his fists.

"How's it feel, boys—oh, 'scuse me, ladies, and girls—after all these years? Fifty–sixty years making fun of us dumb rednecks? For dunking ourselves in muddy rivers and speaking in tongues. Now us dumb rednecks are right beside you on the bridge of the good ship *Sodom-on-the-Hudson!*"

"Let me interpose," said his lead attorney, a silky-smooth Atlantan called Lamar, "that the Reverend's remarks are without prejudice and not for attribution."

"Don't you worry 'bout that, Lamar." The Reverend rolled right over him. "I don't mind who hears this—or reads it, either. Listen up, boys and girls. I don't want your blood money. I got more money in my back pocket than you ever dreamed of. I want your *humiliation*. Tomorrow, a full-page retraction on the back page of every section. The article? Out of your archives! Paper, microfiche, electronic: *de*-leted! And—he turned to me, the toothy grin of triumph wiped instantly from his face—"a full apology on the front page of next Sunday's edition from this sacrilegious weasel to every

Christian in America, for his antireligious Bible-hating filth! In his own words. Approved by me."

He sat down.

There was a long silence. The board and the attorneys exchanged whispered comments.

Then the editor in chief said, "*Every* section might be diminishing returns, don't you think? How about A, B, Business, National, and Arts?"

"And Sports," said the Reverend.

The newspaper of record agreed. Who could blame them? Seventeen pairs of eyes turned toward me. Another silence.

"Just so's we understand each other," said the Reverend to the room, "this man saying no is a deal breaker."

"He's an independent journalist, Reverend," said Ye Ed. "That's how we do things around here. People think for themselves."

Well, up to a point. Outside the boardroom, they said if I refused they would respect me enormously but they couldn't support the cost of two major lawsuits. They could arrange early retirement, triggering a considerable lump sum that would take care of my legal costs. As for their case, they'd fight it all the way to the Supreme Court.

When I returned to the boardroom—alone, the Reverend rose from his chair, smiling, and invited me to sit next to him. Lamar had vanished. So had the triumphant redneck.

"Sorry about the name-calling, Johnny. Just putting on a show. I hope we can work together on this."

"I'm willing to talk."

"Alrighty, let's talk. What I'd like your apology—if you don't mind me calling it that—to say is that I and my people believe in something, but you and yours don't."

"That isn't true. I believe in America. I want it back."

"I don't think you know what you mean by America, Johnny. I don't think you're certain of anything."

"I know this," I said. "There's one kind of person capable of certainty and another kind incapable of it. The second kind envies the first. The first doesn't envy the second; doesn't even know, in fact, by what right they're alive. In that arrogant ignorance lies most of human tragedy."

The Reverend's pale eyes were the color of muddy water. While we spoke, they'd focused on me, but now they refocused through me, on some greater audience.

"You are a worthy opponent, Mr. Greco. Your apology will say that your America is a place of uncertainty, that your truth is relative, that your morality is like the shifting sands of the desert. You will say that you realize there are those for whom America is different and that you envy them: the believing, the certain, those who know truth and morality. You will also say that just as *you* once legislated respect for *your* own—minorities, feminists, homosexuals, the handicapped—Christian believers now in the ascendant have an equal right to legislate respect for *their* own. You will apologize to them from the bottom of your heart for your lack of respect. In your own words, of course."

◆

It was a mistake to go on the bender; I'd been sober for years. But I needed to die for a while and benders are temporary suicide. I committed it around Tuesday lunchtime. When I came to, it was late Friday. I had an hour to write my apology. Lamar was down in the Risen Lamb headquarters in Atlanta waiting to approve it. *If* I wrote it.

If I didn't, I'd be respected enormously and without a doubt go to jail, where good reporters go for what they believe in. For what they're certain of.

I had it framed just as it appeared on the front page of the Sunday edition. It began: *My America is a place of uncertainty and relative truth.*

The Greco Option, my peers called it. Overnight I became the pariah in the schoolyard again, the runty bookish kid no one wants on their team or tells their secrets to.

Most of those who shunned me had long abandoned outrage; they resisted nothing, watching from behind the curtains as the America they said they loved was demolished by the hard hats of the Lord. Maybe deep down they felt the same shame I did, but they wanted *me* to go to jail for it.

"Shame breeds benders," I concluded. "After two more, the paper fired me. It was a year before I found another job—my proper level, I guess—working for this outfit. That was five years ago.

"I used to hang the Greco Option in front of me wherever I wrote, to remind me of my cravenness. And so I'd never never forget the man whose words they were. . . ."

I'd been staring for a long time now into my flat warm beer. I shook my head to get the memories out and looked over at Kuni.

Fast asleep.

FOUR

THROUGHOUT THE SUMMER and fall, Kuni brought me several Mysterious Stranger sightings, but they were always frustratingly word-of-mouth. There was never any video or audio record. Then a weird little story came up in Morris County, weird enough to make me do something I hadn't done in years. I actually went and investigated it.

One cold morning in October, a young New Jersey state trooper had been driving east on I-78. (He was a big fan of the *Inquiring Mind*, he told me; in fact, he'd been watching the Nut Log on his carputer that morning.) Just past Morristown he'd found a green Super-Size SUV, well off the highway in the undergrowth. The car was empty. No signs of collision. The engine was warm and stalled in drive. He figured it'd been there an hour, tops.

In the driver's seat was what he called a "pool" of clothes: men's boxers inside a pair of pants with the belt done up and the legs hanging over the seat, a shirt draped over the back of the seat with a necktie still tied, on the floor a pair of shoes with socks inside them. "Looked as if the guy had been extracted from his clothes," he said.

He checked in the bushes to see if anyone was dead, sick, and/or naked. Nothing. The car was registered to a Risen Lamb–affiliated church in Morristown. When he called, the pastor's wife answered and said the car sounded like her husband's. She was at the scene in minutes.

The trooper played me the car's audiovisual record. (Against regs, he said, but hey, anything for the *Inquiring Mind*.) He was parked on the shoulder, so the cam couldn't pick up much in the bushes, but the audio was pretty good.

The woman's name was Bobbi Coombs, wife of Pastor Darby Coombs. She appeared briefly on the audiovisual, immaculately groomed, wearing a white fox-fur coat, then disappeared into the bushes to identify the car. The cop said she took one look at the front seat and fell to her knees, yelling over and over, "O Lord, take me too! Don't leave me behind, Jesus!"

The cop didn't have a clue about what this meant and didn't know the proper procedure. The wife seemed hysterical, and he had an abandoned car with possibly a naked husband wandering around.

Then an old beat-up brown GMC van with New York plates pulled up on the shoulder in front of Bobbi's SSSUV. A man in a dark hooded fleece got out and walked around the front of his vehicle into the undergrowth. He looked stocky, but the cam was wide angle and flattened people out. His hood was up so his face wasn't visible.

The newcomer appeared to know Bobbi. The cop said he was big and dark-complexioned, might have been Latino. He spoke slowly, almost soothingly, as if trying to keep a lid on the situation. He said, "Bobbi, what happened here?"

"It's Darby," she said. "He's been Raptured!"

The guy explained to the trooper. "The lady believes her husband has been snatched up to Heaven in the Rapture by Jesus, and she wants Jesus to take her too. Right, Bobbi?"

She nodded, tears running down her cheeks. The trooper said that didn't help him much.

The guy in the fleece got Bobbi gently to her feet. He said, "Bobbi, don't be upset when I tell you this. Your husband hasn't been Raptured."

"But his clothes are the way it's supposed to happen," she protested. "Like in the old *Left Behind* movies? I don't want to be left behind!" She started crying again.

The stranger spoke so quietly here, the audio didn't pick it all up: "Bobbi . . . no knowing . . . death will come . . . nothing . . . Bible . . . invention. . . ." But this could be heard clearly: "There is no such thing as the Rapture."

Bobbi started yelling. "Who are you? Why are you haranguing me?"

The trooper yelled at him too. "I thought you knew her! Get outa here! You ain't helping none!"

The stranger stayed calm. He had something else to say. "Bobbi, Darby isn't with Jesus. He's with your church's financial manager, Sheila. They're flying to Costa Rica today with three quarters of a million dollars in church funds. I'm sorry," he went on, "but right now they're in the Ramada Inn at Newark Airport in Room Four-oh-two, having . . . sex."

She exploded. "How *dare* you! *Who are you?*"

The trooper tried to hustle the stranger toward his van, but he didn't budge. "Call the Ramada Inn at Newark Airport, Bobbi," he said, and gave her the number.

Bobbi hesitated, as if she didn't want to know if the stranger was right, but she repeated the number to her phone. The hotel answered. She asked for Room 402.

The phone rang several times; then a man's voice answered. She started to shake violently. "Darby?" she quavered. "What are you doing, honey?" The man gabbled something and hung up. Bobbi burst into tears again.

The cop said he had a dozen loose ends, but the number-one priority was that if the stranger was right about the couple he could be right about the money. He ran to his car to alert the Newark police. The drama unfolded on his two-way. Everything the stranger had said was correct. Darby and Sheila had checked out in a rush and were getting in their rental car when the cops showed. You could hear them protesting on the radio. They had a briefcase with just under eight hundred thousand bucks in negotiable instruments and two first-class tickets to Costa Rica.

But by the time all the excitement died down and the trooper was ready to take his statement, the stranger and his van had gone.

✦

Why did I have this sudden interest in a sordid tale of Baptists sinning? Because—although this was a very different sighting from the previous ones—I had a hunch this man was our Mysterious Stranger. There were no disciples and no healing, true, and the setting was hardly his usual one, but there was the beat-up van, his manner, and some possibly paranormal power.

Normally I would've lost interest in someone like the Mysterious Stranger, but something about this guy kept niggling at me. It might have been my need after years of humping dreck to report a real story, but I'd begun to toy with an intriguing idea.

"What if," I said to Kuni one night, over our now-regular evening beer, "the M.S. *seems* different because he *is* different? What if he's part of some larger plan, which is why he doesn't fit the usual nut-or-hustler mold?"

"What other category is there besides nuts and hustlers?"

"How about messiah-in-training? Someone being groomed as a religious leader?"

Kuni thought about this. "There's someone behind him, you mean? That would explain why he doesn't take money. But why? And who?"

"Let's say someone way up the Christian fundo food chain has decided there's some future in the one segment of the population they've always ignored: the poor. Not money but power. The working class are all the loyal opposition have left, vote-wise. What better way to get to them than through a charismatic young "messiah," one of their own, who heals folks without medical care, doesn't con them out of their hard-earned dough, but becomes a complete hero to them so they'll do anything he says? Like 'Vote for Sparrow 4.' We'd be outta business for good. The country really would be a one-party state."

"And if you're right, a fantastic story," Kuni added. "But no one would run it, would they? It'd be suicide."

"I think I know someone who might," I said.

Kuni got that hungry, excited look young journalists used to get when they smelled a story. He raised his stein. We clinked. "Count me in," he said.

◆

There was one major aspect of the latest Mysterious Stranger story that fit right into my theory: the Risen Lamb affiliation of Coombs's church. It answered the question: How did the stranger know about Pastor Coombs's new twist on the old staging-your-own-death scam? And when to show up and where the couple were going? Simple: Someone at Coombs's church—or higher up the Pure Holy Baptist hierarchy—had gotten wind of the scheme and told it to the M.S., who'd then ridden in like a hero, using "miraculous" powers to bring crime and sin to justice.

There were "con" aspects. The church wasn't in a poor neighborhood and didn't involve poor people. But word of the incident could make its way onto the grapevine of the poor. The M.S. would look good for exposing the hypocrisy of well-heeled Christians.

There was a coda to the story. It came up when I interviewed Bobbi. Apparently she hadn't told the cop or anyone else this part.

"The stranger was getting back in his van," she said. "I yelled at him to wait and ran over. I felt horrible. The fancy fur coat Darby had just bought me felt like . . . dirty laundry. I asked the stranger who he was. He didn't answer. He just took my hands. And in my head—he didn't say it out loud—I heard the words, *I am your Savior.*

"I had a feeling of being . . . safe . . . with him?" Bobbi went on. "That all the ugliness and sadness of my marriage didn't matter. That in the future he would be there. We stood like that for I don't know how long. Then I said, 'What should I do now?'

"He smiled—he had a great smile—and said, 'Sell all you have and follow me.' Then he kissed me on the forehead and drove away."

The M.S. sounded like he had real charisma, the kind he would need to pull a mission like this off. I was getting surer that something was going on here—and that someone was behind it.

Plus, thanks to the cop's audiovisual, I had his license plate.

FIVE

THE VAN WAS registered to José Francisco Lorcan Kennedy. The address was just off Morris Avenue in the Bronx—as it turned out, his mother's apartment.

María was a petite woman, around fifty. She came from a large Guatemalan family, which had fled the homeland during one of the periodic convulsions required by U.S. foreign policy. She had a perfect high-cheeked Mayan face, the kind that suggests great patience. It was slow to register emotion, putting the burden of expressiveness on her eyes. These were huge, dark, heavily lashed, with a tiny disarming cast. As a young woman she must have been ravishing. She was small and compact and had great self-possession. There was a stillness about her, as if, wherever she chose to be, she belonged in that place. Such people are like trees: As they grow older, their roots come to the surface.

Her dad had been a school principal back in Guatemala and

managed to wrestle a decent education for his large brood out of the New York City school system. María had had hopes of becoming a pediatrician, but having so many siblings had overwhelmed that dream; she'd got as far as pediatric nurse. With the cuts in public medical services mandated by Heaven via its faithful servants in Washington and Albany, nursing opportunities had become nonexistent in the Bronx; she had to commute long distances to suburban hospitals to find work. When there was none, she made ends meet by running a tiny day-care center out of her railroad apartment. Every spare corner was occupied by neatly stacked milk crates of toys, juice, and formula.

I'd got her to agree to talk by saying I represented something called the Faith and Hope Web and we were thinking of doing a piece about her son's inspiring work. I figured if there was someone behind him, this would give her a comfort level about telling me who. She'd agreed to talk. Face-to-face, though, she seemed cagey. I got the sense that if I hit her with a barrage of questions she'd clam up. I needed to get her talking about her boy.

I asked about his unusual name. She said she'd wanted his initials to be J.F.K.; his Irish father hadn't. At the baptism, Papa—whose name was Jake—had added the first Irish name he could find in the baby-name book: Lorcan. (He found out later it meant *little fierce one*, which didn't fit his son at all.) Few people used these Christian names; everyone called her son Jay. What did she call him? José. Never liked Jay—sounded too much like his father. This with a rare smile.

She hadn't seen Jay for months, though he called every now and then. He didn't say what he was up to, but she'd heard the rumors. He'd been living with her off and on since he left school ten years ago; she was used to his coming and going. He liked to travel and had been all over the U.S., abroad to Latin America, even Europe, always paying his way, working when he needed money. But he'd never been gone this long. She figured he'd finally cut the cord.

She hadn't minded his living with her. It was good to have a man in the house. She was never sure when his dad might show up. Every year or so, Jake, who made an excellent living as an itinerant house carpenter framing out new homes, passed through New York. He rarely missed an opportunity to harass his wife. He'd never been physically abusive, but he had a deep need to quarrel with her, enraged apparently, even after twenty-five years, that she'd somehow duped an eligible bachelor like himself into marriage. As for his son, the once-doting father had soured on him long ago. He called José a loser, a layabout, a fag.

José had gone to school, K through 12, at Aloysius Gonzaga in the Fordham Road, a big old Jesuit pile where he'd also been baptized and confirmed and had served Mass. His graduating class turned out to be the last one in its century-old history; after that the archdiocese gave up the ghost and closed it.

At Gonzaga, José was a big man on campus—almost. His academics were excellent, and he played point guard for a season on junior varsity, leading his team to a diocesan championship. Then he quit suddenly for reasons he wouldn't share with his coach—only his mother.

He told her it was the championship game that did it. He couldn't stand the look on an opponent's face when he got beat. He'd felt bad for the kid, whose whole life revolved around this chance to be somebody, to be a winner. He'd realized he himself wasn't into winning. His heart was always with those who lost. He said it just like that, those very words. She never forgot them. It was like a different person speaking.

She grew silent, as if we were now on dangerous ground.

Was José still a Catholic? No, but he'd always had a big interest in religion, unhealthy in her opinion, studying up on different faiths but never settling on one. Was she a Catholic? Not anymore. She went to the Iglesia Pentecostal de la Cruz on Bayler Avenue. Was that affiliated with any of the big groups? She shrugged; she didn't think so.

I said the Faith and Hope Web would find his words about winning and losing beautiful. "And it's a beautiful thing that your name is María and his father is a carpenter."

She stared at me from under heavy care-shadowed eyelids. If she thought it was beautiful she wasn't sharing it with me.

"Now that your son is doing . . . what he's doing, other people must have noticed those things too."

She nodded, on guard.

"Who?" I asked.

She said, "Why do you want to know?"

I said, "Well, of course, we'd want to interview other people about him and his . . . mission."

"People in the neighborhood," she said.

"But no one outside the neighborhood?" I was pressing now.

"You keep asking about other people. Why?"

"Just thinking about the competition." I smiled.

If she was going to tell me anything about any competition, it would be here. Instead, she said bitterly to the floor, "I don't want him on the webs! I don't want him doing miracles! I just want him to find a wife and settle down!"

"Have you seen him do miracles?"

Another silence. "Maybe," she said eventually.

"Can you tell me about it?" I asked, as gently as I could.

This silence seemed to go on forever. Finally she sighed and spoke. "It was almost a year ago, in January, right before he stopped living here. A friend from church, Diane, was getting married to her high-school sweetheart, Deion.

"All the guests are Baptist or Pentecostal, so there's no booze, just lemonade. It's pretty dull. José likes wine or beer now and then, and he's joking with some friends and teasing the Baptist lady who's serving the drinks about there being wine in the Bible.

"So a little later I'm talking to Diane and I see José alone by the lemonade. He does something strange. He passes his right hand real slow over the table and then slumps, like it took all his strength? Then he goes outside. I'm worried—maybe he's not feeling well—so I go after him. But I don't see him. I check all the places he might be. I'm away maybe forty minutes. When I come back to the wedding, the place has really woken up! The band is hot, people are shaking their butts, the joint is jumping!

"Diane and Deion are dancing, and Deion's drinking lemonade straight from a container and hollering, 'This ain't lemonade, baby, it's char-don-nay! These hellfire Baptists don't know what they're drinking!' "

"Someone had spiked the lemonade?" I asked.

"Well, listen. I see José's come back. He's watching Deion like a hawk. I go over to see if he's OK. He seems fine, so I, like, joke with him. 'Hey, *niño*, you spike the lemonade?'

"But he's real serious. He says, 'I didn't think it would work.' Then he says. . . ." María hesitated.

"He says, 'Perhaps my time has come.' "

Bingo. A scripted line if ever I heard one. "What do you think he meant by that, María?"

"That a miracle had happened and it was a sign."

"Like the wedding in the Bible?" She gave a tiny nod, eyes down. "But someone could have substituted wine before the wedding," I said, "and reclosed the containers." She said nothing, eyes still down. I said, "Perhaps someone wanted to make it *look* like a miracle."

"Why would they do that?" she snapped.

I said, "To make José look like . . . Jesus?"

"Then he would have to have known! My son would never deceive people he's known all his life!" Her face was taut with anger, but her eyes were brimming. I smelled a breakthrough.

"These days," I said, "being a religious leader can mean big money and great power."

"José doesn't want money or power."

"What if somebody is using him for money or power?"

"No one could use José. José is his own man."

Her face was impassive—except for the tear rolling down her cheek.

"How many people did you tell this story to?"

"No one."

"Did anyone at the wedding say anything?"

"No. . . . Deion, maybe. He talks a lot."

"María, José should be careful. Whether he's being used or not, what he's doing is dangerous. He could get hurt."

She said nothing. The tear rolled off her cheek and into her lap.

◆

Over our beer, Kuni had outlined how you could "cast" a messiah. Mary and its variants were common names; carpenter was a common occupation. A national identity search for Marias or Marys or Maries with carpenter husbands would probably net you a pretty large group to work with. You'd narrow it by income and age, then further by couples with grown sons, then those with religious affiliations. You'd end up with a group of young men who were messiah candidates. Kuni said if you knew your way around confidential records, like those of government agencies, churches, and banks, it would be a ten-minute job. The hard work would be sorting through the candidates to find someone with the talent and the inclination to pull it off.

There was a snag. If "they" had gone to all the trouble of setting up these hoary reruns of the Gospels, surely they'd promote the hell out of it. Kuni had collected dozens of miracle rumors, but this one had never surfaced. It made no sense. In one way it was the same puzzle as before: Jay the Mysterious Stranger didn't seem to want publicity.

Then something came up that knocked the whole theory sideways.

SIX

YOUR PROBLEM, MR. Christ," said Judge Michael Hartman of the Second Circuit Court, State of Connecticut, "is not that you've committed a crime. You've violated Section 28-11 of the public health code of our great state."

I was getting my first look at Jay, the Mysterious Stranger. Physically he was a surprise. It could've been María's physique, or her husband saying his son was effeminate, but I'd developed a mental image of Jay as a slighter, more compact person.

What I saw sitting on the defendant's side of a shabby courtroom in Hartford on a gray November morning was a heavyset man, bordering on powerful, a little over six feet tall. He had thick, wavy black hair, an olive complexion of the kind that would go darker in the summer, wide deep-set brown eyes. Even from where I was sitting in the back of the courtroom, I could see his face was distinctive. Odd wouldn't be going too far. Perhaps it was the Mayan-Irish DNA. Asymmetrical, lumpy, with a wide snub nose—the kind of face that makes you smile automatically. He was dressed in jeans and a well-worn dark-green hooded fleece. He looked like he'd be affectionate, physical.

But there was nothing remarkable about him. He could've been Latino, Southern Italian, Middle Eastern, South Asian: just one more member of the trying-to-get-by twenty-first century American masses.

"My name is José Kennedy," he said, referring, I guess, to the "Mr. Christ" crack. He had a low, rather husky voice, no accent, no elongated street vowels.

"I apologize, Mr. Kennedy," answered Judge Hartman, eyeing his public. "I presumed you'd prefer the divine honorific."

Scattered cackling came from a peanut gallery of regulars, mostly old biddies, in the front rows. His Honor sounded like one of those lawgivers whose courtrooms double as comedy clubs. Aside from his faithful fans, the place was three-quarters full, a surprising turnout on a cold winter day for a hearing about an obscure health-code violation.

State public health officials had picked Jay up two days before in an empty lot in Hartford's barrio, where he was holding a meeting, a hundred or so people in attendance. He'd begun healing: a young mother called Marisol Gutierrez with advanced leukemia, whose husband couldn't afford the panoply of chemo, stem-cell replacement, oral drugs, et cetera, that might help her survive a year or two.

According to one woman, Jay had picked Marisol up out of her wheelchair and held her off the ground in a bear hug for a full minute. The woman said that color flowed into Marisol's cheeks and then she smiled, which she hadn't done for years. That was when three public health officials, backed up by two Hartford PD patrolmen, stepped in.

Jay was charged with eight counts of practicing medicine without a license: this time, four times in Stamford, and three in Bridgeport. They'd had their eye on him for a while. The cops shoved him toward their car.

There was trouble. The husband was incensed, convinced that Jay was curing his wife's cancer. The crowd was right behind him. The younger of the two cops—he was sitting in court, a pasty-faced pear-shaped lad with a lot of new-cop attitude—had actually drawn his weapon. Jay told his people to be cool and got in the police car.

Unable to make bail, he'd spent a couple of nights in jail. Now he was in court for a hearing to see if there should be a trial. Marisol's husband and parents were there, to testify if Jay wanted them to. Marisol sat between them. She certainly didn't look like the end-product of a miracle; painfully skinny, old-geezer bald, skin fragile as a Chinese lantern. But she was laughing and fooling around with her folks, and they looked ecstatic. They'd been telling everyone Marisol was eating like a horse. The word in the barrio was, it was a miracle. A fund drive had been organized to run comprehensive blood tests and prove it. The results were due any minute.

Jay said to the attorney for the Public Health Department, "It's a crime in Connecticut to cure people with no medical coverage?"

The attorney rolled his eyes. Judge Hartman used his patient voice. "That's not the point. There's a law in this state requiring people who practice medicine to hold a state-approved license. Messiahs are not exempt."

More approving titters from the peanut gallery.

"What ought to be on trial here is that law," Jay said.

The judge said, "Let me explain something, your Almightiness. While you've been up in heaven for the last two thousand years, we've developed a little system down here on earth called tripartite govern-ment. There's an executive, a legislative, and a judiciary. We are cur-rently in the judiciary, where we do not pass laws, we *enforce* them!"

Jay continued, unfazed, doing the quiet, husky thing. He cer-tainly had one talent: He made you listen to him. "Along with all the other laws the Christians in Congress have passed, depriving people like Marisol of health care—"

"I'm confused," said Judge Hartman. "Christ is attacking Christians?"

Jay kept right on going. "You know why? They say Jesus said there's no such thing as a free lunch. Not true. I said no such thing."

It was the barrio's turn to approve. They did so noisily. Judge Hartman banged his gavel. "Look, pal," he said, "you're preaching to the converted. I'm a very endangered species, you know. Only one or two of us left alive in captivity. I'm a Democrat!"

The seniors applauded. No gavel for them.

"Your Honor," said Jay, "what do you do for medical care?"

"That's privileged information," snapped the judge. "And *noth-ing* to do with this case."

"You go to a military hospital in Maryland, right? Where state and federal judges are treated free of charge."

"I'm warning you, Kennedy—!"

"Medical care is free for judges. Why not for Marisol?"

The courtroom erupted into a bedlam of *Amens* and *Olés*. The pear-shaped young cop glared belligerently at the recalcitrant masses. His Honor gaveled the place into silence and then pointed the gavel at Jay. "You listen to me, pal. The medical system isn't on trial here, you are. Or you will be if you keep this up. There's only one question you need to answer. Were you—"

There was a commotion at the courtroom doors. Through them

came a little fireplug of a guy in a ratty down jacket, pulling a Sikh medical assistant toward the bench.

"She's cured!" bellowed the fireplug. "Marisol's cured!" He shoved the Sikh toward the bench. "Tell the judge!"

"Judge, I am so sorry," said the poor Sikh.

"Don't worry!" said the judge. "I love interruptions."

The fireplug grabbed the paper from the Sikh. "White blood cells sixty-three percent normal! That's a thirty percent improvement! Platelets sixty-nine percent normal, thirty-five percent improvement! Red blood cells—"

The courtroom erupted again, into cheers of celebration. Marisol's husband stood up, hands clasped above his head like a world champion. Judge Hartman wielded the gavel furiously. When order was restored, he turned to Jay and snapped, "*You* are responsible for the future orderly progress of this hearing! No more rabble-rousing! Got it?" He turned to the Health Department attorney. "OK. You."

"Thank you, judge," he said. "We couldn't be happier if Marisol is cured. We've found, in cases we've been able to check, that Mr. Kennedy's . . . clients' symptoms have been alleviated, though that doesn't mean medical conditions are being cured. How this is occurring isn't medically clear. But that's not the issue. The issue is certification.

"If Mr. Kennedy will cooperate with our investigation of his cases, we'll pay for training him as a Category B health-care provider. He could be certified within a year and continue doing . . . what he does."

"That's extremely generous! Mr. Kennedy, what do you say?"

"Marisol doesn't have a year. I don't have a year."

"Are *you* sick?" asked the judge. "Physician, heal thyself!"

Jay said, "The laws that prevent these people from getting medical help are unjust laws, yet you administer them. You, your Honor, actually believe them to be unjust."

The judge made a rueful maybe-but-what-can-I-do? grimace at his public. They loved him totally.

Jay went on. "You think you're off the hook by admitting that? Uh-uh. It makes you as guilty as those who made the laws—more so, because you know them to be unjust."

"Mr. Kennedy . . . !" warned Judge Hartman.

"If you were Marisol, you wouldn't want to be judged like this. I remind you of something I said once before—"

"Last warning!" Judge Hartman reached for his gavel.

"—Judge not, that ye be not judged." Jay turned to his public and added, "I'm only going to say this twice."

Marisol's dad stood up and shouted, "¡Tienes cojones, niño!" The courtroom went crazy.

Judge Hartman flushed with rage. "I'm holding you in contempt of court! Sixty days!"

"Bueno," said Jay. "¡Tengo solamente contempt para este corte!"

Over thunderous cheers the judge, banging his gavel furiously, shouted, "And that makes your two months . . . six!"

SEVEN

AS I INCHED home down the Jersey Turnpike—eight lanes each way and still a parking lot every rush hour—I felt conflicting emotions. On the one hand was the unwelcome realization that Kuni and I might have been barking up the wrong tree. On the other was an incipient excitement: Had I just seen a man with a big future?

I had plenty of time to ponder, surrounded as I was by four static stinking SSSUVs: a twenty-five-foot Ford Pharaoh, an even larger Nissan Nebuchadnezzar and—at a mere nineteen feet each—two cute Mitsubishi Magogs. And here was I, saving the planet in my 500-watt Suzuki Sulky, which weighed less than one of their gas tanks.

If there was a *them* behind Jay, would they have let things get this bad? Wouldn't they have bailed him out or provided him with an attorney so he wouldn't have talked himself into jail? Going to jail might be a calculated risk to give him street cred, but why? He had plenty already. Plus, jailbirds were ipsofacto sinners. No messiah sponsored by men of God could have that on his résumé.

Just as damaging to our theory was what he'd said to get himself into such deep shit. The faith-hope-and-no-charity brigade had "reformed" health care into Superb (the ruling class), Basic (the ruled class—including yours truly), and None (the class ruled by the ruled class). Would a right-wing-sponsored messiah say publicly that their reforms were a crock?

The possibility that he was for real, in some as yet unclear way, presented just as many problems. For me the miracle thing was a huge sticking point. To date none of the "miracles" I'd heard about could be explained, except as cons. Even if Jay had paranormal powers of some kind—and I'm convinced that certain people do have the power to cause changes in external phenomena—the results aren't miracles. As the health authorities pointed out, Jay might be alleviating people's symptoms, but that didn't mean he was curing them. And a miracle, I would think, must involve a cure, a dramatic one, preferably of something incurable.

For me, miracles didn't matter. I would never believe in them, however dramatic. What drew me to him was much simpler. I liked the look and sound of the guy. It wasn't charisma—quite. He had a face like something at the bottom of the shoe closet, but I wanted to know him better, and that can be said of very few members of the human race. (The human race, I'm told, feels much the same way about me.)

My attraction was as much political as personal. It seemed to me he might have hit on a formula the post-liberal left—neo-progressives or radical centrists or neocoms, whatever the pathetic remnants of opposition were calling themselves that week—had been seeking for a long time. He could do the Religion Thing.

Over the years, "our side" had rung endless changes on the Fundamentalism Lite approach—the notion that all you had to do to win over the Christian Right was to add a little Evangelical catnip to your left-of-center agenda and they'd desert their fundamentalism like a shot. Formerly lefty pols were always trying to coin right-wing-friendly oxymorons like those the Republicans used to be so good at before they stopped bothering: "Relative Prejudice," "Compassionate Militarism," "Neo–Jim Crow," "Situational Bigotry," "Creative Creationism." The woman who came up with that last doozy—an ex-president of Wellesley who still runs the MacArthur-Brookings Foundation—once proposed an Evolution Summit between prominent Darwinists and Creationists to discuss a "deal." Everything before the Jurassic: created in one Judeo-Christian work week. Everything after: as per Darwin. Fair enough?

A very seductive idea suddenly sidled through my mental doorway and leaned against the lintel, batting its eyelashes at me. What if Jay was—potentially—a new breed of populist leader, with spiritual bona fides that in today's God-inclined world were necessary to be taken seriously? With the help of a little judicious journalism—I could handle that—he could be a sizable thorn in the side of certain people. The selfsame people who, a few hours earlier, I'd thought were controlling him.

This guy had always had a major story in him. Now I was sure I had the angle.

As if to signal that excitement was in the air, the traffic suddenly loosened up. The ten-mile jam hadn't been caused by rush-hour volume after all but by an accident. Braking hard on a tight curve coming into the Fort Lee tolls, a BMW Babylon, the biggest SSSUV on the road, had jackknifed.

Twenty minutes later, I was home in my tiny *pigeonnier* high atop the Trump NJ Towers in Hoboken. It consisted of an astronomically priced living box and sleeping box with an eating carton in between. From my living-box window I could stare across the mighty Hudson at the Great Wall of Trump Towers marching up Manhattan's West Side, guarding it from the barbaric onslaught of sunlight. Once I had lived there, looking at where I lived now. Perhaps one day soon I'd be back over there again.

Blinking on my vidi-message was a Southern Asian woman of mature years. Judging by her haughty demeanor she was a Brahmin. She was Mrs. A. Purna, from Human Resources at NewsWeb in Bangalore, and would I return her call promptly? I hit CALLBACK and identified myself. The screen zoomed out to a lavish office in bright morning sunlight. It was already tomorrow in India. How symbolic.

Seated on a maharajah's throne on a swivel stand, was, according to the sign on her faux–Louis Quinze desk, Mrs. A. Purna. She was enormous and dressed in a rich purple sari. She looked like a giant gold-trimmed eggplant.

"Good morning, Mr. Greco," she said, with that hauteur Brahmins affect, as if all of Lord Krishna's creation was an exclusive prep school they run, on whose front gate they've caught you pissing. "Would you give me, if you please, a status and viability report on the Mysterious Stranger story?"

"Um . . . sure. In a nutshell, I don't think it has legs. But—er, how do you know about it?"

"Your colleague, Mr. Yamamoto-Young, has been documenting for us the inordinate number of hours you spend researching it and likewise the amount of his time that you demand for same."

Kuni, Kuni, you treacherous little shit!

"Has he indeed? Documenting inordinate hours indeed?" I said, trying to keep up prolixity-wise. "He's jolly ambitious, you know—"

"He has credibly reported that today you traveled to the State of Connecticut, there to attend a legal proceeding concerning same— and, to boot, trespassing on the territorial perquisites of the Connecticut *Inquiring Mind*. Further, that you told him of a media organ—other than the one that pays your annual emolument— which would consider publication of the Mysterious Stranger story."

"Absurd! I'm utterly dedicated to the *Inquiring Mind*!"

"Mr. Yamamoto-Young e-mailed us an MP-9, on which you are indisputably heard to say, 'I know who might run it.' "

"Preposterous! Audio forgery!"

"I never relish being the bearer of untoward tidings, Mr. Greco, but you have brought this unfortunate exigency upon yourself. I regret to say we are compelled to let you go."

"What's this really about, Mrs. A. Purna? Payback for the British Raj?"

"In the long view, yes. Good day."

EIGHT

WHERE TWO OR *three are gathered together in My name for eggs and bacon, there am I.*—Matthew 18.20.

The elegant Gothic script signaling the return of Evan Whittaker and Jeanine Sabbath to the *Risen Lamb Prayer Breakfast Club* crawled across my laptop. I was sprawled in bed three weeks after my encounter with Kali, Goddess of Destruction and Syntax, trying hard not to think of how nice it would be to start the seventh day of Hanukkah with a large, lightly chilled gin. Not that I was Jewish, but my few remaining friends mostly were, and at holiday time it's important to celebrate other people's beliefs—even if they did give them up at Princeton.

"Big news this morning," said Evan, "in the Pastor Bob blasphemy scandal. The Third Circuit Court turned down his appeal of a decision ordering that his trademark slogan be removed from all White Light golf products. White Lightning golf balls alone—over two hundred million are estimated to be in circulation—will cost billions to recall and replace."

Normally I'd sooner watch a chicken being plucked in slow motion than any webcast produced by the Reverend. But a headline about Pastor Bob's problems had caught my eye, and it linked me to the *Prayer Breakfast Club*. The story, which I hadn't known about, made me sit up. It looked like the First Shepherd was about to lose major ground in his twenty-year battle with the Reverend for control of the Ocracy.

Pastor Bob was crazy about golf. God, for Pastor Bob, was the Divine Golfer, driving, chipping, and putting the golf ball of each human soul through the eighteen holes of life, before it relaxed for all eternity at His Nineteenth Hole. A huge publishing enterprise churned out products that conflated God, golf, and Pastor Bob's taste for comedy: books, posters, paperware, video games, and other rib-tickling items by the million. All bore his trademark slogan: ONE NATION UNDER GOLF.

According to Evan, a little-known group called Golf Moms for Family Values had accused Pastor Bob of Felony Blasphemy One because of this slogan. Civil and criminal charges had been successfully prosecuted. Pastor Bob could be facing financial ruin and fifteen-to-life in the big house. The GMFV were supposedly White Lighters, but to a longtime Reverend watcher like me, this Golf Moms group had his fingerprints all over it. If that was the case, the Rev had crossed a line scrupulously observed to date by the Christian Right: You don't accuse your own of blasphemy.

"Jeanine, this is a dark day for our good brother," said Evan, who, within the limits of Christian charity, hated Pastor Bob's guts. Others might have forgotten the Aryan Knights of America (which Pastor Bob had never renounced); Evan hadn't.

"I'm with God on this one, Evan," replied Jeanine, in her down-state Georgia singsong, an accent so strong some said it could crack pecans. "If I was God, and God knows I'm not, I wouldn't want My almighty works being compared to hitting little balls with sticks."

She gave him a sidelong look that suggested this was an obligatory rather than sincere opinion, and Evan, normally a very serious young man, allowed himself a tiny smile. They were an unlikely pair, these two, but they always seemed to be sharing unspoken confidences.

Evan Whittaker was intriguing. It was hard to understand how someone who'd recently been so supercool had fallen into the Reverend's clutches. A wild child in his football-playing days, all women and cars and bling, Evan had cut a couple of platinum albums even before he led the Atlanta Patriots to their first Superbowl in their new home. His plan had been early retirement and a second career as a hip-hop singer, but something went wrong. The rumor was that an old steroid bust in Boston had been discreetly taken care of by the Reverend, putting the ex-star wide receiver permanently in his back pocket. I didn't subscribe to that—it sounded too underhanded for Evan—but, whatever happened, he'd discovered not long after that he'd been born again. The Reverend himself had baptized Evan into the Church of the Risen Lamb. He'd joined the Angelic Choir of the Reverend's weekly *Sabbath Hour* and its eyeballs had skyrocketed, flattening every other Bible-believing Sunday webcast in creation. Then—big news in Christian circles—the Reverend, who'd been doing the *Prayer Breakfast Club* with his wife for fifteen years, stepped down in favor of Evan.

Jeanine had always been a second banana, occasional comic relief from the Reverend's Bible-based gravitas, but she blossomed in the presence of a six-foot-five African-American athlete half her age.

She'd always been a bohemian presence in the emotionally corseted world of the fundos; with Evan across the desk, the *Prayer Breakfast Club* must have seemed, to its core audience, downright daring. Its eyeballs skyrocketed also.

A petite redheaded ball of fire, Jeanie—as she was known to le tout America—had successfully preserved, past menopause, the cuteness of her cheerleader childhood. The lost souls I hung with dismissed her as a right-wing ditz, but I thought there was more to her than met the eye. She once said, "I put the fun [or "furn"] back into fundamentalism." For my pals this proved she was a moron. To me it proved just the opposite. That *furn* wasn't the point, but *putting it back*. When in its long history had fundamentalism ever been fun? It was deliciously sly, the kind of joke she shared with Evan that she never had with her husband.

While it was easy to see where the ribald rumors came from, I didn't respond to them. They seemed just plain wrong. For all his ardent Pro-creationism, the Rev had never managed to sire a child with Jeanie (giving rise to still more ribald rumors), and they'd never adopted, although she seemed like a mom to the manner born.

Jeanie's relationship with Evan struck me as maternal, not sexual. Given its genetic impossibility, the bond was fascinating. For his part, Evan, who'd been brought up by his widowed father, clearly responded to her warmth, even looked to her for signals. In bearing he could hardly have been more masculine, but offsetting that was a restless seeking quality, as if he was always looking for answers about his purpose in life. He was so powerful a presence he could get away with what might in others have looked like uncertainty. A year earlier, discussing his conversion and future plans on FoxWeb's Sunday show *Faith the Nation*, he'd said something revealing: "I'm not a quarterback, I'm a receiver. My job begins when someone throws me a ball."

On his and Jeanie's first appearance together, which I'd watched along with most of the nation, Evan read a news story about a multiple-vehicle collision in Texas that was supposedly caused when one of the drivers was Raptured. No one had been killed, but there were many serious injuries. Evan was listing the carnage when Jeanie suddenly burst out, "Rapture Helmets!"

"Rapture helmets?" repeated Evan, without batting an eye.

"If folks'd wear Rapture Helmets," she explained, "they wouldn't be turned into vegetables in these collisions." She and Evan had then exchanged an innocent look, and one of those tiny smiles flickered across Evan's lips. You knew that, devout Pure Holy Baptist though she was, Jeanie had never believed in the Rapture for a second. And now, neither did Evan.

"Pastor Bob's out of options," said the Wall Street analyst whom Evan was interviewing on the implications of the First Shepherd's dire situation. "Whatever he does," continued the analyst, "he'll have to step down as CEO of the White Light conglomerate. And guess who's waiting in the wings."

There was a far bigger prize, apparently, within the Reverend's grasp than the mere satisfaction of seeing his nemesis slapped in the slammer.

Pastor Bob's breakthrough twenty years earlier had been the discovery that while Americans were hungry for spiritual nourishment, they wanted it bland and easy to digest—the religious equivalent of fast food. All that New Testament stuff about self-sacrifice and forgiveness puzzled them mightily. So Pastor Bob preached the Christian virtues of feeling good, relieving stress, getting rich, and hiring abundant deadly force to protect the good people from the bad. Nothing embodied this simple faith like his nationwide chain of gated communities called Heavenly Gates.

All Heavenly Gates communities had massive golden gates as their point of entry; all were manned by a robed and bearded security chief—PETER read his name tag—with similarly robed (and armed) seraphim enforcing his directives. Tight security and comprehensive municipal services provided Pastor Bob's flock with peace and certainty in an ugly and uncertain world. The chain was incredibly successful.

The Reverend's Pure Holy Baptists watched in dismay as Heavenly Gates prospered. The Reverend launched a rival outfit called Pearly Gates, but it didn't take off. Pure Holy Baptists just didn't have the laid-back comfort thing down the way Pastor Bob did. Besides, the faux-pearl finish on the Reverend's gates looked tacky and peeled easily. So the Reverend had taken a different tack: If you can't beat 'em, buy 'em.

"Pastor Bob's commitment to Ownership Christianity," said the analyst, "is his Achilles' heel. Every Heavenly Gates community is a public corporation. The Reverend has been quietly taking them over. He now controls seventy-eight percent of Heavenly Gates. If Pastor Bob steps down, the Reverend will become, de facto, the owner of the Church of White Light."

I sat up even straighter. He'd done it, by God! He was about to become the supreme pontiff of the Eastern and Western churches, the Protestant pope. Doctrinally he would have to merge New Age Rock and the Rock of Ages, but that wasn't hard. White Lighters would believe anything you wanted, so long as you didn't take away their barbecues.

Sure enough, a few hours later, Pastor Bob resigned all his positions at the Church of White Light and announced a plea bargain that kept him out of jail. The Reverend was now the undisputed number-one Christian heavyweight in America.

◆

I'd put Jay completely out of my mind, but the Reverend's ascension to the very pinnacle of power put him back, front and center. I might not have a job but I did have a story, possibly a great story. I needed to get on it.

I owned part of my living boxes and most of my car. I could unload both, rent, use mass transit, keep sober. Since the bastard was pretty much responsible for getting me fired, I might as well put all my eggs in his messianic basket.

Sell all you have and follow me.

◆

The starting point was the medium-security jail where Jay was paying the price for his contempt, Taborsky Corrections Center in Middlesex County, Connecticut. It was there I headed one bitter December morning a week later.

I'd met Jay's group briefly in Hartford Criminal Court, after he was hustled off to the pokey. At that time there were ten or more disciples following Jay around, an eclectic lot from all over the social map. I gathered that their intention was to camp outside the jail, visit him as often as possible, and await his return to the fold.

By the time I arrived, Jay had been in Taborsky more than a month, and most of the disciples had scattered. A core group was still waiting faithfully, sleeping in Jay's van or local churches and shelters, getting moved on from time to time but refusing to be discouraged.

They were very reluctant to talk. At first they wouldn't even give me their names. No one had been allowed a visit with Jay, not even María, who showed up the second time I was there and gave me a very cold shoulder. Apparently she believed that my coming to see her was somehow connected to Jay's falling afoul of the law. Her hostility colored the whole group's attitude. For them, I was trouble.

I persisted. I took a room at a local Days Court 6, showed up every day, offered them coffee and meals. Sometimes when it was really cold they'd go back to the Bronx and sack out for the night in María's place. I'd make it a point to be waiting for them when they got back to Taborsky the next morning. I knew I'd break them down eventually; being a pain in the butt is one of the few things I'm good at.

Two weeks into my stakeout, persistence paid off. They'd had some kind of meeting. They were worried about Jay, who still hadn't been allowed a visit. Jail for contempt of court was often used as a way to silence troublemakers; the months had a way of becoming years. The group figured Jay might be getting into still deeper trouble; perhaps somehow, sometime, I might be able to help.

So they began to talk.

NINE

FOR A WHILE I was a Triple-Xtra," said Angela. "I had a scene in *Very Close Encounters of the Third Kind*, but they cut it out."

Angela, Jay's only female disciple (unless you counted María), seemed to enjoy being back in the spotlight, even if it was only on my pocket-cam. I could believe she'd been in the movies. She was thin and haggard, older-looking than her twenty-six years, but she must once have been stunning. She still had riveting gold-green eyes.

She was referring to that brief shining moment in Hollywood, right after the Reverend's assault began, when certain movie producers, more pragmatic than the private-jet Left, had gone over the hill to hook up with the San Fernando adult film industry. The result was a slew of big-budget Triple-X-rated movies, most of them remakes of former blockbusters. All had spectacular orgy scenes, in which hundreds of extras would fill the Roman arena or biblical temple—or (as in the case of the movie Angela was talking about) the spaceship—with heaving heaps of highly imaginative and athletic prurience.

These movies made fortunes at home and abroad (*He's Titanic* actually pulled in more money than the original). The Reverend soon put a stop to the marriage of power and porn, but for a while there was plenty of work if you didn't mind having sex in front of Teamsters.

"I met this guy Robbie on the set," she went on. "His dad had been a big deal in some eighties sitcom, so he was sort of a celebrity by birth."

She fell in love with the Beverly Hills princeling, and he introduced her to the exciting world of crack cocaine. He omitted to tell her until it was too late that he was also HIV positive. She gave a dry little laugh. "Bastard ended up in that Fox series *Christ: The Early Years*? Played the teenage Jesus."

She fell silent for a long uncomfortable moment, then said, "I tested positive. Robbie dumped me. I didn't have insurance. Spent all my savings on antiretrovirals. Started hooking. Got deeper into drugs. . . ."

She was looking away from me now, eyes unfocused, all her animation gone.

"You got a cigarette?" Her voice had changed subtly. There was a whiff of the street. I shook my head.

"What about your folks," I said. "Couldn't they help?"

She refocused on me. "Yeah, yeah. My mom was . . . a teacher. In Brooklyn. Italian. Sicilian. My dad was from Brazil originally. He was a . . . a chef."

"So they helped?"

"My dad was where I get my skin color from. He wrote a bossa nova song about me once called 'Caramela.' He wrote songs all the time."

"I thought you said he was a chef?"

"He was a chef who wrote songs. There a problem with that?" Her eyes glittered. I shook my head again.

"Anyway, no, they couldn't help. I just couldn't tell them. They were good hardworking people. They found out anyway. . . ." There was another uncomfortable beat. "My mom took her own life. My dad . . . he loved her so much . . . he lost his mind, and one night he walked out of the house in his pajamas and no one's seen him since."

I couldn't think what to say after this tale of woe.

"What's wrong, Mr. Media? Don't you believe me?"

"Sure, sure. Sounds like you've had a pretty tough life."

"But it's all changed since I met Jay"—she smiled—"my savior man."

"OK. Where did that happen?"

"In Camden, at the Fred D—the Frederick Douglass Community Center. Kinda place you end up when you hit rock bottom."

"When was this?"

She said it had been in early February of the previous year (which fit with María's date for Jay leaving home). Jay had shown up at the Fred D and started hanging out there every day, trying to get to know folks. But he was from New York, better dressed than they were, and he had a vehicle. People were suspicious.

"One morning, out of the blue," said Angela, "he started preaching about how he was Jesus returned, come back to set things straight. No one paid much attention. I sort of half listened to him. Then a volunteer told him he couldn't preach on government property; this was one place the Christers hadn't got their claws on yet. She was real mean, so Jay left. And then—"

Her face was alive again, intense with the memory, made beautiful by it, in fact.

"I followed him outside. I don't know why, it was beginning to snow and I only had a summer dress on. But I had this crazy idea. . . . I went up to him, and he turned and said, 'Hi, Angela.' Don't know how he knew my name. And he took my hands. They were so warm? On that freezing morning? And, well . . . I don't trust any man alive, you know? But I knew I could trust him. I told him I'd heard him preaching and I said, 'Can you do miracles? I need a miracle, man.' He said, 'Do you believe I can heal you?' I said I'd never believed in anything, but I could believe in him.

"He took me over to the doorway out of the snow. I had these horrible lesions . . . from the sickness? All brown and purple, on my neck and throat, all over me. He put his fingers on them, sort of pressing and stroking at the same time, and where his fingers touched they went . . . away!"

She said the last word almost breathlessly, still amazed at what happened.

"Wait," I said. "You mean where he put pressure they changed color? Or they disappeared?"

She leaned forward, her green-gold eyes on fire, nodding gently, smiling. "They disappeared! And I could feel something inside, happening all over my body. I said to him, 'You cured me!' and he said, 'Your faith cured you, Angela.' "

The word *autosuggestion* popped into my mind. "Have you been tested since then?" I asked.

"I don't need to be," she said, still smiling that dazzling smile. "The lesions never came back."

Her faith—if that's what it was—was overwhelming, even for someone unwilling to be convinced. She anticipated my last question. "He put his fleece around me, we got in his van, and I've been with him ever since. Turned no tricks, done no drugs, never will. I'm not letting that man out of my sight till the day I die."

✦

In the van, when Angela got in, were two other men. Their names were Rufus and Charlie. They'd also followed Jay out of the Fred D, hoping to get a ride to New York and maybe a free meal. Angela didn't know them, but they knew her by sight from the center. She was hard to miss with those eyes, that summer dress, those lesions.

Both men had witnessed Jay's healing from the van. Charlie was frowning, but Rufus's eyes bulged in his round face. He said to Jay: "How'd you make her marks go away, man?"

Angela said, "He did a miracle."

Jay corrected her. "*We* did a miracle."

The two men were very quiet. Jay headed toward the Turnpike. He got on at Exit 4 and drove into the EZ-Pass lane. To stop cheaters, EZ-Pass lanes were equipped with massive metal teeth that rose from the pavement when a truant car went through, tearing its front tires to shreds.

"Hey, watch it!" cried Angela. "You don't have a tag."

Jay gunned the old van through. Nothing happened. GO EZ-PASS! said the screen hospitably.

Charlie said, "That a miracle too?"

Jay just smiled.

✦

Rufus was the fireplug in the down jacket I'd seen in Judge Hartman's courtroom. He said, "I was brought up church religious, Assembly of Jehovah First Baptist Church of South Boston. Never believed a word. Hated it all: God, sin, speaking in tongues. Just did it for my mom. She sang in the choir. But since that day at the

Fred D, I've believed Jay is who he says he is. Every day since, when I see him heal, I believe more. Ain't a shadow of doubt in my mind."

"Ain't a shadow of anything in your mind," said Charlie, smiling across the table at his friend. Charlie was as tall and stringy as Rufus was short and stout. We were in a blue-collar bar a few miles from Taborsky.

"Better than having no mind at all," countered Rufus. "Just a big old hole where your gray matter should be."

I got the feeling this routine was being run for my benefit. Enough with the snappy dialogue. "Do you believe in Jay like Rufus does?" I asked Charlie.

"I don't have nothing to thank God for," he answered slowly. "But I have great respect for Jay. His words have a lotta power. And I've seen the same things Rufus has. But I want to keep an open mind. I can't believe in Jay like old Rufus does, no, sir. Not yet." He took a sip of beer. "But I'd welcome the gift of belief. I truly would."

Rufus and Charlie had known each other since high school in Boston a quarter of a century ago. What brought them together back in the raging heyday of hip-hop was a common love of jazz. Charlie had been a talented jazz guitarist. "A genius," said Rufus. "Coolest licks I ever heard." He'd played with name groups, even done studio work, but it was no way to make a living, at least not in Boston. Meanwhile Rufus was working at nothing jobs. So they both did a stint in the military, Charlie in the infantry, Rufus in the navy. "The sea's in my blood," he explained. "My dad was Portuguese. A cod fisherman. Till the cod ran out."

Rufus's tour was uneventful, but Charlie found himself in Afghanistan where, on patrol one day, his Hummer ran over a land mine. His right hand was hanging out the window at the time. The blast blew the thumb and three fingers off, leaving the middle finger intact, frozen as the tendons stiffened into the universal gesture of disrespect, a perpetual up-yours to his musical dreams.

They'd gotten back together when their tours were done and had knocked around ever since. Their life together had been a slowly downward-trending spiral as they got older and work grew scarcer; I had the impression it had included crimes punished and unpunished, some good times, some very bad times. They were mutually dependent, supporting each other when things were bad, Charlie being prone to terrible depressions, Rufus being an intermittently serious drunk (which endeared him to me).

Meeting Jay just under a year ago had given them both a common purpose. "Being around Jay, helping to help people, bring them a little comfort," said Charlie. "That's a great satisfaction."

Rufus was more down-to-earth. "We help Jay too. He's young, he's educated. People get suspicious. Us and Angela, we're street people; we been around, seen it all. If we're with him, people know he can be trusted."

"Rufus came up with a name," said Charlie. "Way back when."

The three of them were the Apostle Posse.

◆

Kevin had joined the Posse a few months later. Kevin was nineteen, fresh-faced, funny, smart as a whip. He worshiped Jay, who returned his affection. Kevin said he'd known from the moment he became aware of his own existence—around five—that he was gay, though he had no word for it growing up in a little town in Kansas, called Calvin. He was the only child of Bible-believing parents, his father being one of the elders of the local Pure Holy Baptist

Church. When, in his teens, his sexual orientation became impossible to conceal, he confided in his mother, who, though shaken, said she loved him no matter what.

Not so his father. He took everything Kevin owned, clothes, toys from his childhood, books—Kevin was a voracious reader—and made a huge bonfire of them on his front lawn for the whole town to see. Then he gave Kevin an ultimatum: Renounce your abomination or move out. Kevin was fourteen. His mother came to his defense, so his enraged father moved out and got the church to declare an official shunning of his own son.

The church being the social center of Calvin, Kevin and his mom were completely ostracized. She lost her job at the local high school. His academic record was destroyed when he didn't attend school for weeks because of death threats. Then another church from a few towns over, called the First Church of Christ Homophobe—*homophobe* having become a term of approval in the fundamentalist universe—began picketing their house 24-7, plastering it with charitable slogans like GOD HATES FAGS and demanding that Kevin renounce his sinful embrace of Satan.

One night just before he turned sixteen, Kevin slipped out of Calvin and hitched to New York, where he'd worked at various menial jobs until hooking up with the Jay train at a meeting in Bed-Stuy.

The Posse had immediately warmed to him. Angela especially adored him. Kevin, articulate, widely read, became the unofficial scribe of the group, recording what Jay said and did, noting ideas that came up in discussions and what people's concerns were. He kept track of where they went and took names and numbers of people who wanted to stay in touch or have Jay come back to their neighborhoods.

Between the four of them, they told me many wonderful things

about the miracles Jay had done and the things he said. Unfortunately, in the first eight months or so of their being together, no records had been kept of the meetings, although they must have been
attended by scores, sometimes hundreds, of people. I was told that
if you went to the towns and neighborhoods where they took place,
people were still talking about them. I never did that. Your reporter
is small in stature, with the musculature of the average clam, and
very white.

The accounts of Jay's sayings and doings after Kevin joined the
gang were dramatic in detail and probably more accurate. The kid
had great recall, a good eye, and a fine ear. Much of what follows
came from him.

TEN

THE SAYINGS OF JAY

Selfishness is behind every kind of inhumanity. It's this country's worst failing. USA stands for the United Selves of America.

Screens of every kind kill meaning for those on them and for those watching them. People must talk to people; lives must touch lives. The Revelation will not be televised.

Can't walk with me and carry a gun.

That homeless guy you gave a quarter to while you were gabbing on your cell phone? He'll be in paradise long before you.

Last time I said something perhaps I shouldn't have, something that's been taken the wrong way: "The poor are always with you." At that moment, back then, I wanted my friends' attention.

I meant I was going to die soon, but they would have the rest of their lives to care for the poor.

But the rich have twisted my words to mean something quite different: that there's nothing you can do about the poor. That the poor are part of life, like disease or accidents or hurricanes or getting old. Poverty is natural. You'll never get rid of it, so forget about trying. Don't worry that the poor have so much less than you do. Go eat your big meal, go drive your big car, go sleep in your big house. Let the poor look in the windows. Jesus says it's OK. Well, Jesus doesn't say it's OK. OK?

P&L. It can stand for peace and love or profit and loss. But not both. Take your pick.

Whoever is near me will burn; whoever is far from me will freeze. There's nowhere you'll be comfortable.

THE NEW BEATITUDES

Jay would preach some of these by himself. Then he'd encourage people to call out the first two words—"Blessed are . . ."—and he would say the rest. When people got into it, they came up with both halves by themselves. Jay said that was the whole point: When people truly understood his message, got the right *attitude*, these ideas came naturally. That's why Kevin called them the Be-*attitudes*. Here are some he collected.

Blessed are the homeless, for they shall find their way home.

Blessed are the imperfect, for they know no one is perfect.

Blessed are the lovers, for they become one.

Blessed are the cowards, for they have killed no one.

Blessed are the homely, for without them there's no beauty.

Blessed are the generous, for they know their riches belong to others.

Blessed are the doubters, for doubt is the path to truth.

Blessed are the worms, for they turn death into life.

Blessed are the shadows, for they define the light.

Blessed are the dead, for they know the answer.

JAY'S VERSION OF CREATIONISM

Every human being on earth is descended from the first man and the first woman. How do we know? The Bible tells us so. And so does human DNA. Human DNA tells us Adam and Eve lived and met in the Great Rift Valley of the Horn of Africa; scientists estimate between fifty and seventy thousand years ago. Actually it was 61,522 years ago.

Our original African parents didn't call themselves Adam and Eve. What they called each other was mostly clicks and grunts, so we'll call them Click and Grunt. From the love between Click and Grunt flowed all the tribes and races and nations and peoples and faiths and classes and colors and sizes and sexes of man- and womankind. Just as the Bible says, we are all one family that has endured from generation unto generation. Only the Bible didn't get the number of generations right; since our first parents had their first child, there've been around twenty-five hundred generations. But the Bible has the basic story exactly right. Scientific wisdom doesn't contradict my parents' wisdom; it just helps to bring its genius and generosity to light.

PAYBACK

The final saying is also a doing. It concerns Taborsky, the jail where Jay was incarcerated. Taborsky was only a medium-security facility, but the conditions were murderous. Everyone in there had a blade.

It is said that on Jay's first day inside, in the workroom, one inmate tried to kill another in front of him. It is said he stopped the fight and healed the victim of a serious wound. It is said he then preached against payback.

"So this guy kills that one. Some day someone will kill him. Payback always comes around to bite you in the ass. The way out? Forgiveness. Don't laugh. Guys think forgiveness is weakness. Uh-uh. Forgiveness is strength; payback is weakness. Everyone from the warden to the guards outside that door want us to believe in payback. That's why we're in here. We're being paid back by society, so we pay back someone else. It goes around and around, everyone paying back everyone else, hating and dying. We live in a world of payback. We need to live in a world of forgiveness. It's the difference between death and life."

Someone shouts out he's done bad shit. Is Jay saying he ain't evil? Jay says no, but he can be forgiven. He tells them a parable.

"There's this high school cannot win at basketball. The coach is great, but he never has the players. Then one year in the intake there are two kids who are the best point guard and the best shooting guard he's ever seen. The shooting guard is fifteen, six-four. He has sweet hands and plays great D. The point guard is shorter, but his moves are like lightning and he can shoot three-pointers all night.

"That high school starts beating every other school in the league. The two boys are the whole reason. Then the point guard falls in with some bad kids. Starts messing with drugs. Game goes downhill. His team starts to lose. The shooting guard's a good kid, but he can't do it all by himself.

"Now, which one of those two boys does the coach lie awake worrying himself sick about? Which kid does he care about more? Which kid does he go looking for on the street and do everything in his power to save?"

It's real quiet in the workroom. The same guy says, "The point guard?"

"Straight. And that point guard is you, brother. That's how things are between you and your coach."

◆

It is said Jay later healed many men of ailments. It is said he made visits at night to other inmates: the lonely, the despairing, the suicidal. It is said he just appeared in their cells; steel bars could not contain him.

It is said that after Jay had been inside for a month, prisoners began to disappear. There were never any signs of escape and, once away, the escapees were never caught. This was bad. No one had ever escaped from Taborsky.

Warden Tulliver, a righteous Christian of the New England mold, blamed his officers. His officers blamed Jay. They put Jay in the Hole, but the disappearances continued. Mutiny was in the air.

It is said Warden Tulliver had inmate 2427 K6Z brought before him. It is said he asked Jay if he was helping these men escape. Jay said they'd been able to escape because they were forgiven. Tulliver replied, "The Lord forgives. The State of Connecticut does not." And Jay said, "Then I forgive them. I release them in my Mother's name."

It is said Jay's fearlessness worried the warden. It is said the warden feared him for another reason; the judge who'd sent Jay up had just been diagnosed with advanced pancreatic cancer. It is said that is why, some time before his scheduled release, prisoner 2427 K6Z walked.

ELEVEN

SO HERE I SIT, waiting like a giddy schoolgirl in my room at the Days Court 6, a few miles from Taborsky. It's 8:30 A.M. on a cold March morning, and it's snowing.

Jay must have been sprung by now. Word was it could be as early as 5 A.M., an hour before reveille in the jail, so there wouldn't be any trouble from the inmates. At this point our information is sketchy, coming entirely from María, the only person who's been allowed to visit him. It's three months and nineteen days since he went in.

I'm hoping to convince him to do an in-depth interview with me. I have what I need for the rest of my story, but it's missing the crucial factor: its star. If, and only if, I find Jay not just convincing but worthy of the adulation he elicits from people, will I have a story. Otherwise weeks of my life—months, actually, if you count the spadework I did on the *Inquiring Mind* dime—will be down the drain. And probably with them the last best shot I have of reviving what little is left of my career.

I'm not sure he'll show. Rufus didn't want me waiting with the Posse for Jay to come out, his excuse being that he didn't know if Jay would want to speak to a newspaperman, as he quaintly calls me. The real reason is that Rufus has treated me, from day one, like he wouldn't trust me across the street with his toothbrush.

He has a point. I'm not trustworthy. Nothing I know has convinced me entirely. The information on Jay can be seen either as a slowly crystallizing myth or as a growing mountain of corroboration. I go back and forth on whether the man is a potentially major figure or just another seductive fake riding on the sad needs of helpless people.

Why am I here? What has brought me to this very odd moment in my life? Exposing José Francisco is not in the cards; he's nobody, it's pointless. The only reason can be that I want to find him convincing, that I want—though obviously not in a religious way—to believe in him and then express that belief. Can I rise to this occasion? I'm not sure I can. I can't remember the last time, if there ever was a time, I wrote anything positive about anybody. It's never occurred to me in a lifetime of pursuing the banalities of greed and deception that I might need to. Journalists like to pretend that tearing down and ruthlessly exposing is hard work, gritty, and demanding, requiring tenaciousness and countless hours of shoe leather, but what makes the time fly is that tearing down is fun. It's real easy. Whereas, whatever its opposite is, is fucking difficult.

A knock at the door. I jump so hard my head almost parts company with my shoulders. Before I can say anything, the door swings open and there he stands.

In the motel doorway he seems more imposing than he did in court: tall and solid. He's wearing the old green fleece he wore in court, with the hood up. A dusting of snow on the hood and shoulders gives him a timeless quality. He could be from any century.

Coming from the piccolo end of the band, I find most males taller and solider, but imposing does not translate as intimidating. Everything about him is open; you know immediately that he has no protective shell.

His attention is focused on you and you alone. The eyes are his mother's, down to the tiny disarming cast; he looks at you with head slightly down from under her long lashes. Unlike hers, these Irish-Mayan eyes are smiling.

"Johnny. Good to meet you."

The husky voice is quieter than in court, and the words come even slower. He seems to mean the greeting.

Before I'm out of my chair, one burly arm is around my shoulder and he's enclosed me in a strong affectionate squeeze as if we were old friends and he was doing the welcoming.

He plops squarely onto the bed, shaking back the hood, legs apart like an athlete on a bench. Once at rest he's very still, exuding immobility, in the sense of occupying perfectly the space he's in, of being exactly where he should be. His mother has a similar thing, I recall. I suppose *presence* is the word, but it's inadequate. I mean that he seems at peace.

He couldn't look more normal, but for some reason I can't take my eyes off him. I grope for my recorder.

"Rufus thinks you want to expose me."

Normally this opening would put me right on the scent. Normally I'd ask: Is there something to expose?

"Maybe," I answer.

"Who's this for?"

"Dunno yet." I sit across from him in the only chair.

"So it's for yourself?"

"I'll ask the questions, OK, *niño*?" I snap, regretting it instantly, feeling like some idiot with a press card in my trilby.

"OK, *hombre*." He grins.

I don't know where to start. How do you ask a friendly, open, normal-looking guy if he's God?

"First off—er, about your—you know, claims. I've spoken to a few people: your mother, your Posse, a woman who thought her husband had been Raptured—"

"Bobbi."

"She told me you were her savior."

"I didn't say that. I have no right to say that."

"Did you say, 'Sell all you have and follow me,' knowing those were the words of Jesus?"

"You know your Bible."

"I served my time. Could you answer, please?"

"I did. Knowing they were the words of Jesus. They're words that fit her situation. Shopping makes her go weak at the knees. She needs to strip her possessions away from her self. Find the true person beneath. The person I love."

"You know all that from spending five minutes with her?"

"Yes."

"You said, Follow *me*. Are you Jesus?"

"In a sense, yes. In a sense, no. When I was here before, I was a Galilean named Jesus. Yeshua, actually. I've come back as an American man named José. But I have the same nature and the same mission."

"Which is what?"

"To reveal the God in humanity and the humanity in God, by teaching, healing, and, if necessary, dying."

"Like Jesus?"

"Like Jesus."

"You're willing to accept death to accomplish your goal?"

"If I have the courage. I'm a man, like Jesus. I have free will."

Uh-oh, Johnny; there's an out you can drive a truck through.

"This isn't the only time you've repeated Jesus. The thing Kevin quotes: *Whoever is near me will burn; whoever is far from me will freeze?* That's from the Gospel of Thomas."

"The Gospel of Thomas was about me. I'm quoting myself."

"I thought you said Jesus and José are two different guys."

"They are, but the Dual Nature is common to both guys. You were raised Catholic; you know about the Dual Nature."

"How do you know I was raised Catholic?"

"I sensed it." Again the grin.

"Gospel sayings aren't the only parallel. Your mother thinks you turned lemonade into wine at a Bronx wedding."

"I didn't really mean to. It was a Baptist wedding with no alcohol. I thought it might liven things up. It was as big a surprise to me as it was to everyone else."

"Are you sure someone didn't spike the drinks?"

"I'm sure. It was a sign."

"That Baptists should drink?"

"It was my Mother's way of saying my time had come. My Mother in heaven."

"She must have a sense of humor."

"She does."

"So. Lemonade into wine and you're on your way?"

"No. When I realized it was wine, I had an intense . . ."

He narrows his eyes, groping for words. He's speaking so quietly the audio monitor barely moves.

". . . experience, I guess, of being . . . divine."

My messiah-alert starts flashing like a fire truck.

"You never had one before, huh?"

"Sure. But never this . . . vivid."

"Can you describe it?"

"Not really."

"Could you try?"

"Well . . . My self, by which I mean my sense of self rather than my mind, began to . . . swell . . . until my skull felt as if it was going to burst, but then my self shot free of it and expanded into the stars and beyond the stars to the farthest limits of possibility and beyond that, and for one instant I knew all that had ever been and would ever be. . . ."

Pack your bags, Johnny, this guy's nuts.

"Sounds nuts, right?"

Damn grin.

"But you asked."

"Pal, I've heard this shit before. Not this slick; you got a way with words. But it's old news on the messiah circuit."

"I agree. Words are no way to describe the absolute. Even the most precise words are approximate; the infinite is precise."

While I'm deciphering this—is it profound, pseudo-profound, subtly unhinged?—I say something I'd more or less prepared, "Odd, coming from a man they called the Word made flesh."

"That was a different time. The Word was sacred. When you gave your word it was sacred. Now a billion words change brains every second. Words are a debased currency."

"Isn't that going to make your mission kind of hard?"

It's not a grin this time but a smile, broad and intimate.

"This is going nowhere, Johnny. You're trying to trap me, trick me, cop to my scam. Ask me what's in your heart, not on your list. Be my friend. You might find out something."

Normally when a subject suggests we be friends, I feel the rush of impending victory. This time I feel . . . relief. But I haven't a clue what to say. My head has no words in it.

He says, "Try this. If I *was* Jesus, what would you ask me?"

The kid is telling me how to interview him?

"You mean you're not?"

"Don't do that. It goes nowhere."

Impasse. I'm on the very brink of an unknown void. Could be that the story's a dead end. Could be my entire future. If I step back, he will smile, put up his hood, and go, and that will be that. Ah, fuck it. Jump, Johnny, jump!

"OK. Why have you come back now?"

"I thought you'd never ask." He smiles. "Two reasons. One: to clear up the confusion about what I said before—refresh the message. Two: to fulfill the old law—Christianity."

"Does that mean overthrow it?"

"No, it means to take the very best of the last two thousand years—the most fertile ideas and beliefs, the most exemplary lives women and men have lived and the lessons they teach—and then plant a new faith in that soil."

OK. The first truly Nut Log statement. Pity. I wait for the inevitable segue to the Book of Revelation. Not a Christ I ever came across, however normal-seeming, who didn't right about now start to promise blood pouring from the breasts of whores, and horned beasts with chain saws wreaking God's vengeance on fornicators, and all the rest of the sanguinary garbage. But—nothing. He sits impassive, dark eyes on mine, waiting.

"How will the new Christianity—um, grow?"

"As before: one by one, person by person, self by self. The message that needs refreshing is that everyone is potentially Christ, an incarnation of God. Allowing God to inhabit you is something anyone can do. Hard work but it can be done. A day-to-day thing, reaching out to the God in others, allowing God to dwell in you, becoming another incarnation, another Second Coming, another proof of God's presence and purpose in the world."

"Proof? Is proof possible?"

"It's all about belief, Johnny, helping people believe. Believing is incredibly hard. People need as much proof as is humanly feasible. Why not? Why should people remain in the half-darkness of uncertainty? The only certain proof that God is manifest in existence is people you can meet and touch and talk to in whom God dwells. The only way for people to touch the divine is through flesh and blood, eyes and hands."

"What about the Day of Judgment you promised last time?"

"Oh, the Day of Judgment is at hand. For Christianity."

"Why now?"

"Christianity is unrecognizable to me. Christians have removed me from my own religion. They teach that my teachings don't apply until I return in glory and kill all their enemies. Oh, and reign for a thousand years. I always forget that part. I did so much reigning last time. King of this, king of that."

"Yeah, I remember. They put that sign on your cross."

"Until then, they're free to ignore my only commandment: Love one another, even your enemy. Free to take revenge on whom they please; wage wars; steal from the poor and blame them for their own poverty; allow disease, misery, famine, and environmental devastation, even nuclear war, to sweep the planet, because—bring it on! All these man-made horrors are signs sent by me that I'm just around the corner. That's not Christianity, that's insanity.

"What I promised was that I would return exactly the same as the first time. An ordinary Joe you wouldn't look at twice, an obscure event in an obscure place, which would change the course of history."

"And, just for the record, that has happened?"

"You're looking at it."

Deep in my profoundly shallow soul, something stirs. I have a momentary flash, less visual than felt, of sinking slowly, helplessly, into a bottomless ocean.

He's leaning forward, dark eyes bright from under the lashes, lumpy, smiling face slightly to one side. This messiah doesn't glare but he does glow. Or burns.

I know one thing: I'm glad I jumped.

✦

So there we were in the dingy little room with its ancient forty-inch TV on the wall. Time passed but I didn't notice. Sitting there with him, for that long moment in time, the slurry of resentment and disappointment—in which my rusted, dented mind spends a lot of its waking hours—evaporated. My knee-jerk cynicism—that absolute conviction that anything anyone is saying is in some respect suspect—vanished. The past, the past that lives in every line of your face, every inflection of your voice, every reflexive thought and judgment and mental tic and quirk, went with it. I forgot my plans for the future or for his future.

I don't mean I was some new being, forged in the fire of his spirit. Just that I felt cleansed for the moment of a bunch of irrelevant and useless habits, a moment which, when I looked up and saw the fading light outside, had lasted almost seven hours.

It wasn't until later that I realized what it was. For the first time in a long time, possibly for the first time in my life, I was at peace.

I was completely satisfied with the present. I felt no craving for drink or food or smoke or escape or stimulant or distraction, no need to be someplace, call someone, check in with breaking news, mentally assess my current wealth, worry about dying or impending baldness or whether I was as ugly as I've always thought or would ever get laid again. That dumpster of the mind we pick through all our waking hours.

His words: "that dumpster of the mind." I don't know in what context he said it, but it stuck. The kid had a certain poetry in him. When we got on to the absurdity of interpreting the Bible literally, he said, "A lot of what I said last time was poems and riddles. They were meant to have more than one meaning."

It rang a bell. Long ago, during my holy teen moment, I liked Jesus' words because they often seemed to have a poet's eye and ear behind them: "Consider the lilies. . . ." "Be wise as serpents and gentle as doves. . . ."

He had great passion, but it was quiet and deep, not the sublimated rage that often passes for passion or the hatred elevated by injustice into a noble emotion. He was passionate about injustice to the weak, about personal redemption, about people realizing their own incalculable worth, about the deadly machinations and fathomless possibilities of the human self. I found it striking how nonjudgmental he was, how free of that condemnatory tone of your average man of God, the saved speaking down to the not-yet-saved or the already damned. The last thing Jay wanted to instill in anybody was fear. For him, a universe imbued with the divine was not something to make you bow down but something to reassure you. The divinity of all things is normal, not awesome.

"People think of God as the boss of the universe, far away in his office, all-powerful, all-knowing, intimidating, watching everyone's every move. God *is* like that, but it's irrelevant to humans. The relevant thing is that God is here, now, in this room, looking up at you from the cellulose molecules of your notebook or twinkling up your nostrils from that cup of coffee. We're much less mysterious than the men of God want people to believe. That's how they get power, right? God is so awesome you need a specialist to speak to him. Only we specialists have the guts to get close enough. Do not try this at home!

"True, we're the architect of all existence, but we're also its super. We have to worry about the tiny stuff as well. Why is that microbe dying before it should in the intestine of a sheep in eastern Kazakhstan? How long will it take for the shard of Heineken bottle in your tire to cause a flat—or shall we make it fall out going over that pothole?

"You can't have the awe without the atoms. And atoms need constant care. Most of what we do is unbelievably tedious. My father's few seconds of mad Big-Bang-baseball fun became my mother's quasi-infinite ever-expanding headache."

"What about 'Honor the Lord thy God'?"

"You honor God in the finite, the knowable, not in the unknowable infinite. I never used the word *almighty*. I always spoke of God as a parent: normal, tangible, familiar. *Almighty* is a human invention, a reflection of human frustration at human limitations. It's from worshiping God as apart and beyond, sacred, faraway, all powerful—instead of ordinary, present, and everyday—that human beings get their great contempt for life. That's the beginning of evil."

"Wait. . . . The worship of God is the beginning of evil?"

"If it makes you have contempt for others: for an enemy, for the poor, for the rich, for the helpless, for the different. It's not God you're worshiping, it's your own pathetic projection of omnipotence. But God *is*: the enemy, the poor, the rich, the helpless, the

different. God is the other. All evil begins with this belief: that another's existence is less precious than mine."

✦

When he said *we*, meaning himself and his Father and Mother, the
triune God, or when he said *I*, meaning the one God, I didn't flinch.
It seemed reasonable. Jay's use of these terms seemed normal, given
the norms of his worldview, within the massive sweep of his fantasy.
The whole thing was beautifully thought through.

Frankly, if I were a believer, I would far prefer Jay's version of the
Trinity to the patriarchal weirdness of the Nicene Creed, wherein
God is two guys and a ghost: a father, the son he's begotten without
any help, and a vague birdlike thing fluttering around between
them. There's nothing in the Christian canon quite so rabidly sexist
as the doctrine of the Trinity. We are God. We don't need a woman
to have a son. Here's Jay's version:

"The Father, the He in God, is the forces and laws that bind
space, time, and matter. The Mother, the She of God, is existence,
why and how things are. She is the answer to the question: Why not
just nothing? But these two aspects of God are as entwined and in-
terdependent and inseparable as a couple in love. That love pro-
duces the child in God."

"Which is you?"

"Which is me."

✦

He spoke a lot about María and not much about his father. But there
was this:

"Last spring I went to see my dad, Jake. He has this hunting
cabin near Lake Hopatcong? So I'm sitting on the back porch and

looking at this cold, bleak, barren landscape, and I have a flash of . . . wilderness. But bleak, barren wilderness, the desert at night, still hot from the day's sun. And then—"

He shrugs like I won't believe what he's going to say.

"—the devil spoke to me through my dad. Exactly the same temptation as before. He said, 'OK, Jay, if you have these powers, why not make money for the poor, feed the hungry, cure the sick? Leave the world, when you're old and gray, a better place?' A very powerful temptation. Hard to resist."

"Your dad is the devil?"

"No, the devil isn't a person. The devil is a collective beast that lives deep inside humanity, that speaks and acts sometimes through one person, sometimes through many."

"But your dad is one person the beast speaks through?"

"No. My dad is a prick. But your dad is your dad. It wasn't that long ago he filled your universe, right? Everything he did made little worms of pride wriggle in your tummy. My dad used to sit on my bed with his guitar when I was little and sing old Beatles songs to send me to sleep. He told dumb elephant jokes. He drove an old 'seventy-eight Galaxie. Always the same, summer or winter: one hand on the wheel, one on the roof. The Galaxie I was born in— because he and Mom didn't get to the hospital in time. Back then nothing he did or said could ever be wrong. That's why his temptations were so dangerous. They would have been easy to give in to. It's hard not to look for an easier way out."

"Than what?"

He didn't answer.

✦

I asked him why he or his parents allowed evil to flourish.

"Evil is caused by selfishness, by people acting out of the belief that they and their needs are paramount. And just because our first and only commandment is love, the diametric opposite of selfishness, doesn't mean that we're going to save people from the consequences of their selfishness. If you force the vast majority of people to live in squalor so you can live in splendor, you'll bring on the Black Death. If you allow the rise of a homicidal maniac like Hitler because you see him as a way to beat down those who want equality and social justice, he'll start killing people. Don't blame God."

"What about AIDS? What have we done to deserve that?"

"AIDS has fundamental environmental causes that a team of scientists led by a young woman will soon isolate."

"Who's the young woman?"

"Can't tell you. You might track her down and in some way obstruct her. She's a second-year medical student in a sub-Saharan country, and she'll soon win a graduate scholarship to a medical school in Italy."

"When will she cure AIDS?"

"You don't need to know."

"The public has a need to know."

"No, they don't. That's journalists masturbating. The public has no right or need to know the future."

"Will she become rich and famous?"

"No, she's a truly selfless person. But she'll be venerated as the savior of Africa—which will become the savior of the planet."

"Not the U.S.?"

"Dream on."

◆

Around Hour Four I said, "Frankly, you don't sound quite the same as the quotes I got from Kevin and the others."

"You mean how come a twenty-nine-year-old Hispanic male who never went to college can put sentences and paragraphs together?"

"No, no. I mean is there a Bronx Jay and an Upper West Side Jay?"

"I figure you've got a more extensive vocabulary than most of my friends. Doesn't mean you're as smart as they are. I can do it short and street if you like."

"While we're on that subject, there are those who might say your followers are—well, rather damaged people. Can you really trust them? How do you know Angela isn't just a crack whore with a lively imagination?"

"Which story of her life did she tell you, the underage Cuban sex slave?"

"No, the Italian mom committing suicide, the Brazilian dad going mad."

He nodded. "There are a couple of others. The Hollywood part is actually true. But when it comes to family, Angela has a great hunger. She often feeds it the wrong things."

"What's her real background?"

"She was born in a shelter in Oakland. Her parents went out one day and were killed in a run-of-the-mill auto accident. She was abandoned in the shelter, almost starved to death, grew up in the worst kind of foster care."

"So she could be a crack whore with a lively imagination?"

"A very rich man once said, 'Christianity is a religion for losers.' He was absolutely right. It's always been very hard, even for Chris-

tians, to understand that I don't come for the winners in society—
the successful, the creative, the victorious, even the saints. They have
their reward. I come for the anonymous, the invisible, the forgotten,
the damaged. I come, first and foremost, for the losers."

"OK, key question. Lazarus and Dives. Lazarus the poor man is
on the fast track to heaven; Dives has to squeeze through the eye of
a needle even to take the entrance exam. Blessed are the poor. But
billions of people are now beginning to emerge from poverty. As
they get richer, will fewer people get into heaven? What happens to
Christianity when there are no more poor people?"

"Actually, I said blessed are the poor *in spirit*. The poor aren't
necessarily closer to God but they're less burdened by possessions.
Hunger and poverty may be ended, but the loneliness of possession
won't be. This is the biggest difference from the last time. A house-
holder now needs to own—or thinks she needs to own—a mini-
mum of about five thousand household items. All of them cut you
off from others.

"Modern loneliness is physical as well as spiritual. People live in
hermitages of possession. You need great strength to be a hermit, to
discover God alone. The vast majority of people find God through
community. But the communities Jesus took for granted—the tribe,
the village, the market town—are gone.

"People buy pathetic substitutes for community—sound waves
in a speaker, particles bombarding a screen—all pretending to be
friends or the folks next door. The vacuum they leave when the
screen goes dark, when the recording ends, is filled with a loneliness
worse than ever before."

"What's the answer?"

"Flesh and blood touching flesh and blood. Life touching life.
Yours, mine, everybody's."

◆

"Evolution is a fact. Take it from me. I have an inside source."

"You're not going to be popular in Kansas."

"That's why Christianity hasn't long to live. Christianity has become a gated community where you can live with only a tiny fraction of your brain functioning.

"Creationism is blasphemy. Evolution is a divine work of art, a metaphor for the human spirit. It's varied and creative, full of tragedy and achievement, sheer ingenuity and depth and breadth, eye-boggling beauty created from pure utility, amazing adaptation and survival, the ability to overcome the harshest of conditions and turn them into advantages. Evolution is not just the story of life, it's the ultimate celebration of life—one of my Mother's most brilliant creations. There's no more convincing argument for intelligent design than evolution."

◆

"Have you ever had sex?"

There was a beat. "No."

"Have you ever been in love?"

A much longer beat. "Yes. Once."

"How old were you?"

"Eighteen." Jay was silent for a moment, making a decision. "Her name was Beatriz. She was seventeen. Incredibly beautiful. Incredibly sweet-natured. She vibrated with life. It pulsed in her, crackled along her skin and through her words. Life came off her like perfume."

"Did you want to have sex with her?"

"Of course. I'm a man. And I loved her."

"What happened?"

"Some guy tried to rape her in her schoolyard. She resisted and he stabbed her in the throat. She took a long time to die. He raped her anyway."

"Was he caught?"

"No. But his life is a terrible misery—its own punishment."

"Do you feel rage toward him?"

"Rage is not only a great sin, it's a waste of time."

"Didn't you want to kill him?"

"No. That would be to murder Beatriz again."

"What will happen to him?"

"He will make his peace with me. And I will forgive him."

There was a long silence.

I said, "I'm done."

Suddenly he took my hands in his. In the stillness he existed in, it was a sudden explosion of movement. Compared to my puny mitts, his were the size of shovels, basketballer's hands, strong, dry, warm. Their warmth ran up my arms and through my body.

"Johnny, I know you don't believe in me. Or believe I'm who I say I am."

"I'm not sure I'd . . . go that far."

"You don't think I'm nuts anymore, true. But you're not sure if I'm not a very elaborate con artist."

"Journalists are trained to be skeptics."

"That's why I want you to write my story."

"I'm already writing a story."

"Not this story. This story will be part of my story."

Actually, I was delighted, since I had been going to propose an exclusive arrangement. But I played hard to get. I had something to add to the deal.

"The story up to now? Or do I get the whole franchise?"

"Till the end, you mean?"

"Do you know the end?"

A long beat. His eyes were very dark but somehow full of light. Unfathomable. "No."

"Good. I accept. But I have one condition. There's this old friend of mine in Metuchen? Ex-union organizer. Vinnie Tartikoff. Wife's name is Connie. Their only kid Nickie is nineteen. Totaled his bike three months ago. Came off a curve at about sixty, swerving to avoid some animal. Been in a vegetative state since. Effectively brain-dead. They've already lost their house trying to keep him on life support. They're completely tapped out. They're gonna have to pull the plug or the hospital will. I've known this kid since he was yay high. Watched him play Little League. Like him a lot."

He was still holding my hands, looking down at them as if—I wasn't sure what—as if he was communing with them or with someone else. Without looking up, he said, "Why do you want me to do this?"

I quoted. *"It's all about belief, Johnny, helping people believe. Belief is incredibly hard."*

He looked up at me, and I had the sensation that he was reading the inside of the back of my skull on which was printed something like this: *Do I really want proof that this guy's capable of miracles so I can believe in him, or am I just looking for a great end to my story?*

But he only smiled and said, "We'll see, amigo. I make no promises. God is only human. *Hasta luego.*"

It was 4:55 P.M.

✦

Here I sit in the same place, about twelve hours later. I've just closed my ancient Thinkpad 3000. It's been twenty years since I wrote this much this fast, and—I say this without humility, false or otherwise—this well.

The quart of gin I went out and bought, to get myself kick-started, sits on the bedside table, uncracked.

The story unfolded beautifully. Of course, I've been writing it in my head for a few months now, but still. When I was at Bard I used to write songs for campus bands; when a song is right it just flows like honey from a jar, the words and phrases needing no thesaurus, the rhymes falling in the right places, the hook appearing like a Holy Grail in the forest, there for the taking. And if it doesn't do that pretty early on in the process, you know you've got a dog.

This story came out like a song. I hardly corrected a thing. I have to say that every now and then, in my feverish generation of narrative, I had an eerie sense that Jay was present, watching me with that lopsided smile, cycling along beside me, murmuring encouragement as the miles of the marathon fell beneath my feet.

When I needed to quote him, his words were in my head as if my once vast and total photographic recall had been magically released from the vat of alcohol in which, lo, these many years, it's been pickled to the size of a lentil. The first few times I checked a quote against the disc, it was word perfect. After that I didn't bother.

Some of his quotes are—I hope and pray—inflammatory. On one level the story, or its subject, is all I wanted it to be: an in-depth portrait of a Christianity at complete odds with the foam-flecked humbuggery that's strangling our once-great nation.

On another level, though, it's a holy story, a lives-of-the-saints parable of a miracle worker. Ought to give goose bumps to the most rock-ribbed Evangelical.

I can't be faulted by those most likely to find fault with me for lefty bias. As for the Lefties, they probably won't like that I avoided the carping contempt with which most of my co-politicals discuss anything to do with Christianity.

Whether Jay will like it or not I couldn't say. I don't think I'm going to show it to him until it's too late.

As for the great ending? Well . . .

I started calling my friend Vinnie in Metuchen around 9 P.M., having given El Salvador four hours to work his magic. I couldn't get through anywhere and everything was busy through several other calls I made whenever I came up for air. An hour ago, around 3 A.M., I finally got Vinnie on his cell. He was in tears.

I'd last spoken to him early the morning before, when I first got this idea about "testing" Jay. Unbeknownst to me, things had moved very quickly that morning. The resident ethicist at Metuchen General, where his kid Nickie was, had called Vinnie at 9 A.M. This ethicist's job apparently was not to help the parents with the ethical and emotional issues of their tragedy but to deliver an ultimatum: Pay up or we pull the plug.

Vinnie and Connie spent a desperate few hours trying to raise enough money to pay the five-figure bill they owed and buy Nickie a little more time on earth. They came nowhere close.

Around 3 P.M. the hospital administration "regretfully" handed down the decision that Nickie would have to be taken off life support. He was not expected to survive more than a few minutes.

Obviously, they gave his parents time to give their boy the last rites and to assemble grandparents, friends, and siblings to say goodbye. The deed was to be done at 5 P.M. The family gathered and kept vigil for the last hour of Nickie's life. At five precisely (this detail tells you a lot about modern health care) the machines sustaining Nickie's life were turned off by a central computer located in Guadalajara.

Almost immediately his brain waves began to flatten and his heart and breathing slowed. At 5:03:11 he straight-lined, and at 5:04 the monitors were turned off—also by remote control. He was medically dead.

At 5:05:21 P.M., Nickie blinked once, opened his eyes, and, in a hoarse whisper, asked for his mom.

That would be about ten minutes after Jay had said he'd make no promises, which is as close as they ever get in the Bronx to *yes*.

The miracle in Metuchen is all over the media—which was why I hadn't been able to get through for so long. Vinnie and his wife and family have happily been giving interviews to anyone anywhere in the world. I forgot to say: His tears were tears of joy.

Nickie is fine, sleeping soundly after a solid meal. The hospital, claiming the miracle is fantastic publicity, has forgiven Vinnie and his missus their debt so long as nothing is said about it publicly. They've also offered to let Nickie convalesce at no charge for as long as it takes. Doubtless they want to study him a little, to get to the bottom of why taking this young man in a vegetative state *off* their machines would bring him out of his coma.

The media attention to the miracle, I need hardly add, means that the inside scoop my story now ends with will be an absolute blockbuster.

In the last hour, since I wrote up the ending, I've been sitting here in the motel gloom.

For a long moment after I hung up with Vinnie, a terrifying and utterly unfamiliar emotion washed over me: that some unknown force, possibly benevolent but not necessarily, was about to change my life, possibly forever.

Usually that would be a gin kind of thought: from gin or requiring gin. But the gin remains uncracked.

This emotion, I hasten to add, was not belief that a miracle had occurred. The crucial word here is *belief*. Obviously something unusual occurred. Anyway, the unfamiliar emotion faded and my journalistic common sense began reasserting itself.

The most obvious explanation here was a misdiagnosis—exactly how top-notch is health care in Metuchen these days?—and Nickie was in a far less serious condition than the docs thought. The trauma of taking him off the machines actually worked to his benefit, shocking him out of his coma. Of course, there's the problem of the monitor flatlining, but that could've been malfunction.

The question was and is, How could Jay have known about it? Could Vinnie's horrible dilemma have been more widely known about than I realized and somehow through his bush telegraph Jay knew about it? It's possible—except he's been behind bars for three months.

As I lie down, exhausted beyond measure, the paranormal power factor pushes its way front and center. Perhaps Jay intuited that I would set him this test or knew the situation in Metuchen General—that Nickie was beginning to recover—and therefore accepted, knowing it was simple to appear to be the healer. . . . In fact, it was Nickie's own powers of recovery that healed him.

Actually, I don't care. Great story. Great subject. Doesn't seem like an open-and-shut miracle . . . must be an explanation . . . always an explanation. . . .

Last thing I remember is being suffused again with the warmth that flowed from the big square hands. If I didn't know myself a whole lot better I'd have to say the feeling was . . . joy?

Nah.

TWELVE

THE ANCIENT GULFSTREAM 550 wasn't ostentatious, the Reverend felt. He didn't need a Mach-6 rocket plane like those the macrocorporate boys used to circumnavigate the globe in a day. His lumbering old bird was a modest conveyance in keeping with the needs of a humble preacher.

He called the plane Gabriel and loved to fly over God's Chosen Nation in it, alone with its Owner and Operator. He got his best ideas this way, flying up in the wild blue yonder, "nearer, my Friend, to Thee."

Through the bright crisp April morning, Gabriel banked over the Dominion of Christ (formerly the District of Columbia) and came in to land at Sparrow National, the private jetport used exclusively by top-echelon church, government, and military personnel. The Reverend then transferred to his personal chopper for the ride to the White House. He'd had it equipped with stubby stabilizer wings, so that when it flew near the ground in sunlight it cast a crucifix-shaped shadow. Sometimes folks would run from the shadow and he'd have the pilot chase them. Just a little harmless Christian fun. Jeanie called the craft his Holycopter.

Within minutes, the Reverend was being ushered into a side entrance of the East Wing. Even after countless visits, he still got goose bumps walking into the place. What immeasurable power had been exercised within these walls! What uncountable sums of money dispensed, changing the face of the world forever, from this its true center, the throbbing heart of God's Nation. His Lord and Savior had surely walked these halls down the centuries, weeping over the iniquities of some of its occupants, exulting in the Christian rectitude of others, of whose number the current incumbent, the Reverend felt pretty sure, was one.

President Barnard Bee Sparrow had recently been reelected by a landslide, thanks in large part to the efficiency with which the Church of the Risen Lamb turned out their voters—and disenfranchised the opposition's. Vastly expanded definitions of *felony* had reduced to single figures the percentage of minority voters eligible to vote. For example, if any member of a family (uncles, aunts, cousins) had been convicted of a felony, the entire family was considered a "felon family." None of its members could vote. The Reverend didn't have a big problem with rules like these, but he knew Evan did. One day soon he would have to have a little chat with young Evan about the facts of electoral life.

Barnard Bee was the third Sparrow to occupy the White House. Some religious elders of the Reverend's acquaintance murmured that Sparrow 3 was not exactly an intellectual light in the darkness. Others said his Christian humility led him to hide his light under a bushel. Privately, the Reverend suspected that either the light was pretty small or the bushel was unusually large.

In any case, the president made few policy decisions on his own. His longtime adviser, Curt, a man so influential that he'd never had to divulge his last name to anyone, not even to the previous two Sparrows he'd served, took care of all policy originating in the White House.

During Sparrow 3's first term it had been Curt who'd master-minded that fundamental change in the American educational land-scape, the Slow Child Left Behind Act. The act mandated that underachieving children *should* be left behind, shunted to the "slow track" as young as possible so as not to deprive "faster" kids of scarce education funds. Slow children were to be rotated out of the educational system at the age of eleven and into the workforce, if necessary through the Federal Poorhouse System.

The face of American education had changed dramatically for the better. Scores had risen sharply without the drag of slow kids to hold them down. High-school student enrollment plummeted, which meant more "dollars per scholar." Slow kids avoided wasting years in school, pursuing literacy and numeracy. Plus, they got a jump start on exciting careers in the military, rising through the ranks of the Catering Corps, the Tailoring Corps, the Latrine Corps, and so on.

Despite such legislative triumphs, Barnard Bee's first term had not been all smooth sailing. Within a month of his inauguration, the youngest president in history determined to break free of the Sparrow legacy and announced he was firing Curt. The Reverend chuckled at the memory. Fire Curt? The guy didn't have a specific job, for one thing; for another there wasn't anyone in the entire Dominion of Christ with the guts to escort him to the front gate, even if they could find him. You might as well try to fire fog or infectious diseases.

Outside the East Room, the White House flunkies fell back and Guards took over, their red berets jaunty with the gold cockades, a little triangle of their Kromlar full-body armor peeping like chain mail from the open collars of crisply laundered camo shirts.

The Guards were another Curt brainchild. They'd originated in Sparrow 2's second term as a clandestine White House instant-response group called the Redshirts. After the tragic UN bombing, which some treasonous journalists had claimed was actually their work, the Redshirts had been upgraded into a congressionally funded elite corps called the Republican Guard. Their mission: eliminating direct threats to the president's security and reelection. They specialized in FAMINTIM (family intimidation) and TRANSAB (sabotage involving transportation, usually small-plane crashes). The Guards' bravery, global reach, and impenetrable body armor had so far thwarted all would-be presidential assassins. The Republican Guard GI Joe was the fastest-selling model in the toy's long history.

As two courteous young Guards expertly checked him for evidence of evil intent, the Reverend reflected that, while he had far more raw people-power at his command than Curt, he did envy Curt his access to deadly force. The Reverend was no opponent of deadly force, of course. He preached frequently on its efficacy as an instrument of God's will. But at the end of the day he had no tanks or planes at his command, let alone a loyal and ruthless cadre like the Guard. He really must get to know Curt better. It would help if he knew what the guy looked like.

The Reverend entered the hallowed space of the East Room. During his first term, Sparrow 3 had converted it into a high-security Emergency Ops War Room. The august paneling, the sumptuous drapes, even the portraits of the mighty were gone. (The portraits in particular had fallen afoul of a personal quirk of Sparrow 3: He didn't like to be reminded that anyone had been president before him.)

The leader of the free world was sitting at the head of an immense table. He was in his customary posture of sitting sideways to anyone he was meeting, ignoring them. When he finally acknowledged a guest, he would look at him or her from the corners of his eyes in the manner of a seventeenth-century despot posing for a portrait.

Right now, the president was chuckling quietly as he signed an executive order returning the Statue of Liberty to the French. Getting rid of Liberty had been a major goal of his first term. The current order called for the odious statue to be flown to Southeast England, where two delivery options were possible. Either Liberty would be slung from an old B-52, flown to Paris, and dropped in the general area of the Eiffel Tower, or she'd be chopped up into body parts and shipped over to Calais on a garbage scow.

The Reverend took his seat to the president's immediate right as his Religion Adviser. He was surprised how few other advisers were in attendance for this momentous meeting. It could only mean that it was also triple-drop-dead top secret too.

Normally down his side of the table would sit advisers on oil, construction, pharma, and so on. (Traditional cabinet posts had been eliminated on the rationale that archaic terms like Treasury, State, and Interior were incomprehensible to young Americans, not least the incumbent president.)

Down the left side of the table sat advisers with responsibility for foreign affairs (or, as the president liked to joke, Running-the-World Advisers). Today, to the president's immediate left, sat the Joint Chief, General Nathan Bedford Forrest Sparrow, his cousin and the son of Sparrow 2. Next to the Joint Chief sat the Defense Adviser, Air Force General Sharif Haney (the first Iranian-American to achieve four stars). Next to him sat the Foreign Adviser (formerly Secretary of State), Admiral Carl Kubrick. The only other person facing the Reverend was a fairly lowly functionary, the Infrastructure Destruction Adviser, Brigadier General Hayden. Destroying the infrastructure of small countries and rebuilding them at their own expense had become an important revenue source for the now-privatized Pentagon. His presence must mean, thought the Reverend, that a war was in the works. Interesting.

The president turned slowly to his advisers, scanning them from the corners of his small-mammal eyes. Whenever he did this, it always looked to the Reverend as if he was worried that someone was creeping up behind him. He opened one corner of his wide thin-lipped mouth. It looked rather like a small lamb chop. His advisers knew this meant he was about to be humorous.

About eighteen inches in front of the presidential eyes was a holographic monitor visible only to him. He consulted it for Curt's daily list of spontaneous jokes. He'd been trained to smile around at his audience when delivering a joke, but his eyes were focused on the monitor and not on their faces. He also tried to keep looking at them from the corners of his eyes. The total effect, the Reverend felt, was borderline loco.

"Let me just say," read the Chief Executive, "that seldom has such a lack of talent gathered in the East Room. Not since Jack Kennedy dined here alone." The East Room rocked dutifully with laughter.

"Knock, knock," he added, brightening up, for he knew this joke by heart.

"Who's there, Mr. President?" chorused his advisers.

"Armageddon."

"Armageddon who?" they asked in perfect unison.

"Armageddon *outtahere*!"

The Reverend laughed along, though by his count he had now heard this gem eleven times. Suddenly the president's demeanor changed. "What's so funny?" he demanded. "Armageddon's no joke!"

"Amen to that," intoned the Reverend.

The laughter skidded to an abrupt halt. The president refocused on the monitor.

"The latest international outrage in the United Nations of Europe has brought matters to a head between our great nation and our former allies."

The Reverend felt a quickening of his pulse. This must have something to do with cheese. The latest clash between America and Europe was over who would get to supply newly status-conscious populations in China and South Asia with upmarket cheeses, a specialty of European food producers, especially the French. Prosperous Asians were getting bored with sliced and processed American cheese.

The crux of the fight was between phony American versions of Euro cheeses like Camembert, Manchego, and Gorgonzola, which by law had to be made from pasteurized milk, versus the real versions made by Europeans from raw milk. To retaliate for the phony versions of their cheeses, the Europeans had started making sliced and processed cheese from raw milk to compete with the output of U.S. giants like Kraft. It was widely considered in Asia much tastier than the bland and rubbery American version.

Two days earlier, an American cheese tanker carrying half a million barrels of liquid processed cheese to Bombay had run aground off the coast of Brittany, spewing a million pounds of yellow goo into its legendary shellfish and lobster beds. French president Pierre Marbre-Granit, convinced that the *attentat de fromage* had been deliberate, had had the tanker's captain and crew arrested.

"The time has come," continued Sparrow 3, "to draw a line in the cheese. The army and the air force have pitched me a solution that attacks the problem at its core."

The Joint Chief leaned back with an air of triumph. The Defense Adviser also nodded his satisfaction. The Foreign Adviser—to whom all this was apparently news—frowned.

"Problem, Admiral?" snapped the president.

"No, sir. No one could be keener to hear a permanent solution to the UNE problem. It's just that—"

"Don't worry, Carl." General Nathan Bedford Sparrow spoke without looking at the Foreign Adviser to his left. He was only a cousin, but he had the Sparrow mouth. "We'll find your tub toys something to do."

"Anyway"—the commander in chief smiled, pulling off another of his dizzying changeups—"you have an absolute right to be in the loop. That's why we're here. Nathan B.?"

"As you say, sir, it's time for a showdown with these terrorist-coddling pansies. But we can't just D-Day in there. We need a pretext. Bull, here, has a sweet one."

Air Force General Haney smiled at the compliment and leaned forward confidentially. "Relations between Europe and Israel are at an all-time low, thanks to these new hyper-settlements in the Upper West Bank."

The Reverend had one of his God-sent premonitions. It always happened the same way: His big toes started tingling to beat the band.

"Precisely ten weeks from now, on Independence Day at oh-five-hundred hours, twelve major Israeli targets will be the target of hit-

and-run air strikes by Airbus ATAK-seventeen fighter-bombers, bearing the insignias of French, German, Spanish, and Italian squadrons of the UNE Air Defense Command—"

The President overrode General Haney, excited enough to forget his monitor. "We're appalled by this vicious attack on a loyal ally. We launch a retaliatory strike on Brussels, backed up by a huge amphibious infantry landing at—wait for it—Dunkerque!"

General Sparrow took over. "The invasion force fans out east-north-south: Paris, Rotterdam, Berlin, Milan, Barcelona, Madrid, Vienna. In a week we control Warsaw, Cracow, Budapest, Prague."

"And infrastructure?" Brigadier General Hayden was a man of clear and single-minded vision.

The defense adviser had the answer: "Vaporization of every airport, train station, bridge, tunnel, power plant, microwave relay center, industrial plant, communications complex—you name it! The Euros won't have seen bombing like this since . . ."—for a split second, General Haney stared into the abyss of his own rhetoric—"since *never*!"

Kubrick said, "You think you can occupy Europe in a week?"

"Why not?" snapped the president. "It's teensy."

General Haney capped the presentation. "With massive air support from the Kirghiz, Uzbecki, and Afghan bases in the east and from your carriers in the Atlantic—OK, Carlie boy?" He finally turned to the admiral with a placatory grin. "We'll crush the UNE like bugs in a vise."

The president, his cousin, and Haney glared at the other three people in the room in triumph. There was a long pause. Then Admiral Kubrick said, very slowly, "Just so's I get this crystal clear: The Airbus ATAK-seventeens with Euro markings that originally bomb and strafe Israel . . . will be piloted by Americans?"

"Of course, moron!" The president seemed exasperated with his Foreign Adviser.

"Won't a lot of Israelis get, you know . . . hurt?" persisted the admiral, who was Jewish.

"Who cares?" said the president. "Buncha Christ-killers!"

To the Reverend, the other side of the table looked like a clump of bushes swept by a violent wind.

The president rolled his eyes. "Joke, morons! Lighten up!"

The admiral allowed a grin. Everyone laughed heartily except the president. With pious mien, he turned to Sabbath.

"Reverend, I've prayed about this hard and long. And I'm sure that after all the forbearance on the part of our great Christian nation toward the Beast of Revelation over there in UNE-land, Almighty God has lost His patience!"

"Amen!" murmured the Reverend, his toes tingling so hard they felt as if they were burning holes in his socks.

"Tell me, Jimbo: Could our little patty-cake with Israel trigger the actual Armageddon? Could the Lord mistake us for the *real* Antichrist and decide to come back?"

The Reverend took a beat to get control of his tumultuous feelings. Then he said, "The Book of Revelation clearly identifies Israel as the location of the Final Battle, specifically Megiddo, near Haifa—"

"Haifa's one of our targets!" said Haney, in genuine surprise.

The Reverend smiled and went on. "It also prophesies that the Antichrist will begin the Final Battle by an attack on the Jewish people. But I can assure you, Mr. President, that the Lord would never mistake a great Christian like yourself for the Antichrist."

The President looked gratified at such a compliment from the lips of God's Best Friend.

"However," continued the Reverend, accelerating to highway

speed, "support from all Bible-believing Christians will be off the charts if this brilliant stratagem is presented to them as the start of actual Armageddon! And I'm the one to do it!"

"Jimbo!" cried his intrepid leader. "This is why you get the big bucks!"

Inside, the Reverend was quivering with a somewhat different excitement. What if this *was* going to be the start of actual Armageddon? What if the Lord in His wisdom had chosen His servant Barnard Bee Sparrow as the unwitting rod of His wrath? For through that agency, Europe—which all Pure Holy Baptists knew to be the Beast of Revelation—was to be utterly destroyed. Once the Beast was destroyed, the Savior would return in glory with great power.

Let it be so, Lord! prayed James Zebediah Sabbath in his heart. *And let me be Your prophet!*

THIRTEEN

"**COMING IN FROM** the cold, Greco?"

"You kidding? Writing for this rag is like being a side of beef in a meat locker."

Ted Kaminski was Global Features Editor of the *Journal American* and, despite being a neo-imperialist of the first water, one of my oldest friends. What may have attracted me to him was his size; he was even shrimpier than me. (He denied this, insisting I wore elevator shoes.) Unlike me, he was preternaturally dapper, dressed to the nines in all weathers and climes, which may have given him the absurd impression that he was my superior physically as well as sartorially.

You had to be dapper in body, mind, and soul to work at the *Journal American*. The paper was the one surviving news-gathering organization on the planet anyone remotely trusted; its clout was so enormous even the federal government thought twice before crossing swords with it. For security reasons, financial markets had long since gone off-planet, being located in satellites three hundred miles

above every would-be billionaire's hair plugs and run by astronauti-
cal business majors from the Beijing School of Economics. There
was no longer the identification there once had been between the paper and a gloomy couple of blocks in downtown Manhattan. So the
name had recently been shortened to the *Journal*, with an identifier
indicating national provenance. It had forty-seven thriving foreign
editions, many even bigger than the U.S. one, such as the *Journal Indian*. An added advantage to the name change was that after a decade and a half of Sparrovian foreign policy, the term "Wall Street"
had, for the rest of the world, all the PR appeal of "Bergen-Belsen."

"Never thought I'd see you crawling over that transom," Ted
drawled hospitably.

He took the completed Jay story—I was calling it "The Revelation Will Not Be Televised"—and weighed the forty double-spaced
sheets in one daintily manicured paw.

Diametrically opposed on almost every issue, Kaminski and I
were both prehensile conservatives when it came to the superiority
of the printed page over the screen. Only his very considerable foot-
fall in the corridors of power allowed Kaminski to get away with insisting that all major stories—no matter how illustrious the
writer—be delivered in hard copy.

"Five thousand or a little under," he announced expertly. (It was
4,882 words.) "Paper only at that length; you'll have to do a bullet
version for the web-plebs."

I'd pitched the story to him and him only: the *JA* was the one
surviving news organization immune to blasphemy suits, and my
piece was asking for it. As I'd expected, he'd liked the idea. Ted was
a renegade Catholic (and on his father's side a renegade Jew), with a
vast and omnivorous interest in religion. Somewhere, he said, between agnostic and Gnostic.

He quoted Burke and Hobbes by the yard and, despite his rabid devotion to the free market and manifest destiny, was a fierce egalitarian, a very Lincolnesque Republican, convinced it was America's job to end slavery of any kind in the world. (His favorite movie of all time was *Spartacus*.) He made no secret of being disgusted by the thinly veiled racism of his co-conservatives. It was he who, when we were both still at the newspaper of record, had run my Pulitzer Prize–winning series, which happened to be about wage slavery in the Ben-and-Jerry-style eco-farms of the tristate area.

He shared with me a general loathing of fundamentalism, which he believed inimical to freedom and profoundly un-American, and a particular loathing of the Reverend. But he was far too shrewd an editorial strategist to make that the basis of his pitch to Mount Olympus, as he called his top editors. When he'd presented my proposed story to them he'd argued successfully that there was a fascinating laissez-faire dimension to the new would-be messiah. Here was the Reverend, fresh from a free-market triumph in which he had swallowed whole his largest competitor, and lo, within weeks a cocky little enterprise showed up on his flank with a radically updated, more appealing model of the Reverend's own product.

The God-Mother thing alone, Kaminski argued, was a fantastic add-on to the brand; it could have broad and deep appeal to women of all ages, disenchanted by fundamentalist sexism. Who knew if, in a few years, Jay wouldn't be eating the Reverend whole? He deserved a shot at the title.

Ted liked the finished story. He took out the "egregiously communardy" bits and, to my disappointment, the Miracle in Metuchen, which he said, since Jay hadn't been associated with it publicly, seemed "opportunistic." On the other hand, he said the story would run in two or three days, there being no reason not to bring on, as soon as possible, the putative collision between two versions of Christianity.

As it turned out, his timing was impeccable.

FOURTEEN

"Onward, Christian soldiers,
Marching as to war,
With the Cross of Jesus
Going on before!"

EVAN'S MIGHTY BARITONE filled the Reverend's Cathedral of Light in Atlanta like the voice of God. The Reverend stood before his old rugged cross at its simple unadorned altar, as the serried ranks of the Risen Lamb Angelic Choir behind him hummed the driving melody of the greatest of all Christian hymns, bearing the Reverend up like a seashell on the crest of a vast wave of sound. . . .

"I have a dream!" he cried. "A dream of lights, of trumpets, of earthquakes, of meteor showers brighter than a million suns!"

The great video rood screen behind the choir sprang to life with footage of the flashing, crashing signs and portents whereof the Reverend spoke, stars falling from the heavens, mighty shafts of lightning splitting the welkin, great winds whipping clouds across a bloody moon.

"I have a dream of all God's children who have died through the ages being resurrected in miraculous new bodies and bursting forth from their graves!"

Now the screen showed a montage of huge urban and suburban cemeteries, with actual footage of many (but not all) the graves exploding in showers of dirt as thousands of white-clad Christians rose from them, hands held high, filling the sky with upright figures like some apocalyptic version of a Magritte painting.

"I have a dream of living Christians, floating up through the roofs of their houses and offices and cars and buses and trains and planes, miraculously unharmed!"

Another montage showed cityscapes and highways jammed with colliding out-of-control vehicles, planes plunging from the sky, trains derailing, buildings crumbling—and from them more Christians rising up through the air, even more like a Magritte this time because they were in their work clothes.

"I have a dream of the plain of Megiddo and of a mountain thereon, that which is nam-ed"—the Reverend pronounced *named* with two-syllables—"Har-Megiddon! Where the Mighty Lamb is to do final battle with *the beast*!"

The screen showed a great mountain rising from a bleak and barren desert, and from behind camera (in slow motion, so the gold UNE circle of thirteen gold stars could be seen on their fuselage) came first one, then scores, then hundreds of fighter-bombers. Normal speed resumed as the sky grew black with them. The mountain was engulfed in flame as their rockets exploded on its sacred slopes.

"In my dream I behold the Mighty Lamb, rising from Har-Megiddon and smiting the *Beast*!"

From the mountain burst the Returned Christ, a mile tall, in full battle gear, lieutenant stripes on His muscular arm, blond locks flowing out of His marine battle helmet, assault rifle held high against a tattered Old Glory. Like King Kong on the Empire State Building, Christ batted the fighter-bombers out of the sky until not one was left and the desert was littered with their smoking, burning wreckage.

Evan and the Angels crashed back at full volume:

> "Like a mighty army
> Moves the Church of God,
> Brothers, we are treading
> Where the saints have trod!"

"I have a dream," the Reverend repeated in a dramatic sotto voce, "the sweetest dream of all . . . of *judgment*!"

Lieutenant Christ fired his vast weapon at the ground, and a great fiery chasm opened up at his feet. All the wrecked planes were sucked into it in an instant! Flames shot from the chasm. Now marching from every direction came the armies of the Antichrist! They too were huge in size, though not as huge as Christ, their banners streaming in the wind. FREE TO CHOOSE! screamed one.

"*Free to choose damnation*!" cried Lieutenant Christ, and mowed them down. (If you weren't too excited by all the action, you might've noticed that the voice of Lieutenant Christ was Evan.) The bullet-riddled blood-soaked corpses of the abortionists were sucked into the chasm also.

It was probably the most effective *Risen Lamb Sabbath Hour* the Reverend ever made. The Church must have spent a fortune on those ten minutes or so of "actual footage"—the computer effects alone would have cost the entire budget of the average web-buster. The hordes of Antichrist kept coming: recalcitrant Hollywood stars, drug addicts, terrorists in kaffiyehs, Tibetan monks with (incongruously) machine guns, Frenchmen in berets sneering and spitting, trying to stab the lieutenant with huge stilettos.

Shot to ribbons, every one, by the Risen Lamb's inexhaustible supply of ammo, down, down, they all plunged into the fiery pit. And when all were defeated and damned, the Lieutenant threw away his colossal weapon and ascended rapidly into the firmament, where, at around fifteen thousand feet, he caught up with the still-rising Christians.

The choir of Angels on earth and in heaven (on screen), led by Evan's mighty baritone (or was that Jesus?), resumed:

> "At the sign of triumph
> Satan's host doth flee!
> On, then, Christian soldiers,
> On to vic-to-ry!"

The screen exploded in dazzling light—as Christ and the just reached heaven—and went to black. Again the Angels sank into their seraphic murmuring. The camera now zoomed in for a close-up of the Reverend leaning forward, hands outstretched, speaking in an urgent whisper.

"America, be warned! You have just seen actual footage of what to expect only *weeks* from this very day! The Lord has revealed to me that these *truly are* the end-times! From generation unto generation, false prophets have falsely predicted the Day of Judgment. But verily I say unto you, brethren and sistren, *it is here*!

"America, the Kingdom of Abomination is about to attack! This suppurating cesspool brazenly calls itself the United Nations of Europe! And what does the name of the Beast spell? *Une*! The French for *one*! One world, one planet, one people—the dream of Antichrist!

"I, Jim the Baptist, prophesy, not for myself but for Him whose sandal I am not worthy to unlatch! He is at hand, America! Repent! Your time is not months but weeks!

"I, Jim the Baptist, pledge that on Sabbath Day next I will reveal a further prophecy regarding the Final Days. And so it shall continue for five more Sabbaths. On the sixth Sabbath Day I will reveal the exact date of the *final battle*!"

Evan and the choir cracked into the last almighty chorus:

> "Onward, Christian soldiers,
> Marching as to war,
> With the cross of Jesus—"

But the last line was inaudible. The fully amplified cranked-to-eleven wall of choral sound was drowned out by an earsplitting roar unlike any other the Reverend had ever heard in that holy place, as the ten thousand male and female Christian soldiers, gathered in a vast half-moon around their shepherd and his rugged cross, came to their feet like a great beast awakened.

FIFTEEN

I HEAR THE messiah of Morris Avenue was seriously injured this morning," said Gideon the Idiot at the beginning of his monologue. "Seems he was out jogging and got hit by a motorboat."

Only two days after my *Journal* story had come out, and already the king of prime-time news was doing one-liners about Jay!

Nightly News with Gideon the Idiot was just one of several prime-time news webcasts anchored by comics, but it was easily the biggest. The others soon followed suit. The clown who fronted FoxWeb's NewsBlog offered tips for dating a messiah ("If he talks about eating his body, do *not* throw him out. Find him some bread"). Lame parody B-attitudes were everywhere: "Blessed are the sedated, the caffeinated, the shopaholics, the erectile dysfunctional." One sports shouter on SPN wondered, Could the "Savior in sneakers" save the Knicks from elimination in the playoffs? "Hey, Jay, there's some sick and lame guys over in the Knicks locker room need a miracle!"

Several handles for Jay emerged, especially in New York media, which took a proprietary interest in the local divinity. They all included the Bronx in some way, usually going for alliteration rather than accuracy, such as "The Jesus of Jerome Avenue." The one I liked was "Joe Christ" but it involved knowing that *Jose* was the Spanish for *Joseph*—too big a leap for most eyeballs.

The most outrageous reaction came from the *Inquiring Mind*. Kunihiro Yamamoto-Young ran a piece claiming he'd discovered the Mystery Messiah and I'd stolen his story. It was mostly a montage of messiahs I'd found and turned down (including one who'd given himself stigmata by driving tenpenny nails into his hands and feet), the suggestion being that Jay was just another Nut Log nut. That kid had balls of brass.

I suppose people who believed in Jay might have found all this offensive, but in a way I welcomed it. It got his name around far quicker than the straighter media and made him more accessible to people. We didn't need suite cred at this point; I'd already taken care of the class end of the act with Kaminski. But I did want him to get known, to appear on the radar of the people he'd make see red.

Ironically, the story got a huge boost from the Reverend's electrifying announcement. Unlike his co-religionists down the ages who'd often made the mistake of predicting the exact end of the world and then had seen the date pass without incident, the Reverend was no wolf-crier. He kept his flock on the edge of their seats year in, year out, by not being too specific. The Second Coming/Day of Judgment/Final Battle was "at hand," "coming soon," or "upon us," but never "next Tuesday at 2 P.M." Now, in front of hundreds of millions of souls, he'd said there was an exact day and had pledged to name it in six weeks.

Then, just a few days later, in the most important newspaper in the world, a cocky little ethnic messiah popped up to say that the Reverend's whole scenario—and therefore his pledge—was a crock.

Don't get me wrong. The story got good play, but outside of New York, no one exactly yelled *Stop the presses!*—even if there'd been any presses left to stop. Still, it was a personal vindication: After months of silence, my earphone finally started to buzz. I heard from several good friends who'd been noticeably absent from my life since the publication of the Greco Option five years earlier. Some were aghast and some helpless with laughter that I'd "gone over to the Lord." Much the same was true of my comrades in the underground. Some were incensed—as I'd known they would be—by Jay's "revanchism" on the poor, intelligent design, and so on. One female saw profound sexism in Jay's "trope" of the Father God. Why wasn't it the Mother God who controlled the forces of the universe? Why did she get fobbed off with "existence"? (There's no pleasing some people.) A few of the godless called me ("confidentially, OK?"), in my new role as religious expert. They were the kind of people who'd once been made to go to a church or synagogue; enough had rubbed off that they were now worried the Reverend might be right. (I assured them he wasn't.) Most importantly, a few got the big picture: that there were powerful political implications if Jay and his followers, and the emotions they aroused, could be harnessed, shaped, in some way grown.

But an awful lot of ordinary mortals were *really* intrigued by the idea that there was a guy walking around the tristate area who could do miracles.

Trouble was, I had no idea where the miracle man might be. He and the Apostle Posse had left town several weeks earlier and had not been heard from since. If María knew where they were, she wasn't telling me. With a buzz beginning and Kaminski calling for a follow-up, Jay's lack of whereabouts was frustrating. The media was ready to bump him and his mission (and me and mine) into the stratosphere, and I couldn't produce the goods.

✦

Midday on Saturday of the week the *Journal* piece came out, I got a call from someone monitoring the police scanner; there'd been a spontaneous celebration going on all morning up in the Bronx. The Messiah of Morris Avenue was home for the first time in over a year, and an impromptu fiesta was under way. Jay had been preaching and doing miracles and having a grand old time, and yours truly, the designated scribe, the man most responsible for all the excitement, knew nothing about it.

I got myself over to the Bronx and María's place. She wasn't there but everyone on the street knew about the fiesta, which had migrated over to one of the local parks. Apparently the word was out in all five boroughs that Jay had returned, and the cops were getting antsy about the crowds and the cars.

There must have been several thousand people in the park; a cop keeping an eye on things told me the NYPD had pegged the crowd at around five thousand earlier in the morning. He was a stolid four-square young guy, dark olive skin, oiled jet-black head-bristles glistening in the sun, ALVAREZ on his name tag.

I asked him if he was around earlier. "Yeah, but I couldn't hear much," he replied. "The messiah guy wasn't using a mike. People were real quiet. Then he started healing. I was assigned to the perimeter, so I couldn't really see, but"—he shrugged—"people said there were, like, miracles." He looked away with a tiny half-smile as if he secretly hoped what people said was true.

"Do you believe he can do miracles?" I asked. His eyes came back to mine with a glint of hostility.

"You media?" he asked and, when I nodded, cocked his head toward a far corner of the park. "Your people are over there."

I walked through families and couples on the grass. It was Saturday, people's day off, early May, a beautiful afternoon with a touch of winter chill and that sparkling, wind-washed, laundry-fresh cerulean blue that you never see anywhere quite the same as in New York in spring. A light that made the surly brown tenements of the Bronx look like they might have some hope; against which the gold-green leaf buds fluttered slightly in the brisk nor'wester blowing down the Hudson. Nature's first green is gold.

There were impromptu stands with soda being sold from coolers, barbecues on which chicken and tacos and tortillas were cooking or keeping warm. I bought my first empanada of the year: delicious. Kids were playing soccer; dogs were all over the place; there were a lot of guitars and drums. Though the party was winding down there was still celebration in the air, people chatting in animated rings, some of them quite big, a dozen or more people sitting around sharing memories of the morning. I think they were memories anyway—my Spanish isn't that great. Maybe it was just me and spring: there seemed to be a lot of smiling going on.

I couldn't help wondering if it was like this the first time around. The language of the Bible is pretty flat, but the first time I read the Sermon on the Mount and the Feeding of the Five Thousand (if those two go together, I'm a little rusty), I sensed that it was a happy occasion. The man Jay said he once was had preached to ordinary working folks from a little hill and healed their sick and then fed all five thousand of them. Who cared if the feeding was a miracle or something more banal? It was a huge picnic with happy people, Jesus' little Woodstock.

I realized I'd never seen Jay in action. Perhaps it was always like this.

Still, as I walked among the smiling faces and memories of excitement, that cantankerous spoiler of a voice that always lurks somewhere inside me couldn't help sneering: *Yeah, you're smiling now but it won't always be like this. It won't always be songs and smiles. Just like that other sunny day long ago in Judea; humans will find some way to turn it all to shit. Nothing gold can stay.*

Would I look back on this sunny spring day and all these sunny spring people and say, *That was as good as it got?*

Why was I even wondering this?

◆

The guys and gals of the media were standing around intensely doing nothing, as is their wont. There was no sign of Jay or the Posse. One of them was a former colleague from the *Inquiring Mind* whom I knew well enough to avoid whenever I saw him coming, a Brit half my age and three times my weight. His name was Rodney, and his skin was amazingly white, even whiter than mine, as white as the belly of a Dover sole. So we called him Whitey from Blighty.

Whitey from Blighty congratulated me on my "triff" piece in the *Journal*. I asked where the messiah was and he got all riled up, as if the whole bloody thing was my bloody fault.

It turned out that as soon as the media showed, their humble purpose being (a) to be the first to put the Second Coming on camera and (b) the first to film an actual live miracle, Jay had gone stone-cold silent, stopped healing, and refused to be even still-photoed.

So he really meant that stuff about "The Revelation will not be televised." I'd figured it was part of a nice subversive theory that might be magically forgotten once the cameras showed up.

The local lame and halt and their loved ones, deprived of his services, objected strenuously to the presence of the media. The media were miffed, accustomed as they were to people kissing their butts. Press freedom was at stake. The public's right to know was at stake.

Jay had gone walkabout through the crowd, and when they tried to follow him and shoot him or pick up what he was saying, the crowd blocked them.

Several left in high First Amendment dudgeon. A few others tried to be investigative, shouting at Jay over the heads of the crowd—"What do you have to hide? Why are you scared of the cameras? Are you a charlatan?"—and other fearless shafts. The crowd soon shooed them away.

The ease of mind I'd been feeling began to melt into apprehension. I was media too. I hadn't heard from the guy since my piece came out—hell, since I'd done the interview. Was I in the same doghouse as these bottom feeders? I needed to see him and find out.

✦

At María's place there were folks all over: in the courtyard, swarming up the stairwells, sitting in the lobby, quiet and patient, sitting on every available surface, all waiting for Jay. He'd gone with Rufus and Charlie to help out the worst of the cases who'd come to him in the park. In their homes without the media snooping.

María was animated, all over the place, defending the waiting people against the blustery building super, finding snacks and drinks for the kids, comforting sick babies, being everyone's mom.

For once the marked coolness she'd always shown me was gone. Perhaps the *Journal* piece had convinced her of my good intentions. She even sat down with me for a few minutes, happy to talk.

"It's great to have José back, even though he says some things I don't like."

"Like what?" I asked.

"Well, I said to him I was glad to have my son home, my only real family. He takes my hands and says, 'Mama, I have no home and family now. My family are Angela, Rufus, Charlie, Kevin, all the people God heals through my hands, and whoever else comes to me wanting help. My home is wherever I lay my head at night. Everywhere and nowhere.'"

I asked if there was anything he said she did like.

"*Sí, sí,* a million things. But especially when he preached about God the Mother. That was beautiful. I always knew God was a woman."

"Do you think now your son is the Messiah?"

She shook her head, smiling. "I hope not!"

It was good to see Angela again. She'd put on weight and filled out in the obvious places. She certainly didn't look sick. I asked her if she'd been tested yet, to be sure about Jay's miraculous cure.

"Not yet," she said. "We found out that you need to take these new comprehensive tests: to make sure the hyper-virus isn't present? We just don't have the money. Anyway, do I look like I have the plague?" It was true: A beautiful creature was emerging from the chrysalis of sickness.

A New Yorker born and bred, she was happy to be back in the city; the Bronx had been one of her stomping grounds when she was younger. "I got some . . ."—she hesitated a beat or two—"old friends in a bad place. I'm gonna bring them to Jay. He'll heal what ails them." She didn't elaborate, but she had that same look of devotion on her face as when she spoke of her savior man. If he hadn't been Almighty God, I'd have said Jay was one lucky guy.

Kevin was changed too, more sure of his role, which was emerging as the egghead of the group. "I'm the Apostolic Geek," he said with a smile. "Rufus, Charlie, Angela—they've done things, been places, had terrible things happen to them. When we go into these tough nabes, and people see those three and hear their stories, they know they're in good hands. It helps people believe. Like Jay says: It's all about belief.

"The way I can help people believe," said Kevin, "is by putting things together for them. So they understand that the things Jay says and does aren't just isolated words and acts. There's an overall consistency to them. A purpose. I mean"—he hesitated, as if not quite sure he should say what he was going to say—"I believe . . . I'm living . . . in the presence of God. God made flesh. Sometimes, when I'm with him, I can hardly bear the intensity of that; other times it seems so normal it makes me laugh out loud, you know?" He laughed and I almost did too. His intensity was infectious.

So that others might be helped by them, he wrote down his questions and possible answers, made notes of the paradoxes to which his beliefs led him, kept track of new things Jay said to the apostles or preached about. "I'm keeping a pretty detailed record of what he says and does." Suddenly he got tongue-tied. "Not that I'd dream of trespassing, like, on your turf."

My hackles stirred and went back to sleep. He was a good kid and smart. And he wanted to be a writer. I didn't have the heart to slap him down.

"Far as I recall," I said, "there's room for four of us."

He laughed and relaxed and told me about the impromptu parade that had erupted on the streets that morning. "It was amazing! Never seen anything like it in Kansas. Ribbons and streamers and balloons, Virgins of Guadalupe, thousands of candles you couldn't see in the sunlight so people kept burning themselves with the hot wax? And man, that music! Cuban and gospel and mariachi and bossa nova and Catholic hymns all mixed up together: just total wonderful chaos!"

I asked him if anyone mentioned that Jay had been in the news and he said no, why? He hadn't heard about the *Journal American* piece. He didn't know if Jay had, but he hadn't heard Jay or anyone else mention it, and he'd spoken to scores of people that day.

Of course. No one in the Bronx had read the piece—certainly not the folks who'd given Jay his parade that morning. Why would they? Even if they were webbed, they wouldn't eyeball a publication as high-and-mighty as the *Journal*. They'd more likely spend their scarce free time and money on something like the *Inquiring Mind*.

But the Bronx had its own information sources, as reliable and opinionated as the *Journal*. People had been on the street that morning because Jay was famous in a sphere far out of reach of downtown eyes. His fame was in the bodegas and sweatshops and barbershops and on the street corners where laborers gathered at dawn; in construction sites and volunteer clinics and day-care centers and soup kitchens. It was strong enough to bring thousands out.

Kevin said, "There was a fascinating feeling on the street: like this combo of excitement and reverence? There's an old-time word they used in my church back home sometimes? Deliverance. People talked like they thought Jay would bring them . . . deliverance."

Without witnessing it, I knew what he meant. The 'hood wasn't just fawning on a homegrown star. They believed something more tangible: that he would release them from the grinding lives and miserable places they lived, the systematic exclusion they suffered because some humbug somewhere believed they were worthless and unworthy, the deadbeats of the shining city on the hill.

The question was: Could Jay do that? There was a material component to deliverance that didn't seem to be as much a priority for him as it was for them. These people needed schools and health care and jobs and the safety net their work and taxes paid for but which had been stolen from them. Jay delivered to perfection the message that they were equal, every individual as worthwhile as the next— the original American promise, in fact. But could he deliver the material component? Could he deliver deliverance?

"Later, in the park," said Kevin, "he preached about God the Mother. It was beautiful. A lot of folks were weeping. I've heard him speak about Her before, but never like this. He spoke in Spanish and English mixed together, not Spanglish, exactly, more as if there were some things that were best said in one language and some in the other. It was almost like he was singing or chanting."

Kevin said his Spanish wasn't up to getting it down word for word, and Jay was moving through the crowd so he wasn't always audible, but the sermon was less about specifics than conjuring up the presence of his Mother, bringing Her among the people then and there.

"One thing I could make out," said Kevin, "was that every section of the sermon ended with the same five words, like a refrain, and everyone began joining in: *Ella es amor. Puro amor.* You could hear it spreading across the crowd, so there was a delay from the center to the edges, like a lake being ruffled by the wind."

An old Catholic priest had sauntered up and stood on the edge of the crowd while Jay preached. Everyone seemed to know him; he kept shaking hands and clapping backs. After Jay finished preaching, Kevin collared him.

Father Michael Duffy, born and raised in the Bronx, was the parish priest at José's childhood church, Aloysius Gonzaga, and had been for donkey's years. I knew of him slightly. He'd been a thorn in the side of the archdiocese forever. Brilliant and magnetic as a young priest, he should've made bishop by now; but he was also an activist, unofficial chaplain to a militant lay group called Vox Populi and a host of other excellent troublemaking ventures. That's probably why the hierarchy had left him up here—they hoped—to rot; instead, his parish was an oasis of life in the barren landscape of New York Catholicism. He preached in Spanish as fluently as in English or French (for the Haitians and West Africans) and had an overflowing church every Sunday.

Kevin asked Father Mike whether he knew Jay.

"Sure. Little José Kennedy. He was an altar boy up here."

"A good altar boy?"

"No worse than the rest. Always fooling around at the Consecration, fighting over who got to ring the bell. Good point guard, though. Sweet hands."

"What do you think about him saying he's come to fulfill Christianity?"

"It's about time someone did." At this several hands were presented to Father Mike for him to high-five.

"Is he a threat to the Catholic Church?"

"Anything real is a threat to the Church."

"What do you think the Church will do about him?"

"The Church has made the wrong decision about every crisis

they've faced for the last fifty years. Why would they spoil a perfect record doing the right thing about José?"

◆

And what would any Jay appearance be—without a miracle?

In the park where Jay was preaching, there lived an old bag lady. The locals called her Gaga because that was about all she ever said, other than monumental cursing. She'd shown up the previous summer. She was harmless and pathetic enough that the local shopkeepers gave her food when she stumbled into their bodegas; people tried to make her sleep somewhere warm if the temperature got dangerously low.

When Jay began healing she came stumbling through the crowd, mumbling obscenities. A line had formed in front of him. She staggered near to the front of it and flopped on the ground in a heap. People looked embarrassed, like this was a part of their neighborhood they weren't too proud of but didn't know what to do about. Some guy decided to shoo her away.

"C'mon, Gaga, go home now."

But Jay gestured it was OK and went over and knelt next to her on the ground. She spat a stream of syllables at him.

Someone said, "She just a crazy old woman, Jay, she don't know her name, don't where she is, even. Ain't nothing in her poor old head."

"She got Alzheimer's," a big guy added.

Jay took the woman's head in his hands and looked into her eyes. "Tell us your name," he said. The old woman's face puckered up and twisted, as if she was trying to curse. Then her eyes locked on to Jay's. They blinked and opened wider and blinked again, as if she were peering through a dirty window and someone was sponging away the dirt.

"Al . . . Al . . ." She groped for a word.

People said, "Alzheimer's! She's trying to say Alzheimer's!"

"Al . . . Al-thea . . ." said the old woman slowly.

There was complete silence everywhere around. You could hear people farther back shushing people behind them.

Jay said, "What's your last name, Althea?"

The old woman struggled with a second word. Jay was still holding on to her head, but his eyes were closed now.

"G-g-g . . ." said the old woman, and she screwed up her face with trying. "M-m-m . . . g-g . . . Mc-Gon-a-gal!"

She stopped rocking and twisting her head and stared straight at Jay. Then she repeated her name softly, in a different voice: sweet and cultured like an actress in an old movie.

"Althea McGonagal."

When she said that you could hear people, hundreds of them, go *whoooooh!* in amazement.

"Where do you live, Althea?"

"In Philadelphia." The old woman sat up straight and straightened her back. She looked around, smiling, polite. "I'm sorry—where am I? How did I get here?"

Jay had had his eyes closed all this time. Now he opened them. "You tell us," he said.

She thought for a moment. "Well, there was a very bad situation with my husband. I was diagnosed with Alzheimer's, you see, and he took up with a younger woman. Somehow they got hold of my retirement fund. I remember being evicted from my apartment. I don't remember much after that. I was quite ill. I wonder how I got here."

The big guy who said she had Alzheimer's was staring down at her, his eyes big as golf balls. He and Jay helped her up. She looked a little dazed, but she was smiling.

Jay said, "Your husband died last year, after his woman friend left him. Your attorney has been trying to find you. Do you remember his number?" She nodded. He said, "Can someone lend this lady a phone?"

About a hundred and fifty phones appeared. She took one very graciously and strode over to a tree for a little privacy, shedding years as she went.

Everyone burst into applause.

◆

Kevin's notes were even better and more detailed than his verbal observations, full of little details and character sketches and local color that brought the day alive. He handed them over to me without a murmur. It would have been simple to write them up into an eye-witness account in my own voice. Instead, for the first time in several incarnations, I did something reasonably generous.

The story was called HOMETOWN MESSIAH COMES HOME TO JOYOUS WELCOME. The byline read *By Johnny Greco with reporting by Kevin Duryea.* It ran in the *Journal American* exactly ten days after the first story and made more noise than the first—because of all the you-are-there reportage by Kevin the Apostolic Geek. Needless to say, for that very reason, it was like throwing gasoline on a burning fire.

SIXTEEN

WHERE TWO OR *three are gathered together in My name for eggs and bacon, there am I.*—Matthew 18.20.

Instead of Evan or Jeanie, this episode of the *Risen Lamb Prayer Breakfast Club* opened with a Chicago PD mug shot of Rufus. Evan's voice was heard quietly but urgently narrating offscreen. "Rufus Pereira, forty-one years old: aggravated assault, two convictions; DWI, three convictions; also arrested for robbery, battery, public intoxication."

The screen wiped to an LAPD mug shot of Charlie. Evan intoned again, "Charles Brown, forty-two years old: felony fraud, one conviction; interstate flight, one conviction; sale of narcotics, three convictions."

The screen wiped to a Philadelphia PD mug shot of Angela. Of Angela, Evan said, "Angela Wilkins, twenty-nine years old: public prostitution, eleven convictions; possession of narcotics, three convictions. Here's a look at what Miss Wilkins does for a living."

Although it was breakfast time and this was a prayer club, the screen cut to a quick montage—but not too quick—of a naked Angela in various positions with various men, black and white, alone and in combinations (I'd been right about her being stunning in her younger days). Judging by the discarded costumes, the scenes were from her Triple-Xtra days. The various male members involved were discreetly blurred, as were Angela's salient features, but none so much that you didn't know exactly what was what.

The screen wiped to a formal picture of a teenage Kevin in church beside a large crucifix, in his Sunday best. Evan had this to say. "Kevin Duryea, nineteen years old: supposedly born again but officially shunned by his church in Calvin, Kansas, for self-confessed homosexuality. Duryea lives on the streets of New York. And what do you think Mr. Duryea does for a living, America?"

Finally the show went live to Evan and Jeanie. Normally the setting was a sun-drenched restaurant—the Prayer Breakfast Club in Heavenly (formerly Colorado) Springs—with the two hosts sitting in a booth behind a mountain of breakfast fare. Behind them other tables were filled with extras, who served both as a studio audience and as a chorus for the prayers.

This morning the restaurant was empty, there was no food, and the hosts weren't smiling. Looking uncomfortable, Evan said, "These four criminals call themselves apostles. The apostles of *this* man."

The screen now showed a recent news photo of Jay, holding one hand near his face as if trying to avoid the camera. He was in his beat-up old fleece with the hood up and looked a lot like a Colombian coke mule.

Offscreen, Evan said, "José Francisco—that's J. F.—Kennedy. An unemployed drifter from New York. Just released from jail in Middlesex County, Connecticut, after serving a six-month sentence.

This man claims he is Jesus Christ, our Lord and Savior, returned in the Second Coming."

Without looking directly at her as he usually did, Evan said, "Jeanie, this gang of blasphemers, a convicted criminal who calls himself Jesus Christ and the gang who call themselves his apostles—a crack whore, an openly homosexual man, and two hardened criminals—travel together and often sleep together in an old van."

Replied Jeanie, stiffly, "Evan, I think it's best not to dwell too much on what happens in that van. My first thought is the unutterable pain this false messiah is inflicting on our Blessed Redeemer. It's as if this Kennedy character were driving the nails again into His blessed palms and through His sacred feet."

Evan's imperturbable face registered no reaction; instead, he announced, "As our guest this morning, we're privileged to have the Reverend James Sabbath with us to explain the significance of these blasphemies."

The Reverend was sitting to Jeanie's right. He opened a large black Bible.

"Good morning and God bless you. I want to thank you, Evan, and you, Jeanie, for inviting me on your wonderful show to explain the gravity of this situation. We go as always to the Bible. In Mark chapter thirteen, verse six, speaking of the Final Days, Jesus says, 'Many shall come in my name saying I am Christ and shall deceive many.' Again, in Matthew chapter twenty-four, verse twenty-four, our Savior says, 'There shall arise false Christs' "—he lingered over this phrase before continuing—" 'and they shall shew great signs and wonders, insomuch that if it were possible, they shall deceive the very elect.' *Great signs and wonders . . . that shall deceive the very elect. . . .*"

"The elect is you and me and Evan and all of you good folks testifying with us this morning," added Jeanie helpfully.

"That's right, Jeanie—" began the Reverend, but she wasn't finished.

"I've often wondered, Jimmy: Is that why we win so many elections? Because we're the elect?"

If Jeanie was trying to lighten things up, she didn't succeed. Evan's face was a mask. The Reverend had weightier matters to pursue. Ignoring her, he closed his Bible and leaned forward.

"I know you won't be deceived, dear brethren and sistren. Your faith in this book is too strong. But do . . . rejoice! Yes, rejoice! Because the appearance of this false messiah and his false apostles and his false miracles at this moment confirms beyond a shadow of a doubt that the Final Days are here! The Good Lord prophesied it almost two thousand years ago, and here is His prophesy finally fulfilled. It is amazing, isn't it, how the Lord always delivers? Just as *I* foretold, the Final Battle is only weeks away! So gaze on these features, America! Memorize the face of the false Christ . . . and rejoice that the true Christ is at hand!"

A series of slow cross-dissolves followed of Jay in various poses, starting with a mug shot from Taborsky. All showed him to some disadvantage, distracted from a healing, with his mouth open from preaching, tousled, looking over his shoulder, irritated at being photographed.

At the end of the montage, the Reverend picked up his Bible for a final word, but Jeanie interrupted him. She looked over at her co-host. "Before you go, Jimmy, I'd just like ask my co-host, Evan, what he thinks of the false messiah."

Evan opened his mouth and closed it, as if he was at a loss for words for a moment. Then, still without looking at her, he said, "I would have to agree with the Reverend. We should rejoice that the false Christ has come."

Jeanie, in the middle, looked back and forth at them both and tossed her red hair. "You fellas say what you like, I think he's kinda cute!"

The faces of both men were now masks, the Reverend with either rage or horror, Evan with . . . who knew? But for once no tiny smile played across his lips at Jeanie's bon mot.

Her eyes shining with what looked a lot like defiance, Jeanie drove it home. "That's one savior can save me anytime!"

SEVENTEEN

THE REVEREND'S ATTACK did what I couldn't do and Jay wouldn't do: It put him on-screen—countless screens, in fact. From being a relatively local phenomenon and a heartwarming soft news item, Jay became the Beelzebub of the Bronx for a hundred million fundamentalist Christians. Some ewes of the flock might feel the same as Jeanie, but to the vast and obedient majority, the Antichrist now had a face.

For that same reason, he automatically became a potential hero to the godless, for whom any enemy of the Reverend James Sabbath was a friend of theirs.

The godless were the ones I was interested in, of course. I was on the brink of proving something that had only been a pipe dream a couple of months ago: that Jay had dramatic political potential. But we had to move quickly. Whatever the Reverend was up to, he was using Jay for his own purposes. Having demonized him, he wouldn't go on doing so to the point of a backlash that would do Jay good.

Nor could we let it be Jay's only exposure. We had to answer the Reverend by presenting the true Jay, the cocky, charismatic, ethnic messiah. We had to exploit the fact that he was the underdog. Or should I say the under-god?

We had a window of two to three weeks in which to do it, before everyone forgot who Jay was. To seize this opportunity, bring his refreshed message to as many people as possible, he had to make a major, highly visible move.

There was always the chance that some gun-toting Pure Holy Baptist—every one of whom had a concealed carry permit—would decide to send him to the hereafter earlier than scheduled. Assuming he survived that nugatory threat, the godless, never known for the length of their attention span, would soon move on: the cheese war, Internet nostalgia, something. And—surprise, surprise—at this critical moment the man of the hour had once again left town.

The Posse, up in the Bronx, said they didn't know where he was. He'd left two days earlier, explaining that he needed time to fast and pray.

I asked myself, Where did Jesus go to do the fast-and-pray thing? The desert? No, somewhere else. Something struggled around in my lentil-sized total recall. Then I got it: Jay's account of his meeting with his father, when he'd looked out over the barren New Jersey landscape and said, "Wilderness!"

✦

The van was beside his dad's cabin, but he wasn't around. I walked toward the lake and there he was, under the blooming dogwood trees not far from the water, head down, eyes closed, motionless in the bright spring sunlight. He was kneeling on a carpet of violets and celandines.

It was good to see him, very good. The sight of him was like the moment he was framed in the motel doorway; it evoked the seven hours that seemed to have passed in an instant. Just being near him brought back that sense of timelessness. Peace engulfed me; along with the knowledge that, even before the motel room, there'd been some other time and place I'd felt the same, far away and long ago.

I've no idea how long I stood there; it could have been two seconds or twenty minutes. Then, with that suddenness of his, like a pebble breaking the still surface of a pond, he came over and was doing his one-arm hug.

"Sorry, Johnny. I knew you were there, but I was in the middle of a conversation."

"Calling home?"

He smiled and said, "Have you written anything yet?"

"Didn't you see the *Journal American* pieces?" I asked, a little incredulous.

He nodded. "You haven't written anything yet."

"Are you kidding? People with far more visibility than you would kill for that exposure."

"Only the hidden needs to be exposed."

"You were hidden, Jay, very hidden. As in light under bushel? Now you're nationally known. The Reverend attacked you by name this morning on the *Prayer Club*. You and the apostles: showed mug shots and everything."

"Even Angela?"

"Greatest hits from her Triple-X career."

He winced. "Poor Angela."

"You're on the Rev's radar, Jay. He calls you the false Christ. The battle is joined."

"Isn't that what you wanted?"

"Isn't that what *you* want? Isn't *he* the false Christ?"

"No, he's a false prophet. The Christ he's waiting for doesn't exist."

"Follow that through, Jay! Go on the webs, debate him, preach him into the ground! Show him a miracle!"

"Why?"

"To refresh the message."

"The way to refresh the message is to talk to real people, touch real people, the way we're speaking now."

"Look, Jay, before . . . the first time . . . you could do that. Before, a multitude was five thousand people. That's the number you had in the park the other day. That's peanuts."

He laughed. "*Before?*"

"When you were here before."

"You sound like a trainer talking to his guy before a fight. Pumping him up but not believing in him for a second."

"OK. Forget about *before*. Fact remains: To make any kind of mark you got to persuade millions."

"Flesh, blood—life is all that's real, even if only one person witnesses it. Sooner or later the real will reach millions. Like I said, Johnny, that's where you come in."

"Then take my advice. Next time you preach to five thousand people, use a mike. To spread the truth about Sabbath's lies, go on camera."

"Then it's not me. It's a dead voice coming from a diaphragm, dead particles bombarding a screen. It's you I want to speak through. *You're* my mike and camera."

"What's wrong with the camera? What's wrong with a real-life Jay, young, strong, magnetic, miraculous, dripping peace and generosity, going up against a lying, posturing, hate-driven old bigot with dyed hair and a thousand-dollar suit who hasn't done a generous deed in his life? You'll wipe the floor with him!"

He took my hands. "Johnny, I am the Word made Flesh, not a picture of the Word made Flesh."

It was unanswerable. Then I had a brainwave. "OK. How about this? Not a million people, just fifteen thousand. The Garden. No media. Just you and real people, good people, thoughtful people, people seeking the truth who want to see you and know you better. In the flesh."

There was a long silence. He looked into my eyes from under those lashes, and I had the feeling again that he was reading things on the inside of the back of my skull. And I knew somehow that he was immeasurably sad. But why? At what he read there? That I wanted him to succeed, to leave his mark, to challenge evil, to bring people deliverance? Why would that be sad?

He said, "Go back to our little family and ask them. Tell them what you propose, let them discuss it, pray about it, vote. If they agree, I'll do it."

"How can they decide without you there?"

He smiled. "Oh, I'll be there."

EIGHTEEN

THE PLAN WAS pretty grand—and pretty simple. Where once there'd been something called Lincoln Center, there now stood a huge sports complex. I won't go into the depressing details of how this came to pass; suffice it to say it was here that our good Republican mayor Bob Fitzall had achieved his lifelong dream of building a monument to his billionaire buddies. (And to please the angry-white-whale sports fans of the outer boroughs.) The complex had been built and named for that Ozymandias of urban blight, Old Man Trump. The result was so appalling everyone had gotten nostalgic for the hideous old sixties boxes it replaced.

The horrified locals did extract one concession from the Trumpophiliac City Council: Where the Met had once stood was now a large auditorium for rock and rap revivals, city-wide sporting events, political rallies, and so forth. Madison Square Garden was long gone, so it was called the Garden at Lincoln Center, the only structure in the complex that still bore the name of the Great Emancipator.

It was depressingly easy to book the Garden. It was run-down and losing money and Trump was always agitating to demolish it, but the locals fought for it tooth and claw. It seemed the perfect venue with the perfect spirit for my underdog messiah. I figured that with a little discreet sponsorship from the *Journal American*, I could get him in there within my two-to-three-week window.

But first I had to meet his conditions.

✦

The Posse was still camped out in María's place, waiting for Jay to return from the wilderness. I sent word to María that I had a plan for Jay that he wanted them to consider and would she get them all together for dinner. I came with buckets of ribs and beer. María was deep-frying a small mountain of chicken.

Kevin was writing away. Charlie and Rufus showed up. They'd been meeting some folks who wanted to have another street event with Jay. Among them were Deion and Diane Marshall, the couple at whose wedding Jay supposedly did the lemonade-into-wine miracle. Rufus described the excitement in the community, people who wanted Jay to put down stakes and start some kind of church.

The five of us sat down shoulder to shoulder around María's tiny table. There wasn't room for all the food and plates and hands and glasses. No problem. I couldn't remember the last time I'd done anything this communal: probably decades. I liked it. I liked the feeling of being if not among friends then certainly among allies, of being accepted without question, of having nothing to prove.

Rufus said grace. "God our Mother," he said, "we thank you for sending this food. It looks go-o-od!"

"Amen!" said the table. Nice. Short and sweet. I asked Rufus how they felt about having their mug shots plastered all over the place.

He said, "Had my mug shot taken plenty."

Charlie said, over the wing he was gnawing, "Why don't they never shoot your good side?"

Rufus said, "They both my good side."

"How about Angela?" I said. Rufus looked embarrassed.

Charlie said, "She's pretty down."

Rufus looked as if he was ready burst with anger and indignation at her humiliation. Instead he said, "She misses Jay pretty bad."

We ate in silence for a few moments and then Angela came in. She gave me a bright smile, hugged María, and sat down. She did look troubled. She said a quick silent grace of her own and explained why she was late. She had these friends from the old days; she really wanted to turn them around, turn them on to Jay. But they were tough to convince.

We gorged some more, though Angela just picked. María's chicken was sensational. Charlie snapped a beer and offered one to Rufus. He shook his head. "Man!" he said to no one in particular. "When Jay's here I can drink just one beer, no problem. But when he's not. . . ."

He stared at his plate. A tiny frown crossed Angela's face.

I told them about seeing Jay and that I had proposed something to him, something he wanted the Posse to vote on. I took the Prayer Breakfast Club bull by the horns. I said it was horrible what Sabbath did, especially for Angela.

"It was my doing." She stared at her plate. "It's my responsibility."

I made the argument that there was a silver lining: Sabbath acknowledged that Jay was a threat; he had power.

"Don't need no cracker Reverend to tell us that," Rufus said.

I agreed that was true but it gave Jay the opportunity to take his message to a bigger audience. To demonstrate that there was a completely different kind of Christianity than the one Sabbath was selling. No one, I said, could agree more than me that Jay shouldn't deaden his message by going on TV. And I laid my plan out for them.

There was a silence as the meeting cogitated. Then Rufus shook his head and said, "I dunno."

Charlie shook his too and said slowly, "I got a bad feeling about it. We doing fine talking with ordinary people in ordinary places. Why we need to go play the Garden?"

Rufus said, "That's the longest thing you ever said."

Maria laughed. "José? At the Garden? *¿Porqué no?*"

I said, "Shall we vote?" Rufus asked me if I had a vote. I said I didn't know. Rufus said he didn't think so. No one disagreed with him. Everyone joined hands. Kevin felt for my hand on one side, and I took it. Holding hands with anyone was another first—or the first in a very long time. On the other side, Angela did the same. Her hand was slight, soft, and cold as ice.

Kevin said to me, "This is a prayer Jay taught us around four months ago. Just before Taborsky." Rufus looked over at María and nodded.

"Dearest Mother," said María—and then everyone joined in— "in heaven and in our hearts, blessed be Your name and blessed be Your infinite strength.

Feed us with the food we need, teach us to sow the seed of love, hold our hands when we walk alone and afraid.

Forgive us the evil we have done to Your other children and help us forgive those who have done evil to us.

And take us when the darkness comes, into Your loving arms. Amen."

There was a dense silence. We were still holding hands, heads bowed. Angela's cold hand tightened on mine. "Jay's here with us now," she said.

Everyone murmured *mmh-hmmh* in quiet agreement.

María said, "Say what he tells you to say. Doesn't matter if it's yes or no." There was a long moment of utter silence. I can't say I felt Jay's presence, but somehow I knew the others could. The restless sea of traffic and humanity down on the street ebbed far, far away.

Rufus lifted his head. "Let's vote. I say no. Charlie?" Charlie mumbled no.

"!*Yo dijo Sí*!" Maria almost yelled.

Angela smiled for the first time and said, "The women got to stand up to the men. *Yo tambien. ¡Sí!*"

So it was up to Kevin. He started detailing the pros and cons, but Rufus cut in. "Yes or no?"

Kevin looked at Angela with great love in his face, as if to say, *I'm doing this against my better judgment, for you.* "Yes," he said.

NINETEEN

THE REVEREND AWOKE to the warm Georgia dawn from a wonderful dream. He lay for a while, rising through the layers of wakefulness, in his rocking, sloshing bed.

He was in the Pluribus, a luxury RV of the kind bands used to tour in. The Risen Lamb had bought the resplendent vehicle years ago from country superstar Gert Hambone, when he got too heavy to get up the steps. It boasted a deluxe bathroom, a sunken living room, a games nook the Reverend had made into a Late Perpendicular minichapel, and, best of all, a mahogany-paneled bedchamber with a king-size water bed. Despite its ancient pinko-hippie associations, that water bed was the best thing the Reverend had ever found for his bum back.

He loved the Pluribus with a special passion. It took him back to his early days as a starting-out preacher, roaming the South in his daddy's converted Greyhound, with the big old rugged cross strapped to the roof, the arms a tad wider than the bus, so they had to put a bright red rag on the driver's side arm to alert oncoming vehicles. Those were the days! Driving through warm rain or red dust from this sweaty tent revival to that noisy prayer meeting in an over-air-conditioned civic auditorium, where capacity crowds would gather to see Little Jimmy Sabbath, Archangel of Alabama, lay his hands on the sick and the halt.

Days of faith, pure and simple, when the Lord was shaping him, compliant young clay that he was, revealing to him that his love for Jesus and his love for America were one and the same. That his life task was to heal his beloved country. Physically, one American at a time, when the Spirit lived in his fingertips; spiritually, all Americans—whether they liked it or not—by making God's law the law of the land.

Luxurious though the Pluribus was, it was still a bus. Its windows let the pearly early-morning light in just the way the rounded windows of the Greyhound used to, when he'd wake in his sleeping bag, wedged in among the boxes of robes and tambourines, Daddy snoring softly in the front. When he'd feel dizzy with excitement at the good he'd do that day.

The stately old RV spent most of its life in a garage at Many Mansions, the Sabbath estate outside Macon, but on nights like last night, with spring in the air, the Reverend would have it parked out in the East of Eden grotto and spend the night in it.

There was another plus. A night in the Pluribus meant he could avoid the Jeanie Problem. Not that he wanted to sleep away from his wife; he loved her as much as he did the day he first laid eyes on her, third from the right in the fourth row of that Nashville choir, standing out from the other ninety-nine white-robed songbirds as if the Lord had hit her with a follow spot.

She was still attractive, oh, yes, and then some. She still had It.

And that was the Problem. He'd tried to explain that now she couldn't have babies anymore, they couldn't do it anymore, however much he wanted to. She said that was hogwash and the Lord had made loving as surely as He'd made her a redhead, and since they'd never managed to make a baby anyway, what difference did it make?

But the Reverend didn't see how he could preach to a hundred million people on Sunday morning about how the Lord made sex just for making babies and then break the Lord's commandment on Sunday night. If there was one thing he hated, it was hypocrisy. When the Problem first came up, though, he was confused about what was right, and since he wasn't accustomed to being confused he'd spoken to the Lord about it. Sure enough, the Lord had agreed with his position. Unfortunately, according to Jeanie, the Lord had told her different. The whole situation was a pain in the rear end, but sleeping in the Pluribus allowed him to avoid it for one more night. Jeanie hated water beds.

He always slept like a baby on that water bed. Perhaps like a water baby. Charles Kingsley's wonderful book *The Water Babies* was another thing he and Jeanie disagreed about. (Jeanie thought the Reverend Kingsley was an old English fuddy-duddy and his dusty Victorian book just plain sappy.) But it was the only book—other than a big black Bible—his daddy ever gave him. Bound in green leather, it had been published in 1863 in London, England. The Reverend had read it countless times. He was always deeply moved by the story of Tom, the grimy little chimney sweep who falls into the creek and is washed clean and swims down to the sea to find his playmates, the other water babies. It was a vision of salvation he found deeply comforting and familiar.

He was pretty certain the wonderful dream had had water babies, but he wasn't sure. Only that it had been beautiful. With dawn pinking the curtains, he lay in its afterglow, savoring the fading sensations, wistfully hoping it would turn out not to be a dream. . . .

He had been a water baby! It was coming back to him. And Jeanie had too and . . . Evan! Three beautiful little water babies, frisking and frolicking in a pure mountain stream as it burbled its merry way down to the sea, darting and swooping under the sunlit surface, the light refracting into rainbows on their flawless skin, the green plant fronds waving in the currents they made as they swam.

He lay there rocking in the old RV's water bed, fondly recalling the tricks they played on the fishes, pulling a big old salmon's tail and dropping rocks on the catfish lazing around on the bottom. Best of all were the rides on the trout. Man, those things could book! And they loved racing each other.

He couldn't quite figure out why Evan had been in the dream, though at the time it had seemed completely natural. In fact, the Reverend recalled, although they never said so to each other, he and Jeanie had felt great love for Evan and had known that Evan loved them back. But those very feelings were a tad puzzling. What did they mean?

That was the trouble with dreams. They were great in the Bible or when other people had them; they had a clear narrative and often a meaning, a message from On High. But your own dreams just as often had something like this, which suggested that their origin wasn't the Lord but some mysterious part of you not entirely under your control.

The Reverend wondered if Evan's presence was an issue. They'd all been so happy together in the underwater paradise as little water babies, children forever. The Lord's words came into the Reverend's mind: "Lest you become as little children, you shall not enter the kingdom of heaven."

Could that be it? That the underwater paradise was a foretaste of Heaven, of the thousand years of peace Christ would bring on His return, in just a few short weeks? He remembered now that when they'd swum down to the sea in the dream it was to meet someone, someone very important. . . .

The images began to dissolve, but the feelings didn't. Sweet and unfamiliar feelings: togetherness, security, closeness, love. . . .

The Reverend had never had as much time as he would've liked for the God of Love. There was always so much to do, toiling in the smithy of the God of Wrath. But there was nothing wrong with pure, holy love. And were the feelings so unfamiliar? Or were they just long-ago feelings, connected to something tucked away in a far corner of the Reverend's memory that he couldn't quite reach? Something to do with the way the underwater world looked and felt?

Then he remembered the best part of all: When they'd got to the sea and were about to meet the very important someone, Jeanie and Evan and he had held hands in a circle, facing each other, and they'd closed their eyes and their little water-baby lips had kissed. Or had they?

The Reverend sat up with a start, his back in a spasm, the bed sloshing angrily beneath him. He'd just remembered the bad part! The three of them hadn't kissed, but the Reverend, eyes still closed, had felt a pair of lips on his. It had been a kiss dripping with sweetness. He'd thought it must be Jeanie, but when he'd opened his eyes . . . it was another water baby altogether! The false messiah! His little water-baby face all squashed and Spanish-looking, the smiling incarnation of evil, an inch from the Reverend's, his lips still kissing the Reverend's lips! He'd twisted away and flashed toward the surface, but the false messiah water baby had flashed alongside him, and he could see Jeanie and Evan flashing along too on the other side of the false messiah water baby, laughing. Then they'd broken the surface and he'd begun to wake up.

The Reverend saw the dream's meaning clear as daybreak. It had been a vision of paradise in which the Elect, Jeanie and Evan and he, would soon dwell and which Satan had tried to pollute with sin. Satan knew his days were numbered: five weeks, to be precise. He was redoubling his efforts, corrupting the Reverend's dreams, turning them into nightmares from hell. He'd been sent this vision as a warning. He must take the false messiah seriously. He wasn't just a sign but the very Antichrist. Who had to be fought. Who had to be destroyed.

TWENTY

ANGELA WOKE IN the shell of a burned-out brownstone, shivering from the predawn chill. She felt naked at first, then felt her dress on her top and her legs. But her underwear was gone, and through the haze of the dying drugs came hangover memories of violation. She stumbled up from the rubble, tripping on broken bricks, gulping air, swaying from the crack raging through her system. God, she was sore! What had they done to her? And she was off balance, nodding, her head screaming like a drill. She must have done some smack. That meant a needle. Ah, God, not a needle!

She remembered some things. Walking away from María's earlier in the night. Knowing what she was doing was dangerous, toying with temptation but determined to go through with it. Because once they told her crack was back and better than ever, she could not get it out of her mind. And she'd found the solution, the way to kill her ravenous hunger. Face up to it. Go to where people are doing it, confront it. Banish it from her brain forever.

Then, as she walked through the night to the place where she would face up to her hunger and banish it forever, another idea had come along, more sensible in a way. When she got there she'd just do it once. Just one hit and *then* split, to show she didn't need it. Turn on her heel, go back to the Posse, tell Jay how she'd beaten it forever. See the love and happiness on his beautiful face.

Trouble was, when that sweet white smoke went down into her lungs, bam!—the top of her head went off like a grenade, she never wanted it to stop. Ever again. She didn't want to be good. It felt good to be away from all that goodness for a while. She wasn't being good, yet she felt . . . *great*! What could be wrong with that? Why couldn't Jay take some time off from being good too? Be there with her, do a pipe, just one, to celebrate never ever doing it again?

So she hadn't faced it down. She hadn't turned on her heel. She'd set off grenade after grenade in her head, as if she'd declared war on Angela, wanted to blow Angela to bits. And now the down was coming. God, if only you could get high and then die. Stop existing before the down came, not have to pay that terrible price.

She felt better walking, though she knew from bitter experience she wasn't. The sparkling shanks had begun stabbing in from the edges of her vision. They were bad, very bad. And this was just the end of the high. The down would be unbearable. The fear of the down ran cold through her body.

She stumbled onto a highway, three lanes, very few cars but all blaring at her, flashing their brights. Wasn't this the FDR? How had she got to Manhattan? Confused, she dodged through hurtling metal, blinking to see her way as the shards of light lengthened into daggers. How could she have let guys she didn't know, guys she couldn't even remember, thrust into her, let them jab needles in her arm? Once, twice, who knew how often? A night of daggers, stabbing her.

She managed to scramble over a barrier off the highway. She swayed and stumbled along above the East River. It was still night, but the clouds were tinged with mandarin over toward Kennedy. Now it would start. It always came with the sun. The brighter the day the darker she went inside, seeing nothing ahead but the hell she'd made for herself: no relief, no sleep, not even a beer to push away for a while the end-of-the-world despair.

She'd promised. Once to him, a thousand times to herself: No more tricks. No more needles. What demon possessed her so totally that it could lead her to this madness? Satan must be even more powerful than Jay. She stopped, leaning out over the railings and the river below. Something had occurred to her with deadly clarity: *Don't blame the demon.* She was the demon. She had tempted herself. She had said yes. She had fallen.

She began running along the walkway, Jay's name coming from her chest in sobs, as she fled downtown to nowhere, the useless whore who preferred a lump of burning rock to salvation, the Angela from whom Angela could never escape, however far she ran. She ran anyway, the sheer exertion numbing the pain, holding back the floodwaters of misery.

She had to stop. Her head was bursting with pain, the daggers of light blinding her now. She seemed to be on some bridge. No idea of which one—Manhattan, Queensboro—only that the familiar savage nothingness was gnawing inside her like a wild animal. Cars were blaring at her again. She climbed up onto a girder to get away, then higher, till she couldn't hear their tires. The water was pitch-black below; above was the watery light of the sun playing now-you-see-me-now-you-don't behind scudding clouds. Inside was the plunging darkness spreading through her body like poison.

There'd been hope just a few hours ago, so much hope, hope

she'd betrayed in a single moment, when she pushed that door open. . . . Betrayed Jay, the only man she'd ever truly loved. Lost him. Gone. For a lousy pipe of crack. If only you could go back, start over from that moment at the door, be strong this time! She hated her memory for remembering that moment. She had to stop remembering. She had to stop existing.

It wouldn't be difficult. She was on the very edge of the rusty girder, holding a cable thick as an anaconda. Just let go. "Forgive me, Jay, forgive me," she cried.

She tumbled off the girder, changing her mind in the last nanosecond and grabbing for a handhold but unable to find one on the slimy metalwork of the bridge, gravity tugging at her now, tearing her down faster than she would ever have thought possible, her hip smashing against some hard protuberance as she plunged toward the dark foul water.

Then she saw Jay.

He was far, far below, walking slowly to where she would fall, looking up at her. But how could he be there in the East River?

She felt herself fall more slowly, like someone skydiving, her body turning gently, over and over. Each time she faced downward she saw Jay again, standing in that impossible place on the surface of the water, rocking a little in the chop. There was no boat, no raft, nothing. It crossed her mind that this was a hallucination: the last gift of the drug, life's little bonus before the horror of death. . . .

But the oval of Jay's face grew larger as she fell and he held out his arms for her, head slightly to one side, feet spread to steady himself on the water, waiting as if he had known this would happen from the day they'd met.

She drifted down the last ten feet or so, rocking like a feather. Then she was in his arms, feeling the strong grip of his big hands, looking into his face with its crooked smile. Her savior man, as real as the beer cans and chunks of Styrofoam floating around his boots. Cradling her like a baby, like a lamb, he picked his way across the quarrelsome waves toward the riverbank, where ancient parking stripes speckled the crumbled asphalt and his van stood waiting.

TWENTY-ONE

THE COPS MADE the procession exit the park at 72nd Street and proceed down Broadway to 65th, where the Garden was. It was a Sunday evening in late May—Pentecost, someone told me, though I'd long forgotten which feast that was or what it meant.

When Jay left his mom's place to head downtown, hundreds of vehicles—most as battered as his—had followed, festooned with flowers and streamers and balloons, José-istas, as some were calling themselves, hanging out the windows, blowing and banging various musical instruments, honking their horns and generally finding a way to make as much joyous noise as possible.

The cops were in a tolerant mood. Ignoring the dozens of city ordinances and traffic regulations being violated, they gave the mile-long procession an impromptu escort as it moved in a surprisingly orderly fashion onto the Henry Hudson and drove in tattered stateliness down the mighty river with the late-afternoon sun turning its waters to beaten gold. It exited at 125th Street, passed through Harlem's whooping go-Jay! crowds, and flowed into Central Park in all its spring glory, countless cherry trees with their earthbound cumulus clouds of pink and white blossom stirring in the evening breeze. They were like giant pom-poms lining Jay's path, cheering his team on to certain victory.

On the home stretch across 72nd and down Broadway, the Bronx vehicles peeled off and disappeared, their occupants swelling the crowds along the route. It had been noticed that when Jay got into his van at home he was carrying a ficus plant, and somehow along the route this word had magically spread and other plants had been acquired, some still in their pots, some being waved with their roots dripping potting soil. There were rubber plants and spider plants and ferns of a dozen species, wax plants and umbrella trees and philodendrons; even in springtime, people had found banana leaves.

Broadway was a tropical river of huge green leaves waving their welcome, awash with people shouting for Jay, straining for a glimpse of him, holding out babies and kids to him, weeping and cheering. Eventually, a couple of blocks from the Garden, driving became impossible; we stopped and Rufus and Charlie took the van off to park it and guard it, so relic hunters wouldn't strip it to the chassis.

Jay and María were in the lead, holding hands, pushing slowly through the rapturous crowd, me next, behind me Angela and Kevin, holding hands also. I felt odd man out, no one's hand to hold, sandwiched between apostles and the messiah like a prisoner, a hostile protected from the crowd. Just my usual hyper-egocentricity, I suppose, worrying about myself and how I looked when this moment, more than any yet, was Jay's and Jay's alone. Mea culpa.

But I did feel like an outsider. The Garden was my idea, my vision for Jay's next step up the ladder of visibility and credibility, but I didn't know what he planned to do. Nor did I really know what to expect from the audience.

Jay had insisted that half the tickets be free to those who couldn't afford them, the rest sold at usual prices. This had been honored, and both kinds of tickets went within hours, but I knew that the scalpers' prices were into four and even five figures. Many people with a free pair succumbed to the temptation of getting half a year's salary for them. The Garden would be packed, but it was impossible to say how many of the kind of people who were ecstatically welcoming Jay outside would also be inside.

As for miracles, who knew? When I brought the matter up earlier, Jay had said, "I'm almost done with miracles. Miracles alleviate pain, but only the healed know that. For everyone else, miracles are a fantastic trick, a momentary proof of the divine. I knew that before, but I'd forgotten it. Anyway, miracles aren't proof, are they, Johnny?"

And he smiled a slightly mocking smile, the same smile I got when I'd asked him if Angela's wild story of the night before was true or just a hallucination? A smile that said, If you have to ask, there's no point in answering.

He knew I wanted him to do a miracle, here in the Garden. Just one, to wow the opinion makers and movers and shakers. Or was it something else? That I wanted to see one myself, find out if it *was* proof? After all, unless you count the miracle in Metuchen, which I didn't quite, I'd never witnessed one. I was always somewhere else or listening to someone else's astonishment, someone else's moment of wonder, useless to me.

Jay turned to me as he went up the steps to the entrance, ficus plant still cradled in one arm, the crowds knowing he would soon be gone beyond their reach, their fronds still wildly celebrating his flesh-and-blood presence, adoring faces pressing in on him. He said, "This I remember."

◆

We were taken downstairs to the dressing rooms by security, and standing by the NO ENTRY ARMED ENFORCEMENT sign was a short-haired familiar-looking woman in jeans and a baggy sweater. She was holding a brown-paper supermarket bag and looked a bit scared as we approached. Jay gave her the one-arm bear hug: "Bobbi! You did it?"

She nodded. I wouldn't have recognized her, though I'd interviewed her for an hour. Stripped of the Grecian ringlets, the plastic mask, the body armor of designer clothes, she was a person, not a billboard. Instead of Chanel, she smelled of peace.

She handed him the bag, which was stuffed with bundles of C-notes. My guess was it contained at least a hundred grand. Without even looking at it, Jay gave it to María. "Now I can follow you," said Bobbi.

"You sure can." Jay laughed, hugging her again. And in we went.

◆

The galleries rose to their feet. Fifteen thousand throats welcomed him. From the sound of it, a goodly percentage of them were Latino. But the well-heeled were there in abundance too, especially down nearer the stage where we were. They rose to their feet also as Jay walked briskly down the aisle, delighted faces glowing with admiration and anticipation. Perhaps my message had finally gotten through to the people I most wanted to hear it: that we were about to see the debut of a great leader.

Jay ran up onstage and deposited his ficus plant in the middle. I hadn't been able to persuade him to use a radio mike, but every square inch of the stage was audio-sensitive and he'd compromised on this—on the rationale that he could speak naturally. But I knew what he didn't: there were hundreds of pocket- and palm-cams poking out of handbags and jackets by now, recording his every word and move for the webs. There was supposed to have been a total embargo on cameras, but this was the sort of opportunity that the underpaid Garden staff lived for. A lot of dough had changed hands.

Twenty or so men and women, in two rows, were right next to stage front and center. They had bribed their way into these seats, often for as much as ten or fifteen thousand dollars. Several were in wheelchairs. They were all well-heeled (obviously) and all suffering from a major illness. These were the miracle seekers.

Jay introduced himself, matter-of-factly stating his mission: that he had once been Jesus and had come back as José to refresh the message, to set people straight about what he'd really meant the first time.

"Here's one of my central messages," he said. "The best path to salvation is to sell all you have and follow me. It wasn't too popular the first time around, and it isn't now. It's hard for people to free themselves from their possessions. But someone is here who did it!"

He called Bobbi up onstage, who told her story of being unable to get through a day without buying something new and said how free she felt now. Jay promised her he would be with her always and hugged her again, and the Garden, with the huge head of goodwill it had built up, gave her a thunderous hand.

Jay segued—most professionally, I thought—into a familiar theme. "How can anyone shop till they drop in a world where three billion people live on one dollar a day? A country that doesn't do everything in its power to alleviate that reality can't speak of its moral values. My enemies are not who you're told they are: this country or that, one group or another. No human being alive is my enemy. My enemies are poverty, injustice, untreated disease, violence, and greed. Nothing justifies any of these crimes against humanity, especially not my words in the Bible. And none of these enemies of God can be defeated by war. The only war that must be won is the war on war. Love your enemies. I'm only going to say this twice."

The Garden gave him a solid laugh.

He spoke of things we'd spoken of in our first meeting. That without love the Ten Commandments were mere regulations. He spoke of technology and loneliness and community. He spoke of payback and retaliation, of how his words had been corrupted beyond recognition to justify these outrages against the miracle of life.

He mentioned the Reverend by name, wondering out loud what a Risen Lamb was, exactly, whether there was a recipe for it. He spoke of "Disney salvation," in which all you have to do is listen to a hymn and watch a video of grass waving in the wind to be saved. "Sorry, folks, but *feeling* saved is not *being* saved." He had a word or two about the Rapture—"Frankly, it's Crapture"—and the Final Days—"sounds to me like a fall sale." He announced that no one should expect the Second Coming because it had already happened: "You're looking at it."

The Garden gave the Second Coming a rousing ovation.

He introduced his audience to the real Trinity: God the Father, God the Mother, and God the Child. "We revolve around each other, One and Three. We are love eternal and incarnate. Between us we begot and hold together every atom in existence. We are the ultimate nuclear family."

He said that last time he came in the name of his Father, but that this time he'd come in the name of his Mother. He moved to the edge of the stage and looked up into the galleries. "Let me tell you about my Mother," he began.

A visible ripple of anticipation went through large segments of the crowd.

"From Her all love comes. *Ella está aquí, ahora mismo entre nosotros.* She is here, moving among us. *¡Mi madre! ¡Tu madre! Sé su hijo!* Abandon yourself to Her! *Ella es amor. Puro amor.*"

From thousands of Latino throats came a humming sound like bees in a sunny meadow, people murmuring their approval.

"*No me refiero a la madre que tengo ahora*—my sweet mother, María." He pointed to María, sitting a few seats away from me. "*Me refiero a mi Madre del cielo. Todos conocemos a Dios nuestro Padre.* But God is Mother too."

As he spoke he moved slowly around the stage, including everyone now, in the galleries or on the floor, his hands moving with the rhythm of his words. I'd never seen him in action before. He was riveting. What had I been missing?

"She is the mother of all existence. *La razón por la cual todos nosotros existimos.* The Mother of every child that was ever born. *De ella procede toda dulzura. Ella es amor. ¡Puro amor!*"

This time many people echoed him. "*Ella es amor. ¡Puro amor!*" The words went around the Garden and rose into the rafters. Heads were nodding, bodies beginning to sway.

"*Ella es el hombre que amas. ¡Oh, sí! Ella es la mujer que amas. ¡Oh sí!*"

"*Sí, sí!*" answered the Garden, like waves on a seashore.

"She is the lips you kiss! *Ella es la mano que sostienes. Ella es el cuerpo que acaricias.* She is the love you make! *¡Oh, sí! ¡Ella es amor! ¡Puro amor!*"

At least three quarters of the audience chanted the refrain this time. It was as if Jay was singing a hymn, a hymn with its own music and lyrics and long supple rhythms, and they were his chorus. A hymn as far from the Reverend's bellicose war chants as one could possibly be. It was sad and joyful, evocative, regretful, deeply comforting. Even down among the well-heeled where I was, people were beginning to be borne away by the surging sea of emotion. It was impossible not to be. Eyes were closing, coiffed and shaven Manhattan heads were beginning to sway. Some faces seemed swept by grief, but others were transfigured by delighted smiles, ecstatic recall.

Suddenly I saw my own mother's face, her brown eyes smiling as she kissed me good night, the auburn waves of her hair brushing my cheek as I sank safe into the pillow. My mother young and tan from the summer day, years before the evil spoor consumed her from within. If there was a God, a God of love, why wouldn't God be a mother? What strong force in the universe was stronger than a mother's love? In Jay's soft incantatory words, it made utter sense. Two seats from me, a woman in a designer gown that must have cost thousands, with jewelry to match, was rocking gently back and forth, holding her hands to her face, tears seeping through her fingers, murmuring over and over, "Momma . . . momma. . . ."

Jay began moving again, his whole frame pulsing as he walked the perimeter of the stage.

"*No seas orgulloso, o inflexible, o duro, porque te sientes solo.* You are not alone. *Tu madre está a tu lado.* If you are sick, if you are empty, *si estas perdido, no te asustes.* See your Mother waiting for you at the door. . . . *Ella es amor. Puro amor.*"

Every human being in the Garden repeated the refrain with him now, well-heeled and welfare case alike, the Bronx and Manhattan one vast swaying, living thing. The soft Spanish words rolled around the stadium like honeyed thunder. Jay circled back to the center of the stage.

"*¿Sientes su beso en tu mejilla?* Do you feel God's softness? Do you feel God's warmth? Do you feel God's tenderness? *Ella es cielo. ¡Ella es morada! Ella es donde tú perteneces.* Here, now, forever. *¡Dios tu madre! ¡Ella es amor! ¡Puro amor!*"

He was done but they were not. Five times the Garden repeated the refrain. Fifteen thousand voices in unison celebrated mother love and then broke into cheering, whooping, weeping, stomping, joyful applause.

If only he'd left then.

But he knew as well as every other person in the place that there was some unfinished business. As he stood in the center of the stage, solid and silent, with that intense stillness of his, smiling and acknowledging the crowd but seeming not to move, completely at rest, the applause and cheers began to fade and soon the place was deathly quiet. I realized that fifteen thousand fickle brains had returned to feverishly anticipating what they'd really come for.

He played the moment.

"OK, I know! What's the damn plant doing there?"

"*Yessss!*"

"I figured people would come to see miracles. You've heard about some of them. My friend Johnny, the guy who wrote the stories in the newspaper, doesn't believe in miracles, even though he described a lot of them. He thinks there's always an explanation. He may be right. From God's point of view, miracles are tricks. Something medicine can do or will someday, but that we do quicker now to make a point.

"The problem with miracles is they're like drugs. People always want more. People say, Wow! that's amazing! Then they say, Now do a more amazing one. I don't want to get into that game. I want you to believe without miracles.

"There was a miracle I did last time that stuck in people's minds. I got annoyed at a fig tree because I was hungry and it had no figs. So I withered it. Like this."

He pointed at the ficus plant, and before fifteen thousand pairs of eyes it died. Turned brown. The leaves were suddenly so dry and brittle a couple fell to the floor of the stage.

I have no idea how he did this. The stadium was absolutely quiet.

"If your faith is only based on a miracle, that's what will happen to it. It will wither and die."

He had them in the palm of his hand.

"A great English writer named C. S. Lewis said miracles are just speeded up versions of the miracle of existence. Existence is my Mother's greatest miracle. Not the amazing, miraculous universe— that's my Father's work—but the fact that it exists; that it *is* when there is no need for it to be. That miracle is thanks to Mom.

"I'm no different than before: an ordinary man from an ordinary place. I am not nor was I ever a demigod, a saint, a mighty conqueror, a king, a prince, a lord, or a pretty-boy soap star, as you can see. Above all, I am not you in a mirror. I am God and I am an ordinary man. The ordinary reveals God. The ordinary is a miracle, just because it *is*. Instead of *not* being. All existence is a miracle. Especially you. Every one of you is a miracle."

Then he added, "You know, I feel bad for that poor old ficus."

There was a palpable rustle throughout the stadium as thousands of palm-cams and cell phones focused on the ficus. He pointed at it again, and it revived instantly, putting out fresh new green leaves that pushed the dead ones off the revived stalks to the floor.

Led by the Spanish cheering section, the place burst into wild applause. This time he could have left. Instead he said, "OK. Any questions?"

There was a long line of questioners at the mike. Some questions were idiotic: What's Hell like? ("Driving through the Lincoln Tunnel for all eternity"); Did the Big Bang happen? ("Yes, but it wasn't very big").

Then up to the mike stepped a geeky-looking type. Late twenties, designer glasses, uncertain gender, from downtown, Tribeca or somewhere, just the kind of person I was hoping to reach politically . . .

"How do we know the miracle you did on the little tree wasn't some advanced holographic technique?"

. . . and precisely the kind of post-lefty who couldn't see beyond his own knee-jerk prejudice against religion.

Jay said, "You don't. What you're thinking right now is what I warned of. The ficus plant is sitting there, alive and fine, and you're beginning to forget how you felt when I withered it. So you want me to do another miracle, one that will really convince you. There's no such thing."

"You have these very sick people down in front," said the voice of Tribeca reason. "Couldn't you heal one of them? Wouldn't that prove that you're who you say you are?"

"You tell me."

"I think it would."

There was an uncomfortable silence for a beat or two. You could feel that people were waiting again; one part of their brains knew Jay was talking sense, but mostly they wanted to see another miracle. I was one of them. Already my internal explainers were wondering if the withering and unwithering of the ficus plant had indeed been a miracle or was just a demonstration of the same powers other guys use to bend spoons.

"OK," said Jay, "but there's a lot of sick people here tonight as well as these good folks in front. There's a little boy called Rodrigo up in seat C448. How about him? Come on down, Rodrigo." He pointed to the topmost gallery. There was a sudden commotion where he was pointing, a lot of unintelligible Spanish excitement.

"Rodrigo is seven," said Jay. "He has severe cortical visual impairment that makes it almost impossible for him to see. He was diagnosed three years ago, but his parents can't afford treatment so he's been getting steadily worse."

"How do we know he's not a plant?"

Shut up, Tribeca, I said to myself. Why was he still at the mike? There'd been people behind him, but they'd gone.

"You don't," said Jay. "But I can assure you that I picked him at random out of the hundreds of people here tonight who could use a miracle."

"Then how do you know his diagnosis?"

"Because I know all things." He turned to the Garden. "Would you like me to try and heal Rodrigo?"

The geek said something but he was drowned out by the roar of the crowd. By this time, Rodrigo and his mother had reached the stage. Jay took the little boy from her and led him to its center. He was a cute kid, small, dark-skinned, tight curly hair; he moved his head back and forth constantly, as if he had to scan things and people, to see them. He certainly seemed to have a vision problem.

I was gripped by an unnamable emotion, like fear but darker, more opaque. Had the moment arrived? Was I finally about to see an incontrovertible miracle? Would my entire belief system—or lack of it—be thrown into chaos?

Jay squatted down by the little boy's side. "Rodrigo, how much can you see?"

Rodrigo's barely audible little voice said, "It's like I'm looking through Swiss cheese."

Jay said, "How you know what Swiss cheese is?"

"It's my favorite cheese," Rodrigo answered. "I stick my tongue in the holes."

Jay said, "There's your problem, see? Nothing wrong with your eyes. Your head's full of cheese! We gotta get that cheese outa there. Ready?"

He covered the boy's eyes with his thumbs and wrapped his big hands around the little head. He closed his eyes and took a deep breath. There was a moment of utter silence.

Rodrigo said, "Did it come out?"

"Not yet," said Jay, "but it's coming! Get outa there, cheese!" Another moment of silence; then Jay opened his eyes and took away his hands.

I was close enough to see that Rodrigo was blinking rapidly. And smiling. But most people couldn't see those details. I wished we'd had the overhead screens on, but Jay had forbidden it. Rodrigo looked around. Was he scanning or just trying to find his mom? She came from the side of the stage and he walked toward her, without apparently scanning. When they met, he said, *"¡Mama, puedo ver!"* It could have been genuine excitement, or he could have been coached. "I can see! No more holes!" he said, but his words were lost in the swelling applause.

It sounded as if every Spanish-speaking person in the Garden had gone crazy. They lifted the roof for Jay. People surrounded the boy and his mother, yelling and waving and clapping and praising God. A whirlpool of excitement followed the two as they went back up to their seats.

But an awful lot of people were sitting on their hands, including most of those around me. They weren't sure what they'd seen. I wasn't sure what I'd seen. Had it been a miracle and I was just congenitally unable to believe it? Or had nothing happened? Or—worst of all—had something been set up? I couldn't believe Jay would do that. But I wasn't the crowd around me. And, as the cheering died, here was Tribeca back again.

"Come on!" he yelled. "We've seen cures like this for years from these Christian phonies. It proves nothing."

He was loudly booed by the Latinos. Why was no one doing anything about this guy? The mood in the stadium was deteriorating fast.

"Why don't you cure one of these desperately sick people down here in the front?" yelled the spoiler. "Cure this lady with MS! Show us you're who you say you are! Prove it!"

A section of the audience picked up on this and began chanting, "Prove it! Prove it!"

Jay was saying something about another miracle proving nothing, but the noise was too much. He shook his head. It certainly looked as if he was refusing to help the aforementioned desperately sick people.

The geek bellowed into the mike, "Is it because they're *White*? Is it because they're *rich*?"

Things were getting ugly. The Spanish speakers were now chanting back at the chanters. *"¡Callate, callate!"* People were getting up all over, and some were scuffling. Security guys started moving up the aisles. The Garden was engulfed in bedlam.

Jay bowed his head and left the stage.

TWENTY-TWO

FORGET IT, JOHNNY, your guy's a fizzle."

"Ted, when he withered that plant the stadium was quiet as a tomb! You coulda heard a drop of water on a paper towel. Something happened there."

"Yeah. Psychokinesis."

"What about the blind kid?"

"The cheese miracle?" Kaminski laughed. "Giovanni Greco, professional skeptic, where have you gone? The Reverend did more convincing cures back in the sixties."

"There's always an explanation, huh?"

"What happened is your messiah got booed offstage in a very public place with thousands of cameras watching. The rubber plant's all over the webs, dying and reviving on a loop. As in—joke? Wake up, pal. It's over."

"What if I stay on his trail, do another follow-up?"

"No! OK? I went out on a major limb for this guy as it was. There's crazy heat coming down from Mount Olympus. What he had to say in the Garden was Blasphemy One with all the trimmings. Millions of people saw it. This wasn't some gospel meeting in the ghetto. Sorry, guy, he's poison." I began to argue but he held up his hand. "Friend of my youth, go sit in that meat locker for a while. Cool off. We'll do lunch soon. After the world ends."

◆

Backstage, Jay had been serene. He was surrounded by apostles and Latino folks from the 'hood—and Bobbi. He was still delighted by her making the leap. He said there'd been other miracles that evening, but not the kind people could see. He knew who they were; they knew who they were.

"You seem happier about Bobbi than anything else today."

"That's my way, Johnny, one at a time. One becomes two, two become four. Basic principle of life."

What with the après-show chaos—recrimination from the Garden people, the Us-versus-Them tension between Latinos and the well-heeled, the Christian demonstrators who'd materialized outside the stage doors screaming blasphemy, the ravening packs of media people, and the cops, whose mood had soured—I lost contact with the Posse. I roamed the Garden's gloomy environs, checking out local garages, but there was no sign. I'd had plans of trying to find out more about Rodrigo and his condition, but the crowds had dispersed. Anyway, what was the point now?

Hours later, after I'd put some distance and several drinks between me and the disaster, I finally reached María (she and Bobbi's dough having been chaperoned back up to the Bronx where Father

Duffy could use it). She knew only that Jay and Company were hitting the trail again; she didn't know where they were going. I had to admit, to my fourth gin-and-nothing, that I didn't know either. And clearly I hadn't been invited along. Had my shot, I suppose, and blew it.

It was a lonely, lonely night.

TWENTY-THREE

THE REVEREND (THOUGH around these parts folks sometimes still called him "Pastor Jim") sat at his corner table in the Mountain Fountain in downtown Heavenly Springs. It was an unremarkable place in that part of the world, all fake rock and tap-fed mini-waterfalls and rustic furniture made of pine branches. When Pastor Bob had run the town, he turned a blind eye to its one surviving watering hole, the only place in Colorado not subject to the de facto Prohibition the White Lighters had imposed on the rest of the state. The Reverend had decided to continue this policy for much the same reasons as Pastor Bob. One, the Mountain Fountain was run by an ultra-Tridentine Catholic couple with whom he saw eye to eye on most doctrinal matters (if not on the restoration of the Bourbon monarchy and the heretical schism in which the Vatican had languished since the death of Pío Nono). Two, it gave the Risen Lamb Elders a place to relax with a mojito.

As the Reverend sipped his, he felt on top of the world, his body and soul bathed in the cool bright mountain sunshine. Spring in Heavenly Springs! His victory over Pastor Bob was still fresh enough to relish, especially here, in possession of the long-haired hypocrite's former stronghold. His transition teams had met less resistance from White Light management than they'd expected, and the takeover was going smoothly. The squashy-face messiah had been totally discredited, having served his purpose.

And Evan had called that morning, wanting to have a chat, occasions the Reverend always enjoyed. He was fond of Evan, always had been, thinking of himself as Evan's spiritual mentor; sometimes allowing himself a fondness that was almost paternal. The stern, upstanding young man of few words Evan had turned out to be was exactly the kind of son he would have wanted, if Jeanie and he had been able to have one. They'd never really talked about it, but he sensed Jeanie felt the same way. When the three socialized, she called them "The Rev and the Ev."

Of course, if he'd been their son, Evan would have been white. But the Reverend never really thought of Evan as black. He was just Evan, tall, strong, trustworthy, moral to a fault, a magnificent example of how the Lord's grace could transform an aimless, amoral life.

Not for the first time, the Reverend congratulated himself on his freedom from prejudice. Raised in the racial murk of fifties Alabama, when Whiteness was next to Godliness and Blackness something you shot in the back, he'd managed to break free of those chains. Under his leadership, the Pure Holy Baptists had always left the door open for other races, so long as they observed the Lord's commandments and paid their tithes. In fact, he had big plans for Evan, grooming him to become someday the first

black Elder of the Church of the Risen Lamb. Those plans would
have to be put on hold, given the imminence of the Second Coming, but once things had settled down in His thousand-year reign of
peace, he felt sure the Lord would have big plans for the Rev and
the Ev.

And there he was, all six-foot-five of him, towering over the Reverend and his corner table. He seemed nervous. Unusual. People like
Evan didn't have to be nervous.

"Evan, how are you, son? Sit down. Take a load off."

The rustic chair protested as Evan fit his long frame into it.
Heads turned surreptitiously at this meeting of mighty Christians.
The Reverend knew he probably shouldn't, but he still got a thrill
when his public did that.

Evan stared at him for a moment, his face unreadable. "Hi, Jim."

Not *Reverend*? thought the Reverend. Or even *Pastor Jim*? Weird.
"A mojito perhaps?"

Evan shook his head.

The Reverend said, "Well, I'm indulging. It's always a pleasure
to see you, Mr. Whittaker. I've cleared my appointments for the
afternoon."

"You shouldn't have. This won't take long."

Something told the Reverend to proceed with care. He went into
pastoral: smooth and soothing. "We haven't been seeing enough of
each other. What's on your mind, son?"

"I'm troubled, Jim. Have been for some time."

"Comes with the territory, brother. We all have doubts, questions. But often, when things seem darkest—"

"Can it, Jim! I know that spiel. I detest your spiels. I detest what
you make me do and say. Christian Soldiers! Marching to war! I've

never been so ashamed as when you made me the voice of Jesus! With a machine-gun! My God! The words turned to shit in my mouth!" He made a spitting motion at the table.

The Reverend reeled, disoriented, like a champion coming out to meet a contender and suddenly finding himself on the ropes. "Evan, if it's a music thing, we can always change—"

"The fear you live off! The violence and hatred you spread, all with that smooth, silky, wouldn't-harm-a-flea facade!"

Evan was speaking quietly, but it was impossible for people not to notice such vehemence in a man his size. People were watching openly now, straining to hear what was going on.

"Evan! This is the Tempter speaking. But it's not your fault. He can be resisted. Let's pray together."

The Reverend went to take his hands, but Evan held his up in rejection. "I apologize," said Evan, more controlled, the baritone returning. "That was said in anger."

Foreboding raged through the Reverend's soul. Evan calm could be worse than Evan angry. *Say nothing. Listen. However bad it gets, listen. Then act.*

Evan said, "I spent the weekend with my father in Long Island. For Whitsun. He's Episcopal, that's what he calls Pentecost. I was interested in this guy from the Bronx who was written up in the *Journal American.*"

A sudden chill froze the Reverend through and through. Oh, you demon! Vile tempter. What have you done to my son?

Evan went on. "I read the story and the follow-up. A lot of it made sense to me. He was appearing at the Garden on Sunday, so I used the RL skybox to check him out."

"Evan! He is the false messiah! He is the sign that—"

Evan ignored him. "I've been seeking for a while now, Jim.

Really seeking. This man's all the things you say you are, and everything you're not. I'm going to find him and help him if he needs me. So I quit. That's about it."

The Reverend was speechless. He was throttled by an entirely alien emotion: self-doubt. How could he, who knew himself so well, have been so wrong about Evan?

"Hold your horses there, fella!" The Reverend managed a chuckle. "Let me tell you why I made time for you today. I wanted to ask you to do me the honor of becoming the first African-American Elder of the Church of the Risen Lamb!"

Not a flicker of response came from Evan. He went on. "There was someone with me in the skybox: Jeanie. We've been talking for a long time now about how empty we both feel spiritually, how much we disagree with the things you . . . promote. She can laugh about it; I can't. But she's really helped me find my way. She's been kind of a mother to me, I guess. We understand each other. Anyway, she was real taken with . . . Jay also. I don't mean to talk out of turn. I'm sure she'll get around to telling you herself."

"Evan, look into my eyes and listen! I had a dream that foretold this happening! A few nights ago! A warning from God that the false messiah would take you from me!"

"Jim, I owe you a lot. I'll always be grateful for that. But now . . . I'm sorry, I don't believe a word that comes out of your mouth. God bless you. I hope you find your way."

With one fluid motion Evan rose, turned his back, and was gone. The son in whom he was so well pleased. Gone out of his life. Forever. He knew Evan. Once Evan made a decision, it was made.

Heads watched Evan go, rejection and farewell in every step, then turned back to the Reverend, agape at the mighty happenings at the corner table.

The man of God stared into his mojito, his cup of gall. *Now I can say like Job,* he thought bitterly. *Those whom I loved have turned against me.*

But, said the avenging angel inside him, *I'll be damned if I'll take it lying down, like Job. Off to find the Antichrist, are you, Evan? Uh-uh! The Lord's vengeance will find him first!*

TWENTY-FOUR

JAY'S STORY LOOKED like it had run its course. Johnny Greco's career blip was definitely over. I therefore permitted myself—we drunks prefer formulations like *permitted myself*—a no-holds-barred, max-out-the-cards, ranting, raving, roving, barfing bender, at whose molten core was a forty-odd-hour blackout during which nothing I did, said, or stole; nowhere I drank, slept, ate, or shat; no one I insulted, threw up on, or fornicated with will ever be known to me. All I can safely say is that, unlike the old days when I'd of-ten end up in the ditches, fields, or dwellings for hire of cities as far-flung as Tashkent and Auckland, I did not, as far as I could tell from the pocket evidence, leave the tristate area. I'm more cautious and circumspect during my blackouts, now that I'm a mature adult.

When I did come to in my Hoboken living box—helped there, I later found out, by a disgusted neighbor—it was with a hangover from which I would rather never have wakened.

Despite the blinding pain of the hatchet lodged in my skull, I became aware that there were several messages on my land line. All were from María, asking me if I could come to the Bronx; all were urgent, the last quite tearful.

Hours of cold showers, a bowl of three-alarm chili, and a quick hair o' the dog and I was sitting at her tiny kitchen table. Kevin, recently arrived, was washing up.

María had her fathomless patience face on, her pain all the more painful for being borne so stoically. The tiny cast in her huge eyes was more pronounced, perhaps because her tears magnified it. *My tears have magnified my grief.*

"José is in terrible trouble," she said. She didn't elaborate; Kevin would explain. She gave me the impression she held me responsible. "It all started in the Garden," she went on, her voice cracking.

"María, you guys voted on it. I didn't. And you said yes." *But it was your idea and you humped it for your own squalid reasons, so shut up, Johnny.*

She turned away from me without another word and went into her tiny bedroom. A little later I heard bitter sobbing.

Kevin looked battered and exhausted. He told me what Jay and the gang had been up to while I had been partying.

The Posse now comprised seven people: the original apostles, plus Bobbi and a Bronx contingent: Deion Marshall and a pediatric nurse friend of María's called Amarys. After the Garden fiasco they'd all headed out to Fort McGuire in southern Jersey. Jay wanted to refresh the message for the military.

No one knew it at the time, at least not the enlisted men and certainly not Jay: Fort McGuire would be a major staging point for Operation Armageddon, the easternmost point in the U.S. from which troops could be airlifted across the pond to begin the assault through Dunkerque. Armageddon was to launch July 4th, just over four weeks away. Most of the personnel had been given two weeks' leave. When they returned they were to await orders; it was made clear that this would involve shipping out again.

Many of these guys had just returned from combat duty in far-off lands where neither English, Christ, nor Americans were popular and were pretty pissed that they were being called upon so soon to put their lives back on the line. The mood at the vast air base wasn't good.

I never discovered why at this point Jay chose the course he did. Perhaps he knew somehow that an insane and catastrophic war was imminent; perhaps he hoped to get his mission back on track by going after the men of war rather than the men of God. Either way, it was a fateful decision.

What went down was as follows:

Jay and the gang camped not far from the base's main gate when they arrived. (They had three vehicles now: Jay's van, Bobbi's SSSUV, and Amarys's old Trooper). The plan was to be back at the gate early next day, when personnel would be leaving in substantial numbers.

This they did—or, rather, Jay, Kevin, and Deion did. Outside the gate, Jay was recognized by an older couple who were on their way to a sad rendezvous in the base's morgue: identifying the body of their son, a staff sergeant who'd died the night before from wounds sustained three days earlier in Serbia, when an American air base had been overrun by Bosnian-Kosovar guerrillas. (Serbia was now our staunch ally, Bosnia and Kosovo our mortal enemies.)

The distraught mother, who'd seen webcasts of Jay in the Garden, begged him to bring her son back from the dead.

Jay and Deion drove with the couple to the base's medical facility. That early in the morning, it was deserted. Two guards allowed Jay and the mother into the facility, she having the paperwork. According to the mother, Jay didn't wait for attendants to let them in but went into the morgue by himself. A few minutes later—and I emphasize here that I am simply repeating what persons unknown told Kevin—he emerged with her son in a hospital gown, pale and groggy but very much alive.

Thrilling, of course. Biblical déjà vu, of course. Refreshing the message with a vengeance.

And, if true, the most dramatic miracle yet and the least dramatic. The only accounts of Jay's "miracles" I've given so far—with the exception of the fizzles in the Garden—have been those someone gave me full details of. For this there's nothing. No one was in the morgue with Jay except the man he raised from the dead.

According to the unknown someone, the overjoyed couple had taken custody of their dazed son and tried to thank Jay. He told them to leave immediately. It might not be safe for them to stay in the vicinity of the base.

Jay and Deion rejoined Kevin at the main gate. Word was flying all over the base that the Jesus freak who'd done the withering-the-rubber-plant thing in the Garden had brought a dead airman back to life. Could there be a more powerful image for a soldier, a more gut-tugging story than that? Greater love hath no man than that he gives back life to another.

So when Jay got up on a milk crate just inside the gate and started preaching, a fair-sized crowd gathered and kept getting bigger as he went on.

As he had at the Garden, he began by explaining matter-of-factly who he was and why he had returned, which no man or woman present seemed to have any problem with. There are no atheists in foxholes and very few in forts.

Then he said what he'd come to say. "Love your enemies. I do. I have loved every soldier on every side of every war ever fought. I have loved every child of God murdered by another child of God. Because—make no mistake—whenever one of my children kills another on purpose, it's murder. Whether it's from thirty thousand feet or three, it's murder. It's no less murder than creeping into their bedroom while they're asleep and beating them to death with a tire iron."

Remarkably, Kevin said, no one objected. They were rapt.

"Murder is not a mission or a calling or a career. If you went to West Point or the Air Force Academy to get a degree in it, it's still murder. All the fancy words your superiors come up with— retaliation, extreme prejudice, overwhelming force, collateral damage, smart this, and pinpoint that—cannot alter the fact that all these words mean murder.

"Wearing a uniform does not to stop killing from being murder, killing for your country does not stop it from being murder. Clicking on an icon a thousand miles away does not stop it from being murder. Sending a command to a robot does not stop it from being murder. If your sergeant tells you to do it, it's murder; if you are told by your officer to tell an enlisted man to do it, all three of you commit murder. It's murder if a court absolves you of all wrongdoing. It's murder if a man of God blesses the weapon you murder with. It's murder if you vote for someone who tells others to murder in your name. It's murder if the one you murder has murdered.

"And if you say God told you to murder, I say to you it is not God you are listening to."

The crowd was now many hundreds strong. Many people were

holding up recording devices and phones to get Jay and his words down. People on the fringes were being told by people closer in what he was saying. Still, there seemed to be no objections, no puzzlement even.

At this point, MPs began appearing. Some stopped and listened. Others began circling the crowd, looking for a way in, to start breaking things up. Jay continued.

"I have always hated wars waged in my name. *God is on our side! Gott mit uns! Deus Vult! God bless America!* I am on no one's side. I am not on America's side, or Islam's, or Israel's, or Europe's. I have never been on the British, the German, the Spanish, the Dutch, the Catholic, or the Protestant side; I did not uphold the Crusaders, not the Turks or the Golden Hordes, not the sons of Ali or the sons of Muhammad. I did not guide the hand of David or Solomon, or the hand of Caesar or Alexander or Ptolemy. Thou shalt not kill. There are no exceptions."

Officers began to appear. There was confusion, since this didn't seem to be a demonstration or a fight—just a guy talking. Plus it was still early, people were half awake, hung over from last night's beer. The MPs began huddling with the officers and a few officers hurried back into the base, for guidance or reinforcements.

"You are the same blood, you and every child of your Mother in Heaven alive on this planet. When you spill their blood you spill your own. So refuse! If they call you a coward for refusing to murder your brother or sister, be a coward! In your Mother's eyes, you're a hero!

"There are no just wars. War is a collective murder-suicide pact by members of the same family. You may not take from her other children the gift your Mother in Heaven gave you: existence. Love is the only family value that matters."

The crowd was now enormous, a thousand or more. Some official decision appeared to have been taken, and several officers led groups of MPs into the crowd, trying to penetrate to Jay. There were protests, batons swung, several of them pulled from MPs' hands and tossed away. It was the first violence of the gathering.

When the crowd began to realize that the officers and MPs were trying to get to Jay and arrest him, the whole center—hundreds of people with a single thought, it seemed—linked arms and began hustling Jay, Kevin, and Deion through the gate, protecting them from capture and giving them the opportunity to escape. When the crowd came to the apostles' vehicles, a path opened for them. It was a Gandhi moment: as if the crowd had absorbed Jay's message of nonviolence and instantly acted on it in the face of baton-swinging head-butting tough guys.

Deion jumped in Amarys's Trooper and took off. Kevin stayed with Jay. Jay wouldn't get in the van; he said it was too well-known. There was a huddle, and several friendly airmen ran for their vehicles. Jay and Kevin were bundled into one pickup, which took off, followed by another pickup and a jeep. The old brown van was left by the base's perimeter fence, its skewed headlights staring forlornly down the road.

◆

You don't have to be a military attorney to know that matters were ten times more serious than they had been an hour or two earlier. Just skimming the transcript Kevin handed me, I could see grounds for arrest on half a dozen major military charges: incitement to subversion, desertion, relinquishment of weapons, sabotage. In time of war—and when wasn't it wartime by now?—all those crimes were treason, punishable by death.

The airmen with Kevin and Jay hooked up with the other apostles at the camp. The corporal with the jeep had an aunt and uncle in Lancaster County—Amish farmers, old-school pacifists and anti-mechanists. No TV, no electricity, no cell phones, no cars, no computers. Hard to track even with modern snooping. He offered to take Jay and the gang there; it would be safe for a few days.

The other two airmen split before the satellites started to get suspicious of their shiny new pickups. Jay insisted that the Bronx contingent leave. He wanted the Apostle Posse to go back with them too, but they refused pointblank. None of them, especially Angela and Bobbi, would let Jay out of their sight.

So that's where the gang had been for the last three days, with an old Amish couple somewhere in Lancaster County. Since phones and cars could be tracked, Kevin had been the safest way to get a message to me; a day of travel, by bus and on his thumb. The message was: Jay wanted to see me.

✦

Kaminski repeated all my own objections to the Lazarus story, checked while I was on the line with a source at McGuire. Nothing untoward had been reported. No miracles. No messiah sightings. All I had to go on was Kevin.

Anyway, said Ted, the whole antimilitary antiwar rant went against his grain. That was going too far. If a guy was raised from the dead, sure: front-page news. But he'd never given the miracle stuff much credence. Sorry, Giovanni. No sale.

✦

So there I was on a lovely June evening in lovely Lancaster County, walking down a dirt track through fields of young corn. I must've walked a mile already, but I was fresh as a daisy. There were daylilies all along the freshly painted three-rail fencing, their ragged gold and bronze blooms sharp against the white of the rails. Swallows were swooping through the lazy warm air, tucking into their hors d'oeuvres; a rabbit broke cover up ahead and sat for a few moments, beady-eyeing me, before leaping back into the lush and lustrous chlorophyll. It must be fun to jump around in your dinner. If I had Kevin's directions correct, the white complex of stately clapboard house, barn, and silo a few hundred yards up the track ought to be where the people's Christ was holed up.

I was in a benevolent mood, truly excited at seeing the kid again, selfishly craving that aura he surrounded you with where past and future never intruded.

My earphone buzzed. Weird. I could've sworn I turned it off in Newark before getting on the bus. But I'd had a couple of pops in the bar. Maybe I'd forgotten. Hadn't made any calls and I wasn't about to answer this. That was how they tracked you. But the caller recognition voice said in my ear, *Kaminski*. Uh-oh. Must have had second thoughts. Lulled by the balmy evening, I said *yes*, and I was connected to . . .

"Hello? Hello?"

My stomach did knee bends. I ran back down the track to lead them away from the farm and Jay, anywhere, crumpling up Kevin's directions and throwing them in the daylilies. They could still be miles away and there were woods off to the right; maybe they'd block the satellite. . . .

I hadn't gone twenty yards when a chopper-drone—one of the latest stealth jobs whose rotors didn't make a sound—landed beside me in the corn. A dozen bots bounced down on the ground and covered me with their stubby weapons.

They sheepdogged me back up the track at a run, the chopper-drone hovering behind them a few feet from the ground like our shepherd. I was the sheep that had been lost and now was found.

From behind us came the real choppers with the real troops, thundering technology and violence through the soft Amish air: dozens of them, enough to take a small town. The old clapboard house had a simple, unadorned front door; it opened and Jay was framed in it, looking up calmly at the noise and then, as I ran toward him, at me.

I stumbled and fell in front of him and struggled to my knees, winded, blind with shame. "So . . . sorry, Jay . . . my cell . . . forgive me!"

Jay helped me up and gave me the one-arm hug. Was I forgiven?

We stood, me panting, him serene. He was twenty-five years my junior but his arm was a father's arm, strong and sheltering. The horror that was to come, the shame and misery of the past, receded. I was with him. He was with me. That was all that counted.

"What was your message?"

"Don't ever forget our deal."

The troops were Republican Guards, blinding silver in their full-body Kromlar armor with the blood-crimson crosses back and front. This thing was being run from the very top. Half a dozen came in our direction.

He let me go and took my hands, engulfing them as usual. In his hands mine always felt like a child's. I got one last lopsided smile.

"*Hasta luego, amigo.*"

"*Hasta luego, niño.*"

Then the Guards were on us.

TWENTY-FIVE

WE WERE IMMEDIATELY separated. I saw Bobbi and Angela for a flash, being chivvied by female Guards into a chopper. Kevin ran; they caught him in the corn. Rufus and Charlie were nowhere to be seen. Incredibly, given the search equipment the Guards had, they avoided detection by hiding in an old stone root cellar. Years of practice, I guess.

The Amish couple were attending some kind of spring harvest supper at their local church. They were arrested when they got back and, a little later, disappeared.

I was probably taken to the DC area. There was a longish bumpy chopper ride, but I was shackled, blindfolded, and drugged; it could've been anywhere.

I should make it clear that courage has never been my long suit. I'd taken on a few thieves and bullies in my time, but my cojones were always on paper. I'd never once had to confront the probability of violent pain. I was scared shitless. According to reliable sources, the Guards' interpretation of *love your enemies* was: We only torture you to the cliff edge of death, for your own good.

There were two of them in the room. An audio feed from elsewhere had been obligingly left on. Over it could be heard the agonized screams of someone in the early stages of interrogation, when the voice is still working. It took me a few moments, through the fog of drugs and fear, to realize that the begging, pleading man was Kevin.

The Guards had an interrogation policy of never raising their voices, never using epithets of any kind, never using violent or threatening language. There was no good-cop bad-cop. They were all good cops. Their rationale was they interrogated you as Christ would have.

"Good evening, Mr. Greco," said one. "Sorry to say, your situation is dire. The man you led us to, whom we know to be your leader, has fostered a form of religious terrorism even more insidious than other forms we're called on to combat. He is being taken to a secure facility where, after exhaustive debriefing, he will stand trial for his life. Your situation is to all intents and purposes the same. Your media status is no shield. Do I make myself clear?"

He made it clear. My sphincter made it clear.

The other cop was even more compassionate. "Mr. Greco, you have an alternative. It has been proposed at a very high level that you be permitted to avoid debriefing, trial, and certain execution by agreeing to observe the behavior from this point on of your leader and then write an official, objective, unbiased account of the proceedings, with the appropriate oversight and review. If you perform this role satisfactorily you will given your freedom, the only proviso being that you carry for the remainder of your life an intravenous shackle. Will you accept this generous offer? You have ninety seconds to decide."

My overloaded brain spun wildly. The "high level" must be the Reverend. Presumably the Angel of the Lord's vengeance was orchestrating every aspect of Jay's pursuit, arrest, and trial. I'd not only led him to his prey, I'd provided him with a sizable bonus; the man who'd launched Jay in the media would be the most credible witness to his downfall.

It was typical Reverend: brilliant, manipulative, win-win for him, no-win for me. Just like last time. Except now the stakes weren't just my integrity and good name but my life.

The seconds ticked on. I knew agreement was a betrayal, but I couldn't quite crystallize how. Would I be doing anything different from any other journalist? Everyone worked with "oversight and review." If I didn't do it, someone else would. Better me, surely, who might be able to nudge the account nearer to the truth. Wouldn't it be best to seize this opportunity? Live to write another day?

Would agreeing make me Judas? A bit late to worry about that. I was already Judas; I'd led the high priest's men right to him. And yet at that very moment, just a few hours ago, he'd forgiven me and, standing in the sunset with his arm around my shoulders, said, "Don't ever forget our deal."

Wasn't this our deal, to write his story? How could I do that dead? But it wouldn't be his story. It would be the Reverend's. Just like last time. Why was self-preservation always a betrayal?

"You have twenty seconds left, Mr. Greco."

Was I ready to die? I loved Jay dearly, but was I ready to die for him? Why not? *Blessed are the dead, for they know the answer.*

"Mr. Greco?"

"I . . . accept the offer."

The Greco Option, Part Two.

TWENTY-SIX

"ARE YOU THE Second Coming of Jesus, the Son of God?"

"I prefer to be called the Child of God."

"Yes or no."

"I am."

"Yes or no, José!"

"Yes."

"I draw the court's attention to the defendant's frequent claim: I am the Second Coming of Jesus, Son of God."

Jay was sitting in a Def SMod (Defendant Security Module), a large transparent bell-shaped pod, made of hyper-glass, airtight and soundproof. He could hear what was being said in court, unless someone—prosecutor, defense counsel, or judge—imposed a security blackout. Then he could hear nothing that was being said or decided about him.

During questioning, the court could hear him, as now in the

prosecution's final summation, but his voice came out tinny and hollow. A glass pod was talking, not Jay.

All defendants tried by the military for capital crimes—99 percent of them terror suspects—were held in these for security reasons. But the real purpose of the module was to criminalize the guy inside. The very slim chance he or she had of being acquitted became anorexic. The pod said, This prisoner is dangerous, violent, and guilty.

From where I was sitting in a separated observation bay back of the hearing room, Jay was a shadowy figure behind two walls of glass, each one thick enough to be rocket-proof. I couldn't see his face clearly, but he looked slumped and lifeless. That morning it was sometimes hard to remember that it was flesh-and-blood Jay I was seeing, a real man—my friend—whose life was in the balance.

If *balance* is the word. The military prosecutor, a sharp-nosed young officer with a West Texas twang, had a Risen Lamb pin in his lapel. Two of the three judges, air force majors both, were of the same persuasion—as was, even more amazingly, Jay's own military-appointed defense counsel. They'd been ordered by higher-ups not to sport their pins during the tribunal, to ensure their objectivity.

The trial had been moved away from McGuire to a bigger, newer air force base, Fort Oswald, Texas, probably because Christians could be more easily mobilized there than in New Jersey. Several legions of them had been outside the gate that morning, baying for the false messiah's blood, praying for the tribunal to "Execute him! Execute him!"

I might have made a nice graf or two out of a man named Kennedy being tried at a base named for one of the newest Christian saints, but I was still agonizing over what I'd agreed to do. How could I report this trial without conveying that it was a miserable sham?

"José, you have frequently repeated the statement: The Day of Judgment is at hand for Christianity. The Day of Judgment is normally interpreted as the return of our Sav—of Jesus to destroy his enemies with overwhelming force. Do you advocate the violent overthrow of Christianity?"

"No."

"Do you advocate the overthrow of Christianity?"

"No."

"Yet you've also said, I come not to destroy Christianity but to fulfill it. That's a deliberate parallelism of the words of Jesus, who said, 'I come not to destroy the law (of Moses) but to fulfill it.' To do that he launched an entirely new religion called Christianity."

With each question the prosecutor's head lunged forward at the shadowy figure in the DefSMod, his nose like the tip of a broadsword. Another useless irony: Jay was being prodded toward almost certain death for advocating the supreme sanctity of life.

"Do you intend to launch an entirely new religion?"

"Yes."

"Called Christianity?"

"That's not up to me. That's up to those who launch it."

"What will it be called, Neo-Christianity? Christianity the Sequel? Christianity Two? Joséanity?"

"I have no idea."

"But it will replace Christianity?"

"As we know it, yes."

"So you do advocate the overthrow of Christianity?"

"If that's how you define overthrow, yes."

The prosecution's witnesses had provided a ton of evidence. Aided and abetted by defense counsel's cross-examination of them, which bordered on narcoleptic, their lies and innuendos were spectacularly damning.

There was Deion, who looked as if he had been expertly worked over for a night shift or two, his big face puffy and his speech slurred. He sullenly testified that, yes, he was now convinced that Jay had paid people to spike the drinks at his wedding and make it look like a miracle.

There was the chant-leading geek from the Garden, who turned out to be an undercover Risen Lamb operative. He confirmed the hideous blasphemies Jay had voiced before an audience of millions, in particular that God Almighty was a woman. His appearance shocked me for a second, a testament to my idiotic delusion that a Tribeca lisp and rimless Vuitton glasses indicated someone on the side of the angels. But no, they're everywhere, Satan's little helpers.

There was a goateed expert witness from a Pepperdine-affiliated research outfit called the Christian Science Institute. "No relation of Mrs. Eddy," he joked. CSI concentrated on faith-based scientific research; the bearded one being a specialist in miracles and debunking them, especially miracles attributed to Catholic saints. He gave testimony about exceptional individuals with alpha waves outside the normal range of 7.5 to 13 cycles per second, who could learn to harness them to induce the temporary alleviation of symptoms of serious illness. I confess I found some of his testimony persuasive. Example: that Kaposi's sarcoma lesions could be made to vanish for a time.

There was a cavalcade of informers and undercover types who swore up and down that Jay advocated group sex, gay sex, underage sex, socialism, Satanism, animal rights, snuff porn, abolition of golf, and other unspeakable crimes.

Crowning my shame was the most damning evidence of all:

Kevin's transcript of Jay's preachments at McGuire, which had been confiscated from me when I was arrested. A Republican Guard intoned the juicier parts for the benefit of the court in suitably horrified tones, as if he were reading *The Story of O* to an audience of Carmelite nuns.

Finally there was the Reverend himself, who in a masterfully understated appearance was summoned as an expert witness on the deleterious physical and mental effects of blasphemy. Using his soft-spoken, carefully considered persona, he gave testimony directly relating to outrages the court had just heard. He concentrated on the inflammatory appeal of blasphemy, what he called the Three-F effect (for Forbidden Fruit Factor). The egregiousness of Jay's theological errors could easily mislead young and untutored enlisted persons into capital crimes (like those Jay was on trial for). The Reverend was key to the prosecution's strategy of conflating outrages to Christianity (blasphemy) with outrages to the state (treason). I had to admit, in my objective witness role, he did a compelling job.

The contrast between his mastery of the court and the hunched silent Jay was testimony in itself. Behold moral values triumphant: patriot versus traitor, Christ versus Antichrist, winner versus . . . loser.

To hold back the avalanche of negative evidence, defense pleaded insanity, calling one expert witness, a professor of clinical psychiatry at Rice with a specialty in religious delusion. He testified that the incidence of delusional messiahs was rising; Jay exhibited all the symptoms, quoth the Prof. He kept the court in stitches with examples of messianic weirdness, including one on the *Inquiring Mind*'s Nut Log, a Jesus who walked around with tenpenny nails in his hands and feet.

To wrap up his denunciatory summation, prosecuting counsel led Jay through his McGuire preachments, insisting that he answer only "I did" or "I did not." The effect was almost ritual, a litany of self-condemnation.

"Did you say, There are no just wars?"

"I did."

"Did you say, War is a mutual murder-suicide pact between family members?"

"I did."

"Did you say, Cowards are heroes to God?"

"I did."

"Did you say, Killing for your country is murder?"

"I did."

"Did you say, Whether it's from thirty thousand feet or three, it is still murder?"

"I did."

"Did you say, It is murder to murder one who has murdered?"

"I did."

"Did you say, I (meaning God) am not on America's side?"

"I did."

"The prosecution rests."

Defense counsel waived the right to summation, and the prisoner was asked to stand for the verdict. He did. The president of the tribunal, a bespectacled air force colonel with silver hair, probably nearing his half century, who'd said almost nothing during the proceedings, asked the defendant if, in the absence of defense summation, he had anything further to say.

Jay looked at him for a long moment and bowed his head, shaking it slowly. Behind that lying glass, the thick barrier of hardened silica that sucked all the humanity out of him, it looked like a final utter admission of guilt.

The president asked the major to his left for his verdict. The major barked, without a beat, "Guilty on all charges!"

He asked the major on his right, who quietly, with great compassion in his voice, said, "Guilty on all charges. May God save his soul."

Then the president said, "Gentlemen, fellow officers, I'm an American with old-fashioned American values. I'm none too sure how American these newfangled values we hear so much about are. In my America there is no God or Christ or Yahweh or Muhammad or any other religious leader, except in the privacy of a citizen's soul. I am, I hope, a moral if imperfect man. But my beliefs are as irrelevant to the functioning of this tribunal as they are to the functioning of our great nation. To paraphrase the words of a great Christian—she was head of the Church of England when she said them—'We do not make windows into our citizens' souls.'

"It's clear to me that this case is really a battle between two radically different interpretations of the laws and traditions of Christianity. I doubt this tribunal is the proper venue for such a battle. I don't underestimate my respected fellow officers' conclusion that the prisoner is guilty as charged of treason, subversion of troops during time of war, incitement to sabotage, desertion, insubordination and abandonment of weapons, giving aid and comfort to the enemy, and accusing commanding officers in time of war of capital crimes. Nor do I disrespect in any way their verdict that he should pay the price for these offenses, which is, in our jurisdiction, summary execution.

"But in my view, the only offense against the U.S. Air Force the prisoner has committed beyond reasonable doubt is to trespass on its property. For this, ironically, he is not charged. He did, however, trespass for the purpose, hallowed in our old-fashioned American traditions, of expressing his opinion. Now we can recharge him, find him guilty, and toss him in the brig for a few months to show him what happens to trespassers. But as to the other charges, I see nothing substantive in the evidence. Prosecution has failed to convince me that blasphemy as defined by the Church is treason as defined by the State.

"Obnoxious though I find his views, he simply preached what he believed was the truth. In what way is his right to preach his truth less than that of the Reverend Sabbath? Does the Reverend Sabbath or anyone else in this court have a monopoly on truth? What is truth, if we cannot all contribute to its totality? In my opinion, this man has done no wrong. I cannot condemn him.

"Since the crimes he is charged with carry the death penalty, the verdict of this tribunal must be unanimous. It is also required, in the absence of unanimity, that the tribunal duly reflect, on the gravity of the charges and of the sentence, before a second vote is taken. This tribunal is adjourned until nine A.M. tomorrow."

✦

I was driven back to my motel. María had arrived the evening before to keep vigil along with her friend Amarys, who was now with her 24-7, deeply worried about what would become of her should the worst happen. It felt good to be able to bear a little good news for once, my having been the cause of so much bad.

It wasn't Amarys who came to the door of the room but Bobbi. She'd received a very minor charge; she figured it was to sow dissension within the Posse, since Angela and Kevin were still up for the same capital charges as Jay was. Her parents had bailed her out, and she'd just arrived to keep vigil with the other two women.

Jay's mother seemed to get smaller and more defenseless every time I saw her. I wanted to hug her the way Jay would, but I knew it was out of the question. Her heart may have forgiven me, but her body was still thinking about it. So it was a joy—not a familiar feeling to me, I must confess—to be able to tell her the good news. Her face lit up like a full moon peeping over dark woods. The two younger women were ecstatic.

I enlarged. The trial could hardly have gone worse—the evidence, the witnesses, the spinelessness of the defense—but the colonel stood up for his principles in the face of everyone. So long as he stuck to his guns the next day, and there was every indication from his words that he would, the tribunal would be hung again and Jay would go free.

There was a knock at the door. It was my Guard driver. My services were needed. Immediately, please. That Christlike Guards courtesy. I got in the car, and an apparatus like oversize goggles was placed on my face, obscuring my vision, hearing, and all sense of direction.

◆

The torture was under way. I was in a small room with a large one-way mirror through which I could see into the chamber. There was a Guard with me to explain procedures.

Jay was in a long hospital gown cut low on his chest and tied at the back, so that his back and lower end could be exposed. He was hooded. His hands were cuffed behind his back. There was a long white plastic table and a chair. He was slumped over the chair, groaning. In the chamber with him were two Guards in fatigues.

The softening-up stage was over, my Guard told me, simple beating with rubber-covered chains on the soles of the feet, the kidneys, the testicles. Internal damage might have been done in the latter two areas, but nothing would be fatal or visible. These guys, he said, were real pros.

The persuasion stage began. A cylindrical metal helmet was

placed over Jay's hood. My pal explained this was so his screams would be amplified back into his own skull. He was pushed onto the table on his back. One Guard held him down by the throat; the other took a pair of pliers and—with a sadism as ancient as malice—began twisting Jay's nipples with them.

Even deadened by the helmet, Jay's screams were like an animal being butchered. I turned away, groping for the audio to turn down the sound. My Guard restrained me. "Take notes, please."

The twisting went on for about a minute, Jay writhing in agony. Then the restraining Guard leaned down to Jay's helmet and said, "Recant. Say you're a false messiah."

The helmet shook slightly. So it began again; and again it stopped and again they repeated the same quiet message. Again the helmet shook. And again it began.

When the helmet shook again, my Guard explained that Jay was becoming acclimated to the pain so now they were going to increase it. The Guard with the pliers began pulling Jay's chest hair out in tiny tufts, excruciatingly slowly, stretching the skin upward, until the hairs tore free. Dozens of tiny blood blisters appeared where each tuft was pulled out. Some burst. The animal screams were worse than before. Revulsion rose in my throat; I gagged.

The Guard offered me a sickness bag from a handy pile. He smiled. "Happens all the time."

After a while, to my horror, my horror lessened. It became routine, my hatred of the torturers intellectual rather than visceral. Was I becoming acclimated to Jay's pain?

No. Because then they started the electroshock.

At first I thought they were done. They took Jay's helmet off and seemed to be soothing him. They were standing between me and him so I couldn't see. But when they went out of the room, Jay was lying in restraints on the table, one clip on his tongue in the hood's mouth hole, another under the gown on his genitals. Wires ran down to a heavy-duty outlet in the floor.

The angry spasms the current flung Jay's body into, were impossible to watch: an arm-flailing, leg-jerking dance of death. I thought, This is the closest you'll ever be to incarnation, kid, to God in the flesh. The fundamental force of the universe shaking you like a rag doll.

The dance of death stopped. The Guards came back in and sat Jay up. All his motor skills were gone, head and limbs lolling uselessly. They whispered in his ear, "Recant. Say you're a false messiah." He had no response. He was inert. A terrible fear rose in my throat like reflux.

My Guard shook his head in disgust. "Passed out," he said.

I tried something. "Y'know, I think I got all I need. Thanks." To my surprise, he smiled OK and let me stand up. I said, "You guys are something, man. This was intense!"

We high-fived and went to the door.

"Know what?" He grinned. "Before the night's out we'll break him."

But know what? They didn't.

◆

We rose early. The dawn was like scraps of last night's porterhouse, alternate black and blood-colored streaks of cirrus scarring the salmony pink of the eastern sky.

Red sky at morning, shepherd's warning.

By the time we left the motel to go to the base, a bilious cloud cover was settling in and the tips of summer thunderheads were already visible over the horizon, like silver-haired giants coming to the rescue.

The idea was to get on the base early enough to beat the demonstrators, but they were ahead of us. There were thousands of them this morning. Fundamentalists having little to do in the way of evening entertainment, they'd spent much of the night drawing signs of visceral fury.

There were dozens of variants on the red "forbidden" circle: a *J*, Jay's face, or Satan's face with a red line through it; DEATH TO, KILL, or INJECT coupled with same in every conceivable combo; long-haired Christs weeping; one enormous brightly colored tableau held by four men, showing Christ hacking Jay's head off; another where Christ was injecting Jay in the arm with an enormous syringe marked POISON.

The din was immense and María was terrified. If the decision to acquit came down, as I was pretty certain it would, the righteous would be ready to lynch someone, preferably Jay but, failing him, some other nearby Hispanics. They'd never release Jay through the base's main gate. There was no point in waiting there. I left the women in a diner two miles down the highway and headed back for the Big Moment.

They brought Jay out, shackled hand and foot. His face was unmarked if puffy. The careful custodians of the night knew their job. But he moved with enormous difficulty, stooped, head bowed, eyes closed, breathing shortly, as if his strong young body was one enormous throbbing bruise.

They put him in the module and made the usual show of locking and sealing it. Prosecution and defense were already in place. In came the tribunal, the two majors side by side, followed by the colonel. There was a spring in his step as if someone had offered him his own TV show during the night. I thought, *There's a man who knows his mind, who's looking forward to doing some good today.*

They took their places. The colonel rose briskly, greeting the court almost jauntily and getting down to business. He said the court had considered whether any review of evidence was needed and decided no. Without further ado, he asked his colleagues if they'd carefully considered their verdicts, which they had. He polled them: The barking major had not changed his opinion, nor had the compassionate major. Guilty as charged on all counts.

The colonel then said, "I too have carefully considered my verdict. I have taken into account all the evidence presented here yesterday and weighed issues such as our national security, the morale of our brave air force men and women, the right of Americans to speak out in time of war. But America is a nation of individuals, and their freedom is the most precious possession we have. I look upon this individual, what he said and to whom he has said it, and I see— an enemy of my country. Guilty as charged on all counts."

The sentence was effective immediately: death by lethal injection. It would be carried out at an adjacent correctional facility at 1200 hours.

Because there's no public at a military trial and a lot of discipline, there's little drama. The tribunal stood and saluted defense and prosecution, and they all exited in order of rank. Jay was released from the module and led off to his death.

And that was that.

✦

Later in the day, at a rowdy on-base reception, the colonel announced some good news. Due to the elevated likelihood of hostile action abroad, he had been promoted the night before, by special order of the commander in chief, to the rank of one-star general.

TWENTY-SEVEN

LOOMING OVER THEIR heads, the great cross turned under a thunderhead sky, its readout scrolling endlessly across the flat exurban landscape. On one side: CHRIST DIED FOR YOUR SINS! and on the other: NOW IT'S YOUR TURN!

The Risen Lamb Correctional Facility, two miles from Fort Oswald, had been designated for Jay's execution. The jail had only been open a month and no sinners had yet been executed in the Death Center, the facility's multichamber execution rotunda. Jay would be the very first. The Reverend had more than one thing to celebrate that morning.

Lightning on the horizon already impinging on their consciousness, making them jump a little, the twelve Elders of the Church of the Risen Lamb checked their weapons at security. Escorting them was the Reverend in a warden's cap, standard issue Blood-of-the-Lamb crimson, cocked at a jaunty angle.

The nine Brethren unloaded an arsenal of handguns and pocket rocket launchers. The Chief Justice had one of the new hyper-lasers that could burn a dime-sized hole clear through a perp in 13 milliseconds. The other Brethren looked at it longingly.

"Eleventh Commandment," warned the Reverend. "Thou shalt not covet thy neighbor's hyper-laser!"

He'd sent for me right after the verdict. I was trying to sneak away to the diner and tell the women the disastrous news, but he'd insisted I accompany the execution party. "I'd be happy to cover the execution," I'd stuttered, "but can I bring Jay's mother along to say goodbye?"

The Reverend laughed, incredulous. "His mother? She spawned Satan. Get in the car."

As we headed along razor-wire tunnels, the Rev explained features of the facility to such Elders as Cardinal Grise of Los Angeles, who were making their first visit to the facility.

We arrived at the oak-paneled antechamber to the Death Center. Double oak doors opened soundlessly. We went down a wide faux-marble staircase and into the spacious oak-paneled central observation room. Ancient prints of various forms of execution covered the walls. At its center was a lavish circular bar, manned by two smiling vestal virgins in sexy blood-colored versions of a corrections officer's uniform. The room was a giant underground skybox.

Around the room's circumference were ten wide observation windows each giving onto a small lethal-injection chamber about the size of an average bedroom. The death chambers were identical: shaped in a parallelogram, the inner wall narrower than the outer one.

The Reverend, with the singsong babble of the house-proud, pointed out the sliding partitions between each observation post. These could be activated to ensure privacy, if desired; gaily patterned curtains could likewise frame the windows. "Studies show," said the Reverend, "that victims' relatives like curtains. They want the sinner to know that, while he's checking out, they're going on living behind the cheery curtains of home. It helps closure."

Victims, not relatives, could also choose how to dispose of the executionee's corpse. In each observation booth were two large buttons: BURIAL and CREMATION.

I peered into the chambers, every muscle in my miserable body wanting to flee but not daring to, fascinated by the mechanism of legal murder. It was a way to reject the reality, which I could not face, that the young man I'd met a mere three months ago, and who had occupied my every waking thought since, would soon cease to exist.

Facing me in each chamber was a five-foot-wide retina of one-way glass through which the condemned sinner could be observed by the executioner as the lethal drugs were administered. Below each retina were two triads of copper outlets. Each had three flexible tubes color-coded for the three drugs that made up the lethal cocktail; each terminated in a tridentlike attachment that was plugged into an IV. The drugs were administered through both these devices, one in each arm. A death gurney with padded restraints neatly folded over it and armrests at right angles to the top part stood in the center of each chamber.

Well, not quite each. In Chamber A the gurney was missing. It was in use.

The Reverend had been holding forth about Death Row not being Easy Street, but now he got to his big finish. "Compassion marks our faith from all others. We do everything here to encourage deathbed—or lethal-injection-gurney—*conversions*. We alone offer the miracle of salvation.

"Brethren, out in the anteroom of Chamber A is the very first cardinal sinner this facility will execute. A creature so corrupted by evil that he barely merits the name of *man*. But I believe that even this degraded soul can, through the grace of the Risen Lamb, be saved!"

The Brethren gravely nodded their approval. The Reverend swept from the room toward a magically open door. I jumped up to follow him. Was I not his scribe? He put a firm paw in my chest. No coverage needed.

Actually I welcomed the rejection. I couldn't have faced Jay standing beside his captor—my captor—obediently taking notes.

In any case, every last word in that place was taped.

◆

The Reverend comes into the Repentance Area, a bleak white room whose only decoration is a large wooden crucifix. Jay is kneeling beside the gurney on which he's to die. The Reverend crosses his arms: "Hoping for a reprieve, amigo? Don't waste your breath."

Jay rises in agony, straightening up to meet his tormentor. The sudden effort causes blood to well into his mouth. Internal damage has been caused. Still cuffed, he can't stop it from trickling down the sides of his chin.

The Reverend stares at him, bare teeth clenched in a smile—a familiar smile I recognize from a windy March morning in a New York boardroom years earlier. The triumphant redneck is back. He struts, he has on his Tony Lama boots. When he put them on early that morning, he must have known what the verdict would be long before the tribunal made it.

"So you're Hay-soos. I'm supposed to be in here to save your soul, Hay-soos. Don't think I'll bother. Send you back to Hell where you came from."

Jay says nothing, looking at him from under those lashes as if too tired to ask, Will there be more pain?

"I don't get it, Hay-soos. What were you trying to accomplish, boy? Even if you *were* Jesus, what's the point? You ain't the Christ people want. People want someone who makes them feel safe. What ordinary folks mean by *saved* is *safe*. Safe in the world to come, safe to enjoy this world's abundance.

"You got anything to say, Hay-soos? Time's getting short."

Jay has nothing to say.

"Look at you: dirty, penniless, raggedy-ass. Tell you what. If you were Christ and you came back like this, I'd still hunt you down and kill you. We corrected Christianity, Christ. Worked out the kinks. We don't need you. We got things running smoothly: right from wrong, good guys, bad guys, what the Bible says down pat. People don't want more than that. The less they know, the more they understand.

"Got any last words, Hay-soos? Cat got your tongue?"

Jay bows his head. A gesture of humility? Forgiveness? Or just plain defeat?

"God is a woman! Love your enemies! Just the kinda thing a woman would say. God is man, Hay-soos. He made the world in His image. God doesn't love His enemies. He destroys them. That's why I destroyed you—because you're my enemy and I love my God!"

Jay raises his head. It isn't forgiveness or defeat. Just plain exhaustion.

"If you're Christ, turn me into salt. Wither me. Shatter your shackles, make the guards fall into a slumber. Walk out of here in glory!"

Jay upchucks a little. More blood trickles down his chin. The Reverend stares at him with distaste for a long beat, as if turning some final insult over in his mind.

"I wondered, for about a millisecond, if I'd got it wrong. When I heard about you working miracles? If you were the man I met long ago. But I know my Bible, see? I know—"

Jay swallows as he speaks: the blood, no doubt. "I was that man, Jimmy. The day down by the river?"

The Reverend, who has been preening, strutting a step or two every now and then, busy victory in his body language, is suddenly very still.

Jay's voice is a bloody whisper. "I remember the joy in your heart—and in mine. I even remember the tie you wore: your favorite tie that you folded up and put by itself on the changing table."

"What was . . . on that tie?"

"Little crucifixes."

"You're just guessing."

"And little lambs with wings. Rising."

Jay is standing straight now; the Reverend seems to have shrunk.

"Your heart was filled with love that day, Jimmy. When your father let your head up out of the muddy water, it was as if everything but love had been washed away. Remember?"

"No! You . . . Satan! Using truth to defile truth!"

"When I came into your dream the other night, Jimmy, it was to remind you of that."

"Get thee behind—"

"Remember?"

Jay kisses him lightly on the lips. For a split second the Reverend does nothing, staring at the man kissing him. In wonder? Recognition?

Then he recoils as if shotgunned, Jay's crimson blood smearing his mouth like lipstick. He spits and slaps frantically at the blood as he rushes from the room.

✦

Let's draw no pious morals from Jay's death.

It was not on some bleak Golgotha, from whose barren slopes sprang a message of hope echoing down the centuries. It took place in a sterile spirulina-green chamber lit by blinding halogens, on a gurney of black imitation leather. It cost his executioners $1,744.13. Thousands just like it had occurred in Texas jails in the years before his. Jay's death was a mere number in a sequence, of no more consequence than that of a bug at nightfall.

Yes, his arms were outstretched, but not as they were said to have been long ago, against a stormy, spectral sky. He was flat on his back, his wrists bound to the armrests of the gurney by plastic restraints so that IVs could be inserted into incisions made in each forearm and the three poisons introduced one by one into his body.

Let's not make too much of the fact that he died of slow asphyxiation just as crucifixion killed the crucified, the weight of their bodies gradually crushing their lungs. Jay died of slow asphyxiation because, by order of the Reverend, the IVs were deliberately set to miss his veins. Not enough of the pancuronium bromide that was supposed to paralyze his lungs, reached them to kill him. Nor did enough sodium thiopental, designed to render him unconscious, reach his brain. So while he slowly asphyxiated, he was fully conscious. The coup de grâce, potassium chloride, took forever to reach his heart.

An execution that normally takes a very short while took, instead, forty-five minutes of agonized gasping and convulsions as Jay's body fought instinctively for oxygen and the wayward poisons racked it with pain. Even if he'd decided to die with dignity, his reflexes wouldn't let him.

But the Elders did have ample time to sink to their knees on the blood-crimson carpet and pray that the sinner would repent of his blasphemies before it was too late.

And, yes, the blood flowed down his place of execution just as it once had from the nails and the crown of thorns. But the blood welling from Jay's mouth and into his nose, splattering his face and gown as he choked on it, was from internal injuries inflicted by his expert torturers. The blood pooling on the floor gushed from gashes torn in his forearms by the convulsions of a body that was drowning without being able to drown.

I saw no inspiring parallels or portents in the bucking, gasping body on the gurney. I saw only a young man put to death in terrible agony for the crime of saying that men have no right to kill other men, a young man dying on a gurney largely because my petty machinations had put him there, without which he might still be alive and free, bringing relief where there was pain, comfort into lonely and imperfect lives.

Other than my guilt, there was no moral. And certainly no glory. Nor was there any point in begging a nonexistent God— though I did—that the kid would save himself, now of all times, with a miracle.

More than half an hour into the torment, at 12:37 P.M., the Reverend proclaimed the false messiah's repentance to be a lost cause. The Elders got up, dusting off their pants. As Jay's death throes began, the Chief Justice of the Supreme Court and the Cardinal Archbishop of Los Angeles ordered Bloody Marys from the bar.

Suddenly at 12:44 P.M., Jay, who had uttered not a word throughout his ordeal, cried, "*¡Dios! ¡Madre! ¡Nada mas!*"

The Elders cheered. The Chief Justice and his Eminence clinked glasses. The CEO of FoxWorld, the vice president of the United

States, and the man who many hoped would be the first King of Israel in 2,700 years, high-fived. "Praise the Lord!" shouted the Reverend. "Satan cried uncle!"

Jay gave a long shuddering groan. Then the thread of his life snapped and his spirit shot to the stars.

Or rather, the Messiah of Morris Avenue ceased to exist.

TWENTY-EIGHT

THE EXECUTIONER CONFIRMED the exact time of Jay's death: 12:45:03.

The Reverend pressed the CREMATION button. No point in taking chances.

I asked him if I could take the ashes to Jay's mother. Generosity and goodwill must have been flooding that great Christian heart. He agreed, but my full account of the trial and execution had to be at his Colorado office within the hour. "And no horseshit about 'Calvary in Texas.' He had it coming, that animal. Every second of it."

I hurried from the death chamber to find a place to write and to wait for Jay's ashes. I was shunted to a media center a few hundred yards away. Outside, the storm that had been ambling in from the west all morning was now only a mile off, still moving in our direction.

Writing was a terrible betrayal. To recount the happenings of that day and not be able to express a word of love or respect for their victim was to live the whole agony again but from a different angle, as if I were a different person with a dried pea for a soul—one of the Elders perhaps. But there was no point writing anything other than a clinical report. The holy suits would hack it up anyway.

It didn't take long. After a while it was like writing police-blotter stuff for Metro, thirty years ago. I headed it FALSE MESSIAH TRIED AND EXECUTED and hit SEND.

Suddenly there was a colossal crack of lightning overhead and seconds later an enormous rending noise of tearing metal, followed by a thunderous smashing and splintering.

Everyone in the center rushed to the window. The giant cross had been struck by lightning, melting part of its base, and had keeled over, destroying part of the death center, one of its arms smashing into an adjacent unit.

Symbolic? Sure, but only of sloppiness and greed. In the haste of the facility's construction no one had remembered to install a lightning conductor. They had the cross back up within a week. I understand Christianity has survived.

✦

María knew I was coming. She and Bobbi were standing outside the motel entrance when I got out of the car, like they'd been waiting for hours. As I approached, Amarys came out of the little lobby and stood with them, the younger women on each side of María.

Stabat Mater Dolorosa.

She would not cry. She didn't look at me, only at Jay's urn, the final contemptuous insult: a plastic container of the kind you buy your coleslaw in, with his inmate number scrawled on top.

She took it as if it were the Host at Communion and held it tight to her breast. Head down, tearless, she turned away, walked with the others to Amarys's Trooper, and drove out onto the interstate. To the north. Away from death.

Finally, dry-eyed Johnny cried. Wept and wept. Fell to my knees and couldn't stop for I don't know how long, there in the gum-pocked parking lot of a Days Court 6, gulping its humid concrete air beneath the stormy Texan sky.

✦

This all happened on a Friday. That Sunday was only two weeks from the Sabbath on which the Reverend had promised to name the exact date of Armageddon.

For the next two weeks, it seemed, he bestrode the world. He never mentioned Jay again—of course—though the Risen Lamb media took passing note of the fact that the communist weasel who'd launched the false messiah had seen the error of his ways. (To my infinite chagrin, the holy suits didn't touch a word of my account and ran it on their webs with my name above the title.)

What was for me one of the more momentous series of events I'd ever participated in, and which I had thought was pretty momentous to the Reverend, was in the end nothing much to him, a pea at the bottom of a mountain of mattresses, a tiny detail in the mighty structure of his prophecy.

He was everywhere, proclaiming that time was short, that houses should be put in order. His certainty, his eloquence, and his ubiquity inspired his supporters and unnerved his enemies. When someone of the Reverend's vast reach believes something to be true, it becomes fact.

Even the Israelis, long inured to hysterical lunacy from the Christian Right concerning their future well-being, began to get uneasy. After all, it was Jewish prophets from which the Reverend was drawing his rocklike certainty: Daniel, Jeremiah, Ezekiel; substantial numbers of ultra-orthodox Jews had drawn similar conclusions. Might they all be on the right track? Arguments raged in the Knesset about whether Her-Megiddon should be occupied, fortified, *something*! The Tikkun web was deluged with anxious introspective postings about Jewish identity in an apocalyptic world. Just what did that 144,000 figure mean?

Even I—not knowing at the time what the Reverend knew—couldn't help feeling that where there was this much smoke there had to be, for once, a flicker of fire. But I worried about it less than my friends. I was more concerned with my intravenous shackle, a nasty little nano-bot cruising round my circulatory system that could be instructed to cause anything from angina to a massive coronary.

As for Jay's death, I was grieving by myself. I wanted no part of the collective grieving of his followers wherever they might be, in the Bronx or anywhere else. But two ugly chunks of fallout were impossible to avoid.

Kevin and Angela were released a few days after Jay's death, without being charged, Angela on her own recognizance, Kevin on his mother's. Had I known about this apparent act of magnanimity on the Reverend's part, I would have done everything in my power to protect them, but I only found out about it postmortem.

Angela's crushed body was found on the Bronx River Parkway at about 7 A.M., one day after her release. She'd been struck by several cars after being killed by the first, which hit and ran. I tracked down the cop who found her; he said the autopsy showed enough crack in her to paralyze a mule. Knowing her burning faith in Jay after her attempted suicide, I doubt it got there by her own hand.

In Calvin, Kevin wasn't home a day before the Church of Christ

Homophobe got wind he was back in town. Doubtless some helpful intelligence—possibly from his father—found its way to them. The next night hooded men dragged him, in front of his weeping mother, from her house and took him into the countryside to a place where an upturned sharpened wooden fencepost had been secured in a cement footing. On this they impaled him. Needless to say, no one was ever arrested, let alone charged, although the cement footing alone was prima facie evidence of premeditated murder. Poor Kevin must have taken hours to die.

Evan Whittaker, who might have provided a counterweight to the Reverend's onslaught, had gone underground. After Jay's execution and the murder of his apostles, Evan feared for his life at the hands of that avenging angel. The Risen Lamb media explained his disappearance by resurrecting the rumors of his hushed-up steroid bust, reporting that he was on the run from cops in Boston.

There were nobler moments. María returned home to await whatever punishment was in store for the mother of a plastic container full of ashes. The community engulfed her like a rain forest. I can't say what went on in the corridors of retribution, but no move was made against her; I imagine the local authorities were smart enough to know that, if one was, the Bronx would explode.

So a posse of righteous Virginians decided to take the Lord's vengeance into their own hands. They drove up to New York City in three SSSUVs, having been supplied with María's exact address by persons unknown. Their GPS led them unerringly to the intersection of her street and Morris Avenue, where they parked in an alley a block away.

They were getting out of their cars when hundreds of silent people appeared rapidly out of the night, pinning them to their vehicles so tightly, one said later, that two of his ribs cracked. The Lord's shotguns, assault rifles, Uzis, and Colts remained uncocked and use-less until the NYPD showed up to take them away. The arresting of-ficer was a young cop with only three years on the force, named Alvarez.

What in the end did these moments of shame and honor signify compared to the ocean of blood and fire that the Reverend promised at Jesus' hand during the Final Battle? Even the noble parts I must confess only made me more resolved to put as much distance as pos-sible physically and mentally between my recent past and my imme-diate future. That, it seemed to pusillanimous me, was the only way to ensure I had a future.

Not that the future held much. I seemed to have ended up back where I started, back where I had always been: an irrelevant bit player in the central dramas of other people's lives.

Enter a messenger. The messenger speaks. Exit the messenger.

TWENTY-NINE

TWO MEN WALK down a country road in rural Pennsylvania. It's a little after 5 A.M. on a Sunday morning in late June.

The unmowed shoulders are thick with summer growth, shiny with newness, a dozen different shades of green, grasses of all species, in wild hummocks or crawling unchecked, trailing rhizomes over rocks and logs. Truant barley from previous years' crops stands tall and proud amid the lesser breeds, themselves engulfed by lilies and jewelweed and the seductively shining leaves of poison oak and ivy, climbing indiscriminately over everything.

One of the men, clearly not a country boy, slept in a patch of ivy last night and is only now beginning to feel the maddening itch around his ankles and wrists as the toxin begins to blister his skin and his scratching obligingly spreads it farther up his shins and forearms.

Back of the greenery on their side of the road is an old stone row, overgrown with creeper and more poison oak; behind it, thick woods of ash and maple and buttonwood and hickory, many of them, when you peer into the thick undergrowth, old and noble trees. Their branches are heavy with the year's complement of leaves, thick and fat with new life, a dozen more different shades of green.

The men are unmoved by the glorious gold of the slanting sunlight as it strikes through the leaves and spatters the road with new light. Both of them look tired in the early morning, haggard and unwashed, as if it has been long days since they saw anything but the beauties of nature. One of them is muttering inaudible complaints to himself under his breath, his taciturn companion saying nothing in response.

The shorter one turns and peers down the road, listening for the whine of an engine that might transport them out of Eden. But the road, which on weekdays would be thick with the cars and pickups of early commuters hoping to beat rush hour on the interstate, is empty on the Lord's Day, so the men trudge on.

As they pass an overgrown opening in the stone row, a disused path into the woods, a third man steps from the dark of the trees and out onto the dusty shoulder of the road. He calls to them quietly, as if he knows them.

They turn tired and defensive—who's bothering us now?—but as they focus on the third man, squinting through the early morning shadows, their faces change, fatigue dissolving into astonishment. They stand rooted to the pavement, paralyzed it seems by terror, though they're registering something quite different, for which the only word is wonder.

"Whaddup, Rufus?" says Jay.

He throws back his hood, taking the little fireplug in a full-body hug. Rufus for once is speechless, the whites of his eyes wide with amazement. As he returns the embrace, his fingers knead Jay's back, gently testing the solidity of the flesh under the fleece.

A big grin cracks the round face. "I knew it, son!"

But Charlie is more reticent. Charlie accepts a friendly shoulder bump, but he'd rather just hold on to Jay's outstretched hand with his good hand, head humbly bowed. For Charlie has that gift he's hoped for so often, a gift beyond all measuring. Charlie finally believes.

✦

"He walked with us a ways," said Rufus, "and we came to a city sign by the road, one of them old rusty white ones with the black writing? You know what it said?"

"What?" I said.

"WELCOME TO EMMAUS."

"We was saying how that was pretty wild, being in the Bible and all, and we turned around and he wasn't there no more."

Charlie said, "Took us far as Emmaus. That was it."

Rufus said, "The old law and the new."

The little company nodded. We were sitting around the kitchen table in María's apartment: the two guys, María, Bobbi—and me, of course, summoned to bear witness to these wondrous new developments.

It had happened to María and Bobbi too. They were sitting around this table on Sunday, also in the morning.

They were getting ready to have breakfast, but without saying the Dear Mother prayer as they'd gotten used to, because it upset María too much. So they just said a little grace . . . and there he was, standing in the doorway!

"Real as the day he was born," said María now, the joy on her face indescribable, the joy of a mother gazing at the new life she holds—which for her, at that moment, he was.

Bobbi went over to him and fell on her knees. "I was crying," she said, "but I don't know why. I was so happy my whole body was bursting."

Jay gently lifted her to her feet and kissed her forehead, the way he did when he very first met her. Then he went to María and held her tight for a long time.

"There's no light coming off him or anything," says María. "He's just Jay, normal, like he's coming in from one of his trips. He's not cold like a dead person. His face is warm; his hand is warm." His lips are warm on her cheek.

Her fine stoic face was transfigured with the knowledge that this had been bound to happen, it was beyond doubt, because her son had promised it, a reward earned by a mother's grief. An all-too-common grief, across the world and down the centuries, but for once rewarded. For María it wasn't so important that anything had been proved or any law fulfilled, just that he was alive again, her Josélito.

Bobbi said, "He got up and went to the door and smiled at us, and said, *Hasta luego.* Then he was gone."

I looked around at these bright faces, people of whom I was immeasurably fond, brave and good people, and I was happy for them, happy that they'd found a way not to let Jay go, to feel again how profoundly he'd penetrated their lives, to achieve that conviction— against all common sense and human experience, not least what they'd just been through—that something new could flower in the world. Belief of which, however much I might have longed for it, I was incapable.

Memory is plastic, intensely so, creating happiness where there is only misery. Memory can change the world. I wondered if the stories I'd just heard were how all religions got their start—with some version of death-to-life. The death of one bringing to the many a new vision of the world, through the simple power of longing.

What I actually said was that these events were wonderful and inspiring, but they should keep them to themselves. Jay's trial had shown there were informers everywhere. If their stories got around and came to the attention of the Reverend or any of his cohorts, their lives wouldn't be worth a nickel.

I promised to write them down just as I heard them, so there would be a permanent record.

That I did—as faithfully and accurately and convincingly as I could. Because that was our deal. It was the least I could do for the kid.

My plan beyond that, I'm ashamed to say, was to run. These tales of resurrection brought no joy to me. As far as I could see, they upped the ante astronomically. To elevate a dead man into a living God would drive the Reverend to insanities of vengeance. It was the ultimate threat. He would stamp out every last vestige of them.

Specifically, my plan of action, as I sped back across the GW Bridge, was to get my passport and some clothes and then head to northwestern Jersey and the rural home of a friend, retired from Bell Labs, with a vast knowledge of microtechnology. If anyone knew how to neutralize the programmable retribution in my bloodstream, he would. That accomplished, I had vaguer plans of getting out of the country, perhaps through Mexico to Spain, where I'd track down my mother's family and start a new life and so on and so forth.

Fat chance. There was a holy suit—a blazer, actually—waiting for me outside my building with a shiny new crimson sedan. On his breast pocket was the Risen Lamb symbol: a crimson-winged lamb superimposed on a sword.

The Reverend wanted me.

THIRTY

HIS PALATIAL ESTATE outside Macon, Many Mansions, all white and silver with slashes of crimson, stood calm and cool in the waves of Georgia summer heat. To me it looked like the last place I'd seen the Reverend—just another jail.

All through the trip down, on his old Gulfstream, the somber Risen Lamb eunuch at my side, my mind had been churning with fear. No good could come from this summons. Had he already gotten wind somehow of the stories of resurrection? Was I to be given a new mission of betrayal? Or was I just in deep shit of some kind, finally about to get mine like the other Jayistas?

Wrong as usual, intrepid reporter.

He sat on a simple Shaker church bench with no cushions, probably the only uncomfortable item of furniture in the voluptuously appointed living room.

He was subdued, or at rest anyway, the bristling need to act that usually came off him quite absent. Beside him sat Jeanie. They were holding hands.

The Reverend had a story to tell me.

◆

He is spending the night in the Pluribus. He sleeps fitfully, as he often does on Sunday nights, what with planning in his mind for the upcoming week. Finally, he falls asleep in the wee hours and wakes a couple of hours later in the very early light, just a little gray coming through the shaded windows.

And he knows there's someone in the bus.

There are guards outside in the compound. But somehow, someone's gotten in.

Quiet as he can, he gropes for the gun on the bedside table. As his eyes adjust, he realizes it's too late. A man is standing at the foot of the bed silhouetted against the window. A big man.

"Jimmy . . ."

He knows that voice, surely?

"Come to me."

But it can't be.

The voice is not threatening. No weapon is evident. The Reverend believes in angels and knows they often take human form, but he's never seen one. There don't seem to be any wings. Are there wingless angels?

He gets up off the rocking water bed and, as much as he can in the cramped sleeping area, keeps a healthy distance between himself and the dark figure. He wonders if he's dreaming and bends his will within the dream to wake from it. Nothing happens. It's no dream.

He sees that the figure is naked from the waist up. A terrible fear begins to grow in the Reverend's belly. As he comes slowly around the bed, the figure turns to face him and therefore the window. And the gray morning light reveals the man it cannot be. The face poisoned with three poisons and burned to ashes. The powerful arms with deep, long gashes inside the elbows, still raw and unhealed. The gashes he made.

"Come to me, Jimmy," says the husky voice. "All is well."

The Reverend feels as though every part of him, every last cell, is being sucked out of his body, leaving only the empty balloon of his skin, standing there as if he were an inflatable Reverend, with nothing inside but air. And then, with a rush, a new person enters that same balloon of skin, inflating it with radiating warmth and light and love, the love he felt so long ago as a boy down by the riverside. Love he's been without for so long. Love for this man. The man he met that day.

He takes Jay's hand. He can't take his eyes off the wounds that his cruelty and rage dug deep into those arms.

"I hunted you down and killed you. I burned you to ashes. How can you forgive me?"

"There's nothing that cannot be forgiven, Jimmy. When you know that, you know everything."

Jay pulls him into an embrace, and he can feel the strong arms, their solidity and warmth, the blood that is flowing through them, the life in them, the new life flowing from them into him. He is lost in the present, weeping like a baby, with tears of relief and joy.

How long the moment lasts he has no idea, but when he finally reenters time and space, he realizes that Jay is gone.

✦

The Reverend sat looking at the floor for a long time after his tale, a little smile on his face. Then he said, "I was the Antichrist, not him. But he even forgave the Antichrist."

He squeezed his wife's hand.

"Jeanie, here, she was way ahead of me. Evan too. They knew who he was long ago, without needing a miracle."

She squeezed his hand back. "Pigheaded." She smiled. "Always were."

The Reverend spent an hour or so with me, open as a faucet, filling me in on whatever he could think of: Evan, Jeanie, Pastor Bob, his dreams, answering whatever I wanted to ask. He told me the whole strategy that was supposed to unfold in Operation Armageddon. He'd already called the White House to alert them to his change of heart; he'd left the clear message that if the mad scheme wasn't aborted, he'd do it himself by publicly spilling the beans.

He and Jeanie were going to Colorado to do the last *Prayer Breakfast Club* together, at which they both intended to make public their conversion. He was resigning all involvement with the Risen Lamb. What he and Jeanie were going to do after that, they hadn't decided; obviously it would involve going to work for the new faith and obviously it would involve getting back with Evan. Jay would tell them how in his own good time.

And he'd remembered to have my intravenous shackle deactivated. It should have self-destructed by now. Thoughtful of him.

I decided not to return to New York. I had my passport and I was halfway to Mexico, and I badly needed to get away from all this. Religion, doctrine, old law, new law, miracles, and resurrection were all exhausting—and dangerous—things. Plus, I wasn't at all happy I was to have inside info on triple-drop-dead top-secret matters of national security. My concern, as I think the diplomats say, was not unfounded.

The Reverend and Jeanie didn't allow their newfound faith to make them careless about air travel. They quietly hired another jet to take them to Colorado Springs, leaving Gabriel on the ground in Macon, where, an hour after their scheduled departure, the bomb that had been secreted in the massage room aft destroyed the old Gulfstream completely.

Somehow this information didn't find its way to the happy couple, or they would have been more cautious that evening. Stayed home, not gone out to dinner at the Risen Lamb's three-star restaurant, the Upper Room. The long arm of the Guard got them in its kitchen; soon after they'd finished their appetizers, both experienced violent convulsions and were rushed to the hospital in Denver, where they died later that night, Jeanie a few minutes after the Reverend. The exact cause of death was never determined; I was probably the only person outside of the White House inner circle who knew that the toxin's name was Armageddon.

In the event, Operation Armageddon never came to pass. Assuming the plan did actually exist, there could have been all kinds of reasons it was aborted: the Reverend's threats, Admiral Kubrick's concern (or pique), a momentary attack of sanity in the White House. Or even the anonymous tip I sent Kaminski—which I was never able to check, as Ted went to his reward not long after (of natural causes for once).

Or the Reverend could've made the whole thing up.

I wouldn't have put it past him. I may have given the impression in observing the terms of my deal that I believed or sympathized with the Reverend's account of his conversion or re-conversion or re-re-conversion.

Spare me. If my mortal enemy believes Jay rose from the dead and is the authentic Second Coming of Jesus, fine. But why should I believe a word my mortal enemy says? The man who killed the kid? Yes. Jay's central message was, There is nothing that can't be forgiven. But Jay was a much better man than I, and forgiveness is a lesson I have learned only imperfectly. To forgive the Reverend, I'll need to attend a far more advanced class.

Who knows whether his "conversion" wasn't some brilliant preemptive move to get yet another wing of Christianity under his control, to co-opt a promising new sect while it was still a-borning? Maybe his fellow power mongers just couldn't let him do that. Maybe it wasn't the White House who had him killed, after all, but Pastor Bob, plotting his return to power. Which certainly came to pass.

Why aren't these explanations as plausible as that he saw, alive and well, a man whom he'd murdered and cremated? The political explanation for his actions is within the realm of credibility. Whereas resurrection, alas, my good, brave, but ultimately gullible friends, despite all your longing for it, simply isn't.

Don't get me wrong. I understand the sweetness of the vision. Resurrection, were it ever to occur, would be the miracle of miracles. That the mourned face could stir and smile, the lost child walk and play again: a joy impossible to measure. Death is like a sea, relentlessly eroding the shores of your consciousness, its distant roar a reminder that your oblivion is inevitable. To be able to build a permanent seawall against it, shut out the roar forever, is the oldest dream of humanity—and the beginning of all religion.

I was lucky. I didn't need miracles. Even when I saw a couple they did little for me. Jay was right: Miracles are tricks, wizardry, meaningless except in the eye of the beholder. What I learned from José Francisco was far more precious, the simplest of his lessons: that we waste a colossal amount of our lives avoiding contact with life. There is no substitute for flesh-and-blood touching flesh-and-blood. His presence was worth a million miracles. To rest in its shadow was to be at peace. How he did that, I don't know and never will. Perhaps it's just what happens when someone's really good at being good.

Are you're thinking that I feel this way because he didn't appear to *me*? I feel excluded? I didn't get the Big Nod?

No. He won't appear to me because he's dead. Not just dead, cremated. He's not even bones in a box, which might spook some atavistic fear of spirits in me. He's ashes. He's gone. He ain't coming back. There's no *him* to come back.

He's returned to the atoms from which he came, and when his ashes—or, rather, *the* ashes, for they have no person or gender—are strewn in the earth or the air or the sea, a year or a century from now, those atoms will spin out into the void of material things to form, at some distant time, some other material thing, with no more meaning than this cold hard rock on which we pass a few years, spinning round the other cold hard rocks, exploring the nothingness of what we touch and see and smell and hear, until we cease to exist and our senses do too and we become the same atoms in the same endless, pointless rigmarole and roundelay. With no chance, folks, of that particular lumpy face and those particular long dark lashes—and that particular ratty old green fleece—ever reappearing.

He was here for a while. And now he's gone.

EPILOGUE

I SIT OVERLOOKING the lagoon that used to be Sarasota, the young palms swaying beside the new Roman ruins.

The owners of this villa are probably more prosperous than Jay would've liked, but they're his faithful followers and they're more than hospitable. For a tapped-out journalist chasing sixty, without a dime to his name and nothing but memories to peddle, this is a safe port in a long storm.

Actually, that's a little minimal—even ungrateful. I move often from one house to another of such kind and good people, and they're more than welcoming. Since I'm one of the few people who knew Jay to touch and speak to, I'm even—well, revered.

It's a living, being revered.

I wonder if that makes me a Reverend.

There's a very private room in this house, where my hosts go to pray and meditate on the scriptures: Kevin's handwritten accounts, my two *Journal American* stories, and transcripts of interviews: with Rufus and Charlie and with eyewitnesses like Bobbi, Mrs. Althea McGonagal, and Nickie and Marisol, the latter two being energetic young people who move discreetly around the country, celebrating Jay, spreading his word. As some poet wrote once of some other poet—my memory's getting very spotty—now Jay is scattered among a hundred cities.

I am invited to my hosts' devotions in the private room, as I am wherever I go. I partake in them, though their deeper meaning is lost on me. But I like the words of Spanglish they use—the Latin of the new faith—liltingly dropping in and out of English, some of the words even beginning to merge now. *Madre* in the Mother's Prayer can be heard as *mad-re* or *moth-er*. In a generation, it will be the same word. Perhaps, during that period, the varying versions I've tried to give in my account—the reservations I always express that there may be more than one true version—will have merged too. There will be one account, one truth, one Word.

In every private room of every house I stay are three large devotional pictures based on original photos but several creative generations away from them. There's Jay in the center, his uneven features symmetricized, the little cast gone from his eyes, his lashes accentuated, the full mouth, which smiled so much, unsmiling. To his left is Kevin in T-shirt and jeans, looking grander and more muscular than he was in real life, writing in a book, the brutal fencepost tastefully in a murky background instead of poking from his chest the way it was when they found him. The first gay saint in history, or at least the first openly gay one.

To the right is Angela, beautiful, more darkly complected than she was, her eyes rolled up to heaven like an old-fashioned Madonna in a way I never saw her in real life. Her picture is by far the most popular of the three, even more than Jay's, her story of redemption the one that really seems to stir people.

Sometimes the private room will contain a silver reliquary with a Piece of the Fleece: a tiny strip supposedly cut from Jay's hooded fleece, which the Guards took from him after his capture. The story of the Guard who stole the Fleece from storage, was converted by his ownership of it, and then executed for treason is an inspirational favorite. I'm often asked to authenticate these scraps of material. They all look like the real thing, dark green, coarse from frequent laundering, but who really knows?

There are states where it's more than your life is worth to own a devotional item. In states like Florida, there's a degree of tolerance, but it's still best to keep one's devotions private. And this being an election year, violent promises are being made. The ruling junta promises that subversive and "terrorist" sects will be exterminated. The latest member of the clan hoping to inherit the Sparrovian mantle, General Nathan Bedford Forrest Sparrow, links "sects" and "violence" in his campaign appearances.

As usual with the American right, there's a barely concealed racism at work. The faith of Jay is considered a religion for people of color, too wild and woolly for nice people of the white race. But then Jesus was more black than he was white, so there we are—once more refreshing the message.

The great beast of fundamentalism has moved on, having licked the wound of the Reverend and Jeanie's "rumored" conversion into a trifling scar. The Pure Holy Baptists have fallen under the control of the White Lighters, and Pastor Bob is back in the ascendant. The end-time is still upon us and doubtless will be till the end of time.

Evan is a great leader of the new faith and has been highly instrumental in its spread abroad, especially in Latin America and, now, Africa. He became mighty proclaiming the conversion and martyrdom of the Reverend and Jeanie; it's hard to disbelieve someone like Evan. His profound and moving autobiography *I Confess* is already considered one of the new faith's foremost devotional works.

AIDS appears to be on the brink of a final cure, a comprehensive vaccine that has something to do with the stem cells of chimpanzees. The breakthrough was made by a young woman from Angola working with a European-based team. She is very charismatic. If she pulls this off she will have a great future. She did her postgraduate work in Bologna. Of all the things Jay said, this nonmiracle rocks my unbelief the most.

Is the new faith the new Christianity? That's certainly what my hosts believe. They call themselves New Christians, one of the main groups emerging as time goes on. The other main group are the Jayistas or, as they prefer to be known, the Joséans. While solidarity is the overwhelming priority right now, disagreements are beginning to appear.

The New Christians, who are often converts from Protestant denominations, tend to have more liberal and individual interpretations of Jay's surviving words than the Joséans. The Joséans are often ex-Catholics and have an irritating way of bolstering their claims to correct interpretation by pointing out that they were there first and know best. You can see this assertion turning one day into the claim that their original connection with the flesh-and-blood Jay gives them unique authority to decide correctly when there's disagreement. A crabby old skeptic like me might go as far as to wonder if, should New Christianity and Joséanity survive a century or two, they won't be burning each other at the stake.

I still play the same kind of role I did when Jay was alive:

considered a central player but feeling very much like a fringe one. New Christians may venerate me as a member of Jay's inner circle, but I can't come close to María or Bobbi or Charlie or Rufus, who has emerged as a strong and charismatic leader.

There are Joséans—Rufus is one—who see me as Jay's Judas. The one who was standing with him when the high priest's guards came. And—worse than the original Judas—who sat with the high priest in judgment on him. Worst of all, who did not go out and, for shame, hang himself. I'm not so sure I don't agree with them.

The odd thing about growing old in this line of work is to listen to younger people—or, more oddly, people my own age, none of whom ever met Jay or met anyone who met him but know of him only through our few writings—speak with such certainty about who he was, his nature and powers and, above all, what his words meant.

I used to find their certainty irritating and would challenge it in my cups. Increasingly, I envy it terribly. It's like the whiff of a delicious dinner, smelled through a window, that you savor for a moment before walking on down the street, knowing you will never share it.

I miss him, I suppose. I still miss him. That's really what I mean. He was the closest I ever got to certainty. I was only his messenger, but at least I had an entrance.

I long to be walking down a county road of a sunny morning and have him step out from the shadow of a glade, as he did for Rufus and Charlie; or be there at the end of my bed one early morning, as he was for the Reverend, his strong shoulders silhouetted in the dawn light. To hear his slow, low voice, to look into his real eyes behind the real lashes, not the idealized ones of the holy pictures. To have him put his real arm around my ever more stooped and rickety old shoulders.

Just once more. To feel just once more that calm and peace he cast around him like a cloak of light, the certainty that nothing exists or matters except his presence here and now and forever. To have him let me touch the wounds in his resurrected arms as he did the others. To know the bacilli in those healing wounds are as real as the drops of dew on the grass outside . . .

And believe.

THE END

AND THE BEGINNING

ACKNOWLEDGMENTS

A FIRST NOVEL is a daunting thing—especially when it has to be written on a fast track with the clock ticking. It would have been impossible to achieve without the strenuous and dedicated efforts of my editors, Jennifer Barth and George Hodgman. It would have been easy to falter without the relentless optimism of my agent, Jonathon Lazear; the encouragement and reassurance along the way from good friends like George Kalogerakis and Ron Shelton; and above all without the support of my beloved wife, Carla.

Warm thanks also to my dear friend the celebrated Spanish poet Clara Janes for rendering my pidgin Spanish into mellifluous Castilian.

Pax in terra.

ABOUT THE AUTHOR

TONY HENDRA attended Cambridge University, where he performed frequently with friends and future Monty Pythons John Cleese and Graham Chapman. He was editor in chief of *Spy*, an original editor of *National Lampoon*, and played Ian Faith in *This Is Spinal Tap*. He has written frequently for *New York, Harper's, GQ, Vanity Fair, Men's Journal*, and *Esquire*. He lives in New York.

ST. AGATHA WILDCAT
AUCTION
2005

FIRST GRADE PROJECT

THIS BOOK WAS DONATED BY;

David Szolosi

I CHOSE THIS BOOK
BECAUSE:

It COOked
Good

COLOSSAL BOOK OF DINOSAURS

FEATURING THE DINOSAUR DICTIONARY

MODERN PUBLISHING
A DIVISION OF UNISYSTEMS, INC.
NEW YORK, NEW YORK 10022

PRINTED IN ITALY
SERIES UPC#11990

Introduction

The first dinosaur fossils were found approximately 100 years ago. Ever since their discovery, human beings have been fascinated by the prehistoric inhabitants of Earth who lived millions of years ago!

Everyday, archeologists and paleontologists continue to uncover new and exciting information about dinosaurs, and man has learned a great deal about these strange and wonderful creatures. Many questions, however, remain unanswered. How did these huge monsters evolve from the simple reptiles that preceded them? How did they hunt? How did they raise their young? What caused the sudden extinction of the many members and branches of this prehistoric "family."

During the Mesozoic Era—a time period also called "The Age of Dinosaurs"—an astounding variety of creatures roamed Earth. Man has discovered evidence of huge beasts, who weighed several tons apiece; small, quick animals, who ran through prehistoric forests; flying reptiles, who soared through the sky; and fierce predators, who hunted and killed other creatures for food.

This book provides a fascinating look into the Age of Dinosaurs. Adventure-filled stories and exciting, full-color illustrations offer true-to-life accounts of several dinosaurs' daily lives. The "Facts About Dinosaurs" section contains added, concise information about these amazing creatures.

A "Dinosaur Dictionary" is included in this volume so that readers may easily discover pertinent facts about their favorite Sauropod, Ceratopsian, or Pterosaur.

Prepare for a wonderful journey, back in time, to an Earth ruled by the incredible dinosaurs.

Table of Contents

WHAT IS A DINOSAUR?

TYPES OF DINOSAUR

There were many types of dinosaur but among the most famous was the family of sauropods. These were large, four-footed animals with small heads, long necks, large bodies, and long tails. They had quite small brains with a special nerve box in their hip to control the tail and back legs.

Heavily armored dinosaurs like this "node-lizard" ankylosaur were built for protection and combat. They walked on all fours and ate plants. Some were armed with large bony clubs at the end of the tail. Others just had side and back armor. Several types had spikes and plates.

Probably the most feared dinosaurs of all were the flesh-eating carnosaurs like *Daspletosaurus*. They walked erect on two legs; most had very small arms and weighed up to 7 tons. They could move quickly and would eat dead animals as well as kill other dinosaurs for food. All had large fangs.

DINOSAUR GROUPS

Whichever family a dinosaur belonged to it was in one of two groups. The groups were distinguished by the way their hip bones were arranged. These bones are called the ilium, the ischium and the pubis. Saurischian (lizard-hip) dinosaurs had a hip bone arrangement like that seen in the drawing on the right.

ilium

ischium

pubis

SAURISCHIAN

ilium

ischium

pubis

ORNITHISCHIAN

Ornithischian dinosaurs had the hip arrangement shown in the drawing on the left. Here, the pubis lies back along the ischium. Later, some dinosaurs had a different pubic bone shaped to point more forward than previous types and is shown here jutting beyond the ilium. All ornithischians were plant eaters.

THE DINOSAUR WALK

The dinosaur was distinguished by the way its legs were attached to its hips. In the drawings below you can see the squat arrangement of a lizard, the semi-raised posture of a crocodile and the fully developed structure of a mammal or a dinosaur. The way the hip joints developed is also shown. We must not think of dinosaurs as primitive. They were highly developed.

LIZARD   CROCODILE   DINOSAUR

REPTILE   PRE-DINOSAUR

DINOSAUR

DINOSAUR FEET

Some dinosaurs walked on their toes, like *Ceratosaurus* whose leg and foot is shown in the left-hand drawing below. Other dinosaur feet, like those of *Apatosaurus* at bottom right, were adapted for carrying great weights across firm ground. It is wrong to think of giant sauropods like these wallowing in marshy swamps. Studies show they would have become hopelessly bogged down!

11

THE AGE OF THE DINOSAURS

SAURISCHIAN (LIZARD-HIP)

Dinosaurs of this type were found all over the world and lived from the middle of the Triassic period to the end of the Cretaceous. They were both meat and plant eaters, had clawed feet and included the families of sauropods (with five toes like modern lizards), carnosaurs (bipedal meat eaters) and coelurosaurs (similar to carnosaurs but with hollow bones, large brains and possibly warm blooded). Reptiles and crocodiles are shown for comparison.

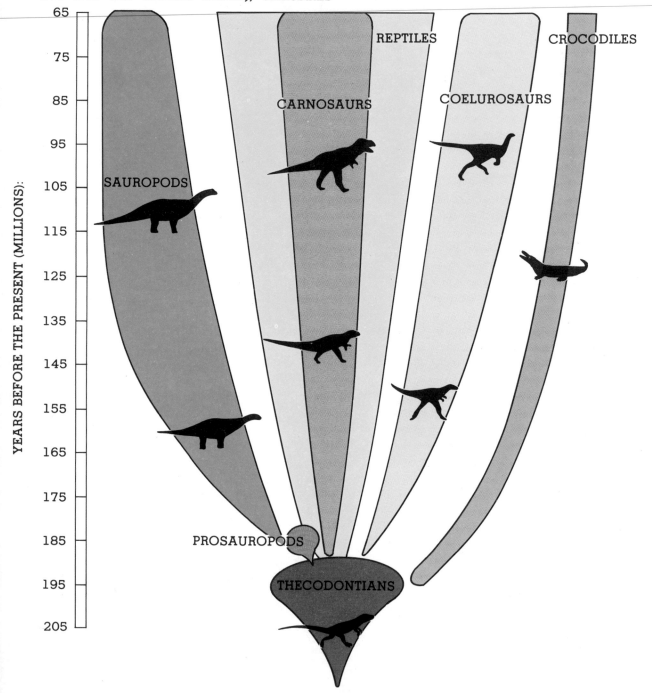

YEARS BEFORE THE PRESENT (MILLIONS):

65
75
85
95
105
115
125
135
145
155
165
175
185
195
205

REPTILES

CROCODILES

CARNOSAURS

COELUROSAURS

SAUROPODS

PROSAUROPODS

THECODONTIANS

ORNITHISCHIAN (BIRD-HIP)

These dinosaurs had hoofed toes, ate plants and most had beaked mouths. Some, like the stegosaurs and the ankylosaurs, had protective armor. Ornithopods were thought to have bird-like feet and ran with tails outstretched for balance. Pterosaurs were not true birds.

Modern birds are thought to have come from Saurischian Coelurosaurs. The age of the birds and mammals are shown for comparison. Like reptiles and crocodiles, they have survived to the present.

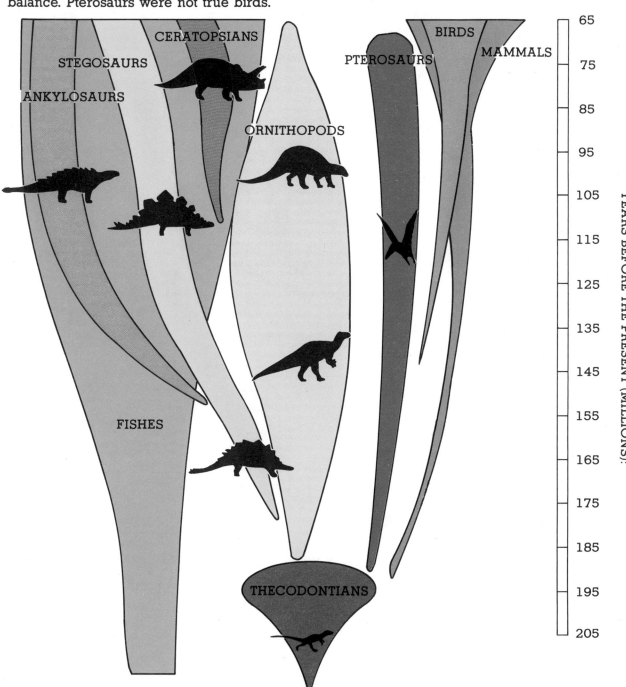

CERATOPSIANS

STEGOSAURS

ANKYLOSAURS

ORNITHOPODS

PTEROSAURS

BIRDS

MAMMALS

FISHES

THECODONTIANS

65

75

85

95

105

115

125

135

145

155

165

175

185

195

205

YEARS BEFORE THE PRESENT (MILLIONS):

13

DINOSAUR SIZES

PLATEOSAURUS

DASPLETOSAURUS

COELURUS

STEGOSAURUS

TRICERATOPS

COMPSOGNATHUS

From the giant Diplodocus to the tiny Compsognathus, dinosaurs came in all shapes and sizes. Here dinosaurs are compared with modern animals like the elephant, the hippopotamus, the rhinoceros, the giraffe, the dog and man. Compare the size of Tyrannosaurus with a rhinoceros and see how Triceratops would have looked to a man!

Many dinosaurs, like Coelurus, were fast, nimble and hard to catch. Others, like Diplodocus, were slow, lumbering animals rather like the modern elephant. Stegosaurus, like the rhinoceros, was well protected and could probably run quite fast too. What a strange sight it would be if all these animals could really be seen around today!

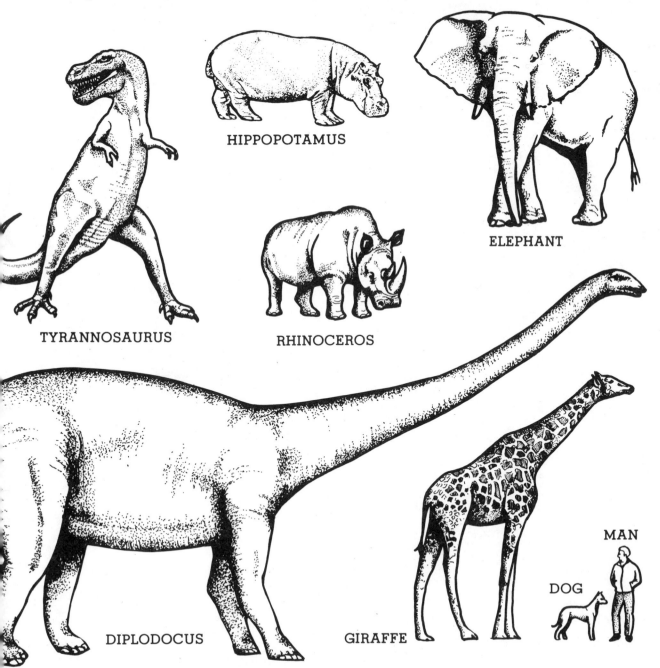

HIPPOPOTAMUS

ELEPHANT

TYRANNOSAURUS

RHINOCEROS

DIPLODOCUS

GIRAFFE

MAN

DOG

Quetzalcoatlus

Parasaurolophus

Deinosuchus

Corythosaurus

Spinosaurus

Oviraptor

16

Anatosaurus

Written by David White
Illustrated by Pam Mara

Pachycephalosaurus

Anatosaurus

Struthiomimus

Scolosaurus

Rutiodon

Psittacosaurus

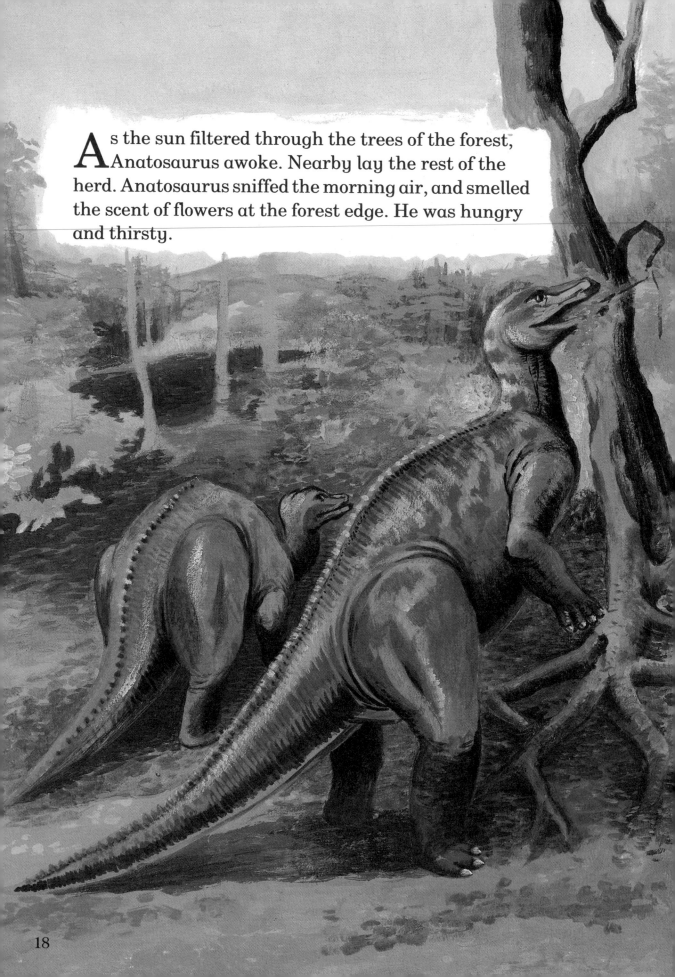

As the sun filtered through the trees of the forest, Anatosaurus awoke. Nearby lay the rest of the herd. Anatosaurus sniffed the morning air, and smelled the scent of flowers at the forest edge. He was hungry and thirsty.

He stood on his hind legs, using his great tail to balance himself, and bit off the branch of an oak. Anatosaurus chewed slowly. His strong teeth could grind any foliage, even pine needles, to make a meal that he could digest. He browsed quietly among the branches of the tree. The forest was his home and his source of food. In it, he could find all the leaves and fruit he wanted.

When he was young, Anatosaurus lived near the water. His mother hatched her eggs on the shore of a lake, so that the hatchlings could run to the water whenever there was danger. Then he had lived on water weeds, sucking them up from the water.

When he grew older and his teeth became
strong, he moved away from the lake and into the
forest. There was always plenty to eat. The forest
contained every kind of tree – pines and firs, oaks, ash,
poplars, sycamores, willows, maples, and birch.

After a morning of grazing, Anatosaurus lay down and dozed in the midday heat. He did not sleep, however. There was always the danger of attack by other animals, especially the fierce meat-eaters.

Luckily, Anatosaurus had sharp eyes and good hearing. Most important of all, he had a keen sense of smell. While it was still far away, he could smell the scent of another animal in the wind. This gave him plenty of warning.

Today, though, there was no wind. The forest was hot and still. Anatosaurus could hear the grunting of the herd as it browsed contentedly in the heat. Suddenly, the grunting changed to a loud croaking. Something had frightened the herd. Animals began to run off through the trees. Anatosaurus got up on his hind legs. He could run fastest this way.

Then the cause of all the panic burst into sight. It was Deinonychus, known as "terrible claw". Deinonychus was only a small animal, but his sickle-like claw made him a fearsome opponent. With his claw, he could wound and even kill animals much larger than himself.

Anatosaurus was no match for Deinonychus, so he did the only thing he could. He ran. He ran through the dense undergrowth of shrubs and small trees toward the lake. He knew instinctively that the water would protect him.

Anatosaurus was as suited to the water as to the land. He had webbed feet and a long flat-sided tail to help him swim fast. Once he reached the lake, he knew he would be safe.

As he ran, he could hear Deinonychus behind
him. He looked anxiously for a sign of the lake. With his
great weight, Anatosaurus was beginning to get tired.
If he stopped for breath, he knew that Deinonychus
would be on his back, tearing at him with his terrible
sickle-claw.

Suddenly, the lake came into view. Anatosaurus bounded across the shore and plunged into the water. He swam away from the land with a few powerful sweeps of his tail. Deinonychus could only stand at the water's edge and watch his prey escape. Then he turned away and loped off in search of other prey.

Afterwards, Anatosaurus returned to the shore. The lakeside was now calm and peaceful. Palaeotringa, long-legged wading birds, probed the sand for shellfish and worms. Plegadornis stood at the water's edge, watching for frogs and water beetles.

Graculavus, who had been diving for fish, shook his wings dry as he perched on a rock by the lake.

Anatosaurus found plenty of food around the lakeside. He ate pistia, or water lettuce, and trapa, water chestnut. If he waded into the lake, he could sample some salvinia, a floating fern.

As Anatosaurus took his pick of the succulent plants, a herd of Brachylophosaurs wandered onto the shore. They were harmless, plant-eating creatures like himself. Yet suddenly, Anatosaurus heard the harsh clash of bone against bone, as Brachylophosaurus battled with Brachylophosaurus.

It was a trial of strength, rather than a fight. One of the younger members of the herd had challenged the herd leader to a contest. The two animals stood face to face. Then they pressed their face plates, made of solid bone, against each other. The winner was the one who forced the other to give way. He could then become the leader of the herd.

Anatosaurus stopped browsing among the greenery to watch the contest. At first, it looked as though the young Brachylophosaurus would win. Then the experience of the leader began to tell. The older Brachylophosaurus started to push the younger one back.

Just as it seemed that the leader would win, a terrifying roar sent the birds of the lake flying into the air. Out of the forest stalked Tyrannosaurus. He saw the herd of Brachylophosaurs and broke into a run. The great creature took short, awkward steps, giving the herd time to scatter. Anatosaurus fled with them.

Tyrannosaurus watched the herd scattering in front of him. He was looking for the weakest and the slowest animal. Finally, he made his move, darting in among the Brachylophosaurs. Anatosaurus saw his chance and ran for the edge of the forest.

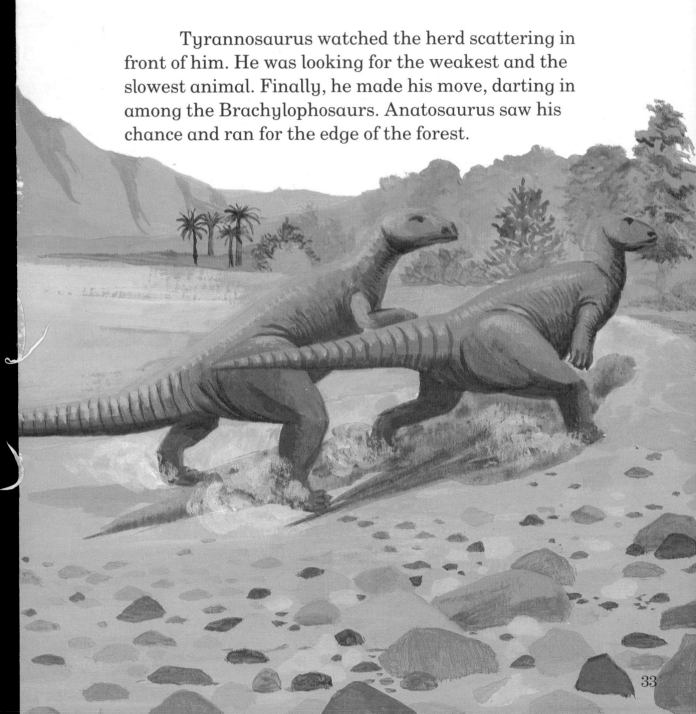

He looked back. Tyrannosaurus stood over a
Brachylophosaurus, tearing at it with his vicious teeth.
The rest of the herd had escaped, and so had Anatosaurus.

In the late afternoon, Anatosaurus rejoined his own herd in the oak forest. He found them browsing peacefully. Anatosaurus was tired and hungry by now. He reached up to the branches of an oak tree and began to eat. The running had tired him. Soon he lay down, curled up his great body in the forest undergrowth, and slept. The light faded slowly in the forest.

Rhamphorhynchus

Pteranodon

Pterodactyl

Ankylosaurus

Dimetrodon

Iguanodon

Tricondon

36

Deinonychus

Written by Rupert Oliver
Illustrated by Roger Payne

Archaeopteryx

Ichthyosaurus

Plesiosaurus

Deinonychus

Nothosaurus

Deinonychus shifted his position to make himself
more comfortable. A sharp twig had been
digging into his ribs. He had been resting in the
shade of the tree for several hours now.

Idly, he raised his great claw and scratched
himself behind the ear. The terrible heat of the noon
sun was too strong for Deinonychus, but it was
beginning to cool down now. His ear still itched.
Deinonychus lifted his foot up again and scratched
himself more vigorously. This time he disturbed a
large insect which flew away. It had been biting him
and sucking his blood. Deinonychus was comfortable
now and he dozed off again. As he dozed a butterfly
flew past on its colorful wings. Deinonychus did not
like the hot weather but it suited the insects.

It was late in the afternoon and the sun was not so hot when Deinonychus woke. The insects still buzzed around Deinonychus, but he did not itch. Slowly he rose to his feet. He felt fresh and fit. Deinonychus yawned and licked his lips. He felt thirsty. The heat of the day had dried him out, even though he had rested in the shade. Deinonychus set off to walk to the river.

Following a well-used track between the trees and bushes, Deinonychus reached the water's edge. The river was full of fresh, cool water. The arrival of Deinonychus disturbed a pair of turtles who splashed back into the safety of the river.

Deinonychus walked out across the mud flats to the water. He bent down to drink. Suddenly, the whole water surface seemed to explode with spray and foam right at the feet of Deinonychus. In sudden fear, Deinonychus stepped back as a vicious pair of jaws snapped shut, inches from his leg. Out of the flying water emerged the head and body of a crocodile. It had been lying in shallow water waiting. Deinonychus had walked right into the trap.

Quickly, Deinonychus scrambled back across the mud to the dry land. The crocodile did not follow Deinonychus. It preferred to sink back into the water and wait for another animal to come to drink.

Deinonychus ran into the trees lining the river. He had not completely satisfied his thirst, but he did not want to go back to the river if the crocodile was still there. Perhaps if he went to another part of the river there would be no crocodiles.

Suddenly, Deinonychus heard a distant crash. He stood still. Then another crash sounded out, much nearer. Now Deinonychus could hear heavy footsteps and the sound of smashing branches. Something was coming and whatever it was, it was very large. Deinonychus was worried that it was a meat-eater. It would be safest to hide.

Deinonychus pushed his way into a thick bush and waited. The sound of footsteps came closer and closer and then Deinonychus could see a looming bulk as the creature came into sight. Deinonychus need not have worried. The newcomer was a Tenontosaurus. This dinosaur was big, but it ate plants and was no danger to Deinonychus.

When it had gone Deinonychus came out of hiding and looked around. The Tenontosaurus had left a path of flattened and broken vegetation behind it as it smashed a way through the forest. Deinonychus decided to follow the path. It would be easier than picking his own route.

Deinonychus walked along the tracks of the Tenontosaurus until he reached the edge of the forest. Instead of finding himself at a river, Deinonychus was at the edge of a wide plain. He could see for miles across the landscape. On the plain was a group of animals. When Deinonychus saw what they were he felt his stomach rumbling. They were Psittacosaurs. Deinonychus suddenly felt very hungry.

Deinonychus knew that he would have to be very careful when hunting the Psittacosaurs. If they saw him they would run away and Deinonychus would have to go hungry.

Deinonychus walked out on to the plain as if he had not seen the Psittacosaurs. He did not walk straight toward them. He walked toward a small clump of trees to one side. One Psittacosaurus looked up from its feeding to watch the Deinonychus. When it saw that the Deinonychus was not coming toward it, the Psittacosaurus continued eating.

Using the trees as cover, Deinonychus was able to get close to the Psittacosaurs without being seen. As soon as he left the trees and moved toward the plant-eaters he was seen. One of the Psittacosaurs gave a bellow of alarm and started to run. The other Psittacosaurs heard the cry and also began to run. If he was to stand any chance of a meal, Deinonychus too had to run. The chase had begun.

Using his long legs Deinonychus bounded after the retreating Psittacosaurs. One of the plant-eaters was slower than the others. Perhaps he was old or ill, either way he would be the easiest to catch. Deinonychus decided to chase him. Across the plain the two dinosaurs raced. Their feet kicked up the dust as they ran.

Deinonychus was gaining on the Psittacosaurus. Then it stumbled. Now it stood no chance against Deinonychus. Deinonychus leapt high into the air. He brought his hind legs up under his body and raised his great claws. He had judged the leap perfectly. Deinonychus landed right on top of the Psittacosaurus. His huge, sickle-shaped claws ripped deep into the plant-eater. The Psittacosaurus gave a roar of pain and tried to escape, but Deinonychus was hungry and plunged his terrible claws into the soft body of the Psittacosaurus again and again. Within seconds it was all over and the Psittacosaurus lay dead at the feet of Deinonychus.

Deinonychus climbed off the still body of the Psittacosaurus. The long chase had made him breathless. Then he began to eat. He bent down and tore great mouthfuls of meat from the carcass.

As Deinonychus began to eat he saw a pair of small Coelurosaurs standing nearby. Deinonychus roared at them angrily, but they did not move away. Deinonychus continued eating. While he was still eating, one of the Coelurosaurs dashed in and grabbed a mouthful of meat. Deinonychus left the body of the Psittacosaurus when he was full. Then both the Coelurosaurs dashed in and began to eat.

As Deinonychus moved away the sun was setting. He felt much better with a full stomach and moved off to find somewhere to rest for the night. Behind him the small animals continued to squabble over pieces of meat, but the sounds of their fight faded as Deinonychus moved away. In the shelter of some bushes Deinonychus found a soft patch of ferns to lie on. He settled down and closed his eyes. It had been a tiring day and Deinonychus was very tired. Soon he was fast asleep.

Quetzalcoatlus

Parasaurolophus

Deinosuchus

Corythosaurus

Spinosaurus

Oviraptor

56

Pachycephalosaurus

Written by Frances Swann
Illustrated by Pam Mara

Pachycephalosaurus

Anatosaurus

Struthiomimus

Scolosaurus

Rutiodon

Psittacosaurus

It was early morning when Pachycephalosaurus awoke. The air was hot, dry and still.

A little way off, a couple of one-year-old males were playfighting. Their noise disturbed the others, and slowly the rest of Pachycephalosaurus' small herd began to stir. The herd had slept in the shelter of a huge overhanging rock on the treeless hillside. It was the dry season. Soon the sun would rise higher, and even in the shadow of the rock it would be uncomfortably hot.

The herd was hungry. They assembled gradually behind Pachycephalosaurus. Slowly they moved down the hillside in search of fresh vegetation and shade.

Pachycephalosaurus felt restless. He was the oldest, largest, and strongest of the males. Therefore, he was the dominant male and the herd leader. This was the mating season, a time when other males would challenge his position. So far he had always won. Pachycephalosaurus knew that one day the outcome would be different, and he would lose his herd to a younger male.

Pachycephalosaurus called his herd in closer. The descent was steep and the ground hard and stony. A Pterosaur flew low over the group. Pachycephalosaurus felt a rush of warm air from its leathery wings. He watched as it glided down toward the valley.

Over the green and yellow treetops he could see the thin blue line of the river. A vast flood plain lay beyond, and the hazy line of a mountain range lay beyond that.

A sudden crack of thunder frightened the herd. They bunched closer together. A lizard darted back into the rocks. The herd quickened its pace.

The descent was less steep now, and the vegetation thicker. The herd stopped to feed on some bushes. Pachycephalosaurus chewed the leaves, but remained watchful. Another clap of thunder shook the valley. Pachycephalosaurus turned. To his horror he saw another Pachycephalosaurus herd standing absolutely still, watching him. In front was a powerful male, his challenging posture unmistakable.

The two males approached each other menacingly, watched by their herds. As the distance between them lessened, both males adopted a butting posture. Heads down, with backs and tails held in a stiff, straight line, they ran at each other.

Their heads met with a dull thud. They retreated and charged at each other again and again. Suddenly the other male withdrew, panting with exhaustion. Pachycephalosaurus had won!

To prove his victory, Pachycephalosaurus chased the challenger and his herd into the thicket of katsura trees. Pachycephalosaurus was shaken, but unhurt.

Pachycephalosaurus needed to get his breath back, so the herd moved slowly into the shade of the trees.

The ground was covered with oval yellow katsura leaves. A shrew-like mammal darted out to catch a beetle, and a line of ants swarmed up the trunk of a breadfruit tree. All seemed still.

The herd moved forward. Above them rose the tall silvery bark and the lime green canopy of sycamore trees. A sudden commotion brought the herd to a halt.

Through the trees they could see two male
Chasmorsaurs locked in battle. The horns on their great
frilled heads clashed together as they pushed and swayed
violently.

The Chasmosaurs were intent on their contest and
the herd passed unnoticed.

Pachycephalosaurus grew uneasy as the day
continued. A strange smell was in the air. A pair of
Stenonychosaurs sprinted back and forth catching insects.
They seemed unbothered.

The smell grew stronger and stronger. Smoke! Pachycephalosaurus was filled with terror. The herd's territory was on the hillside, but the fire had them trapped. Panic stricken, the herd fled deeper into the trees, heading instinctively for the river.

They ran headlong through the thick undergrowth, almost trampling a Panoplosaurus as it lay clutching the ground with alarm.

The smoke was all around them now and the whole forest seemed on the move. The ground shook as a herd of Triceratops charged blindly past them. Small mammals raced across the forest floor, and birds flew wildly above them.

A fleet-footed Struthiomimus raced by, disappearing into the distance. The herd was beginning to tire. Pachycephalosaurus was a large animal and not used to running so far, but terror and panic drove him.

At last the air grew clearer and Pachycephalosaurus could breathe more easily. They were leaving the fire behind.

The herd did not stop until they reached the dry sandy land by the river. Here they drank and rested, in the cover of the tall rushes under the redwood trees.

It was late afternoon before Pachycephalosaurus led his herd out along the river. The air was cooler, sun sparkled on the water, and all along the bank turtles plopped back into the river as the herd passed.

Several half-submerged crocodiles lay in the shallow water at the river's edge. Suddenly, one stood up. With a fast, zig-zagging pace, he made for a clump of tall rushes.

The herd stopped as the dark shape of an angry female Parasaurolophus rose from her nest. She had been sitting on her eggs. Her threatening posture and her size were too much for the crocodile. It turned back and slid quietly into the river.

Pachycephalosaurus had no wish to anger the Parasaurolophus any further. He led his herd around her nest site, and on through the rushes.

As they rounded the next bend there was a sudden explosion of sound. A deafening mixture of bellows, roars, and splashes filled the air. The herd came to an abrupt halt. Pachycephalosaurus looked wildly about him for the source of the noise.

On the far bank of the river a pack of Dromaeosaurs had killed a Coryothsaurus. Quarrelling among themselves, they were already tearing at their kill.

Thundering toward them was a massive Tyrannosaurus. It roared defiantly, hoping to scatter the Dromaeosaurs and claim the carcass for itself.

73

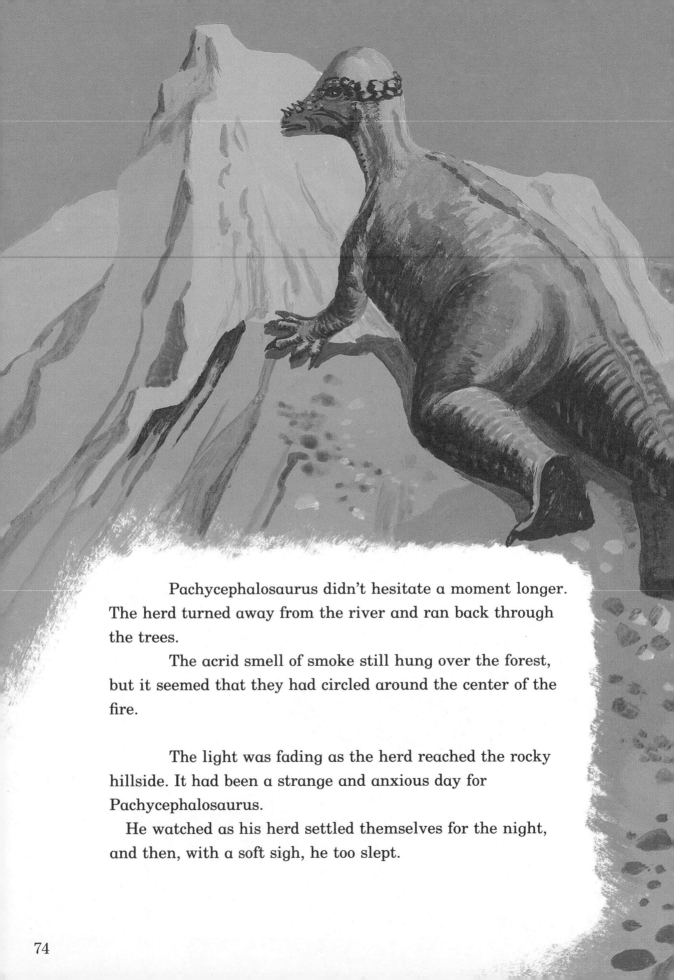

Pachycephalosaurus didn't hesitate a moment longer. The herd turned away from the river and ran back through the trees.

The acrid smell of smoke still hung over the forest, but it seemed that they had circled around the center of the fire.

The light was fading as the herd reached the rocky hillside. It had been a strange and anxious day for Pachycephalosaurus.

He watched as his herd settled themselves for the night, and then, with a soft sigh, he too slept.

Quetzalcoatlus

Parasaurolophus

Deinosuchus

Corythosaurus

Oviraptor

76 Spinosaurus

Psittacosaurus

Written by Frances Swann
Illustrated by Pam Mara

Pachycephalosaurus

Anatosaurus

Struthiomimus

Scolosaurus

Rutiodon

Psittacosaurus

The sun was already climbing in the sky over the distant purple hills as Psittacosaurus slowly awoke. He was hungry and not well rested, because it had been a strangely disturbing night. Thunder had rolled back and forth across the plain. Disturbed by it, the herd had sought out a higher shelter than usual.

The herd gradually assembled behind the older males. They protected the females and their young by keeping them in the middle. Then they moved off, walking quietly over the forest floor. Above them the yellow katsura and ginko leaves shaded them from the rising sun. The sharp smell of fallen ginko fruit filled Psittacosaurus's nostrils as he tested the air.

In a short time the herd reached a steep bank. Here they slowed to let the youngsters cross it. Psittacosaurus looked out over the hardwood forest and across the plain. Below him he could see the great delta that fanned out toward the sea. Several birds soared on thermals above him. On the far side of the plain he watched a huge herd of dinosaurs obscured by a dust cloud moving slowly toward the forest edge.

Hungry now, the herd moved quickly toward their favorite feeding grounds. Every so often Psittacosaurus would grasp a passing cycad leaf, crop it with his powerful beak, and chew it as he walked.

Abruptly, the herd stopped. Over the heads of the animals in front of him, Psittacosaurus could see a small group of large Probactrosaurs. They turned to stare at the herd and then lumbered off a few feet to resume feeding. Noisily they raked down branches with their great thumb spikes. Then they settled again onto all fours to chew enormous amounts of foliage.

The herd moved on past them. They knew that despite their size, the Probactrosaurs posed no danger.

At last the herd settled at a quiet feeding ground. Here they could eat in peace. Moving lightly from plant to plant, the herd grasped, chopped, and chewed the luscious green foliage. Palm-like cycads and big bennettitales leaves disappeared as they browsed. Psittacosaurus chewed idly as he watched the youngsters tackling the ferns of the undergrowth.

The heat of the sun was now beginning to penetrate the forest, and every so often, small lizards would dart in and out of view. A slight movement caught Psittacosaurus's eye. Coiled around a branch was a small snake watching him with unblinking eyes. Psittacosaurus moved past it on all fours, heading for some tasty flowering plants he had noticed.

The herd was now well satisified. With the warm sun on his back, Psittacosaurus rested.

Psittacosaurus felt wakeful and unsettled. Still chewing, he moved a little away from his herd. Suddenly, the peace of the forest was shattered by a commotion just yards away from Psittacosaurus. Frozen with fear, he dropped onto all fours among the tall ferns.

In front of him through the leaves, he could see a lone Deinonychus. The great creature was on its hind legs, its huge body towering over a Shamosaurus. The Deinonychus bellowed as the Shamosaurus swung its heavy tail club at the predator's ankles.

Deinonychus lunged repeatedly at the Shamosaurus, but the Shamosaurus was too agile for it. The Shamosaurus swung its tail club again. This time it drew blood, and the Deinonychus turned to escape. Psittacosaurus heard it crashing through the undergrowth as it fled.

When Psittacosaurus finally stood up again, the Shamosaurus had gone and the forest was calm.

Psittacosaurus rejoined his herd when they started to move. The forest seemed secure and safe again as they ambled on, travelling more slowly now in the sultry heat.

All of a sudden, little mammals startled from
the undergrowth ran toward them. The herd, instantly
sensing great danger, rose on their hind legs and ran
panic-stricken, pursued by a large group of
Deinonychus. Headlong they ran, terror driving them
onward, gaining with every yard over their hunters.

Underfoot, decaying branches littered the
moss-covered ground, and young trees slowed their
progress. Slowly the sounds of pursuit faded behind
them.

Abruptly, the dark shade of the redwood trees gave way to the glare of sun on sand. The herd stood, flanks heaving with exhaustion. On a soft sand bank by the river, Psittacosaurus blinked in the bright light. Shaken by their narrow escape, the herd rested for a while. Keeping close to the edge of the forest, they moved on following the course of the river. Every so often a heron would flap off in front of them or a crocodile would silently slip back into the water. Otherwise all seemed peaceful, and Psittacosaurus began to relax.

Around a bend in the river, the herd came upon three female Bactrosaurs at a nest site. One female was covering her newly laid eggs with sand. The other two moved menacingly toward the herd. Quickly and warily, the herd skirted the nest site.

A sudden thrashing commotion at the river's edge caused the herd to stop and stare. In the churning water Psittacosaurus could see a pair of crocodiles twisting and turning as they tugged at a small dinosaur carcass. Not far from them was a flock of flamingos standing statue-like and unbothered.

The herd moved on, and the ground underfoot became wetter as they reached the edge of a shallow lake. Disturbed by their presence, a couple of basking turtles fell back into the water with a loud plop. In the shallow water Psittacosaurus could make out the darker shadows of darting fish.

A slight sound made Psittacosaurus look up. Across the lake, a group of Segnosaurs splashed toward him through the shallows with their broad feet.

The Segnosaurs posed no threat, and the herd watched them curiously. In the distance Psittacosaurus noticed the vast dark shape of a Pterosaur soaring high above the water.

Slowly the herd turned away from the lake. The air was cooler now. Soon the light would begin to fade. The herd must feed again and find a safe resting place for the night. With a last glance at the lake, Psittacosaurus followed the others back into the shade of the forest. Pleasantly tired, he felt he would sleep well that night.

Quetzalcoatlus

Parasaurolophus

Deinosuchus

Corythosaurus

Oviraptor

Spinosaurus

Rutiodon

Written by David White
Illustrated by Pam Mara

Pachycephalosaurus

Anatosaurus

Struthiomimus

Scolosaurus

Rutiodon

Psittacosaurus

As the sun rose above the horizon of the valley, the creatures of the riverbank began to stir. Rutiodon was already awake. She was keeping a constant watch over the nest of eggs she had laid two days earlier. Soon, they would be ready to hatch.

Rutiodon stretched her legs, which were stiff from the cold. She was hungry after the long night. It was now time for her to go to the river to hunt for fish.

She raised herself on her four powerful legs and moved off in the direction of the river. A small Coelurosaur darted out of her path as she made her way through the ferns and horsetails. The Coelurosaur was no match for Rutiodon, who was a powerful creature. She was almost twelve feet long, with many sharp teeth in her long jaws. She was also well armored against attack.

Soon, Rutiodon reached the river. She slid into the clear waters with hardly a sound. She began to swim upstream. Only her eyes and the nostrils just in front of them appeared above the water.

Rutiodon swam swiftly, her great tail sweeping from side to side, propelling her through the water. Her long jaws snapped shut on the fish. There were plenty for her to eat. Other animals, too, were hunting the fish. On the far side of the river, Rutiodon could see a group of Cyclotosaurs in the water. There were enough fish for everyone.

When she had eaten her fill, Rutiodon returned downstream. She clambered up the bank, anxious to return to the place where her eggs were hidden. She did not dare to leave them unguarded for too long. The eggs of a Rutiodon were tempting food for many animals in the river valley.

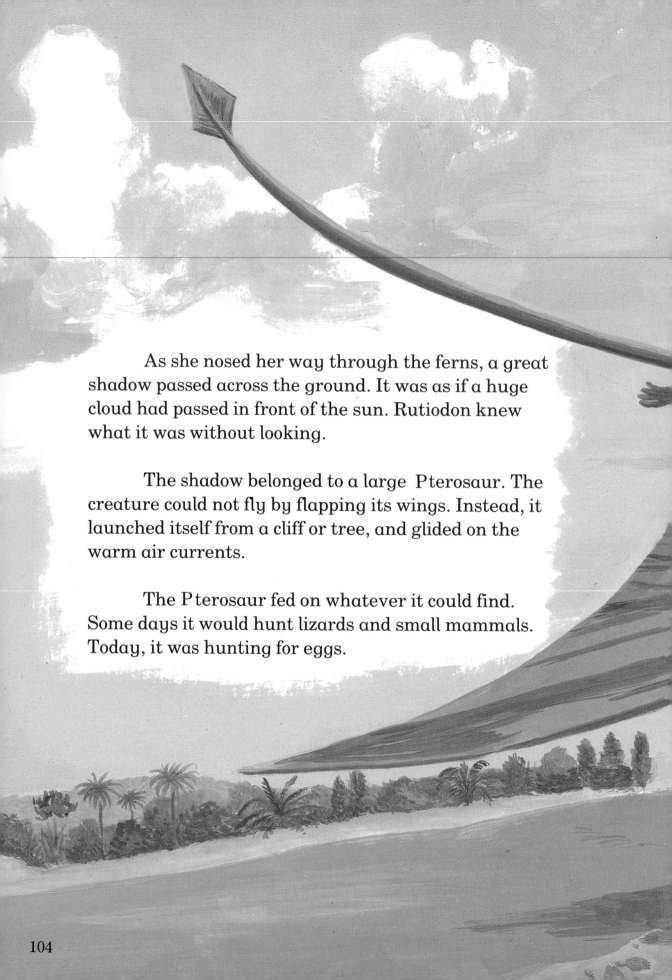

As she nosed her way through the ferns, a great shadow passed across the ground. It was as if a huge cloud had passed in front of the sun. Rutiodon knew what it was without looking.

The shadow belonged to a large Pterosaur. The creature could not fly by flapping its wings. Instead, it launched itself from a cliff or tree, and glided on the warm air currents.

The Pterosaur fed on whatever it could find. Some days it would hunt lizards and small mammals. Today, it was hunting for eggs.

Rutiodon moved quickly to protect her eggs. She covered them with her great body. Hissing through her nostrils, her jaw gaping, she warned off the Pterosaur. The creature swooped once, saw it was useless, and backed away. Then the Pterosaur disappeared to look for easier prey.

The danger had past. Rutiodon could now doze in the midday sun while she digested her meal. Occasionally there were interruptions, and Rutiodon would half open her eyes. She saw Stagonolepis lumbering through the undergrowth. He looked threatening, with big bony plates on his back for protection. Rutiodon knew she need not fear him.

Stagonolepis was not looking for trouble. He was not interested in the eggs Rutiodon was guarding. Instead, he grubbed in the ground for the juicy roots of plants. Eventually he moved away, snuffling as he went.

The sun was now at its height. The air grew sultry. Away to the northwest, the sky began to darken. The sound of thunder rolled across the valley. Forks of lightning shot down from the upper air. Rutiodon knew instinctively what was to follow. A sudden roaring sound grew louder and louder. A flash flood was coming.

The river, swollen with rain, tumbled down the valley. Muddy water broke over the river banks and swept off anything in its way.

Rutiodon carefully put her eggs in her mouth and carried them to the safety of higher ground. Other animals were not so quick to escape. Henodus, a flat-headed creature encased in a thick shell, was swept off his rock. Mastodonsaurus, who was grazing on the river bank, struggled to stay upright as the torrent swirled around his feet. He, too, was swept downstream.

Suddenly, it was quiet. The flood subsided as quickly as it had risen. The river returned to normal. The only evidence of the flood was a thick carpet of mud spread across both banks.

Rutiodon remained near her eggs. In her new hiding place, away from the river, there were new dangers. Rutiodon could see the edge of the pine woods, where herds of Plateosaurs grazed. Suddenly, there was a sound of breaking foliage. The Plateosaurs paused in their eating, their long necks bending as they turned to see the cause of the noise.

Coelophysis scampered out of the woods, pursued by two Ornithosuchus. Coelophysis dodged this way and that, tiring the mighty pursuers. In the end, the Ornithosuchuses gave up the chase. Instead, they turned on a third Ornithosuchus.

Soon the pine woods echoed with the sound of animals snapping and tearing at each other's flesh. The two Ornithosuchus finally brought down the third. The struggle was over.

However, the danger was not past for Rutiodon. Coelophysis headed straight for her after he had escaped from the Ornithosuchuses. Now he circled around the eggs, snatching and biting with his grasping claws and pointed beak. Rutiodon lunged at him angrily. Coelophysis danced away and then danced back again, looking for a way around Rutiodon.

Finally, the Coelophysis gave up. He was hungry, and he was using up valuable energy. He must find easier prey. As suddenly as he had come, he dashed off into the ferns.

Rutiodon could now relax for a while. Soon it would be night again. New dangers would appear. In the dusk, Rutiodon could again leave the eggs to go down to the river for fish. The river was calm and clear, as if the torrent of the day had never happened. Rutiodon swam lazily, enjoying the cool water. Then she returned to her eggs. For the first time that day, she slept.

Quetzalcoatlus

Parasaurolophus

Deinosuchus

Corythosaurus

Oviraptor

116   Spinosaurus

Scolosaurus

Written by David White
Illustrated by Pam Mara

Pachycephalosaurus

Anatosaurus

Struthiomimus

Scolosaurus

Rutiodon

Psittacosaurus

The rocks of the foothills cast long shadows in the first sunlight. A python, which had slept against a tree stump during the night, uncurled and slithered away. All was still. Then slowly, one of the rocks began to move. It was Scolosaurus. As he lay flat against the ground the heavy armor on his back made him look like a piece of rugged rock.

Scolosaurus liked the safety of hills. If he could not find a cave or rock for shelter, his camouflage would always protect him. He could also walk more safely there than he could in the swampy forests. There was no danger of getting bogged down.

Now he needed food. The grasses of the mountains were sparse and dry. He wanted the green and juicy plants of the woods. He set off for the trees in the valley below.

Scolosaurus knew a glade where the most succulent foliage grew. Here, magnolia and climbing roses flowered. Bees, attracted by the bright colors, carried pollen from one to the other.

Scolosaurus browsed peacefully among the undergrowth. The peace was soon disturbed by the sound of an animal crashing through the foliage.

Struthiomimus burst into the glade. He was a tall creature, with long legs and a long neck. His three-toed feet enabled him to run away quickly from any attacker. Now he needed to use them.

Close after him came Dromaeosaurus. He was far smaller than Struthiomimus, but much more dangerous. This fierce little animal had wickedly sharp claws on his hind legs, which he used to slash at his victims.

Struthiomimus ran around the glade, dodging this way and that. Speed was his only defense against Dromaeosaurus. Scolosaurus took little notice of the chase. With his heavy armor, he was well protected against creatures like Dromaeosaurus. Only his underbelly was vulnerable to attack. This is why he took so much care to protect it.

After circling the glade, Struthiomimus suddenly darted into the trees. Dromaeosaurus did not bother to follow. The chase had tired him. He turned and retraced his steps. There would be other prey for him.

Now the sun was higher, and the forest grew hotter and more humid. Scolosaurus felt thirsty. It was time for him to go down to the river to drink. The river ran through a plain beyond the wood. As Scolosaurus left the shelter of the trees, he was glad he had the protection of his armor.

Across the river plain, Scolosaurus saw herds of Parasaurolophus and Trachodons. Like him, they were going to the river to drink. Most animals visited the river at some time during the day. This made it a dangerous place. The meat-eaters could be sure of a kill if they lay in wait long enough.

Today, there were no signs of the meat-eaters. Side by side with the Trachodons, Scolosaurus drank the clear water of the river. The only sound to disturb the peace was the buzzing of flying insects and the flutter of dragonflies.

Suddenly, Scolosaurus noticed that the Trachodons beside him had vanished. He could see the reason for this reflected in the river. The image of Gorgosaurus appeared in the water. Scolosaurus twisted around to face him, just as Gorgosaurus lunged forward. The huge jaws and savage teeth of the mighty meat-eater snapped shut close to Scolosaurus's face.

Instinctively, Scolosaurus took up a defensive position. He tucked his great legs under his body and lowered himself to the ground. There was no gap between his armor and the ground. Gorgosaurus circled around him, roaring angrily.

The meat-eater began to lunge at Scolosaurus in an effort to turn him over. This would be the end for Scolosaurus. Quite unprotected and unable to regain his upright position, he would be easy prey for the sharp teeth of Gorgosaurus. He must do everything in his power to prevent it.

Luckily, he was equipped with a heavy tail, and armed with two spikes at the tip. As Gorgosaurus stood astride him, Scolosaurus lashed upward at the meat-eater. Gorgosaurus reeled back, roaring with pain. Gorgosaurus lunged again and the Scolosaurus's tail hit him again just below the throat. Gorgosaurus was almost thrown to the ground.

Finally, Gorgosaurus turned away. He had enough of Scolosaurus and his spiny tail. He moved off down the riverbank. This time, it was the Gorgosaurus who was trapped. Facing him was Styracosaurus. With his frill of spikes, he was a fearsome sight. Gorgosaurus hesitated for a moment. If he could get around the side of Styracosaurus, he could deal with him.

Styracosaurus did not give him the chance. With a bellow, he began to charge straight at the meat-eater. The dust flew up behind him as he approached. Gorgosaurus tried to sidestep him, but he was too slow. Styracosaurus landed a stunning blow on his right side.

Gorgosaurus lost his footing and crashed to the ground. Scolosaurus did not wait to see what happened next. Wisely, he took the chance to slip away from the river, across the flood plain toward the woods.

By now it was late afternoon. The shadows had begun to lengthen. The woods looked darker and more threatening. Scolosaurus moved quickly through the undergrowth, as dozens of smaller creatures scampered across his path.

Soon he emerged from the woods, and began the long climb up the foothills to his home. As he climbed, he saw the shape of other animals in the dusk. There was Ankylosaurus, searching for a crevice in the rocks in which to spend the night. Like Scolosaurus, he was safe in the open of the plateaus. He, too, carried heavy armor on his back, and his tail wielded a fearsome club.

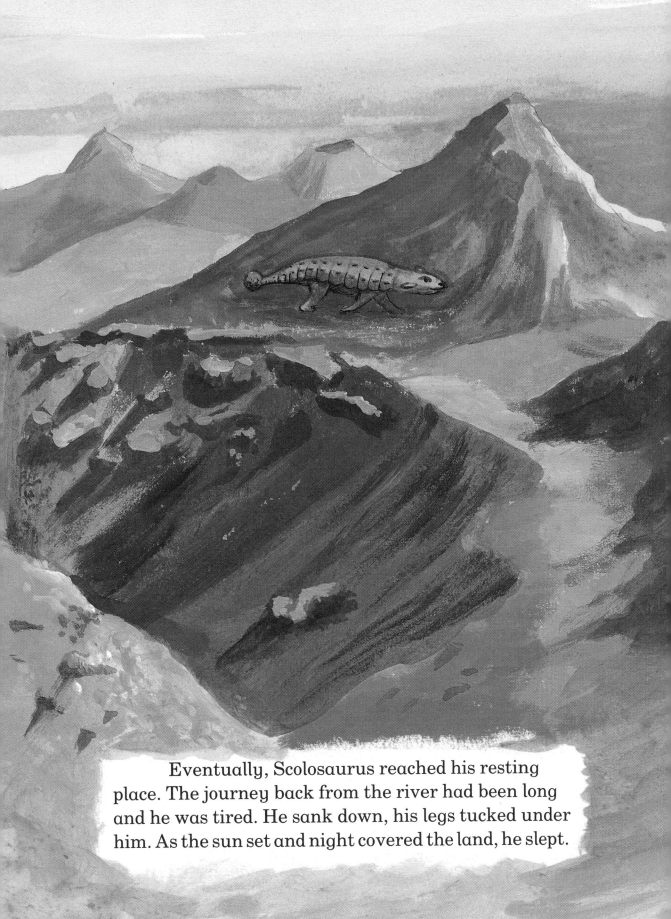

Eventually, Scolosaurus reached his resting place. The journey back from the river had been long and he was tired. He sank down, his legs tucked under him. As the sun set and night covered the land, he slept.

Quetzalcoatlus

Parasaurolophus

Deinosuchus

Corythosaurus

Spinosaurus

Oviraptor

Spinosaurus

Written by David White
Illustrated by Pam Mara

Pachycephalosaurus

Anatosaurus

Struthiomimus

Scolosaurus

Rutiodon

Psittacosaurus

The dawn arrived suddenly at the edge of the desert. One minute, the plains were cloaked in darkness. The next, they shimmered in the harsh subtropical sun.

Although the sun was above the horizon, the air was still chilly with night. In the shadows cast by a rocky outcrop, Spinosaurus and his mate woke and stirred themselves.

Slowly, Spinosaurus raised himself from the squatting position in which he had slept, until he stood on all four limbs. He knew that he must get warm quickly. Once his blood was warm, he could move fast – faster than the creatures whose blood was still cold.

Spinosaurus emerged from the shadows into the sunlight and looked around him. Then, purposefully, he turned his body until one side was facing the sun. This was so that the sun's rays could heat the blood circulating through the great sail on his back.

Spinosaurus felt the warmth coursing through his veins. His limbs loosened and his brain became more alert. Soon, he was ready to hunt for his prey.

He moved off across the plain, his lowered head swinging from side to side. He was searching for tracks in the sand. Soon he found what he was looking for. There were three pairs of tracks, left by large, three-toed creatures. The hunt was on.

Spinosaurus found his prey on the broad plain of the river. Three Ouranosaurs were feeding on the vegetation that grew near the river. They stood on their broad hind limbs, tearing at the plants which grew in the crevices of the rocks.

Scenting Spinosaurus in the wind, they lowered themselves onto all fours and began to lumber away from the danger. Spinosaurus gave chase.

However, the Ouranosaurs were not easy prey, for they could run as fast as Spinosaurus. This was because their blood, too, had been warmed in the sails on their backs.

Yet Spinosaurus was able to keep up with the Ouranosaurs. He would have caught one of them but they suddenly split up. As each Ouranosaurus ran off in a different direction, Spinosaurus hesitated. Which one should he pursue?

His hesitation allowed the Ouranosauruses to escape. Spinosaurus halted and watched them go. Slowly he returned to the banks of the river. If he could not eat, he could at least drink. He drank warily, watching for the giant crocodiles that inhabited the riverbank. These enormous animals would lie in wait for dinosaurs who came to drink at the river.

Spinosaurus returned to the open plain. In the distance, he could see a great cloud of dust. This was a clear signal that a herd of Sauropods was on the move.

As Spinosaurus approached the herd, he could see that it was a large one. Some 20 to 30 Brachiosaurs were making their slow way across the plain. The adults stayed on the outside of the herd, while the young were kept inside. This was to give them protection from attack.

Spinosaurus was interested only in the young Brachiosaurs. However, the adults made a defensive wall with their bodies, so that it was impossible for him to reach them. Spinosaurus angrily snapped and tore at their massive legs, but to no avail.

Finally, he turned away in frustration.
Spinosaurus was tired and dusty and hot. The sun was
now high in the sky. There was no shade on the plain,
so Spinosaurus turned toward the sun, so that the
sun's rays did not strike his sail head-on. When he was
cooler, he continued the hunt. He saw flying reptiles
circling in the distance—a sign that some large
creature had died. As he approached, he saw it was the
carcass of Titanosaurus, a Sauropod.

Several Quetzalcoatluses were perched on the carcass, tearing at the flesh. Spinosaurus chased them away. He was hungry, and he eagerly began to eat. But his meal was interrupted by a roar. Tyrannosaurus, too, had seen the flying reptiles and had come to feed on the carcass. Now it was Spinosaurus's turn to be chased away.

Spinosaurus was no match for Tyrannosaurus. Besides, a fight could damage the precious sail on his back.

Disappointed and still hungry, Spinosaurus returned to the riverbank. His arrival surprised Gallimimus, who was foraging for insects and lizards. The hunter lunged at his prey, but Gallimimus was too fast. As Spinosaurus's jaw snapped shut, the creature sprang away, disappearing into the foliage.

Spinosaurus decided to rejoin his mate on the higher ground. Together, they moved across the plain in the heat of the afternoon, ever watchful. Eventually, they found what they were looking for – the undisturbed carcass of a Parrosaurus. The animal had been killed by a Tyrannosaurus when it became separated from the herd. The Tyrannosaurus had eaten its fill, and left the rest to the scavengers of the plain.

Spinosaurus and his mate ate eagerly. This time they could eat as much as they wanted without being disturbed.

As the shadows lengthened, Spinosaurus and his mate returned to the rocky ledge. The evening was cool after the intense heat of the day. Spinosaurus settled down to sleep.

FACTS ABOUT DINOSAURS
Anatosaurus and the Late Cretaceous World

The skeleton of Anatosaurus compared in size with a man

The time of Anatosaurus

The Mesozoic Era, known as the Age of the Dinosaurs, lasted from 225 million years ago to 65 million years ago. Palaeontologists divide this age in to three periods: the Triassic, the Jurassic and the Cretaceous. Anatosaurus lived in the second half of the Cretaceous period, some 70 million years ago. We know this because bones and even pieces of mummified skin have been found in the rocks that were laid down in that period. Anatosaurus lived right up to the end of the Mesozoic Era, until the point when, mysteriously, all dinosaur life on Earth ended.

The land of Anatosaurus

Toward the end of the Age of the Dinosaurs, the world began to look more like it does today. The two supercontinents of Laurasia and Gondwanaland had broken up to form the present continents, which were separated from each other by vast oceans. Dinosaurs were no longer free to roam the world.

Anatosaurus lived in great numbers in North America. The land looked very different then. It was generally flatter. The central range of mountains had not yet been formed. It may also have been intersected by a vast inland sea which extended from the north to the south.

The family tree of Anatosaurus

Anatosaurus was one of the first of the Hadrosaurs, or "duck-billed" dinosaurs. Hadrosaurs were by far the most successful of all the ornithopods living in the Late Cretaceous period. The first Hadrosaur, Batractosaurus, lived in Mongolia 100 million years ago. By 60 million years ago they had spread to Asia, Europe and North America.

There were three main groups or branches of the Hadrosaurs: the flat-headed Hadrosaurs, the solid-crested Hadrosaurs, and the remarkable hollow-crested Hadrosaurs. (Scientists are not certain what these crests of

156

hollow bone were for, but they think they may have acted as recognition signals). The group that changed least during the 40 million years of their existence were the flat-headed Hadrosaurs, among them Anatosaurus.

Other plant-eaters

Plant-eating Hadrosaurs were the most successful dinosaurs of the Cretaceous period. They completely dominated the North American and Canadian forests, browsing among the trees at the forest's edge. Brachylophosaurus was one of them. Brachylophosaurus had a strong bony face-plate which was probably used in combat with members of the herd. However, Hadrosaurs, like all plant-eaters, were docile creatures, and they would not have used their hardened skulls to fight off predatory meat-eaters.

The meat-eaters

If the Hadrosaurs had been allowed to browse undisturbed, they would have stripped the forests bare. They were prevented from doing so by the meat-eating dinosaurs, the lizard-hipped Carnosaurs, who attained a terrifying power and size during the Cretaceous period. The best known is Tyrannosaurus Rex. This was the largest flesh-eater of all time, almost **45 feet long and weighing 10 tons.** However Deinonychus, a far smaller Carnosaur, was probably more fearsome even than Tyrannosaurus.

Although it was only 6 feet long, it wielded a sickle-shaped claw which enabled it to overcome plant-eaters much longer than itself.

Birds and plants

Much of the bird and plant life of the Cretaceous period would have been recognizable to us today. Besides the older trees, such as conifers and ginkgoes, there were pines, firs, oaks, ash, poplars, maples and sycamores. Among the birds, Graculavus looked much like a present day cormorant and Plegadornis resembled a heron or a stork.

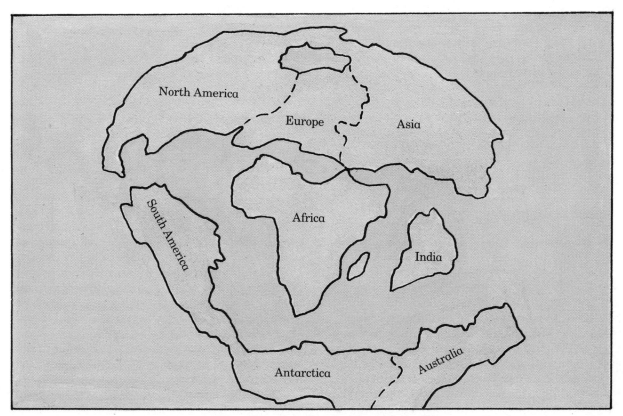

Map of the Cretaceous World

Deinonychus and Early Cretaceous North America

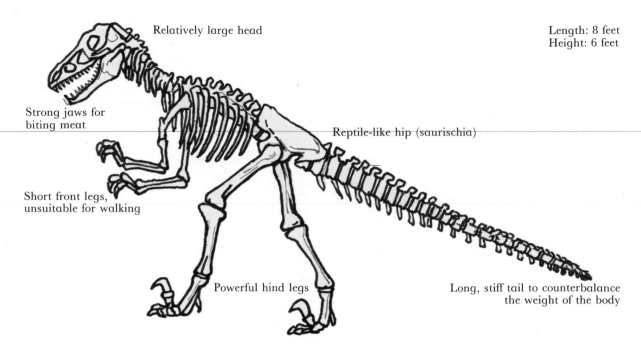

Relatively large head

Length: 8 feet
Height: 6 feet

Strong jaws for biting meat

Reptile-like hip (saurischia)

Short front legs, unsuitable for walking

Powerful hind legs

Long, stiff tail to counterbalance the weight of the body

Skeleton of Deinonychus

When did Deinonychus live?
The Age of the Dinosaurs began about 225 million years ago and lasted for some 180 million years. Scientists have divided this era, which has been called the Mesozoic, into three periods. The first was the Triassic, the second the Jurassic and the third the Cretaceous. Deinonychus lived during the early part of the Cretaceous. It lived about 125 million years ago.

Where did Deinonychus live?
The fossils of Deinonychus have been found in Montana in the United States but Montana was a very different place 125 million years ago. There were no Rocky Mountains. The earth movements that were to result in the Rockies **had not even begun. [The landscape was very much like that depicted in the story about Deinonychus and would only become mountainous toward the end of the Cretaceous period.]**

It is also interesting to note that western North America was not linked to the eastern part of the continent. It is thought that a shallow sea ran from Canada down to the Gulf of Mexico. Instead, scientists believe, the western part of the continent was linked with Asia. The fact that dinosaurs similar to Deinonychus have been found in Asia but not in eastern America, seems

to support this idea. Indeed, Deinonychosaurs may have first evolved in eastern Asia.

The Terrible Claw
Deinonychus means 'terrible claw' and it is easy to see why scientists gave it this name. The second toe on each hind foot ended in a 5 inch long claw. There can be little doubt that this was its main killing weapon. Deinonychus could also run very fast. When it saw a likely victim its speed would enable it to run the victim down. When Deinonychus had reached its prey it would leap upon it and kick and slash at it with its claw, just as some birds do.

Some scientists think that Deinonychus may have hidden in ambush for its prey, alternatively it may have hunted in packs as lions do today. It certainly had a larger brain than other dinosaurs and may have been intelligent enough to hunt in groups.

Deinonychus Ancestors
Deinonychus was a meat-eating dinosaur of the Saurischian, (lizard-hipped) group. All the meat-eating and some plant-eating dinosaurs belonged to this group. All plant-eating dinosaurs belonged to the Ornithischian, (bird-hipped) group.

Deinonychus clearly represented a distinct form of meat-eating dinosaur. Scientists have therefore placed it and a few similar dinosaurs, in a special family known as Deinonychosaurs. It is thought that this family was an offshoot of the highly successful Coelurosaur family which survived throughout the entire Age of Dinosaurs. The fast-running and agile Deinonychosaurs were certainly very different from the larger and more ponderous Carnosaurs such as Tyrannosaurus rex. They were much more like the small Coelurosaurs which could scamper around in the undergrowth. It is thought that one type of Coelurosaur changed into the Deinonychosaurs at the start of the Cretaceous period, about 135 million years ago. Phaedrolosaurus, a dinosaur from China, may have been one of these ancestral Deinonychosaurs.

A Time of Change

Deinonychus lived during the early part of the Cretaceous period, a time of great change for the dinosaurs. Throughout the previous ninety million years the Saurischian dinosaurs had ruled the world. The future belonged to the Ornithischians.

During the long Jurassic period, the most important type of plant-eater had been the Sauropods. Sauropods were giant Saurischian dinosaurs with long tails and long necks. Brontosaurus was a kind of Sauropod. By the time Deinonychus hunted in North America, Sauropods were becoming rarer. Their place was being taken by many new kinds of Ornithischians.

Tenontosaurus, was one of these. It belonged to the Iguanodontid family of dinosaurs. This family included the famous Iguanodon from Europe which was related to the highly successful duckbilled dinosaurs. Psittacosaurus was also an Ornithischian dinosaur. It was probably the ancestor of the Ceratopsian dinosaurs, a group which included the mighty Triceratops.

Other animals were changing as well. The flying reptiles were changing from the longtailed forms, such as Rhamphorhynchus, to the short-tailed Pterosaurs. Birds had evolved from reptile ancestors and were developing into a wide range of species.

The early Cretaceous period was an important time for life on Earth.

The Deinonychus with (inset) the large sickle-shaped claw on its hind leg with which it attacked its prey.

The Skeleton of Pachycephalosaurus Compared in Size with a Man

Length 26 ft (8m)

Pachycephalosaurus and the Cretaceous World

The age of the Dinosaurs

The word dinosaur is derived from two Greek words meaning "terrible lizard." All the dinosaurs lived in the Mesozoic Era, 225 to 65 million years ago, when the continents were much closer than today. At one time, much of the land was one giant continent called Pangaea. This great mass broke up over many millions of years, and segments drifted apart to become our present continents.

No man has ever seen a dinosaur – man did not appear on earth until a mere 2 to 3 million years ago. So how do we know so much about dinosaurs?

Fossil Finds

Our knowledge comes from fossils, which have been discovered all over the world. Fossil skeletons, eggs, nesting sites, tracks, dung, imprints of skin, and even mummified stomach contents have been found. New finds constantly update our view of the dinosaurs and their world.

When Pachycephalosaurus lived

The Mesozoic Era is divided into three periods— Triassic, Jurassic and the Cretaceous. Pachycephalosaurus lived at the end of the Cretaceous period, which lasted from 135 to 65 million years. The word Cretaceous means chalk. During this time great beds of chalk were formed and the continents took on their present shapes. At the start of the Cretaceous period the weather was mild, but by the end it was quite a lot colder.

The land was low-lying, and it was a time of high sea levels, with many deltas, rivers, lakes and swamps. Many new types of plants evolved during the Cretaceous period. Flowering plants appeared for the first time. Many of these plants have survived and would be familiar to us today.

All about Pachycephalosaurus

Pachycephalosaurus belonged to a group of dinosaurs called Pachycephalosaurus, meaning "thick-headed reptiles." At 26 feet (8m) long, Pachycephalosaurus was the largest of a group of thirteen known types. These have been found as widely apart as North America, Asia, England and Madagascar.

160

Pachycephalosaurus was a herbivore (plant eater) who walked upright on its hind legs. It probably lived in small herds in the drier highland areas, much as goats do today.

Pachycephalosaurus had a high domed skull with a massively thickened skull roof. It is presumed that the males would have defended their territories by having "head-butting" contests. Present day goats and rams behave the same way.

Pachycephalosaurus lived 75 to 64 million years ago. The relationship of Pachycephalosaurus to other groups of dinosaurs is still unclear.

**

Stegosaurus (above), like Pachycephalosaurus, was discovered in North America.

Psittacosaurus and the Cretaceous World

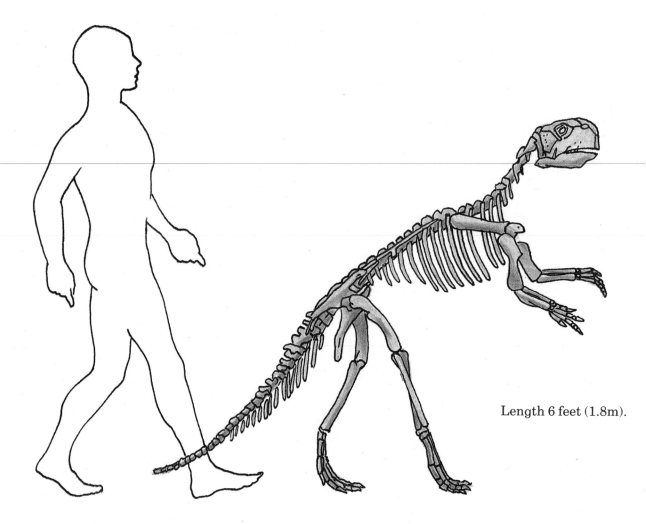

Length 6 feet (1.8m).

The skeleton of Psittacosaurus compared in size with a man

The Age of the Dinosaurs

The word *dinosaur* is derived from two Greek words meaning "terrible lizard." All the dinosaurs lived in the Mesozoic Era, 225 to 65 million years ago, at a time when the continents were much closer to each other than today.
At one time much of the land was one giant continent called Pangaea. This great mass broke up over many millions of years—and segments drifted apart to become our present-day continents.

No human being has ever seen a dinosaur. Humans did not even appear on Earth until 2 to 3 million years ago. How then do we know so much about the dinosaurs?

Fossil Finds

Our knowledge has come from fossils that have been discovered all over the world. People have found fossil skeletons, eggs, nesting sites, tracks, dung, imprints of skin, and even mummified stomach contents. Every day new finds change our view of the dinosaurs and their world.

When Psittacosaurus Lived

The Mesozoic Era is divided into three periods: Triassic, Jurassic, and Cretaceous. Psittacosaurus lived in the middle of the Cretaceous period, which lasted from 135 to 65 million years ago. The word *Cretaceous* means "chalk". During this period, great beds of chalk were laid down and the continents took on their present-day shapes. At the start of the Cretaceous period the weather was mild, but by the end it was quite a lot colder.

The land was low-lying and it was a time of high sea levels with many deltas, rivers, lakes and swamps. Many new types of plants evolved during the Cretaceous period. Flowering plants appeared for the first time. By the end of the Cretaceous period many trees and plants that are familiar to us today existed.

All About Psittacosaurus

Psittacosaurus lived in Mongolia. He was a Ceratopsian (horned face) dinosaur. It is probable he could use his hands both to grasp foliage and to walk. The long tail was used as a counterbalance when he ran; he would have relied on speed to escape predators.

The arrival of many new types of plants probably caused the evolution of Psittacosaurus's parrot-like beak, which enabled him to crop them.

Two of the tiniest dinosaur remains ever found were skulls of baby Psittacosaurus. The young would have been 16 inches (40cm) and 10 inches (25cm) long. They had large eyes, and their teeth were already worn from eating plant food.

Psittacosaurus probably laid eggs like Bractrosaurus, but no one knows how much parental care they gave their young.

Psittacosaurus and Pterosaur (above) have similar parrot-like beaks.

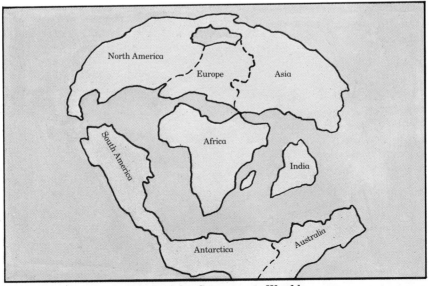

Map of the Cretaceous World

Rutiodon and the Triassic Era

The skeleton of Rutiodon compared in size with a man

The time of Rutiodon

The beginning of the Mesozoic Era was the Triassic Period. It was called Triassic because three rock layers ("tri" means three) dating from this period were found in Germany.

The Triassic Period was between 225 and 193 million years ago.

Rutiodon lived during the Late or Upper Triassic Period; that is, in the second half, some 190 million years ago.

The land of Rutiodon

By the Late Triassic Period, the vast supercontinent Pangaea had split up to form Laurasia to the north and Gondwanaland to the South. Laurasia included modern North America, Europe and Asia. This is where Rutiodon lived.

Rutiodon lived near pools and rivers, just as crocodiles do today.

The family tree of Rutiodon

Rutiodon belonged to the Thecodonts, or "socket-toothed" reptiles. These were very important families since they led to the crocodiles, dinosaurs and Pterosaurs.

The family tree of Rutiodon

Thecodonts evolved 226 million years ago, right at the beginning of the Triassic Period. The first were the Proterosuchians. These were heavy sprawling creatures. They were followed by the Pseudosuchians, which were much lighter and more nimble. Then came the Aetosaurs, the armored plant-eaters, and finally the flesh-eating Phytosaurs.

Rutiodon was a Phytosaur. Fish-eating Phytosaurs dominated rivers and pools until they were replaced by crocodiles. They looked very similar to crocodiles. The only difference was that their nostrils were close to their eyes, while a crocodile's are at the end of its snout.

Other flesh-eaters

During the Triassic Period, two kinds of meat-eaters evolved: large and small. The small meat-eaters were called Coelurosaurs. They made up for their size with their speed. One of the most successful was Coelophysis. This creature was about 10 feet in length, with a long thin tail to balance it when it ran. Its bones were thin and delicate to keep its bodyweight light.

The large meat-eaters were the Carnosaurs. Many scientists think that Ornithosuchus was the first of the Carnosaurs. It was the most fearsome dinosaur of its time. Its only real enemy was another Ornithosuchus.

Among the fish eaters was Cyclotosaurus. As large as a crocodile, Cyclotosaurus had weak legs and needed to stay in water to support its body. It opened its mouth by raising its skull rather than dropping its lower jaw.

Plant-eaters

Plateosaurus was a lizard-hipped dinosaur, almost 20 feet long, that lived in the lowland swamps. It was a Prosauropod and the forerunner of giants like Diplodocus. It shared its environment with numerous amphibians. Among the amphibians, Mastodonsaurus was by far the largest. Its skull alone was over three feet long.

Stagnolepis looked fiercer than it was. It was an Aetorsaur, one of the armor-plated plant-eaters. It had a pig-like nose and weak teeth.

Henodus was a reptile which looked like a turtle. In fact Placodonts like Henodus did eventually evolve into marine turtles.

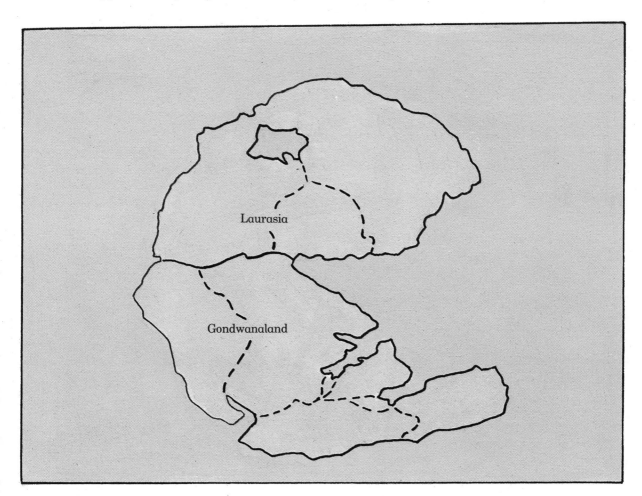

Map of the Triassic period

Scolosaurus and the Cretaceous World

The skeleton of Scolosaurus compared in size with a man

The time of Scolosaurus

Although fossilized remains of Scolosaurus are very rare, there is enough evidence to suggest that Scolosaurus lived at the very end of the age of dinosaurs; that is, in the late Cretaceous period, between 100 million and 65 million years ago. The reason there are so few remains is that Scolosaurus lived in the upland areas, where no sediments were formed. Most of our evidence about dinosaurs comes from sedimentary rocks.

The land of Scolosaurus

The Cretaceous period was a time of immense change. Seas divided the northern supercontinent of Laurasia in two, to form Asiamerica (eastern Asia and western North America) and Euramerica (Europe and eastern North America). The collision of Europe and North and South America, which were joined for the first time, began to push up the present day Rockies and the Andes.

Scientists think that Scolosaurus probably lived at the foot of these new mountain ranges. Scolosaurus must have been a successful dinosaur, since remains have been found throughout the northern hemisphere, in Asia, Europe and North America. No remains have been found in the southern continents of Africa, India, and Australia.

This is because the continents had separated from the northern landmass, so the dinosaurs were no longer able to move from one to the other.

The family tree of Scolosaurus.

Scolosaurus belonged to the family of Ankylosaurs, or "armored dinosaurs." The earliest Ankylosaur was probably Scelidosaurus, who lived in early Jurassic times, 195 million years ago. The family of more than 30 types of Ankylosaurs developed into two distinct branches. On the one side there were the lightweight Ankylosaurs, with narrow heads and without tail weapons. On the other side there were the heavyweight Ankylosaurs, armored like tanks and armed with a spike or club on their tails.

Scolosaurs, an advanced member of the Ankylosaur family, belonged to the armored branch.

Other plant-eaters

Plant-eating dinosaurs dominated the late Cretaceous period. Besides the Ankylosaurs, the other main plant-eaters were the Hadrosaurs and the Ceratopsians. Parasaurolophus, was a striking-looking Hadrosaur, with a hollow crest that measured over six feet from the snout to tip. Trachodon, or Anatosaurus as it is alternately named, was a flat-headed Hadrosaur. Both these creatures were harmless and inoffensive creatures. Their defence lay in flight rather than fight.

Other plant-eaters, however, were not so docile. Ceratopsians were like rhinoceroses, with heavy bodies, sturdy legs and horns on their faces. Some of them, like Styracosaurus, had a frill of spikes round their necks. Their formidable features were enough to drive away any meat-eating dinosaur.

Meat-eaters

Carnivorous dinosaurs had an important function in the late Cretaceous period. By preying on the plant-eating dinosaurs, they prevented the forests from becoming over-browsed. The most impressive meat-eaters were Tyrannosaurus and his cousin, Gorgosaurus. But other, smaller meat-eaters could be equally fearsome. Dromaeosaurus, one of the family of Coelurosaurs, made up for his size with a sickle claw, which he used to attack far larger creatures.

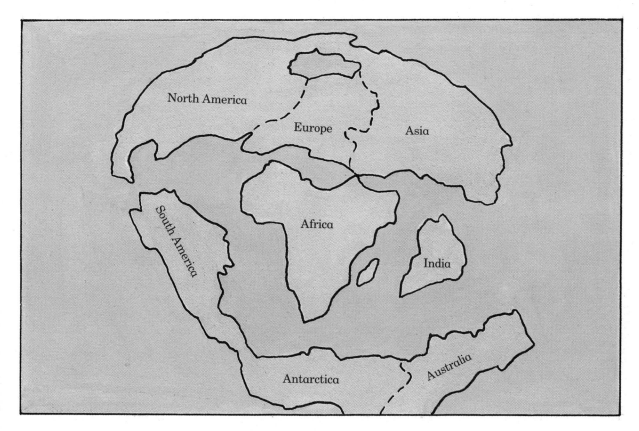

Map of the Cretaceous World

Spinosaurus and the Cretaceous World

A speculative skeleton of Spinosaurus compared in size to a man.

The time of Spinosaurus

The Mesozoic Era, or the "age of dinosaurs" as it is sometimes known, was between 225 million years ago and 65 million years ago. Geologists divide the era into three periods: the Triassic, the Jurassic and the Cretaceous.

The first two periods are much shorter than the third. The Cretaceous Period lasted for 71 million years. Spinosaurus lived at some time during this period.

The land of Spinosaurus

In the Cretaceous Period, the continents separated and acquired something like the shape they have today. The continent of Africa separated from Europe and Asia.

Spinosaurus lived in North Africa. Fossils have been found in Egypt, which is why Palaeontologists have called it *Spinosaurus aegypticus*. The climate of North Africa was then subtropical and more moist than it is today.

The family tree of Spinosaurus

Spinosaurus belonged to the Carnosaur family. Carnosaurs evolved in the Triassic Period. They soon achieved large sizes. Teratosaurus, who lived 200 million years ago, was 20 feet long. In the Jurassic Period, Carnosaurs like Megalosaurus (the first dinosaur to have been discovered in 1822) and Allosaurus appeared. This branch of the family developed into the fearsome Tyrannosaurus in the Cretaceous Period.

Another branch resulted in Spinosaurus, who is an interesting example of how a Carnosaur adapted to climatic conditions. Most Carnosaurs lived in forests, swamps and jungles. Spinosaurus lived on the edge of the desert. It evolved its sail to cope with the intense heat, just as Dimetrodon did in the Permian Period.

Other meat-eaters

Spinosaurus had many meat-eating

competitors. Chief among them was his Carnosaur cousin, Tyrannosaurus. But there were others like the enormous Quetzalcoatlus. This was a Pterosaur and probably the largest flying creature that ever lived. The creature had a wingspan of 39 feet and weighed more than 180 pounds. It scavenged for food, feeding on the bodies of dead dinosaurs.

Plant-eaters

Once the southern continents, like Africa, had separated from the northern continents, the dinosaurs were no longer free to move throughout the world. This meant that dinosaurs evolved differently in different parts of the world.

In the northern continents, like North America, a new generation of highly successful plant-eaters evolved – the Hadrosaurs, the Ankylosaurs and the Ceratopsians. However, these same types never evolved in the southern continents such as Africa. In these continents, plant-eaters continued to be slow-moving, slow-witted Sauropods like Brachiosaurus and Parrosaurus. They were easy prey for the meat-eaters.

Some plant-eaters did evolve that were able to escape from Carnosaurs. One of these is Ouranosaur.

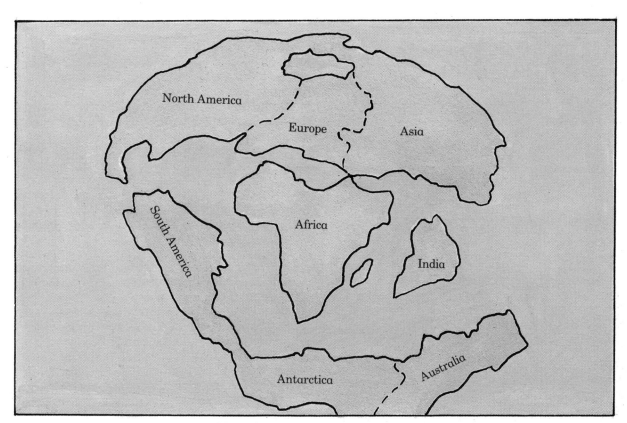

Map of the Cretaceous World

Albertosaurus
(al-BER-tuh-sawr-us)

Albertosaurus was a carnosaur. Carnosaurs were giant flesh eaters with big heads carrying powerful jaws and huge teeth. They had large bodies with powerful back legs and very short front legs. Albertosaurus had slightly longer front legs than *Tyrannosaurus*, a close relative.

Many skeletons of Albertosaurus have been found in the western United States and Canada, and in Mongolia. It is one of the most frequently found kinds of dinosaur fossils. For a long time, scientists thought that certain fossil bones discovered in different places were from separate kinds of dinosaurs. Now, they recognize them all as belonging to the Albertosaurus.

Because Albertosaurus was lighter than *Tyrannosaurus*, it was probably faster. Albertosaurus was about 16 feet tall. It had more teeth than *Tyrannosaurus* and could slash its way into the flesh of its victims, tearing them to pieces before swallowing them.

Length: 26 feet
Weight: 2 tons
Lived: Late Cretaceous
Found: North America

Allosaurus
(Al-uh-sawr-us)

Allosaurus is one of the most fearsome eating machines of the dinosaur age. Remains of these gigantic, flesh-eating dinosaurs have been found in North America, Africa, Australia, and Asia. In one field, scientists found remains of more than 40 Allosaurus.

Allosaurus had a head more than 3 feet long. With jaws hinged like those of a snake, it could swallow its prey whole. Its teeth were curved and up to 4 inches in length. Allosaurus was different from other flesh-eating dinosaurs. It had a ridge along the top of its skull and strange bumps above its eyes. The animal had powerful muscles and a strong tail to give it balance. With only small front legs it had to run and fight on its two powerful back legs. Allosaurus had a single claw 6 inches long on each finger. With these it could slash and tear the flesh of its prey. On each foot were three toes, each with a claw-like talon.

Allosaurus belonged to a family that lived successfully for about 100 million years. It would attack slow, lumbering dinosaurs like *Apatosaurus*. One fossil *Apatosaurus* skeleton has been found with Allosaurus tooth marks on its tail bones.

Length: 36 feet
Weight: 2 tons
Lived: Late Jurassic
Found: North America, Africa, Australia, Asia

Altispinax
(al-tuh-SPY-nax)

This unusual dinosaur lived over 120 million years ago. Fossil bones have been found in England, and it is likely that the animal roamed throughout Europe. Altispinax means "high thorn." Its name comes from the large spines on its back. Each spine was four times longer than the individual back bones it was attached to. A skin probably covered the spines, giving the dinosaur a sail-like fan across its back.

Altispinax was not as big as others in its family. With a length of about 25 feet it was not as big as *Spinosaurus*, which was 40 feet long. All members of this family were flesh eaters. They had sets of small, very sharp teeth. Like other flesh eaters, Altispinax had strong back legs and small, short arms. The sail, or back fin, probably helped the animal cool down in hot climates. Some scientists believe it may have been used to frighten other animals.

Length: 26 feet
Weight: 3 tons
Lived: Early Cretaceous
Found: Northwest Europe

Anatosaurus
(ah-NAT-uh-sawr-us)

One of the last dinosaurs to become extinct, Anatosaurus lived 65 million years ago. Anatosaurus was a duckbill dinosaur and belonged to a family that had jaws shaped like a duck's beak. They were called hadrosaurids and lived for more than 60 million years. Anatosaurus was a typical hadrosaurid. It had up to 1,000 tiny teeth in its mouth for munching vegetation. Many types of Hadrosaurids had a crest, each type shaped differently. Anatosaurus had no crest, but had instead a smooth, rounded head. Anatosaurus had strong back legs and could probably run very fast.

Anatosaurus was built to eat plants, leaves, and small shrubs. One set of remains has been found with pine needles in its stomach, along with seeds and fruit! They could stand erect on their back legs and nibble high branches or rest on their front legs and munch plants. If threatened, they could probably rear up and dash away at great speed. They had strong tails that provided balance when they were running on their back legs. Some Anatosaurus remains have been found with pieces of skin preserved. This is a very unusual find, and scientists have studied the skin carefully. Anatosaurus skin had a pebbly texture, like the skin of a lizard.

Anchiceratops
(ANG-kee-sair-a-tops)

Length: 30 feet
Weight: 3 tons
Lived: Late Cretaceous
Found: Canada

Anchiceratops was on earth for only a few million years, beginning about 69 million years ago. Like all the other dinosaurs, it became extinct 65 million years ago. Anchiceratops belonged to the ceratopsian (horned dinosaur) family and was about 17 feet long. All ceratopsians had a frill made of bone growing from the back of the head. Attached to the frill were very powerful muscles that worked its big jaws. Anchiceratops had a particularly large frill and a massive parrot beak. Three horns grew along the top of its face, two above its eyes and one on its beak.

Anchiceratops roamed the vast plains of Canada during the Cretaceous period, when lush vegetation was plentiful. It liked to crunch tough roots and probably grazed in large herds. They did not eat meat but their tough hides would have protected them well. Only vicious flesh eaters like *Tyrannosaurus Rex* would have been a match for Anchiceratops.

Length: 19 feet, 6 inches
Weight: 7 tons
Lived: Late Cretaceous
Found: Canada

Ankylosaurus
(ang-KILE-uh-sawr-us)

This was the largest, heaviest, and most heavily defended of the ankylosaurid (fused lizard) family to which it belonged. It was more than 32 feet long, weighed 5 tons, and had lots of armor plates over its body. Ankylosaurids were armored dinosaurs with short legs and barrel-shaped bodies. They had short necks and stood low on the ground. Bony slabs, plates, and spikes were set into its skin, under which the flesh grew thick like panels of leather. Dinosaurs of this type had small teeth and jaws with very little muscle power.

Ankylosaurus was one of the most successful of its family at surviving. A great many of them were around at the end of the dinosaur age. They had evolved from earlier types more vulnerable to predators. Several fossil skeletons have been found in Canada, and most seemed to have survived by hiding under their armor. Ankylosaurus had a large bony club at the end of its tail. With this, the dinosaur probably lashed out at flesh eaters, knocking them off their feet or crushing their skulls.

Length: 35 feet
Weight: 1—5 tons
Lived: Late Cretaceous
Found: United States, Canada

Apatosaurus
(ah-PAT-uh-sawr-us)

One of the largest dinosaurs that ever walked the earth, Apatosaurus appeared around 155 million years ago and was a member of the great sauropod (four-legged plant eater) family. All sauropods had stiff limbs and thick legs. Animals like these were slow, lumbering beasts that spent most of their lives eating leaves and large plants. Big animals need a lot of food to satisfy their hunger, and dinosaurs were no exception.

Apatosaurus was once called *Brontosaurus*, or "thunder lizard," because people assume it must have shaken the earth when it walked. After all, it did weigh more than 30 tons. Apatosaurus had a very long neck that stretched more than 20 feet from its shoulder to its head. Scientists used to think the head was small but recent discoveries have shown it to be quite large. It had small teeth shaped like pegs and spent a long time chewing its food. Because these dinosaurs had small brains, scientists used to believe they were stupid. Modern scientists now suspect that they were more intelligent.

Length: 70 feet
Weight: 33 tons
Lived: Late Jurassic
Found: United States (Colorado, Oklahoma, Utah, Wyoming)

Archaeopteryx
(ar-kee-OP-ter-ix)

Although many scientists do not consider this a dinosaur at all, others think it was. Its name means "ancient feathers," and it is the earliest known animal to have feathers like a bird. The collarbone and some hip and foot bones, though, are more like dinosaur bones. Archaeopteryx had small muscles and three claws on each foot, with three-clawed fingers half way along each wing. Unlike birds, which have no teeth, this animal had small teeth. It also had scales on its face. From these facts it is possible to show that Archaeopteryx could not have flown very well. It would have fluttered around just above the ground like a frightened chicken.

Archaeopteryx is believed to be the link between land dinosaurs and true birds. For that reason, some scientists claim it is not a dinosaur at all, but the first real bird. It probably got its feathers from scales that split and allowed air to pass through. This would help Archaeopteryx get airborne – but just barely! It was probably descended from *Compsognathus*, which had a long neck, a very long tail, and light bones, just like Archaeopteryx.

Length: 3 feet
Weight: 20 pounds
Lived: Late Jurassic
Found: England, southern West Germany, United States

Bagaceratops
(bah-gah-SAIR-uh-tops)

A ceratopsian (horned dinosaur), this little plant eater was only 3 feet long. He was an earlier member of the family to which *Anchiceratops* belonged. Bagaceratops had a relatively small face with a parrot-like beak. This helped the animal tear up small roots and shrubs to eat. He had no teeth.

Horned dinosaurs are famous for their neck frills made of bone and their several large horns. Bagaceratops had only one small horn just above its beak. It also had a small neck frill and would have been easy prey for flesh-eating dinosaurs. Bagaceratops has been found in Mongolia, and it is not known if they were common throughout the world. Compared to other horned dinosaurs, Bagaceratops looked like a small rhinoceros and may have lived in small groups for survival. Unlike other horned dinosaurs, Bagaceratops could not stand on its back legs.

Length: 3 feet, 3 inches
Weight: 1000 pounds
Lived: Late Cretaceous
Found: Mongolia

Barapasaurus
(bah-RAH-puh-sawr-us)

Barapasaurus means "big leg lizard" and is a combination of Indian and Greek words. It is called Barapasaurus because it had large legs. Unlike most other sauropod (lizard feet) dinosaurs, Barapasaurus did not have thick legs. Its limbs were long and slim, and it had a short head and spoon-shaped teeth. Some scientists believe it should belong in a family of its own. [Most put it among a group of lizard-foot dinosaurs separate from other groups like *Diplodocus* and *Brachiosaurus*.] The most notable difference between Barapasaurus and other sauropods is that it had longer legs, a taller neck, and a comparatively shorter tail. Scientists used to think dinosaurs like these spent all their life in lakes or rivers. They now think Barapasaurus lived by grazing and eating almost continuously. Dinosaurs like Barapasaurus first appeared almost 200 million years ago. They led to large numbers of giant plant eaters found all over the world. Barapasaurus probably died out around 150 million years ago.

Length: 60 feet
Weight: 28 tons
Lived: Early Jurassic
Found: Central India

Brachiosaurus
(BRAK-ee-uh-sawr-us)

This dinosaur has a length of more than 75 feet. It is one of the biggest ever found. The first Brachiosaurus was discovered in 1900 at the Grand River Valley, Colorado. When scientists put its bones together they discovered that its front legs were much longer than its back legs. This is why they called it Brachiosaurus, which means "arm lizard." All other dinosaurs had their longest legs at the back.

Brachiosaurus has a very long neck and a small head with little teeth. Its back is strong and arched with a relatively short tail. Brachiosaurus was very bulky and probably weighed more than 75 tons. It could have looked over the top of a three-story building and probably munched vegetation from tall trees.

Some people used to think Brachiosaurus lived in water, keeping only its long neck above the surface. Scientists now think it roamed around on land. It may have had a long trunk from the two big nostrils on the top of its head. No one knows for sure. Its been 130 million years since Brachiosaurus roamed the earth, and only the bones have survived.

Length: 70–90 feet
Weight: 80–100 tons
Lived: Late Jurassic
Found: United States (Colorado), Algeria, Tanzania

Brachyceratops
(brak-ee-SAIR-uh-tops)

One of the smallest of the short-frilled ceratopsids (horned dinosaurs), Brachyceratops has been named from a group of only five fossils. These were found together in one place in Montana. Each dinosaur was about 6 feet long. Some scientists thought they were not just small ceratopsids. They thought they were baby *Monoclonius* dinosaurs. The bones certainly looked like them and had the same features. Then the fossils of an adult were found, and now most scientists agree that these five examples represent a special type within the family of horned dinosaurs.

Brachyceratops had a very short neck frill made of bone. It was not unlike *Bagaceratops*, although it had two horns above its eyebrows in addition to a large horn on its nose. Brachyceratops lived about 75 million years ago, or 4 million years after Bagaceratops. It may be an early member of the family that led to *Monoclonius* and the giant *Triceratops*. All these were short-frilled dinosaurs.

There were many members of the short-frilled ceratopsian family, including *Centrosaurus, Eoceratops, Monoclonius, Pachyrhinosaurus* and *Styracosaurus*. All had horns, short neck frills made of bone, and scaly skins. Some had holes in their neck frills, while others did not. Some members of the family had bony spikes, and all known members of the family came from North America. Of course, it is always possible that some fossil remains may be found outside this region, but it is unlikely.

Length: 6 feet
Weight: 500 pounds
Lived: Late Cretaceous
Found: United States (Montana), Canada

Brontosaurus. See *Apatosaurus*.

Camarasaurus
(KAM-uh-ruh-sawr-us)

Camptosaurus
(KAMP-tuh-sawr-us)

In several ways, Camarasaurus is similar to *Brachiosaurus*, except it is smaller. Like all other dinosaurs (excluding *Brachiosaurus*), its back legs are longer than its front legs. It has nostrils on top of its head, its neck is fairly short, and it has a deep skull and small teeth. The discovery of baby Camarasaurus fossils has helped scientists understand how dinosaurs looked as they grew up. When born they had big heads, short necks, and stubby tails. They changed as they developed.

The brain of Camarasaurus was small compared to its body. Its nose was on top of its head, just in front of its eyes. These dinosaurs must have led a lazy, peaceful life. Their size and tough hide would not make them good prey for flesh eaters, who probably left them alone. Camarasaurus probably wandered through the swamp and forest continually munching. Its little mouth had to feed a very large body.

Length: 60 feet
Weight: 20 tons
Lived: Late Jurassic
Found: United States (Colorado, Oklahoma, Utah, Wyoming)

This one animal gave its name to an entire family of dinosaurs called "bent lizards" (camptosaurids). They are known to have lived more than 140 million years ago, during the late Jurassic period. Camptosaurids had strong back legs with hooves on their feet. This allowed them to run away from trouble quickly. Camptosaurids are named for their thigh bones, which were bent. They would sometimes stand erect and use their long tongues to pull leaves and foliage from shrubs.

Camptosaurus varied in size from 4 feet to nearly 20 feet. It had a small horned beak with which it could cut leaves and thin branches. Like many other dinosaurs, Camptosaurus could breathe while it chewed. This was possible because the passage that led from its mouth to its stomach was different from the passage that led from its nose to its lungs. Camptosaurus has been found in Europe and North America. It was an ancestor of the family of *Iguanodon*. It was more primitive, however, with four toes on each foot and without a spike on its thumb.

Length: 23 feet
Weight: 1,100 pounds
Lived: Late Jurassic/Early Cretaceous
Found: Western Europe, western North America

Centrosaurus
(SEN-truh-sawr-us)

This dinosaur belonged to the family of short-frilled ceratopsians (horned dinosaurs). Others were the tiny *Brachyceratops* and the much larger *Monoclonius* and *Pachyrhinosaurus.* These were almost as big as Centrosaurus. Like *Monoclonius,* Centrosaurus had a single horn on the top of its nose that curved forward instead of back. It also had a bumpy frill with two pieces of bone shaped like hooks. Centrosaurus had small hooves like a rhinoceros and very thick legs. Each back leg had four stumpy toes and each front foot had five "fingers." Centrosaurus had very strong jaw muscles to help it grind tough food. Scientists believe Centrosaurus traveled in herds. A single fossil find of eighteen separate animals has been discovered in Alberta. The most famous ceratopsian dinosaur is *Triceratops.* They lived mostly in great herds and roamed far and wide for root food and plants. In this way they must have been like great herds of bison ambling across the prairie.

Length: 20 feet
Weight: 2 tons
Lived: Late Cretaceous
Found: Canada (Alberta)

Ceratosaurus
(sair-AT-o-sawr-us)

Ceratosaurus means "horned lizard" and was so named because it belonged to an unusual family of horned flesh eaters. It is thought to have been related to *Allosaurus*, another flesh eater. But Ceratosaurus is the only dinosaur of its kind known to have had a horn on its nose. Ceratosaurus was up to 20 feet long and had a row of small, bony plates running down its back. It had short front legs with four fingers, each with a small claw. Each foot had three toes, also clawed. Ceratosaurus had a large head and a lightweight bone structure. Its teeth were shaped for tearing flesh and killing large animals.

Ceratosaurus probably hunted in packs. Scientists have discovered sets of Ceratosaurus footprints, suggesting that they roamed in groups. It probably lived about the same time as *Megalosaurus* but a long time before *Tyrannosaurus*, another flesheater. Dinosaurs like these would have been feared by all other animals. They were big and powerful and had large appetites.

Cetiosaurus
(SEET-ee-o-sawr-us)

This animal is one of the earliest plant-eating dinosaurs discovered. It probably lived at about the same time *Barapasaurus* roamed the earth. Cetiosaurus belonged to the same group of dinosaurs as *Diplodocus* and probably appeared around 190 million years ago. Scientists can tell that it is an early type, because its bones are not as well developed as other dinosaurs of its family. While others had lightweight back bones, hollowed out to save weight, Cetiosaurus had solid back bones. This observation helps scientists place Cetiosaurus several million years before *Diplodocus*, *Brachiosaurus*, and other types.

Cetiosaurus looked a lot like *Camarasaurus* and had a tail similar to *Diplodocus*. It was smaller than *Camarasaurus* and weighed about 10 tons. Cetiosaurus may have wallowed in rivers and lakes. Scientists are not sure how it lived. They think it probably went down to the water to cool off and wash just like the hippopotamus does today.

Length: 20 feet
Weight: 1 ton
Lived: Late Jurassic
Found: United States (Oklahoma, Colorado, Utah), East Africa

Length: 45–60 feet
Weight: 9–12 tons
Lived: Middle to Late Jurassic
Found: Western Europe, North Africa

Chasmosaurus
(KAZ-muh-sawr-us)

Chasmosaurus was a member of the ceratopsian (horned dinosaur) family and similar to *Anchiceratops*. Although smaller than its cousin, Chasmosaurus was a typical horned dinosaur. It had a large neck frill made of bone. Large holes in the bony plate reduced the weight of the neck frill. This made it easier for Chasmosaurus to move its head around. Strong neck muscles were attached to the frill. It needed these to pull out the roots of tough plants. Chasmosaurus had the parrot-like beak of other horned dinosaurs. The frill was longer than the skull itself and covered with skin.

Many Chasmosaurus fossil bones have been found in Alberta. Skin impressions on rock show it had small button-like scales all over its body. With these, its hide was probably quite tough.

Animals like *Tyrannosaurus* would have had a hard time trying to bite through its leathery skin. Their best defense would have been to run away!

Length: 17 feet
Weight: 3—5 tons
Lived: Late Cretaceous
Found: United States (New Mexico), Canada (Alberta)

Coelophysis
(see-lo-FISE-iss)

One of the very first dinosaurs, Coelophysis was known to have lived more than 210 million years ago. In 1947, scientists found more than a hundred skeletons at Ghost Ranch, New Mexico. There were many animals of different ages, and they ranged between 3 feet and 10 feet in length. This discovery has led scientists to believe that they lived in colonies and wandered about in large herds.

Coelophysis was a nimble dinosaur and could probably run very fast. It had slim legs, a long neck and tail and a pointed head with sharp teeth. Feeding on a diet of meat, Coelophysis had three fingers on each hand and a strong muscle joining its hips to its spine. This muscle probably enabled it to twist and turn as it ran, chasing small animals on which it fed.

Some fossil remains of a Coelophysis show babies inside what would have been its stomach. This causes some people to wonder if they were cannibals, eating their young when other food got scarce. Some scientists think they gave birth to live young. Other dinosaurs laid eggs.

Length: 10 feet
Weight: 65 pounds
Lived: Late Triassic
Found: Southwestern West Germany

Coelurus
(see-LURE-us)

Although Coelurus (hollow tail) first appeared around 160 million years ago, it was directly descended from *Coelophysis*. Coelurus was a small, nimble animal about 6 feet long. It had hollow bones for lightness and only three fingers on each hand. The thumb was short but the other two fingers each had a small claw. Coelurus was similar in appearance to *Ornitholestes*, another member of the same family.

Coelurus's head was slightly smaller than a man's hand. In its mouth were rows of small but jagged teeth. These helped it tear small pieces of flesh. Coelurus probably fed on small birds, tiny animals, and dead mammals. With its light weight and strong muscles, it could easily tear through the undergrowth, its head held low, grasping and snatching at wildlife within reach. Some of these small dinosaurs might have fed on the eggs of bigger dinosaurs. They may also have eaten berries or large seeds.

Length: 6 feet, 6 inches
Weight: 30 pounds
Lived: Late Jurassic
Found: United States (Wyoming)

Compsognathus
(komp-so-NAY-thus)

These small, fast running dinosaurs lived at the same time *Coelurus* was known to have been in North America. Compsognathus fossils have been found in Europe. They are among the smallest dinosaurs known. The adults were no more than 2 feet long, about the size of a chicken. They had long necks and very long tails. The stiff tail helped them run very fast and gave them balance. Each hand had two fingers and each finger had a claw. Their legs, twice as long as their arms, had three toes on each foot.

Compsognathus means "pretty jaw." Its long, pointed head held two rows of sharp teeth, and it is known to have eaten meat. It had hollow bones, which made it very light. Each animal probably weighed less than 7 pounds. This little dinosaur

may have been an egg hunter. There would have been many eggs around in the dinosaur age. Some would have been large enough to provide a juicy meal for these nimble-footed animals.

It is hard to think of this little creature as a real dinosaur, yet he is as much a dinosaur as big *Tyrannosaurus* or giant *Apatosaurus*.

Length: 2 feet
Weight: 7 pounds
Lived: Late Jurassic
Found: Southern West Germany, southeast France

Corythosaurus
(ko-RITH-uh-sawr-us)

Corythosaurus, whose name means "helmet lizard," had a large crest on top of its head. Corythosaurus belonged to the family of duckbill dinosaurs called hadrosaurids. Among other hadrosaurid members were *Bactrosaurus*, *Lambeosaurus* and *Edmontosaurus*. Corythosaurus appeared after *Bactrosaurus* but just before *Edmontosaurus*. It was the only group of duckbills to have a crest on its head. The crest was hollow, narrow, and shaped like a dinner plate. Females and young had smaller crests than males.

Corythosaurus was probably used to feeding on small lizards, insect colonies, and plants. It had a toothless beak with which it would scoop up its food. From fossil remains it seems to have been about 30 feet long and probably weighed around 3 tons. Its big, heavy tail would be useful for keeping it balanced while it stood on its back legs and slowly munched food.

Length: 33 feet
Weight: 2—4 tons
Lived: Late Cretaceous
Found: United States (Montana), Canada (Alberta)

Dacentrurus
(day-sen-TROO-rus)

Belonged to the family of stegosaurid (roof lizard) dinosaurs of which the most famous was *Stegosaurus*. Decentrurus was only 15 feet long, about half the length of *Stegosaurus*, and weighed less than 1 ton. It was one of the earliest stegosaurids. Members of the stegosaurid family were divided into two groups. Some had bony plates down the top of their backs with spines on the tail. The others had mostly spikes and no plates. Dacentrurus had two rows of spikes along its back and tail. Because of its longer legs it stood higher off the ground than some other stegosaurids. Remains of this dinosaur have been found in England. Like other members of the family, it had three toes on each foot and four fingers on each hand. Dacentrurus had a small head and short teeth for eating soft plants. If attacked, stegosaurids would have little defense against meat-eating dinosaurs. They had large fleshy parts and no means of protecting themselves except with their spikes. If attacked, they could lash out with their spiked tail and damage a predator.

Length: 13 feet
Weight: 1,500 pounds
Lived: Middle to Late Jurassic
Found: England

Deinonychus
(dyne-ON-ik-us)

This dinosaur was one of the most efficient hunters of them all. It belonged to the family dromaeosaurid, or "running lizard." Terrifying flesh eaters like *Tyrannosaurus* would tear large dinosaurs to pieces with their huge teeth and massive jaws. Yet they could probably not move very fast. One dinosaur that could was Deinonychus. This dinosaur was the largest in his family, which also included *Dromaeosaurus* and *Velociraptor*.

Deinonychus means "terrible claw." It was given this name because it had a sickle-shaped toe and claw on each foot. The other three toes on each foot were shorter. When running it would lift the claw up and put the outer toes to the ground. The toe with the big claw would be used to rip the bodies of other dinosaurs. Balancing on one leg, it would slash viciously using strong muscles in its thigh. Its tail had long pieces of bone to make it stiff when running. Small arms and hands each had three clawed fingers. Deinonychus had a large head, good eyesight, and sharp teeth.

Length: 10–11 feet
Weight: 250 pounds
Lived: Early Cretaceous
Found: Western United States

Dicraeosaurus
(dye-CREE-uh-sawr-us)

A member of the same family as *Diplodocus*, this smaller relative appeared in the late Jurassic period, more than 150 million years ago. Dicraeosaurus was one of that large group of lumbering plant eaters that lived for more than 100 million years. It was only 40 feet long and stood 10 feet tall. Its name means "forked lizard" and refers to the bones that make up its spine. Some of its back bones are divided to look like a giant Y. The branches on top had large muscles attached to them. Unlike *Diplodocus*, Dicraeosaurus had solid back bones.

This dinosaur weighed about 6 tons and probably spent most of its life peacefully munching plants and lush vegetation. This peace could end, though, if it was attacked by one or more of the fearsome flesh-eaters. It had little or no defense and might have escaped by walking into deep water. Dinosaurs could not swim and would probably not go into rivers and lakes unless attacked. Large, four-footed ones could wade in and escape.

Length: 43–66 feet
Weight: 6–9 tons
Lived: Late Jurassic
Found: Tanzania

Dilophosaurus
(dye-LO-fuh-sawr-us)

This animal belonged to the megalosaurid (great lizard) family that appeared very early in the Jurassic period, around 200 million years ago. It was related to *Megalosaurus*. Dilophosaurus had a large head and two thin bony crests running from the top of its nose to the back of its head. These gave it its name, which means "two-ridged lizard." When first discovered, scientists thought the crest belonged to another animal because it was found some distance away from the skull. Later discoveries proved the crest came from this dinosaur.

Dilophosaurus had five fingers on each hand. The two inner fingers were very small. The outer fingers had long claws like fangs. These would have been used to lash out at victims, easily ripping into flesh. Its powerful jaws would have easily crushed flesh and bone as it sank its huge teeth into the animal's body. On its feet were three clawed toes and a small "big" toe turned backward.

Length: 20 feet
Weight: 1,500 pounds
Lived: Early Jurassic
Found: United States (Arizona)

Diplodocus
(dih-PLOD-uh-kus)

Diplodocus is one of the most famous of the four-legged prehistoric plant eaters. A complete skeleton of Diplodocus was dug up by the famous Scottish-American millionaire, Andrew Carnegie. It was 88 feet long, including a 26-foot neck and a 45-foot tail. The head was quite small and had two rows of peg-like teeth. These were used to pull leaves from tree branches like a comb rakes through hair.

With its long neck, the dinosaur could see over trees and across great distances. This was just as well. It would not have been a fast mover and proved an easy prey to the big flesh-eaters. Diplodocus weighed more than 11 tons. It needed a special skeleton to support that weight. The dinosaur takes its name, which means "double beam," from small bones beneath the backbone. These had a piece that ran forward as well as another piece that ran back – a double-beamed bone. Diplodocus is one of the longest dinosaurs that ever lived. It is not the heaviest. In fact, for its size, Diplodocus was light. Compare Diplodocus with *Apatosaurus*, which weighed 33 tons and yet was nearly 20 feet shorter in length.

Length: 87 feet
Weight: 7—11 tons
Lived: Late Jurassic
Found: United States (Colorado, Montana, Utah, Wyoming)

Dromaeosaurus
(drom-ee-uh-SAWR-us)

Dromaeosaurus was one of the dromaeosaurid (running lizard) dinosaurs like Deinonychus, but smaller. Fossil remains show it to have been about the size of a man and to have weighed approximately 100 pounds. Its tail was made stiff by rods of bone and helped keep it balanced when running fast. Dromaeosaurus had a large head which contained a big brain. The dinosaur would have been able to balance itself on one leg with the help of its stiff tail while savagely attacking its prey with its clawed toes.

Dromaeosaurus appeared later than its relative, *Deinonychus*, and stalked the earth in the late Cretaceous period, about 70 million years ago. Because Dromaeosaurus was so much smaller it probably had best pickings among the tiny animal life. Many small reptiles and mammals would have been attacked by this fast-moving dinosaur. Dromaeosaurus lived about the same time as *Velociraptor*, although it appeared earlier.

Length: 6 feet
Weight: 100 pounds
Lived: Late Cretaceous
Found: Canada (southern Alberta)

Dromiceiomimus
(dro-miss-ee-o-MY-mus)

This dinosaur belonged to the family of orntho-mimids (ostrich dinosaurs). They were called this because they looked like ostriches with a long tail and no feathers. Unlike most other dinosaurs, ornithomimids were very fast. Nothing could catch them. At full speed, Dromiceiomimis was quicker than a galloping horse. It had a long slender neck and a large head. Although about 12 feet long, its thin, light bones gave it a weight of only 220 pounds. Its neck was long and slender, supporting a large head with a big brain and huge eyes. They had no teeth, but each foot had three toes. Each hand had three spindly fingers, each with a tiny claw.

Dromiceiomimus means "emu mimic." It was named this because it looked like an emu. The dinosaur was in the same family as *Ornithomimus* and *Struthiomimus*. Unless surprised while feeding, it is unlikely that the Dromiceiomimus was easy prey. It probably fed on seeds, small eggs,

insects, or other pickings in woods and on plains. If disturbed, it would lift up its stiff tail, raise its head, and run quickly to safety.

Dromiceiomimus lived at the end of the great age of dinosaurs. Members of the ornithomimid family spanned 100 million years, from the mid-Jurassic to the end of the Cretaceous period. Most ornithomimids lived during the middle to late Cretaceous period. They represent the end of a long line or ostrich dinosaurs that began with the coelophysids in the late Triassic. The most famous coelophysid was *Coelophysis*, which weighed less than one-third the weight of Dromiceiomimus.

Length: 11 feet, 6 inches
Weight: 220 pounds
Lived: Late Cretaceous
Found: Canada (southern Alberta)

Dryosaurus
(DRY-o-sawr-us)

A member of the large group of "bird-footed" dinosaurs, this one belonged to a family known as the gazelles of prehistoric animal life. They were all small and quite fast, with five-fingered hands and four toes on each foot. They chewed plant food and vegetation with small teeth inside horny beaks. These were very successful survivors. The families in this group lived for more than 100 million years. They were among the first "bird-footed" dinosaurs to appear and lived among types like *Camptosaurus*.

Dryosaurus, which means "oak lizard," was the biggest of the group. Some were up to 14 feet long. A nearly complete Dryosaurus skeleton was found in Utah. From this scientists have discovered it had long, agile legs, which gave it speed when in a chase. It had little else to defend itself with. It would probably forage among vegetation and plant life, always bobbing its head up to watch for big preying flesh eaters!

Length: 9–14 feet
Weight: 120–180 pounds
Lived: Middle to Late Jurassic
Found: Eastern England, Romania, Tanzania, United States (Utah)

Dryptosaurus
(DRIP-tuh-sawr-us)

This animal is one of the most mysterious dinosaurs, because nobody has been able to build up a full skeleton. At least 12 fossil specimens have been found, however. The best skeleton was dug up by a famous dinosaur collector in 1866. He called the dinosaur Laelaps. Because somebody had already given that name to an insect it was changed to Dryptosaurus, which means "tearing lizard." This was an appropriate name. Dryptosaurus was a large meat eater like *Tyrannosaurus*. It was about 25 feet long with curved teeth and three large claws on each foot.

Some scientists think this dinosaur may have been a different member of the *Tyrannosaurus* family. Others think it was closely related to *Megalosaurus*. A few have even linked it with *Iguanodon*! The picture shows how Dryptosaurus might have looked when he roamed the earth around 70 million years ago.

Length: 25 feet
Weight: 1 ton
Lived: Late Cretaceous
Found: United States (New Jersey, Maryland, Colorado, Montana, Wyoming)

Edmontosaurus
(ed-MON-tuh-sawr-us)

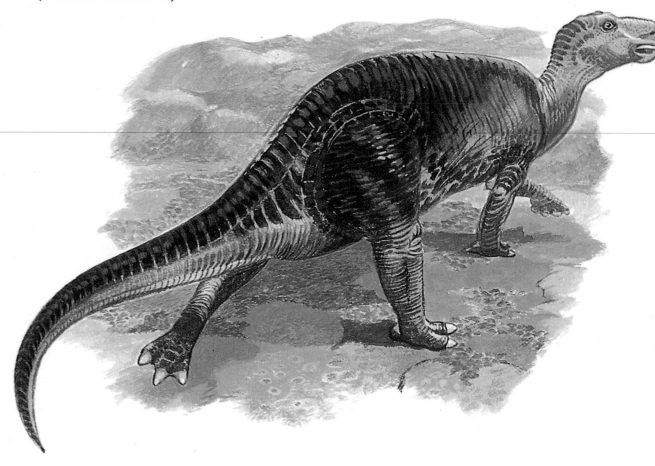

This dinosaur was one of the giants in the large family of duckbill dinosaurs. It was as long as 43 feet and could weigh more than 3 tons. It belonged to the group of "bird-foot" families and appeared during the late Cretaceous period, about 72 million years ago. Edmontosaurus were plentiful: they were known to have lived all over the earth.

Edmontosaurus did not have a bony crest on top of its head, as other duckbills did. Its skull was low in front and high at the back. It fed on plants that needed to be chopped up before being swallowed. To do that it had about a thousand teeth in its soft mouth. Scientists know quite a bit about this dinosaur because they have found so many skeletons.

Some scientists think Edmontosaurus had flaps of skin on each side of its nose. When it blew these up like balloons, they made a loud bellowing sound. Like many other animals, dinosaurs probably used these loud noises to communicate.

Length: 33–42 feet
Weight: 2–3 tons
Lived: Late Cretaceous
Found: United States (New Jersey, Montana) Canada (Alberta)

Elaphrosaurus
(eh-LOFF-ruh-sawr-us)

One of the earliest ornithomimids (ostrich dinosaurs), Elaphrosaurus was a relative of *Dromiceiomimus*, *Gallimimus*, *Ornithomimus*, and *Struthiomimus*. It was probably one of the earliest members of that family and fossil bones have been found that date back to the late Jurassic period. Most "ostrich dinosaurs" are found from the Cretaceous period. A distant relative is *Ornitholestes*, a small dinosaur only half the size of Elaphrosaurus.

With long, slender legs and a stiff tail, Elaphrosaurus would have easily sprinted from danger. It had keen eyes and a quick brain. Its diet probably depended on where it lived. Near the sea it might have grubbed around for shellfish or shoveled sand for tiny creatures. Some lived far inland and others foraged among woods and forests. Since it had no teeth, Elaphrosaurus could not have eaten meat.

Length: 11 feet, 6 inches
Weight: 220 pounds
Lived: Late Jurassic
Found: Algeria, Tanzania, Morocco, Tunisia, Egypt, Niger

Eoceratops
(EE-o-sair-uh-tops)

This medium-sized dinosaur belonged to the large family of ceratopsian (horned dinosaurs). The most famous and largest member of this family was *Triceratops*. With a length of about 20 feet, Eoceratops was much smaller than *Triceratops*. Horned dinosaurs varied in size and had different types of horns. Some, like *Brachyceratops*, were no larger than 6 feet and had only one small horn. These appeared around 75 million years ago. *Triceratops* was huge and had three big horns, two of which were 4 feet or longer. *Triceratops* appeared about 67 million years ago. Eoceratops was an early horned dinosaur. It is thought to date back almost as far as *Brachyceratops* and is best known from fossil bones dug up in Alberta. Three small horns on its face crowned a 3-foot-long skull. A short bony neck frill protected the back of its head from the fangs of meat-eating dinosaurs. Eoceratops means "early horned face." It was probably the earliest of its family type.

Length: 20 feet
Weight: 2—5 tons
Lived: Late Cretaceous
Found: Canada (Alberta)

Erlikosaurus
(er-LIK-uh-sawr-us)

Euhelopus
(you-heh-LO-pus)

One of the big plant-eating dinosaurs similar to *Camarasaurus*, Euhelopus, or "good marsh foot," had a longer neck and nose. Like *Camarasaurus*, it had strong teeth that grew around its jaws. Other dinosaurs of this type had teeth growing only in front. Euhelopus had large nostrils on top of its head. Because of this, some scientists think it had a long trunk. That would have made it look very strange. Both *Camarasaurus* and Euhelopus were camarsaurid (chambered lizard) dinosaurs, with hollow chambers in the backbone.

Euhelopus was a little slimmer than *Camarasaurus*, but large members of the family may have weighed as much as 24 tons. The biggest could have been up to 50 feet in length – without trunk. In this picture, Euhelopus is shown without a trunk. From fossil remains, scientists believed they were at home in marshy land at the bank of muddy rivers or in swamps. They would have been safer there than on dry or wooded land where the big flesh eaters roamed.

This flesh eater was found among remains dug up in Mongolia. It belonged to a strange branch of the big carnosaur (flesh lizard) group. Other families belonged to types like *Tyrannosaurus*, *Allosaurus*, and *Megalosaurus*. Erlikosaurus belonged to the family of "slow lizard," or segnosaurid, dinosaurs. It was named in 1980, and most scientists think it was a direct descendent of *Megalosaurus*. Erlikosaurus appeared late, more than 100 million years after *Megalosaurus* first walked the earth.

Erlikosaurus did not look like *Megalosaurus*, though. It looked more like *Deinonychus* in size, but had longer arms and smaller teeth. Its top lip ended in a toothless beak. It had four toes, each with a long claw. It is believed its feet may have been webbed like a duck's. Other members of the same family were even bigger than Erlikosaurus. One, called *Segnosaurus*, was 30 feet long and stood more than 8 feet tall.

Length: 13 feet
Weight: 280 pounds
Lived: Late Cretaceous
Found: Mongolia

Length: 33–50 feet
Weight: 18–24 tons
Lived: Early Cretaceous
Found: China (Shantung)

Euoplocephalus
(you-op-luh-SEF-uh-lus)

Named for its "well armored head," Euoplocephalus was a member of the family of ankylosaurs. These "fused lizards" were best known by the bones of *Ankylosaurus*, the biggest of them all. There were at least twelve different types within the family and Euoplocephalus was typical in size and weight. It probably weighed nearly 3 tons and has been dug up in places as far apart as Alberta and Sinkiang, which is in northwest China.

All ankylosaurs were about the size of a modern battle tank. They had different arrangements of armored bands down their backs with ridged plates and blunt spikes. Euoplocephalus had round nostrils and a horny, toothless beak. Row upon row of armored back plates helped protect it from predators. At the end of its tail it had a large, bony club. Ankylosaurids were among the last dinosaurs to appear before all dinosaurs became extinct 65 million years ago. Euoplocephalus was well adapted to munching plants and lush greenery while protected from attack.

Two closely related families of ankylosaurs were the "fused lizards" and the "node lizards." Both appeared from a common ancestor at the beginning of the Cretaceous period and have been found all over Europe, North America, and Asia. Node lizards included *Acanthopholis*, *Hylaeosaurus*, *Nodosaurus*, *Panoplosaurus*, and *Silvisaurus*.

Length: 23 feet
Weight: 3 tons
Lived: Late Cretaceous
Found: Canada (Alberta), China (Sinkiang)

193

Fabrosaurus
(FAB-ruh-sawr-us)

Gallimimus
(gall-ih-MY-mus)

With a long neck, bony tail, and strong legs for running, Gallimimus was the largest of the ostrich dinosaurs (ornithomimids). Its name means "fowl mimick" because it seemed to copy the behavior and appearance of certain fowls we know today, like the ostrich and the turkey. With a length of 13 feet, it could probably move quickly on its long legs. Other relatives were *Dromiceiomimus* and *Elaphrosaurus*. Gallimimus had poorly developed hands. They would not have been much use for grasping tiny lizards or tearing open insect nests. Each member of the family of ostrich dinosaurs differed in some way from its relative. Gallimimus had an unusually long snout with a broad, flat end.

Like other members of the family, Gallimimus would quickly sprint away from danger. With long loping legs, it would have looked like an ostrich as it ran. It may have snapped and pecked at dinosaur eggs. Dinosaur eggs were small with thin shells similar to chicken or turkey eggs. A good strong peck from Gallimimus' beak would have been enough to break them open.

Fabrosaurids, or "Fabre's lizards" were among the earliest dinosaurs known. They were small, the largest as tall as a man, and light-boned. Fabrosaurus was only 3 feet long and had hollow limb bones with small arms and long legs. Each hand had five fingers and each foot had four toes. In its relatively small mouth were two rows of ridged teeth. With these, it could grind small roots and shoots. Fabrosaurus had a broad jaw with holes for new teeth to replace old ones.

Fabrosaurus was closely related to *Lesothosaurus* and *Scutellosaurus*. It appeared late in the Triassic period, more than 200 million years ago. Dinosaurs of the fabrosaurid family lived for at least 70 million years and were like the grazing animals of today. They would have been the gazelles and deer of the dinosaur world. From this line of ancient animals came *Heterodontosaurus*, *Hypsilophodon*, *Camptosaurus*, *Iguanodon*, *Hadrosaurus*, *Bactrosaurus*, and many other duckbills, boneheads, and other groups.

Length: 3 feet, 4 inches
Weight: 40 pounds
Lived: Late Triassic/Early Jurassic
Found: South Africa (Lesotho)

Length: 13 feet
Weight: 250 pounds
Lived: Late Cretaceous
Found: Southern Mongolia

Geranosaurus
(jer-AN-uh-sawr-us)

This tiny dinosaur was a close relative of *Heterodontosaurus*, Geranosaurus was among the very first dinosaurs that appeared. They were ancestors of "bird-footed dinosaurs," such as *Fabrosaurus*. Scientists believe they eventually led to the great families of the bonehead dinosaurs like *Pachycephalosaurus*. More than 130 million years before the bonehead dinosaurs, however, the little Geranosaurus roamed large areas of South America and South Africa. At that time, the two countries were joined together. Since then, over millions of years, South America and Africa drifted apart.

Geranosaurus means "crane-lizard." It had tusks as well as teeth that were used for grinding food. Perhaps only males had tusks. Geranosaurus had small tusks in the lower jaw but no sockets for them in the upper jaw. It is believed these little dinosaurs died out around 200 million years ago. Heterodontosaurids did not lead to other, more developed descendents. Yet they came from a line that also produced the "bird-foot" dinosaurs, and scientists think they may still find remains of later members of the heterodontosaurid family. It would not be surprising if they turned up in South America.

Length: 4 feet
Weight: 50 pounds
Lived: Late Triassic/Early Jurassic
Found: South Africa

Hadrosaurus
(HAD-ruh-sawr-us)

This was the first dinosaur from North America to be named. Its bones were dug up in New Jersey, and in 1858 it was given a name that means "different foot." This became the family name for a large group of hadrosaurids. The family also included *Edmontosaurus*, which was much bigger and heavier than Hadrosaurus. All duckbills had flat heads with solid bone crests or humps on top. The shape and size of these features varied among different members of the family. Hadrosaurus had a deep, narrow face. It had two rounded humps, one above each eye socket. Scientists have discovered fossil remains of Hadrosaurus that date back 78 million years, making Hadrosaurus older than *Edmontosaurus*. In fact, they were not very closely related. Both came from an unknown ancestor believed to have been on earth more than 80 million years

ago. Some scientists, however, think both types were much older than this. They have found fossil footprints 120 million years old that look just like those made by Hadrosaurus.

Length: 26—32 feet
Weight: 1—5 tons
Lived: Late Cretaceous
Found: United States (New Jersey, New Mexico), Canada (Alberta)

Herrerasaurus
(her-RAY-rah-sawr-us)

This fearsome meat eater belonged to the group of prosauropod ("before the lizard feet") dinosaurs. Prosauropods go back to the beginning of dinosaur life, 220 million years ago. From these different families came the great and gigantic plant eaters like *Cetiosaurus*, *Brachiosaurus*, *Camarasaurus*, and *Diplodocus*. Herrerasaurus was not the earliest prosauropod, but it was the biggest of its family. Its big head had two rows of teeth shaped like sickles. With long back legs and large front legs, it was probably able to move quickly across rough ground. Its front legs probably helped it climb across rocky land.

From bones dug up in Argentina, Herrerasaurus is known to have been about 10 feet long and to have weighed around 220 pounds. Others in the family have been found in China. Not many are believed to have existed. They did not seem to survive beyond the early Jurassic period, about 200 million years ago.

Length: 10 feet
Weight: 220 pounds
Lived: Late Triassic
Found: Northwest Argentina

Heterodontosaurus
(het-er-uh-DON-tuh-sawr-us)

A close relative of *Geranosaurus*, Heterodontosaurus was more advanced and larger. These small dinosaurs would have been on earth at the same time as *Herrerasaurus* and *Fabrosaurus*. All three kinds date back to the late Triassic, more than 190 million years ago. Heterodontosaurus remains have been found in South Africa, Argentina, and China. This animal had one thing in common with people: three different types of teeth. It had sharp, cutting teeth at the front, fangs at the front of the lower jaw, and molars in the back for grinding.

Heterodontosaurus had three toes on each foot and a claw at the back of its heel. It had five fingers on each hand. Like most other members of this family, Heterodontosaurus was small, about 4 feet long. Some of these dinosaurs had muscles in their cheeks. They probably had a mixed diet of small insects and plant roots, with seeds, nuts, and primitive forms of fruit. Heterodontosaurus had small, grasping hands that could forage and grub around for juicy food. There were no defensive weapons on its body. Only the speed of its legs would help it escape attack.

Length: 4 feet
Weight: 50 pounds
Lived: Late Triassic/Early Jurassic
Found: South Africa

Homalocephale
(ho-mah-luh-SEF-uh-lee)

Its name means "level head" because it had a flat top to its skull. There were several bumps on the top of its head and a pattern of small pits. Most remains come from Mongolia and it was probably about 10 feet long. Homalocephale was one of the large family of "bone-head" dinosaurs that lived about 70 million years ago. They are thought to have descended from the family of *Heterodontosaurus* dinosaurs, which lived more than 110 million years earlier. Homalocephale was closely related to *Pachycephalosaurus*.

Like other members of its family, Homalocephale had a very thick skull. This may have been used to attack others that tried to invade its territory, or it may have been used to play. Animals of today often butt heads in play. Homalocephale probably lived on high slopes and on the sides of mountains. Most of its fossil remains have been washed down from high places by fast-flowing streams. These animals walked on their back legs, using their tails as props when standing.

Length: 10 feet
Weight: 200 pounds
Lived: Late Cretaceous
Found: Mongolia

Hylaeosaurus
(hy-LAY-ee-uh-sawr-us)

This primitive ankylosaur ("armored dinosaur") was closely related to *Acanthopholis*. It lived about 120 million years ago and belonged to the "node lizard" group of ankylosaurs. The other group, called "fused lizards," included *Ankylosaurus*. Hylaeosaurus means "woodland lizard," and it was discovered in southeast England as long ago as 1833. It probably had spikes along the sides of its body and plates jutting up along the tail. Underneath, it had a heavily armored back from its head to its tail.

Unlike the "fused lizard" ankylosaurs, Hylaeosaurus and its relatives did not have a thick, bony tail club. Instead of hitting the attacking predator, it may have stood higher on its legs to run away at the pace of a trotting horse. Hylaeosaurus had weak jaws and small teeth. It would spend its time eating ground plants and large insects. Dinosaurs of the ankylosaur families account for one in ten of all dinosaur remains.

Length: 20 feet
Weight: 2—5 tons
Lived: Early Cretaceous
Found: England

Hypselosaurus
(HIP-sih-luh-sawr-us)

This is one of the lesser known members of the sauropod ("lizard foot") dinosaurs within the family of titanosaurids, or "giant lizards" and was a distant relative of the big plant eaters like *Diplodocus* and *Apatosaurus*. The members of the "giant lizard" family each had a steep, sloping head set on a short neck. Their teeth were peg-shaped and their mouths were small. These dinosaurs also had long, slim tails. Hypselosaurus means "high ridge lizard," and this dinosaur was called so because it had a particularly high back. At 40 feet long, it was a relatively small member of the family. Other members of the family were up to 70 feet long.

Scientists have discovered eggs from Hypselosaurus that may be the biggest of all dinosaur eggs. Each egg is 12 inches long and 10 inches in diameter. It could contain almost 6 pints of liquid. The surface of each egg is rough and pitted. Clusters of five eggs have been found in nests. They are the only eggs positively known to come from a specific dinosaur.

Length: 40 feet
Weight: 30–40 tons
Lived: Late Cretaceous
Found: France, Spain

Hypsilophodon
(hip-sih-LO-fuh-don)

This particular dinosaur survived for more than 100 million years. It first appeared at the end of the early Jurassic period and lived until all the dinosaurs died out 65 million years ago. Hypsilophodon belonged to the same family as *Dryosaurus*. It was smaller, perhaps only half the size of its larger relative. These were among the most fleet-footed dinosaurs ever. They could run fast and keep their balance at great speeds. They had horny beaks, and most had small upper teeth. Each foot had three toes and their small hands had five fingers.

Hypsilophodon had a special set of self-sharpening teeth in its cheeks. It may have had two rows of bony studs down the length of its back, and some of the studs may have continued onto the tail. Various skeletons show Hypsilophodon to have been between 4 feet, 6 inches and 7 feet, 6 inches long. Specimens have been found in England and Portugal as well as South Dakota. At least 20 partial skeletons have been unearthed.

Length: 6 feet, 7 inches
Weight: 130 pounds
Lived: Early Cretaceous
Found: United States (South Dakota), England, Portugal

Iguanodon
(ig-WAN-oh-don)

Named "iguana tooth" because it had teeth like modern iguana lizards, Iguanodon is one of the most famous dinosaurs. It belongs to a family similar to *Camptosaurus* but larger, heavier, and better equipped to eat. Its mouth was large, with teeth in the cheeks. In front was a bony beak like *Hypsilophodon*. Iguanodon usually stood on all fours. It had big, strong thighs and three-toed feet. Its smaller front legs each had four fingers and a spiked thumb. When it reared up to rest on the base of its tail, it would have stretched up to 16 feet tall. It had a length of almost 30 feet.

Iguanodon first appeared more than 120 million years ago and lived 55 million years, becoming extinct at the same time as all the other dinosaurs. Other members of the Iguanodon family included *Muttaburrasaurus* and *Ouranosaurus*. Iguanodon probably roamed swampy countryside, wading through hot marshland looking for food. It could wrap its long tongue around reeds and thick grasses. Sucked into its large mouth, small branches and tough roots would be crunched with its two rows of cheek teeth.

Length: 29 feet
Weight: 5 tons
Lived: Early Cretaceous
Found: Europe, Romania, North America, North Africa, Mongolia

Ingenia
(in-JEN-ee-ah)

Oviraptorids, or "egg thieves," was a family with two members. One was called Ingenia, which means "genius." The other, which gave its name to the family, was called *Oviraptor*. Both belonged to a very large group of separate, closely linked families. The group members were called coelurosaurs, or "hollow tailed-lizards," because they all had thin, fragile bones, long legs, and shorter arms. Other important families included *Avimimus*, *Compsognathus*, *Ornithomimus*, *Dromaeosaurus*, and *Stenonychosaurus*. In all, 60 different types of dinosaurs in 14 families made up this group.

Ingenia was discovered in 1981 and had thicker fingers than *Oviraptor*. Of three fingers on each hand, the first was longest, followed by the second. Each finger had a curved claw. At about 6 feet long, Ingenia was a little smaller than *Oviraptor*. It was found in southwest Mongolia, and it is likely that others lived elsewhere in Asia.

Length: 6 feet
Weight: 60 pounds
Lived: Late Cretaceous
Found: Mongolia

Kentrosaurus
(KEN-truh-sawr-us)

One of the stegosaurid, or "plated dinosaur," family, Kentrosaurus means "pointed lizard." It was named for the spines on its back. Other members of this family included *Dacentrurus*, *Stegosaurus*, and *Tuojiangosaurus*. All these dinosaurs walked on four legs and had very tough skins. Kentrosaurus had pairs of short, triangular shaped plates on its neck and shoulders. Halfway along its back, the plates were replaced with long spikes. The spikes were set in pairs along the back and the tail. An extra spike grew from the top of each thigh.

Plated dinosaurs changed from their first appearance in the middle of the Jurassic period 160 million years ago. Various members of the family appeared at different times. Kentrosaurus was known to exist as far back as the late Jurassic, about 150 million years ago. Compared with giants like *Stegosaurus*, Kentrosaurus was quite small. It was little more than half the size of its larger relative.

Length: 17 feet
Weight: 1 ton
Lived: Late Jurassic
Found: Tanzania

Kritosaurus
(KRIT-uh-sawr-us)

Some scientists think this dinosaur was a very close relative of *Hadrosaurus*. It had a flat, broad head and a humped nose. It belonged to the duckbill family and lived toward the end of the dinosaur age. Kritosaurus means "noble lizard." Its humped nose reminded some people of the nose of a noble Roman senator!

Remains of Kritosaurus have been dug up in New Mexico and Baja California. Skeletons show it to have been about 30 feet long and up to 15 feet tall. It probably weighed nearly 3 tons. Duckbill dinosaurs had webbed feet and could probably swim. They would only do this to escape predators. Most of them lived in forests and woods.

Female Kritosaurus laid eggs in nests and stayed to look after them. Most male dinosaurs roamed away from the nest while females nursed the eggs until they hatched. Then they tended the young until they had grown up.

Length: 30 feet
Weight: 3 tons
Lived: Late Cretaceous
Found: United States (New Mexico), Mexico (Baja California)

Labocania
(lab-o-KAY-nee-uh)

A relative of *Tyrannosaurus* and *Megalosaurus*, this Cretaceous dinosaur was a fearsome flesh eater. It was much smaller than *Tyrannosaurus* and has not yet been attached to a known dinosaur family. It probably belonged to a group of more than 15 similar dinosaurs. Labocania had a much bigger head than *Tyrannosaurus* and a much bigger body. In many other ways it was very similar to its bigger relative. With enormous teeth and sharp claws on its toes, Labocania would have been a frightening predator. Yet its weight, which averaged about 3 tons, probably slowed it down and allowed it to be attacked by other flesh eaters. Some scientists think it had a very thick skin, which would have made it tough to kill. Only a few bones of Labocania have ever been found. They were dug up in the La Bocana Roja rock formations in Baja California.

Length: 25 feet
Weight: 3 tons
Lived: Late Cretaceous
Found: Mexico (Baja California)

Lambeosaurus
(LAM-be-uh-sawr-us)

A member of the duckbill family, Lambeosaurus was named after Lawrence Lambe, a Canadian scientist who spent much of his life studying dinosaurs. Literally the word means "Lambe's lizard." There were two types of duckbills. One group had head crests made of hollow bone, and the other group did not. Lambeosaurus was a member of the crested group and was the largest crested type known. Remains have been found in western North America, from Canada to Baja California.

With a very large tail and an enormous crest, Lambeosaurus was a monster, almost four stories tall on his back legs. Some skulls have been found with a crest bigger than the head. Others look like they might have had a small neck frill made of bone. One type had a very deep tail, which would have made it a good swimmer. This would be unusual, since it is not thought dinosaurs were happy in water. Rock impressions of its pebbly skin show Lambeosaurus to have had a leathery hide. Lambeosaurus is known to have lived about 85 million years ago.

Length: 49 feet
Weight: 2—5 tons
Lived: Late Cretaceous
Found: Mexico (Baja California), United States (Montana), Canada (Alberta)

Lesothosaurus
(leh-SOTH-uh-sawr-us)

Named after Lesotho, the country in Africa where it was first discovered, Lesothosaurus was a very close relative of *Fabrosaurus*. It was a member of the "bird-footed" (ornithopod) family. Built for browsing and running away if attacked, the back legs were strong and had three main claws on each foot. In addition, each foot had a small claw higher up the shin. Each tiny hand had four main fingers and a tiny, stub-like thumb. Like *Fabrosaurus*, Lesothosaurus was only 3 feet long and lived in the late Triassic, more than 200 million years ago. Unlike its close relative, it had narrower teeth. Its front teeth were smooth and pointed. Some scientists say the cheek teeth look like serrated arrow heads.

Small dinosaurs of this family are thought by some to have been the ancestors of almost all the "bird-foot" dinosaurs. No larger than a big dog, they survived at least 70 million years before dying out. Eventually, long before they vanished, other more powerful "bird-hips" had arrived.

Length: 3 feet, 4 inches
Weight: 40 pounds
Lived: Late Triassic/Early Jurassic
Found: South Africa

Lexovisaurus
(lex-OH-vuh-sawr-us)

This dinosaur is one of the oldest relatives of *Stegosaurus* known to have been found anywhere. It was very similar to *Kentrosaurus* but lived several million years earlier. It was discovered in remains found around the town of Lyon in France. An ancient Gallic people called Lexovi once lived in the area. Because of this, scientists called it Lexovisaurus ("Lexovi lizard"). Other bones were found in other parts of France, and fossil remains were also discovered in England. Those found in England are for an animal about the same size as *Kentrosaurus*. Some scientists think they have found more remains that suggest some members of the same family were much larger.

With more varied plates and spikes than *Kentrosaurus*, Lexovisaurus had narrow plates on its back and spines on its tail. Like its descendent, it had large spikes protecting each thigh. It is likely that dinosaurs of this type roamed across large areas of the earth. Several members of the same family would cross the same paths many times. More than 4,000 miles separate England from Tanzania, where *Kentrosaurus* was found!

Scientists are not sure why Lexovisaurus, and other members of its family, had bony plates along its back. Some people think it was for protection, although the animal would have been exposed along the sides of its body. Others believe it helped the animal radiate heat and keep its body temperature comfortable.

Length: 17 feet
Weight: 1 ton
Lived: Mid Jurassic
Found: England, France

Lufengosaurus
(loo-FEN-guh-sawr-us)

Distantly related to *Anchisaurus*, but larger, heavier, and stronger, Lufengosaurus belonged to the "flat lizard" (plateosaurid) family. It is known to have appeared about 210 million years ago. This member of the plateosaurid family was found in Lu-feng, making it the oldest dinosaur from China. It had strong jaws and short, widely spaced teeth. Because of this, scientists think it ate small animals as well as munching plants and small trees. Lufengosaurus probably walked on all fours. To get food they could rear up on their hind legs, using their long, strong tails for balance.

For a while, Lufengosaurus and its family relatives may have dominated large parts of the earth. It was the time when dinosaurs were just beginning to appear. Another famous relative, which gave its name to the entire family, is *Plateosaurus*. Different family members have been dug up in North America, Europe, and Africa. They are not thought to have lived long. They probably died out by the early Jurassic period.

Length: 20 feet
Weight: 1,800 pounds
Lived: Late Triassic/Early Jurassic
Found: China

Maiasaura
(mah-ee-ah-SAWR-uh)

Maiasaura is called "good mother lizard" because it was found with nests and babies. It belonged to the group of duckbill dinosaurs. Other members of the same family were *Edmontosaurus* and *Hadrosaurus*. They had flat heads without crests and a long, straight bottom jaw. They would browse among trees and long grasses munching food as they slowly ambled along. Maiasaura was dug up in Montana and had a bony spike growing from the top of its head. This dinosaur was discovered in 1978. With it were several nests, each one 7 feet across and more than 2 feet deep. Each nest was in the form of a mound. The eggs, shaped like sausages, were set out in the mound like spokes in a wheel. Each layer of eggs was separated with a layer of sand. The top layer was completely covered over. The young were found near the nest. This suggests that when they hatched they stayed close to home. These newly hatched Maiasaura were about 18 inches long and had badly worn teeth. The mother probably brought them food.

Length: 30 feet
Weight: 1—2 tons
Lived: Late Cretaceous
Found: United States (Montana)

Mamenchisaurus
(mah-MEN-chee-sawr-us)

This unusual dinosaur was a close relative of *Diplodocus* and *Apatosaurus*. Dinosaurs in this family were unusually long. Mamenchisaurus was discovered in south-central China and named from the area in which it was found – Mamenchi. From its bones, scientists guess that it was about 72 feet long, with the longest neck of any dinosaur yet discovered. In fact, its neck was so long it contained 19 neck bones, called vertebrae. From its "shoulders" to its head, Mamenchisaurus measured 33 feet!

Some of the vertebrae had struts to help stiffen the neck. Some scientists believe it may have developed this neck to reach very high branches of tall trees. Others believe it spent most of its life in rivers and ponds, sweeping its neck around to feed from the bank. This is not very likely. It probably combed leaves from twigs on trees. It may even have reared up to rest on the base of its spine. If it did, it could have reached leaves 50 feet above the ground.

Length: 72 feet
Weight: 10 tons
Lived: Late Jurassic
Found: China (Mamenchi)

Massospondylus
(mass-o-SPON-dih-lus)

Massospondylus was a close relative of *Lufengosaurus* and *Plateosaurus*, and a distant relative of *Thecodontosaurus*, and its name means "bulky spine bone." In most aspects it was similar to its close relatives, except that it was smaller. Dinosaurs of this type were common over 200 million years ago, during the late Triassic and early Jurassic periods. Fossil remains of Massospondylus were found in southern Africa. Bones similar to this type have also been found as far away as India.

Massospondylus had much larger hands than any of its relatives. In each thumb was a large, curved claw. This may have been a defensive weapon, but it is more likely that the claw was used to increase its diet. Instead of munching plants and small animals, it could dig up juicy roots and tear out small trees. This dinosaur had stones and pebbles in its stomach to grind up food. Its primitive teeth were not capable of tearing up plant food in its mouth.

Length: 13 feet
Weight: 1,200 pounds
Lived: Late Triassic/Early Jurassic
Found: South Africa

Megalosaurus
(MEG-uh-lo-sawr-us)

This was the very first dinosaur to be named. It was identified in 1824 and called "big lizard" because it was so large. At that time people thought it was just another old reptile. They did not know it belonged to a completely different group of animals that lived many millions of years ago. Described by Oxford University Professor Robert Plot in 1677, the thigh bone of Megalosaurus was said to come from a giant man! Nearly 150 years later it was identified as belonging to a relative of *Allosaurus*. Megalosaurus belonged to a family of at least 17 different types of flesh-eating dinosaurs.

It was a big, heavy predator distantly related to that terrifying meat eater, *Tyrannosaurus*. Megalosaurus had curved teeth with a saw-tooth edge and strong claws on each toe and finger. By studying footprints of this beast found all over Europe, South America, Africa, and Asia, scientists guess that it waddled like a duck, its tail thrashing from side to side as it stumbled along. This is because its toes pointed inward.

Length: 30 feet
Weight: 1 ton
Lived: Early Jurassic to Early Cretaceous
Found: Europe, South America, Africa, Asia

Melanorosaurus
(mel-AN-or-uh-sawr-us)

Dinosaur hunters are unsure about Melanorosaurus. Some think it is the same animal as Euskelosaurus. Others identify it as very similar but different. Whatever it is called, it was a member of the "flat lizard" family named after *Plateosaurus*. These dinosaurs had broad hands and feet. Their legs probably stuck out sideways and they walked on all fours. Some, such as *Lufengosaurus*, could stand upright on their back legs. They all had blunt teeth and chewed plants and possibly small animals.

Melanorosaurus was the longest of the early dinosaurs and had legs like an elephant. Its bones were solid, like those of most dinosaurs of this period. Later, more advanced dinosaurs developed hollow bones to reduce their weight. This gave them greater agility. It allowed them to run and escape danger. They probably survived longer this way. With lighter bones came a better method of moving blood around the body.

Consequently, advanced dinosaurs were able to shed body heat as they ran. Long before that, though, Melanorosaurus was an important early dinosaur.

Scientists have thought a lot about how Melanosaurus and other similar dinosaurs moved around. Some think they were able to trot or run fast to escape danger. Others believe they were more like reptiles, unable to run fast and shed extra heat. Melanosaurus was certainly well developed, and although it appeared early in the age of dinosaurs it was more advanced than some that appeared later.

Length: 40 feet
Weight: 2 tons
Lived: Late Triassic/Early Jurassic
Found: South Africa

Microceratops
(my-kro-SAIR-uh-tops)

Literally named "little horned face," this tiny plant eater is one of the smallest dinosaurs yet discovered. Fully grown, an adult would stretch little more than 2 feet long from beak to tail. It belonged to the family headed by *Protoceratops*. Its other well-known relative was *Bagaceratops*. These were small, primitive, horned dinosaurs. Each had a differently shaped horn or bump on its face. Microceratops had a short neck frill made of bone. A horny beak helped it grovel among the undergrowth for food and a place to hide. Being so small, it would have made easy pickings for meat eaters.

Fossil bones found in Mongolia and east China show that Microceratops had longer back legs than its relatives. These legs were slender and strong enough to support its weight. Microceratops probably foraged on all fours. It would rear up and run on its back legs when startled. This little dinosaur was not around long and soon died out.

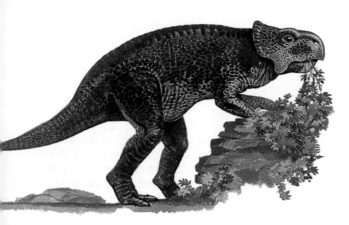

Length: 2 feet, 6 inches
Weight: 25 pounds
Lived: Late Cretaceous
Found: Mongolia

Microvenator
(my-kro-ven-AY-tor)

Microvenator is one of the smallest "hollow-tailed lizards" (coelurosaurs) discovered. Its name means "small hunter." This turkey-sized hunting dinosaur was dug up in Montana and lived in the early Cretaceous period. Its hollow bones made it lightweight. Microvenator stood only 30 inches tall, although its total length was almost 4 feet. It had a long neck with a small head. On its short arms were three fingers. Its long tail was built to help the dinosaur balance itself when standing up on its back legs.

Microvenator was related to *Coelurus*, *Ornitholestes*, and *Ornithomimoides*. These fast-moving, pecking little predators existed on earth for several million years. As a group, these families of dinosaurs survived for about 100 million years. All of them were descendents of the late Triassic *Coelophysis*. Although none could fly, they were the equal of pecking birds today. They would have cleaned up food left by larger animals.

Length: 2 feet, 6 inches
Weight: 14 pounds
Lived: Early Cretaceous
Found: United States (Montana), Tibet

Monoclonius
(mon-uh-CLO-nee-us)

This animal is one of the earliest horned dinosaurs to be discovered in western North America. It was called Monoclonius ("single stem") because it had a single horn on its nose and was a member of the family of horned dinosaurs called ceratopsians. There were two types of horned dinosaurs. One type, like Monoclonius, had short neck frills made of bone. The other type had longer frills. Other members of the short-frill type included *Brachyceratops*, *Centrosaurus*, *Pachyrhinosaurus*, and *Styrachosaurus*. The most famous relative was *Triceratops*, the biggest and the most feared.

Some people think *Brachyceratops* was a baby Monoclonius. *Brachyceratops* was about two-thirds the size of Monoclonius. Monoclonius was little more than half the size of *Triceratops*. Its head was large, about 6 feet long, and a single horn grew from the top of its nose. A small bump grew above each eye. The back edge of the neck frill had a row of bony knobs and two spikes that pointed forward. Monoclonius may have used its horn to topple small palm trees and its parrot-like beak to forage for juicy roots.

Length: 18 feet
Weight: 1–8 tons
Lived: Late Cretaceous
Found: Western North America

Muttaburrasaurus
(mut-tah-BUR-rah-sawr-us)

This large relative of *Iguanodon* was named after the place in Australia, called Muttaburra, where it was discovered. First named in 1981, it is one of the few dinosaurs to come from that country. Muttaburrasaurus has a close link with the *Camptosaurus* family. Many of its bones look more like *Camptosaurus* than *Iguanodon*. Because of that, some dinosaur scientists classify it with the *Camptosaurus* rather than the *Iguanodon* family. The differences between the two families are slight. Along with many others, they are all part of the "bird-foot" group called ornithopods. Muttaburrasaurus had a low head with a broad skull. Its mouth swept gently upward and it had teeth like garden shears. These sharp teeth would have helped it eat meat, although no one knows exactly what it did feed on. Like several dinosaurs, it probably ate meat as well as plants and roots. It had a spiked thumb on each hand, like *Iguanodon*, to help it forage or fend off attackers. Members of the *Iguanodon* family appeared at the beginning of the Cretaceous period, about 125 million years ago. Muttaburrasaurus dates from about 105 million years ago.

Length: 23 feet
Weight: 4 tons
Lived: Mid-Late Cretaceous
Found: Australia (Muttaburra)

Nemegtosaurus
(NEH-meh-tuh-sawr-us)

Skull bones found indicate that this dinosaur was a late member of the *Diplodocus* family. It has been named after Mongolia's Nemegt Basin where it was found. *Diplodocus* is not found in rocks from the late Cretaceous. The skull named Nemegtosaurus is very similar to a *Diplodocus* skull. It has the same sloping shape. Other Nemegtosaurus bones have also been found. It may be that *Diplodocus* lived in this later period also, but that no bones have yet been found in rocks that date from this time. Nemegtosaurus was probably as long as *Diplodocus*, with a slender body, long neck, and long tail.
Nemegtosaurus is related to *Mamenchisaurus*. It does not, however, have that dinosaur's extremely long neck. Other members of the family came from the late Jurassic, about 50 million years before Nemegtosaurus roamed these hidden places deep in Asia. It is possible that isolated groups of dinosaurs lived on for millions of years after their relatives had died out. The headless skeleton of another dinosaur was found with Nemegtosaurus. Some scientists believe it was part of the same animal.

Length: 87 feet
Weight: 12 tons
Lived: Late Cretaceous
Found: Mongolia (Nemegt Basin)

Nodosaurus
(no-doe-SAWR-us)

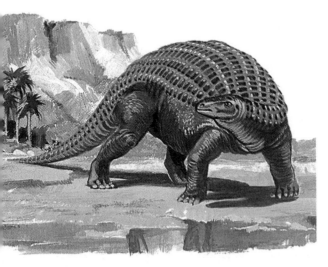

This medium-sized armored dinosaur has been found all over North America, from New Jersey to Wyoming. It had rows of large and small plates down its back and its sides, or flanks. Its skin had bony buttons, called nodes, between its ribs. Small spikes were attached to the plates. It would have been a tough beast to eat! None of these bony plates and spikes were attached to its skeleton. For this reason, dinosaur scientists are not exactly sure where they were positioned.

In some families of armored dinosaurs, each member had a bony club at the end of its tail. Nodosaurus belonged to a group that had no club. Instead, its tail just trailed along the ground as its low head foraged for food. Node dinosaurs have been found in many countries, including France, Spain, England, India, China, and Australia. The largest members of the family were about 25 feet long and weighed more than 3 tons.

Length: 18 feet
Weight: 2—3 tons
Lived: Late Cretaceous
Found: United States (Kansas, Wyoming, New Jersey)

Opisthocoelicaudia
(o-piss-tho-SEE-luh-caw-dee-uh)

When Polish scientists were looking for dinosaurs in the Gobi Desert of Mongolia, they found remains of this animal without its neck bones or a skull. They called it the "backward hollow-tail dinosaur." It had four legs of almost equal length, and its tail was held high. Rigid bone links kept the tail level but about 5 feet off the ground. When they looked further, the scientists found a skull that they called *Nemegtosaurus*. Some experts think the two are the same animal. Others say the head does not match the skeleton found several miles away.

Opisthocoelicaudia may have sat back on the base of its tail. With its front legs and neck up in the air it could have reached very high trees and branches to feed off leaves. Scientists say the bones of this dinosaur are similar to the bones of freshwater turtles. Some turtles prop themselves up on the base of their tails. Some turtles curl their tails round big stones to anchor themselves. The dinosaur may have done this also.

Length: 40 feet
Weight: 15 tons
Lived: Late Cretaceous
Found: Mongolia (Gobi Desert)

Ornitholestes
(or-nith-o-LESS-teez)

A lightly built meat eater, Ornitholestes was called "bird robber" because it was believed to chase primitive bird life. Scientists used to think it was the same as *Coelurus*, but they now see it as a different member of the same family. It had long and slim back legs with short front legs, or arms. With tough feet and a tiny claw on each of three toes, they were fast-running dinosaurs. Capable of dashing through undergrowth and across grassland, they may have preyed on the dead flesh of other dinosaurs. In this way they may have been the jackals of the dinosaur age, tearing up the flesh of dinosaurs killed by the great meat eaters like *Tyrannosaurus*.

With small hands, each supporting three fingers, they probably lived by rummaging and foraging. An almost complete skeleton of Ornitholestes was found in Wyoming. From this, scientists have pieced together a lot of information about the tiny predator. Lizards, frogs, and small mammals would have been easy prey for this fierce little hunter.

Length: 6 feet, 6 inches
Weight: 30 pounds
Lived: Late Jurassic
Found: United States (Wyoming)

Ornithomimus
(or-nith-uh-MY-mus)

Found widely in North America and Mongolia, this dinosaur was called "bird imitator" because it looked like an ostrich without feathers. As a member of the same family as *Dromiceiomimus*, *Elaphrosaurus*, *Gallimimus*, and *Struthiomimus*, Ornithomimus was lightly built with a delicate bone structure. It was basically all neck and tail, held together by a short, plump body. All members of this family had keen eyesight, were quick, and could leap about at great speed. Ornithomimus had a long mouth with no teeth and a small head. It had a large brain and was not stupid. There were three toes on each foot and three fingers on each hand. Its arms were so small they were useless for real work and would have been good only for scratching the ground for things to eat. Feeding off insects, eggs, seeds, and small grubs, Ornithomimus would have little means of defending itself if attacked. This kept it alert for danger. With a top speed of around 35 MPH, Ornithomimus could outpace any other animal.

Length: 11 feet, 6 inches
Weight: 220 pounds
Lived: Late Cretaceous
Found: Western North America, Tibet

Othnielia
(oth-NEEL-ee-ah)

The bones of Othnielia were originally called Nanosaurus. They were discovered in 1877 by the fossil hunter Othniel Charles Marsh. Exactly one hundred years later they were renamed after the man who discovered them. The dinosaur was a small member of the "bird-foot" family named after *Hypsilophodon*. It was much older than others in the same family, such as *Parkosaurus*. Othnielia was very like *Hypsilophodon*, except it had hardened enamel on both sides of its teeth. Its jaws were built to chop plants and chew them up before swallowing. The tip of the pointed mouth had a small beak-like pincer. Its jaws had strong muscles to cope with tough food. It also had an unusual hinge in the back of its mouth. When its upper and lower jaws came together, they swiveled around so both sets of teeth met exactly together.

Like others in the family, Othnielia had three toes on each foot and fingers on each hand. These dinosaurs were among some of the most successful at surviving. They lived about 100 million years before they died out.

Length: 4 feet, 6 inches
Weight: 50 pounds
Lived: Late Jurassic
Found: Western North America

Ouranosaurus
(our-AHN-uh-sawr-us)

One of the strangest dinosaurs, Ouranosaurus was discovered from remains found in West Africa. It belonged to the family of *Iguanodons* and was close in size to *Muttaburrasaurus*. It was a typical duckbill, with a flat head and an upturned mouth. It would often drop down on all fours but could also stand up on its back legs. Members of the *Iguanodon* family have been found all over the world. They stayed on earth for a long time, and Ouranosaurus may have been an ancestor of the duck-billed dinosaurs that appeared in the late Cretaceous period.

One other feature set Ouranosaurus apart from its relatives. It had a thin sail made of skin running from the back of its neck to the end of its tail. There may also have been a piece of skin under its chin. The skin probably carried blood vessels. These would remove heat from the body of the dinosaur. The heat would be carried to the surface of the skin and radiated away into the air. In this way the dinosaur would cool itself in hot weather. In cold conditions, the sail would have gathered heat from the sun. The blood would have carried heat to the body, arms, and legs to warm them.

Length: 23 feet
Weight: 4 tons
Lived: Early Cretaceous
Found: West Africa

Pachycephalosaurus
(pak-ee-SEF-uh-lo-sawr-us)

This dinosaur was a very large member of the "bonehead" family. All members of the family had thick skulls. Some had a thick knob on top of the skull that looked like a crash helmet. Some of these animals were quite small, less than 3 feet in size. A relative, *Homalocephale*, was 10 feet long. Pachycephalosaurus was the biggest of the boneheads and towered above its relatives. It also had the thickest skull, with which it could charge its enemies and knock them senseless. There was only one problem with a thick skull. It left little room for brains!

Scientists have carefully measured the skull of different boneheads and found that Pachycephalosaurus had a dense cap of bone 10 inches thick. It had some small, bony spikes jutting up from its nose and sharp knobs around the back of its head. Charging at full speed, it would have made a terrific impact. It may also have used its head to ram others in its family. Some animals do this today to claim territory or to warn off others. Pachycephalosaurus lived in North America, but others in the large family have been found all over the world.

Length: 15 feet
Weight: 450 pounds
Lived: Late Cretaceous
Found: Western North America

Pachyrhinosaurus
(PAK-ee-rye-no-sawr-us)

Bone hunters in Alberta dug up the fossil remains of a very unusual member of the "horned dinosaur" family. The most familiar member of this family was *Triceratops*. Others included *Centrosaurus*, *Eoceratops*, *Monoclonius*, and *Styracosaurus*. Each had one or more horns on its face. Pachyrhinosaurus had no horn but had a squat stump on the top of its nose. The stump, shaped like a plate, was 22 inches long and 14 inches wide. The bone was 5 inches deep with a volcano-shaped crater in the middle. Bone knobs had grown above the eyes.

All horned dinosaurs had either a short frill or a large frill. Pachyrhinosaurus belonged to the short-frilled family. It had short spikes of bone growing from the back of the frill. Like all horned dinosaurs, it had a parrot-like beak with which it groveled for food. The stump on the nose of this dinosaur might have been used to ram other animals or to knock small trees down by charging them with its head.

Length: 18 feet
Weight: 1—2 tons
Lived: Late Cretaceous
Found: Canada (Alberta)

Palaeoscincus
(pay-lee-o-SKINK-us)

Panoplosaurus
(pan-OP-luh-sawr-us)

Because of its bony plates and protective spikes, this dinosaur was called "fully armored lizard." It was one of the last armored dinosaurs from North America. Its back was protected by hard plates made of bone. Large slabs of bone were attached to its skull. These protected its neck and the sides of its head. Its skin was covered with bony lumps set in the thick skin.

Panoplosaurus had a massive head. It was arched on top and had a narrow snout. This too was covered with bony plates. In its mouth, Panoplosaurus had small teeth with ridges. From the teeth, scientists believe it fed on roots and dug out small bush plants. Dinosaurs like Panoplosaurus were very heavily defended and protected with bony armor. Yet they had weak jaws and poor teeth. They would have spent a lot of time gathering up food with their bony snouts. Protected from attack inside their bony plates and a skin several inches thick, they were little more than eating machines.

Known only by a single tooth and some odd bones found in Montana, this dinosaur is a member of the "node lizard" family. Some scientists have said it is the same as *Panoplosaurus*, but most agree it is different. Node lizards (called nodosaurids) were very heavily armored, four-footed dinosaurs. They are known to have lived throughout North America, Europe, and Asia. They probably descended from *Hylaeosaurus* about 125 million years ago. Some scientists think *Hylaeosaurus* was descended from *Scelidosaurus*.

Palaeoscincus was larger than some other node lizards. Scientists believe there were about 19 different types. Some were only 7 feet long. Others were up to 25 feet in length. They walked well above the ground but their heads were low. The neck was short and allowed little movement. Safe inside their bony armor, they would have been troubled by few dinosaurs.

Length: 23 feet
Weight: 3—5 tons
Lived: Late Cretaceous
Found: United States (Montana)

Length: 23 feet
Weight: 3—4 tons
Lived: Late Cretaceous
Found: Western North America

Parasaurolophus
(par-ah-sawr-OL-uh-fus)

A large member of the duckbill family of dinosaurs, called hadrosaurids, Parasaurolophus was a close relative of *Lambeosaurus*. Most duckbills were divided into two groups. One had a flat head with no crest. The second group had tall, bony head crests. Each family had a different crest style and families would recognize each other this way. Parasaurolophus had a very special crest. It was a curved, hollow horn that attached to the front of the head and swept backwards.

The horn was more than 6 feet long. Inside, two tubes went up to the top and two came back down. These were breathing tubes. Each pair of tubes going up into the crest was attached to the nostrils in the dinosaur's nose. The down tubes went to the lungs. Scientists have measured the tubes. They believe Parasaurolophus could make a very loud bellowing sound by snorting through these sound tubes.

Length: 33 feet
Weight: 2—4 tons
Lived: Late Cretaceous
Found: United States (Utah, New Mexico), Canada (Alberta)

Pinacosaurus
(pin-AH-kuh-sawr-us)

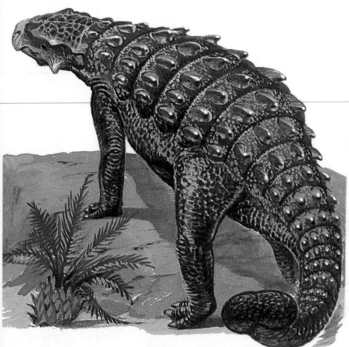

This dinosaur was called "plank lizard" because it had a heavily armored back. It was a member of the "fused lizard" group, which also included *Ankylosaurus*, *Euoplocephalus*, and *Sauroplites*. It had a broad mouth and a beak-like face. Its legs were directly below its body and held it off the ground. All members of this family had a big bone club at the end of a long tail. Pinacosaurus had sharp spikes along its back and sides. Bones from this dinosaur have been found in China and Mongolia.

Pinacosaurus was one of the smallest in the "fused lizard" group. It was only half the size of the massive *Ankylosaurus*. It lived in hot, dry climates high above sea level. Food might have been difficult to find where it lived, but it probably went around without challenge. Not many dinosaurs liked very hot places.

Length: 18 feet
Weight: 2 tons
Lived: Late Cretaceous
Found Mongolia, China

Plateosaurus
(PLAY-tee-uh-sawr-us)

This was the most common of the early dinosaurs known to science. Plateosaurus means "flat lizard," and it has given its name to a family of at least seven different types. Others include *Lufengosaurus* and *Massospondylus*. Plateosaurus was larger than either of these. It had a very thick tail with strong muscles. It would have been able to use the base of its spine as a prop. By doing this and rearing up on its hind legs, it could tear down branches of high trees or munch the tops of palms.

These dinosaurs date from the end of the Triassic, more than 200 million years ago. They and their relatives have been found all over the world. Plateosaurus must have been particularly common in Europe, where many fossil bones have been found. These dinosaurs lived for many millions of years before they died out. Some scientists think that they were the true ancestors of the giant, four-footed sauropods like *Apatosaurus* and *Diplodocus*.

Length: 26 feet
Weight: 1 ton
Lived: Late Triassic
Found: Germany, France, Switzerland, England

Podokesaurus
(po-DOE-kee-sawr-us)

This little dinosaur may never have existed. Its name means "swift-footed lizard." Was Podokesaurus a separate animal or was it really a *Coelophysis?* It is known to have lived during the late Triassic or early Jurassic period. It belonged to the family of "hollow form" dinosaurs called coelophysids. Dinosaurs in that group were named after *Coelophysis*. They are known from the skeletons of many animals that lived and died together. It is believed they were all caught by a sudden sandstorm and buried alive. Many dinosaur scientists believe that Podokesaurus was a different animal, but very similar to *Coelophysis*. This little meat eater, alive at the dawn of the dinosaur age, would have stood only 2 feet tall. It was lightly built and had a long tail. It also had long hind legs and a pair of short arms with tiny hands. The bones of this little creature were found in Massachusetts, and no more have been found anywhere else.

Length: 10 feet
Weight: 65 pounds
Lived: Late Triassic
Found: Massachusetts

Prosaurolophus
(pro-sawr-OL-uh-fus)

This dinosaur was the ancestor of *Saurolophus*. It had a sloping face with bumps over the eyebrows. Its mouth was flat and its lower jaw was straight. Prosaurolophus belonged to the family of duckbills that had flat heads or skulls. They did not have large crests or domes on their heads. Prosaurolophus did have a small bony lump that ended in a spike.

Compared to other duckbills, Prosaurolophus was not particularly large. Although some duckbills were only 12 feet long, others, like *Hadrosaurus*, were up to 32 feet in length. Prosaurolophus was 26 feet long, with a strong tail that it usually held straight out behind itself as it loped along on its hind legs. Prosaurolophus laid its eggs in mud mounds shaped like saucers. Some scientists think the adults gathered the young together to look after them. They may even have gathered food for them. Some had flaps of skin that could be blown up like balloons. They may have done this to make loud calls to others in the family.

Length: 26 feet
Weight: 1–4 tons
Lived: Late Cretaceous
Found: Canada (Alberta)

Protoceratops
(pro-toe-SAIR-uh-tops)

About the size of a pig, Protoceratops is the earliest known member of the family of horned dinosaurs. Its name means "first horned face." Many skeletons were discovered by an American expedition to Mongolia in 1922. This expedition also found nests with unhatched baby Protoceratops curled up inside eggs. The baby dinosaurs were only 12 inches long. The eggs were only 6 inches across and had been placed in rows around a bowl-shaped nest. The eggs were separated from each other by layers of sand. These were the first dinosaur eggs to be found.

The closest relatives to Protoceratops were *Bagaceratops* and *Microceratops*. Protoceratops had a large face and a small neck frill. It had a large beak and bumps on its nose and above its eyebrows. These bumps were the first signs of horns that would develop in later dinosaurs. Later horned dinosaurs like *Styracosaurus* and *Triceratops* had big horns and were much larger than Protoceratops.

Length: 6 feet
Weight: 1—2 tons
Lived: Late Cretaceous
Found: Mongolia

Psittacosaurus
(SIT-uh-ko-sawr-us)

This man-sized dinosaur is a member of the "parrot lizard" family. It is linked with the "horned face" dinosaurs. Psittacosaurus looked a bit like *Protoceratops* but had no bone neck frill. It had a beak like a parrot and a deep jaw. Its front legs were quite short, while its back legs were long and very strong. It probably ambled along on all fours and stood on its back legs to reach plants and branches.

Psittacosaurus had four toes on each foot, one of which was a stump like a short thumb. It had four fingers on each hand and claws on each finger and toe. These dinosaurs lived in the early and mid-Cretaceous period. They may have descended from the *Heterodontosaurus* family of the early Jurassic more than 90 million years earlier.

On one bone hunt, scientists found a baby Psittacosaurus only half the size of a pigeon. It is the smallest baby dinosaur found anywhere.

Length: 2 feet, 7 inches to 5 feet
Weight: Up to 50 pounds
Lived: Early Cretaceous
Found: Mongolia, China, USSR (Siberia)

Saichania
(sye-CHAY-nee-ah)

Some very good fossil bones of this dinosaur have been found in Mongolia. Its name, which means "beautiful one" in Mongolian, refers to the unusually good state of the fossils and not to the dinosaur's appearance!

Saichania belonged to the late Cretaceous family of armored dinosaurs (ankylosaurids). Members of the same family included *Ankylosaurus*, *Euoplocephalus*, *Pinacosaurus*, *Sauroplites*, and *Tarchia*. Saichania's size was about average for the armored dinosaurs, although much smaller than a huge *Ankylosaurus*.

Saichania had a larger skull than *Pinacosaurus*, with more bumpy bone on top. It had a large number of bone knobs, studs, and spikes in rows across its back and along its tail. Where the back legs were attached to its spine, separate bones were welded together for great strength. The bony club on the end of its tail was similar to the club on *Ankylosaurus*.

Length: 23 feet
Weight: 2—5 tons
Lived: Late Cretaceous
Found: Mongolia

Saltopus
(SALT-o-pus)

This tiny dinosaur was a member of the "hollow tail" (coelurosaur) family. Because the scientist who discovered it thought it was a jumping dinosaur, he called it Saltopus, which means "leaping foot" in Latin. In fact, Saltopus was probably a fast runner. It is one of the oldest dinosaurs known and was found in a quarry in Scotland during a bone hunt in 1910. Scientists think it fed on small insects and lizards. It was closely related to *Coelophysis* and *Procompsognathus*.

Saltopus had small arms with five fingers on each hand. The fourth and fifth fingers were very small. It had strong muscles at the top of its back legs. These helped it move very fast over rough ground. Saltopus had a pointed face and mouth with rows of small teeth. It was only about the size of a domestic cat and stood 8 inches high at its hip.

Length: 2 feet
Weight: 2 pounds
Lived: Late Triassic
Found: Scotland

Saurolophus
(sawr-OL-o-fus)

Because it had a large piece of bone sticking out the back of its head, this dinosaur was given the Greek name for "crested lizard." It belonged to the group of "bird foot" dinosaurs and to the family of duckbills. It appeared just as *Corythosaurus* was dying out. It lived at the same times as *Lambeosaurus*. Examples of this dinosaur have been found in North America and Asia. It is a very advanced duckbill and is believed to date back only 75 million years.

Saurolophus looked a lot like *Edmontosaurus*, but it had a long head shaped like a spoon. The dinosaur probably stood 17 feet tall on its back legs and would have reached leaves and branches as high as the roof on a house. It had three hoofed toes on each foot and four webbed fingers on each hand. Two fingers on each hand were also hoofed. Its tail was big and flattened, with strong bones and muscles. This helped the animal control its balance as it shifted from four legs to two. Like all duckbills, it had no teeth in its beak. It did have sets of teeth in its cheeks.

Length: 30 feet
Weight: 1—2 tons
Lived: Late Cretaceous
Found: East Asia, North America

Sauroplites
(sawr-uh-PLY-teez)

This is one of the oldest of the "armored dinosaur" (ankylosaur) family and dates back to the early Cretaceous period. Its name means "stone-like lizard" and is taken from the name Hoplite, a heavily armored ancient Greek soldier. Its remains were found on the border between China and Mongolia.

Not many bones of Sauroplites have been found. Enough exist, however, to form a good picture of this early ankylosaur. It is smaller than *Saichania*, another member of the armored family which came much later.

Sauroplites was covered with bony segments set into its skin. It also had plates of bone in rows down its back and on its tail. Bony spikes were attached to the side of its body just behind the neck. These would have given it good protection from the flesh-eating dinosaurs of the Cretaceous period.

Length: 20 feet
Weight: 2 tons
Lived: Early Cretaceous
Found: China

Segisaurus
(SEE-gih-sawr-us)

This very early member of the "hollow-tail lizard" family was probably a descendent of *Coelophysis*. It was about the size of a goose and was found in Arizona. Some scientists have likened it to *Procompsognathus*. However, both *Coelophysis* and *Procompsognathus* had hollow bones, while Segisaurus had solid bones.

Segisaurus was named after Segi Canyon, Arizona, where it was found in 1933. Unfortunately, only parts of the skeleton were found, without a head. This has made it very difficult to build up an accurate picture. The artist here has shown what scientists think its head might have looked like. The animal had long, slim back legs and feet very similar to *Procompsognathus*. These would have helped it run quite fast. Because the teeth have not been found, it is impossible to know precisely what it fed on. However, scientists believe it to have been interested in small lizards and tiny animals.

Remains of Segisaurus continue to puzzle scientists. The back-jutting hipbones have tiny holes in them, and the animal has a collarbone. The collarbone had almost disappeared in dinosaurs, even the early ones. Apart from its feet, there were other similarities between Segisaurus and *Procompsognathus*. The hipbones were almost identical, and the arm bones looked as though they belonged to the same family. Much of the work of comparing Segisaurus with *Procompsognathus* was carried out by Professor John Ostrom in 1981.

Length: 3 feet, 4 inches
Weight: 20 pounds
Lived: Early Jurassic
Found: United States (Arizona)

Shanshanosaurus
(shan-SHAN-uh-sawr-us)

This small dinosaur was found by fossil hunters in China. So far, this is the only specimen that has been discovered. The skeleton was built of very thin bones for light weight and flexibility. Its name is taken from the Shan-shan area of China, where it was found. A close relative, called *Noasaurus*, was found in Argentina. Each was like a cross between *Deinonychus* and *Dromaeosaurus*. *Noasaurus* had a terrifying claw on each foot like *Deinonychus*, but it was flexible and more sharply curved.

Shanshanosaurus had a large head shaped like a wedge. Its teeth were very sharp and its eyes were small. No doubt it had poor eyesight. It had a long neck, short arms, and long, muscular legs. On them, this fierce little predator could have moved fast across rough ground. It probably fed on small plant eaters or baby dinosaurs, such as the young of *Diplodocus* and *Apatosaurus*. Only big meat eaters like *Tyrannosaurus* could have gone after fully grown plant eaters. Dinosaurs like Shanshanosaurus probably had to make do with smaller animals.

Length: 6 feet
Weight: 25–30 pounds
Lived: Late Cretaceous
Found: China

Shantungosaurus
(shan-TUNG-o-sawr-us)

With a flat head and a huge body, Shantungosaurus is easily the biggest duckbill yet discovered. It turned up in Shantung, China, and belongs to the large family of hadrosaurine duckbills. It is closely related to *Edmontosaurus*, *Hadrosaurus*, *Maiasaura*, *Prosaurolophus*, and *Saurolophus*. Some members of the family may have been up to 50 feet long and stood 25 feet high. Shantungosaurus had a low skull with a flat top to its head, a flat beak, and no crest, as did some hadrosaurids.

Shantungosaurus was very similar to *Edmontosaurus* but much bigger. It dates from the late Cretaceous period and would have been an impressive sight. A full-scale reconstruction has been set up at the Natural History Museum in Beijing, the capital city of China. A full-grown man standing beside the reconstruction only comes up to the dinosaur's knee. Were it in existence today, Shantungosaurus would be looking over the tops of three-story houses!

Length: 39–49 feet
Weight: 3–4 tons
Lived: Late Cretaceous
Found: China

Spinosaurus
(SPY-nuh-sawr-us)

Several dinosaurs and other animals had large spines on their backs covered with skin. This gave these animals the appearance of having sails on their backs. *Ouranosaurus* was one. Spinosaurus is another. Both lived in the early Cretaceous. Spinosaurus was large and carried 6-foot spines on its back. Both *Ouranosaurus* and Spinosaurus were found from remains discovered in Africa. Skeletons of Spinosaurus also show it to have been a meat eater. It had teeth serrated like steak knives, but they were straight and not curved like those of some other dinosaurs.

Spinosaurus has been put in a group called spinosaurids. The group included several families, among them Altispinax. They were large carnivores and hunted widely for food and prey. The sail may have helped them warm up more quickly than other dinosaurs by taking in heat from the sun. This would have been an advantage when they set out hunting.

Length: 40 feet
Weight: 7 tons
Lived: Late Cretaceous
Found: Niger, Egypt

Staurikosaurus
(stor-IK-uh-sawr-us)

This dinosaur belongs in a family of its own. It has no known relatives. It is, however, part of a group of families known as prosauropods, or "before the lizard-feet dinosaurs." They included the first of the big, four-footed plant eaters like *Plateosaurus* as well as smaller, lighter animals like *Thecodontosaurus*.

Staurikosaurus was named after the Southern Cross, a group of stars best seen in the southern hemisphere. Staurikosaurus was found in southern Brazil. They were among the very first dinosaurs and are known to have existed more than 210 million years ago.

Dinosaurs of this family walked and ran on two legs but could have dropped to all fours if necessary. They had large heads, compact bodies, and sharp teeth. They had five fingers on each hand and five toes on each foot. The middle toes and fingers were the longest.

Length: 6 feet, 6 inches
Weight: Up to 66 pounds
Lived: Middle Triassic
Found: Brazil (Santa Maria)

Stegosaurus
(STEG-uh-sawr-us)

Stegosaurus was first discovered in 1877 from bones found in Colorado. Nobody really knows why it had such big, bony plates on its back. Some scientists think they were there to radiate excess heat from the animal's body. Others believe they were a protection from flesh-eating dinosaurs. Stegosaurus was closely related to 'Kentrosaurus, *Lexovisaurus*, and *Tuojiangosaurus*. Its name means "plated lizard" and refers to all the plates, spikes, and spines on its back and tail.

Stegosaurus had a very small, tube-like head, small teeth, and a brain the size of a walnut. Nevertheless, it could defend itself by lashes from armored spikes on its tail. Its front legs were only half the length of its back legs. The dinosaur probably munched small plants and tree roots, nibbling leaves from small trees or foliage from bushes. Many Stegosaurus bones have been found in Oklahoma, Utah, and Wyoming. Others have turned up in Europe, Africa, India, and China.

Length: 30 feet
Weight: 2 tons
Lived: Late Jurassic
Found: United States (Colorado, Wyoming, Oklahoma, Utah)

Stenonychosaurus
(sten-ON-ik-uh-sawr-us)

If brain size is an indication of intelligence, Stenonychosaurus must have been one of the most intelligent dinosaurs to exist. With a large brain and huge eyes, it was very similar to *Saurornithoides*, its relative. In other ways, it was like the family of *Dromaeosaurus*. It had a long, stiffened tail, long arms, a second toe with a claw, and strong back legs. It also had wide-set eyes for good focusing. It would have judged distance well. Clearly, Stenonynchosaurus was agile, quick-moving, and quick-thinking. It probably stalked its prey like many animals do today. Most dinosaurs survived by instinct. Stenonynchosaurus could get the better of its prey by using brain power to respond to its developed senses. These included sight, sound, and smell. It probably had fast reflexes and could dart about at great speed. Fossil remains have been found in Canada, and they date back about 80 million years.

Length: 6 feet, 6 inches
Weight: 60 to 100 pounds
Lived: Late Cretaceous
Found: Canada (Alberta)

Struthiomimus
(strooth-ee-uh-MY-mus)

Because scientists thought this dinosaur looked like an ostrich, they called it Struthiomimus, which means "ostrich mimic." It had a short body, a long tail, and a curving neck. Its head was small, it had no teeth, and its eyes were quite large. Scientists think that it may have been fairly intelligent, compared to most other dinosaurs. Struthiomimus probably lived on open river banks, pacing around for a juicy morsel. It might have caught some of the many kinds of water life that lived in the late Cretaceous. Perhaps instead it used its strong, curved claws to tear open insect nests or eggs.

This dinosaur was a member of the family of *Ornithomimus*, which belonged to the broad group of "hollow-tail lizards," or coelurosaurs. Other members of the family included *Dromiceiomimus*, *Elaphrosaurus*, and *Gallimimus*.

Length: 11 feet, 6 inches
Weight: 220 pounds
Lived: Late Cretaceous
Found: United States (New Jersey), Canada (Alberta)

Styracosaurus
(sty-RAK-uh-sawr-us)

This is one of the most dramatic members of the short-frilled, "horned dinosaur" family. It was related to *Brachyceratops*, *Centrosaurus*, *Ceratops*, *Eoceratops*, *Monoclonius*, *Pachyrhinosaurus*, and *Triceratops*. Each of these animals had a different arrangement of horns and frills made of bone. Seen from head on, as pictured on the front of this book, Styracosaurus was a fearsome beast. It had a long head with six large spikes that were attached to the back of its neck frill. There was a long horn on its nose and a curved beak for tearing stubborn roots or tree trunks.

Styracosaurus was probably about 6 feet tall and would have weighed around 3 tons. Scientists have calculated that it could have reached a speed of more than 20 MPH in full charge. In some ways it was the equivalent of today's rhinoceros, but much stronger and more dangerous. For all its frightening appearance, however, it was little more than half the size of *Triceratops*.

Syntarsus
(sin-TAR-sus)

This strange dinosaur was found in southern Africa. It dates back to the earliest period of the dinosaur age. Most pieces of the skeleton were found, and experts have put together a good picture of how it must have looked. The bones in its hands look similar to those from *Coelophysis*, and the two lived at about the same time. Syntarsus's foot bones, however, look more like those from a member of the *Heterodontosaurus* family. Its ankle bones look very primitive. They are fused together and not well developed.

Scientists wanted to show dinosaurs with feathers and plumes on their heads, so they drew pictures of Syntarsus this way. Today, very few scientists think it had those features. It would have been surprising to have found feathers on a member of the Coelophysis family. Syntarsus had sharp teeth in its pointed mouth. It was probably quite fast and could run after small mammals and large insects.

Length: 18 feet
Weight: 1—2 tons
Lived: Late Cretaceous
Found: United States (Montana), Canada (Alberta)

Length: 10 feet
Weight: 65 pounds
Lived: Late Triassic
Found: Zimbabwe

Teratosaurus
(teh-RAT-uh-sawr-us)

Members of this family were the first of the big meat-eating carnosaurs, or "flesh lizards." They emerged around 200 million years ago, at the dawn of the dinosaur age. About 100 million years later, the big carnosaurs like *Tenontosaurus* and *Tyrannosaurus* would appear to scavenge the earth. Dinosaurs like Teratosaurus, however, were much faster and more agile than their giant, lumbering descendents. Teratosaurus was found in West Germany. Others from the same family have been found in England and Africa.

Teratosaurus had a large head, a strong neck, and a short body. It had fangs in its mouth and claws on its fingers and toes. Each arm had three fingers and each foot had four toes. Compare this arrangement with dinosaurs like *Tyrannosaurus* and *Tenontosaurus*, which had almost lost the use of their arms.

Length: 20 feet
Weight: 1,500 pounds
Lived: Late Triassic
Found: West Germany, England, Africa

Triceratops
(try-SAIR-uh-tops)

Along with giant meat eaters like *Tyrannosaurus*, Triceratops is probably one of the most famous dinosaurs ever found. It has been fully examined by scientists, thanks to the discovery of a large bed of skeletons in western Wyoming. Along with *Torosaurus*, Triceratops is one of the last of the large group of horned dinosaurs called ceratopsians. Its name comes from the Greek name for three large horns.

Triceratops had a relatively short frill, especially when compared with that of *Torosaurus*. The frill had no holes to make the bone lighter, as some others did. It did have small bumpy pieces of bone on the back edge of the frill. The skull and frill together span a length of more than 6 feet. The two main horns are each more than 3 feet long.

Animals of this family would have been well-protected by their thick, leathery skin and their bony head decoration. They were probably quite slow-moving and would have used their horns more for wrestling than for charging their enemy.

Length: 30 feet
Weight: 6 tons
Lived: Late Cretaceous
Found: United States (Montana, Wyoming, South Dakota), Canada (Alberta)

Tsintaosaurus
(chin-TAY-o-sawr-us)

This was one of the last of the crested duckbills to appear on earth before all dinosaurs became extinct. Very unusual, it is of particular interest to scientists. It was found in China, and its name means "Chinese lizard." Some people think Tsintaosaurus was a descendent of *Sauroplophus*. The bony knob on the top of a *Sauroplophus* skull looks like a primitive form of the main crest on Tsintaosaurus.

Because its crest is so unusual, scientists want to know if it was used for show or developed by nature for fighting. The crest is known to have been a hollow tube. Many crested dinosaurs had hollow tubes that were probably used for making loud, booming sounds. Tsintaosaurus may have had a flap of skin stretching from its beak to the top of the crest. This would have been for show. Many animals develop parts of their body for frightening away enemies or attracting other members of their kind.

Length: 33 feet
Weight: 4 tons
Lived: Late Cretaceous
Found: China

Tyrannosaurus
(tye-RAN-uh-sawr-us)

This is certainly the biggest meat eater and may have been the most frightening dinosaur. It was more than 40 feet long and would have stood more than 18 feet tall on its huge back legs. Its strong tail probably helped balance the animal as it lunged forward and crashed into its prey. Its head was massive and very strong. In the specimens available, some back bones were welded together. This would have resulted from collisions to the head, which then sent enormous shocks down its back. Before the bones welded, the dinosaur would have suffered terrible pain from arthritis.

With legs like giant pillars, Tyrannosaurus would have had a top speed of nearly 20 MPH. It could have kept up this pace for only short distances, though. Probably, it lay in wait for easy prey and gave a short chase. After finally crashing into its next meal, it stunned it with a massive blow from its head. Then Tyrannosaurus would kill its prey with a bone-crushing bite from its huge jaws. Its 3-foot jaws held 60 teeth, each shaped like a dagger and up to 6 inches in length.

Length: 39 feet
Weight: 7 tons
Lived: Late Cretaceous
Found: Western North America

Velociraptor
(veh-loss-ih-RAP-tor)

Velociraptor means "swift plunderer," and this dinosaur was very likely just that. Lightly built for speed and agility, it had a long, low head and a flat skull. Although some of its relatives, including *Dromaeosaurus* and *Deinonychus*, have been found in North America, Velociraptor comes from Mongolia. The shape of its head and mouth suggests that it was a variety of coelurosaur ("hollow-tailed lizard") that developed around the diet it got. One skeleton has been found with its hands clutching the head of a *Protoceratops*. Both dinosaurs seemed to have died in this final fight to the end.

Velociraptor had long fingers, each with a large claw. This would have made it efficient at killing its prey before eating it. Each foot had four toes. The "big" toe was turned in, the first toe had a large claw and the other two were used for standing on. It could run quite fast and probably lived and hunted alone.

Length: 6 feet
Weight: ?
Lived: Late Cretaceous
Found: Mongolia, China

TERMS TO REMEMBER

Ankylosaurs   "Fused lizard" dinosaurs with heavy bodies, short limbs and protective armor.

Carnosaurs   Means "flesh lizard"; the large and powerful flesh-eating dinosaurs.

Ceratopsian   "Horned dinosaurs", which were among the last to appear and among the most abundant of all dinosaur groups. A type with large beaks and neck frills.

Coelurosaurs   Means "hollow-tailed lizard"; a group of 16 separate dinosaur families, all of which were small and slightly built.

Cretaceous   The most recent period of the Mesozoic, generally considered to have begun 135 million years ago and to have ended 65 million years ago.

**

Fossil   A remnant, impression, or trace of an animal or plant of past geological ages, preserved in the Earth's crust.

Gondwanaland   The Southern Continent that resulted when Pangaea split up in the late Triassic period. This land mass later split again to form South America, Africa, India, Antarctica, and Australia.

Hadrosaurid   A category of duck-billed, plant-eating dinosaurs with a hollow crest on its head, which enhanced its sense of smell.

Herbivore   Any plant-eating creature.

**

Jurassic   The middle period of the Mesozoic, generally considered to have begun 190 million years ago and to have ended 135 million years ago.

Laurasia   The Northern Continent that resulted when Pangaea split up in the late Triassic period. This land mass later split again to form North America, Europe, and Asia.

Mammals   A class of higher vertebrates including man and other animals that nourish their young with milk secreted by mammary glands and are usually more or less covered with hair.

Mesozoic Comes from the Greek meaning "middle life" and refers to the geologic period between the Paleozoic and the Cenozoic. The Mesozoic is divided into three periods; the Triassic, the Jurassic and the Cretaceous.

Ornithopods "Bird feet" dinosaurs capable of walking on their back legs.

Ornithischian One of two families of dinosaur which means "bird-hipped" animal.

Paleontology The science of dealing with past life from early geologic records and fossil remains.

Pangaea The supercontinent that contained all of the Earth's land masses in pre-Mesozoic times.

Phytosaurs The earliest known flesh-eaters, these creatures were among the first dinosaurs of the early Triassic period.

Prosauropods Means literally "before the lizard feet" dinosaurs, or Sauropods.

Proterosuchians Enormous, heavy creatures which evolved from the pre-dinosaur reptiles known as the Thecodontians.

Pseudosuchians Lighter, more nimble descendants of the Proterosuchians, which evolved from the early Triassic reptiles known as the Thecodontians, ancestors of the dinosaurs.

Pterosaurs Bird-like "winged lizards" which were not dinosaurs at all but a group of animals capable of gliding long distances.

Quetzalcoatlus The largest flying creature that ever lived. This Pterosaur had a wingspan of 39 feet.

Reptiles Animals that crawl or move on their belly or on short legs. The body is usually covered with scales or bony plates.

Saurischian One of two families of dinosaur which means "lizard-hipped" animal.

Sauropods The family of "lizard-feet" dinosaurs which included some of the largest animals known to have lived.

Stegosaurs "Roof lizard", or plated dinosaurs with bones or spikes protruding through thick skin.

Thecodontians Socket-toothed reptiles which first appeared about 230 million years ago and are thought to have given way to the dinosaurs.

Triassic The earliest period of the Mesozoic, generally considered to have begun 225 million years ago and ended 190 million yeas ago.